# SOMNISCOPE

# SOMNISCOPE

## A DREAMPUNK CONVERGENCE

edited by cliff jones jr.

ISBN: 979-8-88785-030-6 (Paperback)

Library of Congress Control Number: 2024930451

Any references to historical events, real people, or real places are used fictitiously. Names, characters, and places are products of the author's imagination.

Book design by Allison Chernutan.
Cover illustration by Brent Houzenga.
Edited by Cliff Jones Jr.

Printed in the United States of America.

First printing edition 2024.

emily@fracturedmirrorpublishing.com
Fractured Mirror Publishing
Knoxville, Tennessee

*www.fracturedmirrorpublishing.com*

For all the dreampunks out there—
the misfit mystics, the somniloquent
psychonauts...

May our dreams live on
long after we've gone.

Sleep is just another mode of living,
Often overlooked but no less real.
Much of life is harsh and unforgiving,
Numbing us to pain and hope and zeal.
In dreams, we find a place to truly feel.
Step into a world beneath the waves.
Chase the rabbit; walk the balance beam.
Own the night; explore the deepest caves.
Pretend that things are solid as they seem.
Everything is always just a dream.

# TABLE OF CONTENTS


prologue 13

1. looped 15
dez schwartz

interlude a 23

2. dreamsicle skies 25
sonya deulina williams

interlude b 35

3. replaced 37
alessandra ress

interlude c 43

4. dream dance 45
steven r. brandt

interlude d 67

5. man, startled by strange phenomenon 69
jeff noon

interlude e 83

6. pale shadows of the five 85
barry hale

interlude f 99

7. the red smoke 101
david pierre

interlude g 111

8. a lioness named midnight 113
yelena calavera

interlude h 125

9. a long-awaited interview  
courtney locicero **127**

interlude i  **135**

10. a kiss to build a dream on  
cliff jones jr.  **137**

interlude j  **149**

11. parasomnia  
tessa b. dick  **151**

interlude k  **161**

12. clayborn  
igor goldkind  **163**

interlude l  **169**

13. tethered  
ragnar martinson  **171**

interlude m  **183**

14. nova  
matt watters  **185**

interlude n  **195**

15. no good deed  
kurt wagner  **197**

interlude o  **207**

16. brain candy  
j. osman  **209**

interlude p  **217**

17. the songbird run  
blake jessop  **219**

interlude q  **241**

18. my forever ghost  
stephen coghlan  **243**

interlude r  265

19. unalike  267
v. s. santoni

interlude s  277

20. ari  279
jeb r. sherrill

interlude t  291

21. darlings  293
david michael williams

interlude u  305

22. euphoric  307
kristin jacques

interlude v  317

23. signs point to no  319
joseph e. green

interlude w  329

24. the hypnotherapist  331
elizabeth roderick

interlude x  343

25. the secret undoing  345
anna tizard

interlude y  363

26. falling  365
j. r. r. r. hardison

interlude z  381

27. reset  383
l. b. shimaira

epilogue  393

# PROLOGUE

**_Another lonely night, another borrowed dream. I know I'll_** never get to sleep on my own, so why bother trying? It'll only waste time, and I've got to be up in six hours. Five and a half now.

What is it about other people's lives that satisfies that gnawing hunger in my chest, if only for a moment? Living in someone else's skin scratches an itch that can't be reached any other way. All the little parts of myself that aggravate like a pebble in my shoe…they're just gone. Sure, everybody's got problems, but they don't have *my* problems, not exactly. It's this momentary relief that keeps me coming back night after night.

So I pull out the device, plug it into the wall beside my futon, slip on the headset, and lie back onto my pillow. I close my eyes and listen to those ten hypnotic clicks, my countdown to dreamland. Precisely one second after the tenth click, I lose consciousness. There in front of my eyes is the loading screen: "Somniscope."

# I. LOOPED

## by dez schwartz

*'Here. Take your medication, get some sleep, and you'll feel* better in the morning."

Brody didn't believe the nurse's promise. Every night he took his meds, and every morning he didn't feel any better. But considering his situation, taking them was non-optional, so he shoved the pills into his mouth and washed them down with the water she'd handed him. He clamped his fist around the little paper cup, crushing it into a ball, and threw it past her shoulder into the small wastebasket at the back of his room.

Without another word, the nurse and the security guard who'd been shadowing her left, and Brody fell back onto his bed.

Another thirty days of this routine still awaited him before he'd be allowed to leave, and even then, that depended on his doctor saying they'd seen progress. In the meantime, Brody suspected things were actually getting worse.

As he waited for sleep to overcome him, he recounted the day in his mind, trying to make sense of what he'd experienced. He'd awoken to an empty building and a surreal turn of events. The situation had grown increasingly bizarre until he'd returned to find that everyone had magically reappeared in their usual routines back inside the institution. He tried to confront the nurse, but she'd brushed off his concerns, as usual.

For now, things appeared to have returned to normal, and the more he tried to remember, the more clouded those memories became until they were nothing but a blur.

Brody allowed his eyes to flutter closed, and he fell into a deep sleep.

He woke to sunlight pouring over him. Strange, considering his room didn't have windows.

Apparently, it did today.

Brody jumped up from the bed and ran to the new window to peer outside. The staff and the other patients were out in the courtyard participating in some strange kind of workout. Instead of their usual uniforms and scrubs, they wore black robes tied at the waist with a golden rope cord—an item they'd never usually be allowed to have.

"What the hell?" Brody narrowed his eyes, trying to understand what was unfolding while everyone danced in strange formations to music he couldn't hear.

He left his room, deciding to sneak outside to get a closer look.

Sneaking wasn't a problem. No one else seemed to be inside the building. The common area, which was usually full of patients watching pre-approved television shows or playing card games, was not only empty but pristine, as though no one had even gone in there this morning.

The nurses' front desk and staff areas were similarly untouched.

Brody strode through the main hall toward the front doors of the institution with a sense that the entire building was nothing more than a façade he could knock over simply by pushing on one of the walls.

Instead, he pushed on one of the metal doors and let it swing open. As the bright sunlight engulfed him, he thought about ducking behind one of the freshly trimmed hedges in front of the building to keep anyone from spotting him. He was the only one not wearing a weird robe, after all. Nor had anyone woken him up to let him know they were having a special event that day, so something was clearly amiss. He'd been purposefully left out of the loop.

However, there seemed to be no need for hiding. None of the others cared or even noticed he'd joined them outside. They continued their strange flowing dance, and now that he was among them, he realized he hadn't been able to hear their music inside because there was no music at all. Yet somehow, they all moved to the same silent beat.

Curiosity getting the better of him, Brody approached the group. He fully expected one of the staff to hand a robe over to him and give him instructions on how to join in. But none of them broke their trancelike dancing. In fact, everyone's eyes were closed, and as he weaved through the group it became clear they were all in some meditative state. Entranced. Spellbound.

He raised a hand, tempted to tap a young girl with big red curls on the shoulder to see if she'd snap out of it.

A horn honked in the distance, distracting only Brody. The others kept swaying to the silent music, their faces pointed up toward the blinding sky.

A nondescript black sedan was parked at the front gates of the institution, and a familiar man wearing sunglasses leaned against the hood. He lit a cigarette and waved for Brody to join him.

Brody's heart catapulted into his throat at the sight of his ex-boyfriend, James. A mix of relief and anger.

James had been the reason Brody had ended up in this place, after all.

With no one caring to stop him, Brody jogged down the dirt road and joined James by the large iron gates, which had been left ajar.

What on earth had the staff been thinking? Anyone could come in without permission. More importantly, anyone—in this case, Brody—could escape.

James took a final puff of his cigarette and tossed it to the ground without bothering to put it out. He opened the back door on the driver's side, obviously intending to help Brody make a break for it.

"What's going on?" Brody asked, approaching the vehicle.

"This was a huge mistake," James answered. "I should've never let you take that pill. Get in the car."

"What pill?" Brody hesitated. He couldn't remember anything.

James sighed. "We don't have much time. I'll explain later. Just get in."

A loud crack emanated from the sky above them and caused the ground to rumble.

"Shit!" James grabbed Brody by the arm and tried to push him into the car.

In seconds, dark purple clouds rolled overhead, and lightning cracked in horizontal zigzags across the skyline.

Brody glanced over his shoulder at the institution. The robed patients and staff stood still, facing the ominous storm but keeping their eyes sealed shut.

Nothing felt safe. Nothing felt sane. Not even the hands of his ex.

Brody broke free and ran, pumping his legs as hard as he could push them down the road. He'd escape on his own terms, but first he had to seek shelter from the storm.

"Come back! The only way out of this nightmare is with me!" James shouted, his voice growing more distant. "It's going to happen all over again! Don't you understand? Don't you remember?"

Brody ran off the road and into the overgrown brush behind the institution. He'd have a better chance of fleeing if he remained out of sight.

However, he hadn't expected the brush to conceal a deep drainage ditch.

Brody tripped and tumbled forward. Unable to catch himself when his body hit the cool, mossy earth, he continued to roll downhill and finally came to a stop in front of a small concrete edifice.

He pushed himself upright on scraped hands and glanced over his shoulder to make sure no one had followed him.

He was alone. No car or institution in sight. He couldn't even see the road from where he'd landed.

Turning his attention back to the unmarked concrete building, Brody reasoned it must be a facility shed of some sort for the institution. A decent enough place to hide out until the storm subsided.

Thankful to find the door unlocked, Brody slipped inside the dark structure. The door fell shut behind him. He fumbled for a light switch but couldn't find one, so he turned back and pressed against the wall where the door should have been. No handle, no gaps…Nothing budged.

He'd trapped himself.

"What the hell is going on?" Brody ran his hands over his buzzed scalp, letting his nerves catch up to his heart rate.

He'd have to wait until someone found him, and there was no telling how long that would take.

He spun around to survey the room and found himself faced with a vast cosmos.

It took him a moment to recognize the ground had given out beneath him. He was floating in place in the middle of an unknown galaxy.

*Am I dead?* he wondered, letting his fingers glide through a stream of stardust coursing past him. Then his memories came flooding back to him.

He'd gone to James's condo to demand his chance at a once-in-a-lifetime opportunity their breakup had deprived him of. James had developed a drug which facilitated lucid dreaming, but he hadn't had enough time to test it before he'd lost his job at the pharmaceutical lab. He'd managed to steal enough of the drug to continue his research and development in secret, and he'd promised Brody he'd let him try it once it was ready.

But despite Brody's interest, James had broken things off without much explanation.

Romantic rejection was something Brody could handle, but being declined existential answers—not so much.

He'd shown up on James's doorstep. They'd argued. Finally, James gave in and allowed him to be a test subject. Brody had taken the pill, and the next thing he recalled, he was being institutionalized. But who had put him there? James? Police? Or was this all just the effects of the drug?

Voices.

Brody snapped out of his thoughts and strained to pick up on what they were saying and where they could possibly be coming from.

The voices of two distinct people, or entities, were arguing.

He tried to ignore the pounding of his heart and focus on their words.

Then he realized he wasn't hearing them with his ears, rather inside his mind. Like he'd tuned into a psychic radio station and just caught the last bit of a morning talk show.

"You have to stop this," one of the voices said. "You'll kill them all."

"They're killing themselves," the other snapped back. "I'm just making it more entertaining for the rest of us."

"This isn't how it's supposed to happen," the first voice insisted. "They're supposed to transform."

"And so they are. Transforming to ash and dirt," the second said with a bit too much glee in their inflection. "You!"

Somehow, Brody understood he'd been seen. They were addressing him now.

"I told you to stop coming here!" the sinister one screeched. "You're not welcome!"

Brody kicked his legs and flailed his arms backward into space as though he was hoping to swim his way through the universe in retreat—even though he had no real idea of where they were or where he could go.

"Leave!" the first voice added. "And don't come back!"

Brody felt a push of gravity like a punch in the gut. It knocked the wind out of him, and he sailed backward through the cosmos so fast that slamming onto the ground at the front entrance to the institution was a welcome relief from the nauseating propulsion.

He bolted upright near the front steps of the building, as though waking from a terrifying dream.

The gates at the entrance to the property were now closed. James and the black car were gone.

The courtyard was also empty.

The sky cleared up as though the surreal thunderstorm had never been, but now darkness began to fall. Somehow, an entire day had passed him by.

Unsure what else to do, Brody retreated back inside the institution where nurses and staff walked their daily rounds and patients could be heard chatting, laughing, and crying in the common room.

"Brody! There you are," one of the nurses said when she spotted him. "I was on my way to look for you. Did you get left behind in the courtyard?"

"What were you all doing out there?" Brody demanded.

"Our daily stretches, like usual," she answered. "Brody, are you all right? You look shaken."

"Of course I'm shaken!" Brody's adrenaline still raced through his veins. "You were all dancing around in robes like a bunch of cult nutjobs!"

Three other patients who sat a few feet away in the common room stopped playing their card game to watch the exchange.

"Brody!" the nurse reprimanded. "You know we don't like that word here. You need to calm down."

"What kind of storm was that?" he pressed. "And what the fuck are you keeping in the maintenance building out back? It's going to kill us! I heard them! It wants to kill us!"

The common room had grown quiet; everyone was staring at Brody.

The nurse held up her hands and repeated in a stern tone, "You need to calm down."

"No!" Brody slammed his fist onto the counter of the nurse's station knocking over a ceramic vase, which flew to the floor and smashed into a dozen pieces. "I need answers!"

In no time, a member of security was on him, pulling his arms behind his back to prevent him from lashing out again.

"Take him to his room," a second nurse instructed from behind the desk.

The guard dragged Brody back toward his assigned room.

"I know you're hiding something here! This place is evil!" Brody accused. He tried to struggle against the man's grip but wasn't strong enough to break free.

Where would he go, anyway? It wasn't safe outside either, and his one chance for escape had already driven away.

His best option now would be to play their game and let them think he'd calmed down. He could plot an escape overnight.

Once Brody was back in his room, the nurse entered with the security guard waiting beside her to make sure Brody didn't get aggressive again.

"I'm sorry you had a bad day, Brody," the nurse said in a pandering tone, as though she were a schoolteacher and he was a child throwing a tantrum. "Sometimes the best way to reset is to just get some rest. You look exhausted, and that can cause stress."

Brody slumped onto his bed, not arguing. Not saying anything.

She frowned with concern but handed him a paper cup filled with water and placed two capsules into the palm of his hand.

"Here. Take your medication, get some sleep, and you'll feel better in the morning."

# INTERLUDE A

**I don't feel better in the morning. And I've made up my mind** about my meds: I'm done with them. Even if I wanted to start back on the pills again after everything I've been through to get that stuff out of my system, it's just too damn expensive. I'd need some real corpo insurance to afford that, and those days are gone for good. No respectable corp is going to hire a low-cred.

Why did I wake up thinking about meds and insurance and all that? Recorded dreams are supposed to offer some escapism, not extra stress. I'll have to keep adjusting my settings until I find that elusive sweet spot: engaging, exciting…but nothing so wild that I wake up more exhausted than I started out.

It would also be nice to remember a bit more of these dreams once the session is over. I'm paying for them after all. Well, I *would* be paying if I could afford to. And if it weren't so easy to find pirated dreamcaps online.

*That reminds me…*

I check my inbox for news on the firmware mod I ordered last week, but there's nothing yet. *Damn.*

The mod is supposed to let you burn through dreamcaps in a fraction of the time, allowing multiple sessions a night, no problem. A few hours can feel like weeks or even years away from the waking world. Sounds all right to me. The more time I spend living life in somebody else's shoes, the better. I got sick of my own shoes a long time ago. They're more like sandals anyway.

My mind wanders a moment as I recall a trip to the beach I took as a kid. That was back before the pandemic…and the war…and the shutdown. Things were different back then.

Maybe there's time for one more session before I *really* have to get up. It's not like I have a corpo job to get to at a particular time, just the same old hustle. I never make much money in the morning anyway. Folks are stingy on uppers; they get more generous on downers.

I haven't even removed my headset yet, so it's easy to start the Somniscope back up with a new dreamcap. Hopefully this one will calm me down, help me forget about…everything. *Wouldn't that be nice?*

# 2. DREAMSICLE SKIES
## by sonya deulina williams

*It all started with the annual family beach trip. Malcolm's* parents, cousins, uncles, aunts, and grandparents all congregated in a big beach house or condo once a year in Hilton Head, South Carolina. They would stay for a week and hit up the various attractions—quaint little shops, seafood restaurants, and of course the beach—usually as one noisy mob.

It was a hot Wednesday afternoon, but the breeze on the beach felt amazing. Malcolm stood, cradling an oversized black inner tube under his arm, ready to jet for the water and bodysurf the breakers with his cousins Kristen and Dustin and his older brother Nick. He hopped from foot to foot on the hot sand, trying to find relief for his scorched feet. As soon as Nick headed toward the water, Malcolm gave his giant donut a big push forward and ran after it.

It was at that most inopportune moment that a gust of wind caught hold of the tube, changing its course and sending it rolling down the beach instead of toward the water. Malcolm jetted after it, trying to catch up, but the wind was powerful and would not let up. Malcolm pumped his legs as hard as they would go. He wasn't a slow runner, about average for a boy his age, but the inner tube was always just out of reach, skipping along the sand.

He narrowed his focus, the people on their beach towels to his right and the ocean to his left falling away. All that was left was the inner tube and the stretch of beach it was rolling on, rolling and rolling unobstructed near the edge of the water.

He could just make out the corners of sky in his peripheral vision, a creamy tangerine orange that was becoming whiter by the second.

*Like someone's eating a big dreamsicle up there,* he snickered to himself. A question emerged from the back of his mind: *Why would the sky get lighter and not darker at sunset?*

After a while, Malcolm's legs started to get tired; he had literally run that far after this stupid float. Still, he kept on after it, his focus laser sharp. It just didn't make any sense: whenever he would get within arm's reach, the tube would seem to roll a little faster, like it was taunting him. It reminded him of a nightmare he'd had once where he was running through a hallway toward a door that he could never reach. He could never escape until he finally woke himself up screaming.

Finally, by some stroke of pure magic, the joke was over, and the tube slowed down and fell on its side. Nearly keeling over, Malcolm rested his hands on his knees with his head between his legs. He took several big breaths before pouncing on the inner tube in case the wind gods wanted to spite him again. He lay belly-down in the center of it, eyes closed. He was exhausted. He rested his chin on the firm rubber and let the wind play across his back. He was too tired to fight the sleep that was quickly taking him.

When he finally picked his head up and looked around for the first time, he did not recognize where he was. He looked back in the direction of his family, but they were out of sight. In fact, the buildings were completely unfamiliar as far as the eye could see. The structures had changed from large condos and hotels to pastel-colored beach houses. He couldn't even see the top of the yellow, fifteen-story condo where his family was staying. This was the landmark he could always count on to get him back if he wandered too far away, and it was gone.

How far had he gone? Was this a different beach? The sun was even lower in the sky now, which had turned to dark orange and pink, no bright inverted dreamsicle. Malcolm frowned. Why had no one helped him? Grabbed the inner tube for him? These were fleeting questions because he now saw his brother Nick approaching from a distance, a tan figure in navy shorts. Malcolm stayed where he was, wary of what would follow, and waited for Nick to catch up to him.

Once Nick was in earshot, he slowed to an easy jog and asked, "What are you doing?"

"The inner tube rolled away. I ran after it," Malcolm responded flatly.

"And then what?"

"What do you mean?"

"Do you know how long you've been gone?"

"No."

"Over an hour! Mom sent me after you."

"What?!" Malcolm's head was spinning. *Over an hour?! How could the tube have rolled for that long without me catching up? No. That's impossible.* "No, I wasn't. Stop lying!"

"I'm not. It's almost six o'clock."

"*Whoa*…what the—"

"So, you want to tell me what you were really doing?"

"I swear I was just chasing the inner tube."

"Whatever." Nick rolled his eyes and started walking back. "Come on. Mom and Dad are pissed."

Malcolm gulped as he started making the long trek back to his parents, his brain racing over the very real consequences that would undoubtedly be awaiting him when he returned. None of the other strangeness mattered to him suddenly; he was in *big* trouble.

After a surprisingly long walk, he made it back to his family— the remaining members of it, that is. The rest of them had already packed up and left to get ready for dinner, but his mom and dad had stayed behind. Malcolm stared down at his feet, wanting to put off looking at their faces for as long as possible. He had been gone nearly three hours now. The consequences would be dire.

"Malcolm!" He heard his mother snap. Still, he didn't look up. "Look at me, Malcolm."

Okay, this was the moment of truth. He couldn't avoid trouble any longer.

Slowly, he lifted his eyes, his gaze moving from his mom's black sandals to her hands placed firmly on her hips, to her billowing white T-shirt, then to the straight, disapproving line of her mouth, and finally up—

Malcolm froze. His stomach bottomed out into a sick, hollow feeling. No, it wasn't from the anger in his mother's eyes. That was there too, but what was worse was the fact that her eyes were dark and dilated, her pupils huge, saucer-like. It completely freaked him out, but not as much as his next realization: He didn't recognize her, not at all. He looked over to his father and shuddered. There were the same large, horrifying saucer eyes.

Wide-eyed, Malcolm turned to face his brother with the question burning in his mind: *Are you seeing what I'm seeing?*

"Don't look at me," Nick shrugged him off.

*No, he doesn't see it! But how is that possible?*

"But…" Malcolm stammered.

"Where did you go? Do you know how worried you had us?!" The woman who was supposed to be his mother commenced with an angry onslaught of questions. That part made sense.

"I…I…" He looked from parent to parent, trying to make sense of what was happening.

"What were you thinking being gone for so long?" His supposed father finally spoke, the man's voice shaking as it rose to higher and higher decibels. "Never *ever* do that again. Do you hear me? We almost called the police!"

Malcolm had never heard his dad talk to him like this before. This level of anger was unprecedented. This couldn't be his real dad. Still, what was he supposed to do? His brother was acting like nothing was wrong. He shot Nick another fearful look, who once again proceeded to shrug his shoulders and look away. No, Nick really didn't see what he saw. He was completely alone with the horrific and mind-boggling realization that *these were not his parents.*

So he did all he could think to do. He grabbed his inner tube, beach towel, and flip-flops and made his way back to the condo. He would have to pretend that everything was fine, because what else was a seven-year-old to do? He was completely outnumbered, and no one would believe him anyway.

Several years later, Malcolm had moved on with his life, and for the most part he'd forgotten about his strange and disorienting experience at the beach. He was a sophomore in college now, focused on school, partying, and hanging out with friends. His parents lived less than an hour away, and he would still visit them sometimes, the parents that he'd learned to accept and normalize.

Malcolm sat in his bedroom in a beat-up leather recliner. His face was pointed toward the ceiling, and he was snoring loudly. His friend Calvin walked in carrying a brown grocery bag.

"Hey, man."

Malcolm blinked open his eyes and adjusted his gaming headset, which was hanging off his right ear. In his blurred field of vision, a large figure emerged from his doorway and moved toward him. Calvin came into view with some sort of orange popsicle in his mouth.

Calvin smiled, extended a popsicle to Malcolm, and then plopped down in a swivel chair near his bed.

"What's this?"

"Dreamsicle," Calvin said between bites.

"Dreamsicle," Malcolm repeated aloud, robotically.

He peeled away the blue and white plastic and took a small bite, still in his half-asleep state. He was exhausted from staying up late the night before, gaming. The confection was creamy and delicious…

Within minutes, Malcolm's head was swimming. As he floated up and away, the room seemed to change around him, to become a living, breathing being. The walls moved outward, making his room seem much bigger than it was. His breath quickened, and he gripped the arms of his chair as a long-forgotten agoraphobic feeling set in.

"Dude, are you sure there's nothing in this ice cream?" he squeaked out.

"Hahahaha, positive. It's that good, right?" Calvin sat there grinning up at the ceiling and spinning slow circles in his chair.

Just then, Malcolm's phone rang. He looked down at the screen to see "Mom." He hesitated, not wanting to pick up the phone in the state he was in. He would have to call her back in several hours, or even in the morning based on how he was feeling now. He let it ring.

"Mom," he said aloud.

"Huh?" Calvin grunted from his chair.

"Mom," he repeated in the start of an explanation, but then the meaning changed as he began to feel a different long-forgotten feeling that he hadn't experienced in years, one that he'd hoped was just a childhood nightmare.

It must have been Malcolm's hypnotic state of mind, or the way the room expanded, or his mother calling—hell, probably all of it combined—that somehow jogged his memory. The dreamsicle sky…He could see it so clearly now, the orange reverting to white, the endless beach, his parents' eyes…He shuddered and then inhaled a shaky breath to bring himself back to center.

"Listen," Malcolm started aloud, not sure if Calvin was even listening, "something happened to me when I was little…something really scary."

"What?" Calvin asked, still staring up at the ceiling.

"I think my parents were replaced when I was a kid, at the beach."

"Shit, man, like abducted?" Calvin turned to look at Malcolm.

"No, like they were replaced…by exact look-alikes."

"What?!" Calvin giggled. "What *did* they put in your ice cream?"

"I'm serious though. They looked the same, but they *weren't* the same."

"People can change, man."

"No! It's not like that. I don't really know how to explain it; I just know that it wasn't them anymore. And yeah, I guess their personalities changed too."

"Well, have you asked them about it?"

"What?"

"You should ask them who they really are."

"You're joking. They would think I'm crazy! There's no way I'm going to do that, especially after all these years have passed. I was seven."

"Listen, how else are you going to know for sure?"

"I don't know. I guess you're right, there's no real way to know for sure unless I ask…"

Malcolm decided to confront his parents the next time he came home for a weekend visit. He waited until Friday night dinner because it would just be the four of them. He didn't mind for his brother to hear because, well, he was there too when it all happened.

He waited a long time, until everyone had started on their ice cream sundaes, before he began talking. He put down his spoon and waited until there was a lull in the conversation. "Hey, do you guys remember that day at the beach when I was seven? You know, the day I got lost chasing that inner tube?"

His parents exchanged a glance. "Oh yeah," his mother said, "we remember all right. That was the day we almost called the police after you."

"Okay, but do you remember anything odd from that day? Anything that seemed out of place?"

"What? Apart from you running away?" His dad snorted, taking another bite of ice cream.

"Yeah, um…do you remember anything else being…off?"

His mother looked down for a moment, swirling her ice cream around in the bowl. "Yes, actually," she began after a pause, "the day you ran away, I remember the sky looking strange…"

A rush of adrenaline erupted inside Malcolm's head and moved down his spine. He swallowed down his surprise and waited for her to finish.

"I remember there was a white light that took over the sky. It was the strangest thing. At first, I thought it was just the glare from the sun setting, but it was much brighter and took up most of the sky."

Nick put down his spoon. "What? I don't remember anything like that."

Malcolm's dad frowned. "Me neither."

"But I do," Malcolm said. "I wasn't looking at the sky head on, but I remember the white taking over the sky, washing out the orange."

"Yes, exactly!" his mom agreed.

"I don't remember anything off about that day other than you running away," his dad continued, "and that I had vertigo."

"Vertigo?" Malcolm asked. "You mean when you get really dizzy and nauseous?"

"Exactly, except that day it was different than usual. I was walking toward the trash can to throw something away, and I distinctly remember the trash can getting further and further away. It was like I could never reach it, no matter how much I would walk toward it. And it was only like thirty feet away."

*Oh…my…*

Now things were starting to add up. Malcolm turned to look at his brother.

"Nick, do you remember anything at all being weird that day?"

"No. We were about to go swimming, and then you were gone, and Mom and Dad sent me after you. That's it. It was a long walk."

*Wow. So it was only me, Mom, and Dad that saw the changes.*

"Mom, Dad, I'm going to ask you something, and it's going to sound strange, but just bear with me."

"Okay…" Malcolm's mom said nervously. His dad just stared at him.

"Did something happen to the two of you that day at the beach, after you saw that weird light? And Dad, after you had that vertigo experience? Did something…*change*…about you two?"

His parents exchanged a knowing look. Malcolm detected concern in his mother's eyes. After a pause that only twenty-five years of marriage could make decipherable, his mother spoke again. "Malcolm, I'm not sure how to say this, but something did happen to *you* on that trip, not us."

"It did?" Malcolm's eyes widened. "It's funny you should say that…"

"No, not funny at all," Malcolm's dad interrupted, completely cutting off Malcolm's train of thought. "You really scared us. You just didn't seem right when you came back to us that day."

"What do you mean I didn't seem right?"

Malcolm's mom spoke slowly: "You were just acting so…*odd* after you ran away. We were worried about you…Do you remember going to see Kathy Lineman?"

"Kathy who?"

His mother looked at him sideways. "Your therapist at the time. We took you after that trip because, well, you just didn't seem like yourself anymore."

Malcolm shuddered at the possibility that maybe, just maybe, his parents were thinking exactly what he was at that moment. Though they would never admit to such a thing.

"Remember," she continued, "she would make you draw those pictures, and you would bring them home to show us?"

A flashback of a childhood drawing of a beachscape with a vibrant orange sky flashed into his mind, and then all the pictures of his parents he drew, with those giant black eyes.

"Yeah, I think I actually do remember her."

"Well, she said you were suffering from something. Some kind of delusional disorder or a sleep-based disorder. But she wasn't quite sure because she said your symptoms didn't fall under any official diagnosis. We even took you to see a neurologist, but they didn't find anything wrong with you. What she did say was that we needed to keep a close eye on you and check in on you frequently. Eventually she discharged you because she said that you were doing perfectly fine."

*There was absolutely nothing wrong with me! I don't think I even told that therapist what happened. Did I?*

Malcolm felt sick to his stomach, but he knew he wasn't crazy. Something must have happened that day—to the three of them, not just to him. So he did the only thing that there was left to do. The thing that he swore he would never ever do.

"Mom, Dad, just answer one question for me, and be honest… When I came back to you from chasing that inner tube, did you think I was the same person?"

"What…what do you mean?" His mother's voice trembled.

His father went white as a sheet.

"Just answer the question."

His parents just stared at him, and in that moment, he could have sworn that their eyes were as big as saucers.

# INTERLUDE B

**That was a creepy one. I can almost remember the whole** dream this time. I *definitely* remember those eyes, at least. I wish I didn't.

It's getting pretty late in the day now, well past time to get moving. But I have to go ahead and check my inbox first, and I'm not disappointed. The firmware mod I ordered to speed things up and give me more in-dream subjective time is finally ready.

Installation only takes a few minutes, and now I find myself facing a dilemma: Should I get dressed, hit the streets, and try to make some cred today, or can I spend a little more time with my Somniscope? I opt for the latter, rationalizing my laziness by telling myself the extra energy I'll have after just one more dream—a really *good* one this time—will more than make up for the time I'll lose. I can afford to run just one more session, particularly since this one will be sped up and probably take just a few minutes.

Mostly, I'm just impatient to try out my new toy.

I head back to my futon and dive in for one last session. A quick one. Then I'm done.

# 3. REPLACED
## by alessandra ress

*Tasia's way home from school led through a residential* neighborhood. Single-family houses with spacious gardens were lined up here, and in spring the trees and bushes were home to countless birds whose songs always accompanied Tasia's way. Lately, she had sometimes noticed how the songs repeated themselves, but she thought nothing of it. After all, Mr. Meurer greeted her every day with the same "Well, school out already?"— regardless of whether she was walking past his garden at two in the afternoon or five.

Normally, Tasia appreciated her walk home, especially on sunny days like this. Today, however, the three kilometers dragged like chewing gum. Her head was pounding after eight hours of school, and she regretted not taking her bike in the morning.

She was all the more relieved when she finally reached her family's house. She threw her backpack in the corner and made herself a sandwich. She'd have a hot meal later, when her parents came home.

The snack did nothing to relieve her headache. On the contrary, the throbbing now became a constant squeeze that made Tasia feel dizzy.

She went upstairs. Girls' voices were coming from her little sister's room; someone was laughing. Apparently, Lilli had invited a friend.

"Hey Lil," Tasia called from the hallway. "I've been here for half an hour, by the way."

She waited a moment, but Lilli did not deign to greet her sister.

Shrugging her shoulders, Tasia turned away and went to her own room. She changed her sweaty T-shirt, then threw herself on the bed, not even bothering to close the door or get under the covers. Just a little nap…

The sensation of falling out of bed made Tasia startle. Irritated for a moment, she looked around. Her alarm clock had stopped. It still showed 3:34 p.m., but the evening sun told her that it must already be much later.

She yawned. She would have liked to close her eyes again, but she knew that if she did she'd regret it later. Besides, her parents must have come home by now.

With a sigh, she stood up. At least her headache was gone. And luckily, her mother hadn't come up—she always got mad when she saw Tasia lying in bed with jeans on.

Tasia heard a clattering from downstairs, so she ran down to greet her family. A slight flicker appeared before her eyes, probably just an aftereffect of sleep. Unfazed, she jumped the last steps as she always did. It was traditional for her mother to respond with "You're going to slip someday!" but this time she didn't seem to notice.

Tasia's mother stood in the kitchen clearing groceries out of the basket. Lilli carried them further into the pantry, and another girl stood next to her, seemingly undecided whether she'd be able to help or just be standing in the way. When she saw Tasia in the doorway, the strange girl blinked in apparent irritation, and then a somehow unpleasant smile appeared at the corners of her mouth. Tasia had never seen this girl before, evidently a new friend of Lilli's.

"Hi, everyone," Tasia said.

"Crap, the yogurt has a hole in it," her mother remarked, lifting up a package of oatmeal on which thick, white stains announced a run-in with the damaged yogurt cup.

"If it just happened on the way, it doesn't matter," Tasia countered. "Do you want me to clean the package?"

But her mother was already tearing off a paper towel herself and wiping the oatmeal with it. "Everything okay at school?" she asked.

"In English, we're writing a—" Tasia put in, but Lilli babbled off at the same time, "Mr. Rimand said we'd be dissecting pigs' eyes in biology class next week."

"We did that once, too." Tasia shrugged. "Wasn't as exciting as it sounds."

"Teachers still make you do that?" her mother muttered absentmindedly as she scanned the basket for more traces of yogurt. "How about you, Fiona?"

"Nothing special," the strange girl replied. "But Xaver is on crutches now. He broke two toes playing soccer."

Tasia wondered a little at the girl's familiar tone. Had she been around more often after all? Tasia eyed Fiona more closely. She was wearing striped tights and a horse-print dress. Pearls were braided into her curly brown hair. No, Tasia would have remembered her for sure.

"So how was work, Mom?" she asked finally. "How did your presentation go?"

"Poor guy," her mother replied. "But toes heal pretty quickly, I think."

Tasia frowned. "And at work?" she asked again, a little annoyed that everyone was ignoring her today.

But her mother didn't answer. Instead, she glanced outside, where a car had just turned into the driveway. "Ah, there's your father. I asked him to bring pizza. Go ahead, open the door for him."

Amid Lilli's shouts of "Yay, pizza!" Tasia went to the front door. She tried to open it, but the handle wouldn't turn. "The door is stuck," she called toward the kitchen.

Fiona sauntered over to her.

"I can't wait to see him," the strange girl said softly. "I've seen him on the screen many times, but that's not the same."

Tasia blinked. "In photos, you mean?"

Fiona just grinned and opened the door without a hitch. With a bright smile, she faced Tasia's father, who turned the corner with four pizza boxes in his arms.

"Hi there!" He passed the boxes to Fiona and gave her hair a playful tousle. "Hey, everyone!" he called into the house, taking off his shoes and following the babble of voices from the kitchen.

Fiona went after him, carrying the pizza boxes in front of her like a trophy, while Tasia watched them both with her mouth open. Her father hadn't even given her a glance! And why was everyone treating Fiona as if she were part of the family and not just some girl Lilli had brought home?

"Wash your hands, and we can eat right away," Tasia heard her mother call. A moment later, Lilli and Fiona ran past her to the bathroom.

As Fiona went by, Tasia heard her say, "The bug is kind of annoying."

"Eww, a bug? Where?" Lilli asked, but Tasia couldn't hear Fiona's answer. She went into the kitchen, where her father was pulling out cutlery.

"The hand washing thing applies to you too!" her mother teased him.

"Mom? Dad?" asked Tasia timidly, her voice quavering slightly. "Do you hear me?"

"I did when I came in," her father asserted. "By the way, how did your presentation go?"

"Tell me, are you kidding me?" Tasia crossed her arms in front of her chest. "Is this some kind of joke? Is it April Fools' Day or something?"

"All right, I guess," her mother said. "At least the technology cooperated and I got out everything I wanted to say. Now let's see what comes of it…"

Tasia left the room in a daze. Once again, Lilli and Fiona ran past her.

"Lilli?" called Tasia, but her sister paid no attention. Choosing not to go along with this game, she added a sarcastic "Ha ha," and pursed her lips.

# replaced

The pizza smelled inviting, but Tasia decided to go upstairs for a bit first to gather her thoughts. She was headed for her bedroom but stopped at the open door. Breathing became difficult, and she had to lean herself against the wall, trying incredulously to take in what she saw inside the room.

There was no longer a trace of her Linkin Park poster, the quilt with the Milky Way on it, or her easel with the watercolor she had painted in summer school. Instead, the whole room was full of horses. They galloped on posters and wall hangings, her desk pad was now adorned with a foal, and the bedspread was emblazoned with an entire family of mustangs. There was another flicker before Tasia's eyes.

"What the—" muttered Tasia. She took a deep breath and closed her eyes. The dizziness that had seized her at the sight of this strange room soon subsided, but when she opened her eyes again, the horses were still there.

Tasia blinked and looked at her hands. Now a slight flicker emanated from them as well, coming and going every few seconds.

As if in a trance, she turned around. She had to force herself to stop staring at her hands. Her legs trembled as she walked downstairs. The door to the dining room was open. Tasia stood in the frame and watched the people sitting around the table. The man who was cutting his pizza. The woman pouring herself a glass of water. The little girl chewing with obvious pleasure. And the other girl, the one in the horse dress, who was sitting in Tasia's place.

"Oh, what a perfect family life!" Fiona purred, and the others at the table laughed.

Tasia had to make one more attempt to be noticed. She went to the table and reached for the water carafe her mother had just poured from. But she couldn't make it budge. At first, the carafe felt heavy as lead. Then Tasia's hand began to flicker again, like a TV screen during a thunderstorm, and she flinched in shock as her hand passed right through the carafe.

"Fortunately, tomorrow is Friday," the man at the table said.

"Indeed it is," his wife countered. "By the way, can you check on the oven light this weekend? I think it needs to be replaced; it keeps flickering."

"Can I do that?" asked Fiona. She smiled thoughtfully, and her gaze went to the end of the table where Tasia was standing. "I love replacing things in this game."

# INTERLUDE C

**Well, that was fast. How long was I out—five, ten minutes? If** that's how quick a dreamcap runs with this mod, then maybe I have time for one more before heading to work. That last dream really shook me up, and I'd hate to start the day off on the wrong foot.

It felt too real, too much like my waking life. I was a different person, of course—a very different person—but that sensation of being powerless, just being a passive observer in somebody else's story, was all too familiar.

Why do dreams have to be in the third person? They tend to have a main character, but it's not the same as in real life, where you're always sure who you are, and it never changes. Or if it does change, at least, you don't notice the transition. Maybe you hop from head to head, but every time you do, you have all the memories of that particular person and it doesn't feel like anything's different from one moment to the next.

Except it does, doesn't it? Every moment feels different.

If I'm going to run one more dreamcap, I'd better go ahead and dive in. The music's already started; time to join the dance. How about you? Will you join me? Won't you please? Won't you join the dance?

# 4. DREAM DANCE

## by steven r. brandt

**It was another late night in Dream Utilization and Testing,** the research lab known on campus as "the DUaT." Seth opened a bag of cheese balls, stared at the screen filled with random pixels, and listened to the steady stream of white noise.

The mostly meaningless sounds and images were attempts by a computer to decode the dreams of an elderly gentleman in the next room.

The man lay on a comfy foam bed and wore a funny wire-mesh cap, part of a device called a Somniscope. A data cable ran from the Somniscope, across the door, under the desk, and up to the computer. The computer read tiny electronic fluctuations in the signal and attempted to decode them.

Usually, it failed.

Once every hour or so, Seth would see an image flash on the screen or hear a couple of words through the white noise. He was here to watch for these events.

For an instant, he thought maybe he saw a farmhouse. He typed that into the log, which he was supposed to do even if he wasn't sure. The time appeared next to his entry: 1:35 a.m.

Seth yawned.

"*Szzt*—giant cockroach—*szzt.*"

Did he really hear that, or was it his imagination? Seth shrugged and made another log entry.

According to Dr. Khepri, no visual or auditory impression was too subtle to ignore. The professor himself would sift through all the data later, after the sleeping person in the other room awoke and wrote down their dreams.

Seth tossed a crispy, cheesy puffball into the air and caught it in his mouth.

Sure, this gig only paid minimum wage, but it was a cutting-edge, first-of-its-kind experiment. Everyone involved would have their names recorded in the history books.

Of course, Dr. Khepri would get most of the glory. He was the one who figured out how the neuron phreaking, nano-amplifiers, and neural net decoders worked. Seth, however, would be famous for writing down the early recordings of the machine. He'd be as famous as Pavlov's dog, Bierka.

"*Szzt*—Edgar suit—*szzt.*"

What was an Edgar suit? It didn't matter. Seth wrote it down.

Later on, he thought there were laser blasts or something. That was more fun than usual.

Finally, at 4 a.m., when Seth was too tired to catch cheese balls any longer, he called it a night. He yawned, shrugged on his hoodie, and went out into the cold Baltimore night.

*Edgar suit.* What could it mean?

He kept thinking about the phrase "Edgar suit" as he biked home, climbed up the stairs to the apartment he shared with his grandpa, and brushed his teeth. Halfway through, he spotted a giant cockroach and skillfully struck it with a shoe.

What if it wasn't actually a cockroach but an alien monster planning to destroy the Earth? What if he, Seth, had just saved the human race?

He laughed.

That was the kind of crazy idea that went through a young man's brain after being up all night.

Laughing to himself, Seth got undressed and crawled into bed. Nefertiti, his big orange tabby, cuddled up next to him. He stroked the cat's head.

"Let's hook the Somniscope up to you, Neffer," he said, wrapping his fingers over the cat's head and pretending that his hand was the device.

Nefertiti purred.

Seth fell asleep.

Seth dreamed he was back in the DUaT and Neffer was hooked up to the Somniscope. An image of the cat chasing a mouse behind the big green sofa in the living room flashed on the screen. While Seth was writing this down, an alarm went off.

What did the alarm mean? Should he panic?

Seth blinked awake to find his phone ringing.

Bleary-eyed, he picked up the phone and struggled to focus on the screen. It was the DUaT—and it was 8 a.m.! Didn't they understand that he'd only been asleep a few hours?

He almost silenced the phone and put it down.

But what if he'd made some mistake at the lab? What if he needed to apologize for something?

He answered the call: "Hello?"

"Hello, Seth," Dr. Khepri said in a breathless voice. "Have you watched the movie *Men in Black* recently?"

What was the doc asking? It made no sense. "Um. What?"

"The movie, Seth. When did you last see it?"

"Nah, man. I don't watch old movies. I mostly watch NuToob and PickPock. Stuff like that. What is this about?"

"Seth, you are—you're unusually perceptive. Very few of the other students I had monitoring the Somniscope were able to correctly read the output. Until I started going through your logs and comparing them with what our subjects reported from their dreams, I thought I'd failed—that my device didn't work."

Seth rubbed his eyes. "So that means what? I get a raise maybe?"

Silence.

Had he really just said that out loud? The professor was probably going to laugh at him. That was what usually happened in previous jobs where Seth had asked for higher pay, better hours, or to not be insulted.

"Sure. I can't afford a huge raise, you understand. It's just—I need you, Seth. You're the key to making this work."

Seth laughed. "Me?"

"Yes! Think of it. We're going to be famous throughout the scientific world."

"So, you're the mad scientist, and I'm your pet monster?"

There was a pause. "I thought you didn't watch old movies."

"Well, I'm not totally ignorant. I had a classic monster movie elective in my senior year."

Dr. Khepri laughed. "Well, good. We're going to do great things, Seth. You and me. We're going to change the world. When can you come back to work?"

"Um, I need like six more hours of sleep at least."

"Good. I'll see you in about six hours."

"No, man, I'll need food and a shower."

"Seven then. Good. See you soon, Seth."

Before Seth could argue any further, the professor hung up.

When Seth got to work seven hours and three minutes later, Dr. Khepri was standing outside the door, hopping from foot to foot. "There you are! I thought you'd never get here."

"Sorry. I had to make breakfast for my grandpa and the cat."

"It's okay. I've arranged for a new patient. She's waiting inside. This one could be a big deal. I mean, *really* big. If the experiment works."

"Did you hook her up?" Seth asked as he dismounted and locked his bicycle.

"I—I don't like to touch people," Dr. Khepri said.

Seth nodded. "Okay, doc. Where's the lady at?"

"She's on the table already." Dr. Khepri danced up the front steps and held the door open. He grinned like a child as Seth approached. "Do you know what's special about her?"

"Tell me," Seth said, stepping inside.

"She's in a coma. Possibly brain-dead."

A tingle ran over Seth's spine. But why should making contact with a person in this condition bother him?

What if he saw the world of the dead? What if he saw things no mortal was meant to see?

Maybe comparing the doc to a mad scientist was not far off the mark.

Seth stopped in the doorway and turned around.

"Joy was a dancer on Broadway," Dr. Khepri said. "Her mother, Kait, is a special agent for the FBI. She's getting ready to pull the plug on her daughter. I'm counting on you to tell me if there's any brain activity. Is she dreaming in there, or is she dead?"

Seth said nothing.

"Did you know that I was once in a coma?" Dr. Khepri asked.

Seth looked into Dr. Khepri's eyes. It was horrible to imagine that great mind being trapped. Seth shook his head.

"When I was—in that place, I was alone, isolated. If we could reach out to one person like that and make contact, think what that would mean."

Dr. Khepri's gaze became distant.

Given the explanation, it made sense that Dr. Khepri wanted to use his device on this woman.

"You'd be a hero, Seth."

Fame was one thing, but being a hero? To live a life that really mattered?

Still, though, he worried. Could a dead person come out of the Somniscope somehow? Take over a living person? Displace their soul and possess them?

"Will I see her dreams if she's dead?" Seth asked.

Dr. Khepri laughed. "You're funny, Seth. Do you know that? No. My Somniscope reads brain activity. Electrical impulses, that's all. Dead people don't have any. Our coma patient has some, but no one knows if it's meaningful. We're counting on you to tell us. Look inside her. Let us know if there's a reason for her mother not to pull the plug on the machine keeping her alive."

Put that way, Seth's reservations sounded like superstitious nonsense.

But even smart people sometimes believed they knew more than they really did. Superstition sometimes proved true in the end. Who was right this time?

There was no way to know, but this was his chance to be a hero. An opportunity like that always came with risk.

"Okay, let's do this," Seth said.

Joy was beautiful; there was no mistaking that. If not for the feeding tube, the wires, the IV and fluids, and all the machinery, she could have been Sleeping Beauty from a fairy tale.

Seth carefully placed the electrodes on Joy's head as Dr. Khepri had taught him. First a little conductive gel. It reminded him of his mother's perfume—a bit like cherry cough syrup.

The girl's mother, Special Agent Kait, watched with a heavy stare. She made Seth feel like he was guilty of something, though he didn't know what.

Worse, the mother's despair was palpable. What would it be like to have a child and see her end up like this? Seth understood why Dr. Khepri didn't want to be here. Still, he thought it unfair to be left alone with Kait.

"Have you done this before?" Kait asked, making it sound like an accusation.

If she'd shone a bright light in Seth's eyes, it would not have felt more like an interrogation.

"With someone in a coma?" Seth said. "No, never."

"How long will it take before you know if she's in there?"

Seth shrugged and tried to make the movement look casual. It felt more like a spasm. "For normal sleeping patients, I sit and watch the screen for about six hours, since that's how long a person sleeps. Also, I get tired after that long."

Kait nodded.

"Dr. Khepri told me that, for Joy, we might have to wait longer. Like, I might need to do several shifts at the machine. The signal might be fainter, or something."

Seth looked up, and the woman met his eyes. It was a mistake he felt to the depths of his soul.

This woman was hurting, drowning in an ocean of emotional pain. One of Seth's many challenges in life was his strong sense of empathy. He had to do something to make this woman feel better. He just had to.

"Don't worry," he promised. "I'll find her. She'll be all right."

It was, of course, an insane promise. But he could no more take it back than he could have prevented himself from making it.

The woman took his hand. "Thank you."

On his way back to the observation room, Seth tripped on the data cable. The small carpet patch that covered it was supposed to keep that from happening, but it somehow kept sliding off.

Seth crawled under the desk and checked the connection. Sure enough, he'd pulled the data cable out of the computer again. He plugged it back in, tugged the carpet back into place, got in his chair, and picked up the unfinished bag of cheese balls from yesterday.

Then he let out a sigh and settled back in his chair. With a smile, he popped a cheese ball in his mouth. It was only a little stale. Still good.

Would it be a long wait before Joy responded? Frequently, Seth had to sit here for about an hour before he saw something. Of course, normally, he had to wait for the patient to fall asleep. That wasn't an issue this time. He turned up the volume on the speaker. Sometimes that helped.

"*Szzt.* Dance with me. *Szzt.*"

Wow, that was fast. Seth reached over to the keyboard and typed in the message. As soon as he was done, he glanced up at the snowy image on the monitor. Maybe he'd catch a glimpse of the person this woman was imagining as her dance partner. Would it be a movie star, or someone real?

Seth watched, waiting for an impression.

Suddenly, the woman was there, staring back at him from the screen. It was the most vivid image Seth had ever seen in the random fuzz of the monitor.

For a few seconds, he was too stunned to write down what he'd seen.

She'd been looking right at him.

That never happened. Normally, he saw things from slightly above and behind the person, as if a camera on a boom had been inserted into their dreamscape.

Well, this was his first coma patient. Some things had to be different. It was unsettling, though. It was as if the woman were looking through the monitor, like it was a window. She could not, of course, be seeing him. She was lying in a bed in the next room. Motionless. Eyes closed. There was no way she could know Seth was even here.

Seth popped another stale cheese ball into his mouth.

"*Szzt.* Put down your snacks and dance with me. *Szzt.*"

Normally, the messages were just a couple of words. Longer sentences were rare. With trembling hands, Seth quickly logged what she'd said.

As soon as that was typed in, he sighed and smiled to himself. Here he was, alone in the DUaT, and a beautiful woman had just asked him to dance.

The sad thing was that was the closest thing he'd had to a date in the past year, what with taking care of his grandpa and trying to finish his undergraduate degree at Thrice Great University.

Things went back to normal after that. Almost an hour of nothing but white noise and random pixels. On most nights, he cheated a little. He'd turn off the sound and listen to the radio for a while, or leave the white noise on and play a game on his phone with the volume off. Trying to focus on both a fuzzy monitor and hissing speaker was just too mind-numbing.

But this whole situation was different. Her early responses had been so promising; he didn't want to take a chance on missing anything.

"C'mon, Joy. Talk to me," he muttered.

Nothing.

She'd asked him to dance. Well, she'd asked whoever she was dreaming about.

If only she knew that Seth was here wishing he could speak to her.

If only she could dance.

"I'd be happy to dance with you," Seth whispered.

He sighed.

"*Szzt.* Please, Seth. It's been so long since I danced with anyone. *Szzt.*"

Startled, Seth dropped his bag of cheese balls. A few spilled out. Keeping to the five-second rule, he snatched them up and popped them into his mouth.

As he crunched, he got his fingers ready on the keyboard. Should he actually log that last message? Would Dr. Khepri think he'd gone crazy? Would Agent Kait decide he was a sicko who wanted to take advantage of her daughter?

And how was it possible that Joy knew Seth's name?

The easiest explanation was that she didn't. It wasn't all that unusual a name. There'd been two other Seths in his high school.

Still, though, it was kind of spooky.

Not wanting to mess up the experiment, Seth pushed his nervousness aside and typed in the latest message. Hopefully, he'd hear something or see something on the screen soon that would break the illusion that this woman somehow knew Seth was here.

He stared at the monitor and pictured Joy's beautiful face.

If only he could take her hand and help her up from the bed where she'd lain immobile for the last month. If only he had magical powers like the characters in comic books, he would save her by transporting her back into the real world.

And of course, it would be fine if she was grateful. Seth had never had much luck with dating, and he'd never had the courage to even talk to a woman as beautiful as Joy. What would it be like to share love with such an amazing woman?

He imagined dancing with her, holding her shoulder with his right hand just as he'd learned in that evening class he'd taken last year. They twirled around the floor together, her smile beaming joy and light into his cold, dark, lonely soul.

Seth jerked awake.

He'd never fallen asleep while at his station before.

It was a struggle to stay awake for the remainder of the session. Every time he closed his eyes, he was with Joy on the dance floor.

When his eyes were open, she often repeated her plea that he dance with her. Sometimes, he heard music playing. He didn't know the melody, so he couldn't specifically write what he was hearing in the log.

Finally, it was time to go.

Resolving to do better at staying awake next time, he threw on his jacket and rode his bicycle home. The whole way back, he kept thinking about Joy—her haunting smile, her graceful dancing… Even if he'd only imagined those things, they captivated him.

She stayed on his mind until he stepped through the door.

He wrinkled his nose.

The whole apartment smelled like rotting meat.

"Grandpa?" he called out. "What's that smell?"

There was no answer.

Seth sniffed and looked around. The odor seemed to come from the old yellow couch where his cat was sitting, regarding him with a regal, half-lidded expression. In his dream, she'd killed a mouse on the side nearest the window.

"What did you do?" he said to Nefertiti.

She flashed her sapphire-bright eyes at him.

He pulled the couch away from the wall and found a mouse carcass, partly eaten and left to rot, exactly where he expected to find it.

"Neffer," he sighed. "I appreciate that you guard us from mice, but could you do it without making such a mess?"

Her eyes shone at him with piercing yellow light, the wrath of a small angry goddess. How dare he, a mortal, question her actions?

Sleep was delayed a good twenty minutes as Seth scraped up the remains of the mouse and applied some pine cleaner to the floor.

# dream dance

As he washed his hands, his thoughts returned to Joy. "I won't fall asleep while I'm with you again," he promised.

With that resolve firmly in his mind, he went to bed.

Seven hours later, Seth's alarm went off, interrupting a dream. Once again, Seth had been dancing with Joy.

Normally, dreams seemed like insubstantial things, a washed-out version of reality. This dream, however, was different. Reality seemed washed out and faded by comparison.

Groggily, he got to his feet, the music of the dance floor still echoing in his head.

"Today, I will be a hero for Joy," Seth said.

When he got ready, he made an extra effort to shave and comb his hair. He tried to tell himself that Joy would never know the difference, but somehow, he couldn't help himself. He wanted to look his best. If by some miracle she did wake up, he wanted to be ready.

After preparing food for the cat and his grandfather, he hopped on his bike and started toward the DUaT.

On the way, his thoughts returned to that dead mouse he'd found. It had been in the same location where he'd dreamed it was when he was using the Somniscope on Neffer. It was an odd coincidence, but it was unnervingly accurate.

Thankfully, Dr. Khepri wasn't in the lab when Seth arrived. Seth doubted he could have explained why he was wearing a button-down shirt instead of the usual T-shirt he rarely washed, or why his hair was combed, or why he'd worn dress shoes.

Before he settled into his chair, he went into the next room where Joy lay, peaceful and motionless.

There was something mysterious and haunting in her beauty, like the pattern of her features and her coloring were some secret key to his soul. Seth didn't think of himself as shallow, but neither could he explain how this woman's appearance could affect him so.

"Hey, I'm back," he said. "Just help me out, okay? Your mom needs to know that you're in there and you want to live."

She didn't reply, not that he expected her to.

Summoning his courage, he took a breath, then reached out and took her hand in his. With the full force of his mind, he willed her to get up.

It was stupid, of course. He didn't have psychic powers. But still, he had to try.

After a few seconds, he sighed, let go of her hand, and walked toward his desk. On his way through the door, he tripped over the data cable again. Cursing, he got to his feet, pulled the carpet back over the cable, and walked toward his chair.

Dr. Khepri had to find a better solution for that cable. Maybe he could get a longer one and loop it over the top of the door or something? Though Seth had a feeling that, left to his own devices, the doc would never fix the problem.

Seth settled into his chair.

"*Szzt.* Thank you for dancing with me, Seth. *Szzt.*"

Seth put his hands to the keyboard. He was about to type what he'd heard, but again he hesitated. He could not escape the feeling that Joy was referring to the dream he'd had.

He glanced up at the display from Joy's visual cortex, only to see her watching him with a smile.

He blinked.

Normally, the images were only flashes, single moments of the patient's dream. This persisted.

"Uh, hello?" Seth said.

"*Szzt.* Hello, Seth. I can't tell you how good it was to be on my feet again."

"You…" Seth licked his lips. "You can hear me?"

"Of course I can. *Szzt.* I've been so alone, until you found me. *Szzt.*"

Seth rubbed his eyes. He was definitely awake.

"I, um…I'm glad I can talk to you. Your mother will be happy to know that your mind is intact, that it's still working after— after whatever it was that happened to you. When I play back the recordings of these sessions—"

"*Szzt.* She'll see and hear nothing."

# dream dance

Seth paused. "Why? Your messages are clear. Anyone should—"

"Check the cable. *Szzt.*"

Glancing toward the door, Seth began to wonder: How did she know about the cable? Hadn't he checked that it was connected after the last time he'd tripped over it? He couldn't remember. He must have though. Otherwise, how could he be hearing Joy?

He got to his feet, walked to the door, and bent down to look under the cabinet. Sure enough, the data cable was disconnected.

Staring at this unbelievable sight, he felt his fingers and toes go numb. What was happening?

"*Szzt.* Dance with me again, tonight, Seth."

Seth thought about the mouse, about his dream, and his cat. Then he thought back over his time in the DUaT. Seth was always the one to connect the Somniscope. Dr. Khepri didn't like touching patients. What if…What if Seth had the power to hear people's dreams? What if all the Somniscope did was to make him believe he could, thereby enabling his power?

Slowly, he got to his feet and walked over to the next room where Joy lay on her bed. He reached over, placed his fingertips against her forehead, and closed his eyes.

*Joy?* he said inside his mind.

At once, he found himself in the ballroom he'd dreamed he was in the night before. He could see the stars of light thrown by the crystal chandeliers, hear the rich sounds of the wood and wind instruments used by the band. He wore a tuxedo of black silk. Joy was dressed in a sari of nearly transparent linen. Gold adorned her wrists and neck. At the sight of her, he could barely breathe.

The ceilings were high and painted with murals in the style of ancient Egypt. Arched doorways led to a moonlit night. Pyramids stood along the skyline.

"Is this real?" he asked.

It felt real. It looked real. The scent of steak and perfume lingered in the air. It even *smelled* real.

She stepped closer and took his hands in hers. "I've spent the last month creating this world, each and every detail. We are on an island in the midst of a sapphire ocean. There are mountains, cities of marble, floating gardens, rivers lined with a thousand types of flowers. I can make anything—except a companion.

"Or rather, I can, but they aren't real—more like puppets, doing and saying only what I command, when I command. Tell me that you're here, inside my dreams. Tell me I haven't just gotten better at imagining."

Seth laughed. "I'm sure that if you'd imagined someone, he'd be more handsome than me."

She reached up and placed a hand against his cheek. "Never."

Seth's heart thumped. "Then, um, maybe we should dance?"

The tempo of the music suddenly increased, and they whirled together, spinning in each other's arms, twirling around the dance floor.

Everything was more real than reality itself had ever been.

"It's like the world has always had a secret," Seth said. "And I've just learned it."

She leaned in to kiss him—and the world shattered, vanishing as quickly as it had appeared.

Seth tasted blood from where Joy's mother had punched him. One of his teeth felt loose. Those angry eyes bored into his, piercing him, flashing with venom.

Agent Kait stood between him and Joy, her hands balled into fists. Though the gun at her side was discreetly holstered, it stood out in Seth's vision like a beacon.

"What else did you do besides kiss her, you little sicko?" she barked.

It took several seconds for all that to sink in. In the dream, Joy had been about to kiss him. In the real world, apparently, he had bent down to kiss her.

"It's not what you think," Seth said.

How was he going to explain it, though? Would this woman believe he had the power to enter dreams, to see and hear the thoughts of sleeping people? Would she understand that he'd connected with Joy enough to visit her internal world?

"Tell me," Kait said. "When did you take Dr. Khepri?"

Seth blinked. "What?"

"I know what you've done."

There was such certainty in her voice—but what on earth could she be talking about?

"As far as I know," Kait said, "he's the only coma victim who's ever been kidnapped. Did you abuse him too?"

Seth slowly pulled himself up to his feet, blinking. Kait kept her fists raised, her eyes burned like flaming swords.

"I don't know what you're talking about. I spoke to Dr. Khepri just yesterday. He's not in a coma."

"Stop being stupid. We searched your apartment and found him lying there, feeding tube in his stomach, respirator plugged into a large battery. I know."

The room spun; Seth leaned against the wall. "You went inside my apartment?"

"I had a warrant," Kait said.

"I swear to you, he— I—"

Thankfully, Dr. Khepri stepped through the door.

"Look," Seth pointed. "He's standing right there. Doc, I know you don't like talking to people, but please, tell her what's going on."

Kait glanced in the direction Seth had pointed.

Dr. Khepri said nothing. He just looked sadly at the floor.

The fire in Kait's eyes dimmed. "There's no one there, Seth."

"Of—of course, he—he's there," Seth said. "Look!"

But the cold feeling in the pit of Seth's stomach said otherwise. Memories floated through Seth's mind—mixing Dr. Khepri's food, pouring it into the feeding tube.

"Do you know what this means, Seth?" Dr. Khepri asked.

Seth stared at Dr. Khepri. He shook his head.

"It means my invention doesn't work."

Seth rubbed his eyes.

What was real? What wasn't? His lip was bleeding; presumably, that meant Joy's mother was real—and Joy, too.

"Do I—do I own a cat, or did I imagine Neffer also?" Seth asked.

Seth looked again at Kait. Her fists were lowered. There was wariness and pity in her expression now. Was that better or worse than hatred?

"Your cat is real," Kait affirmed.

If the cat was real, then maybe the dead mouse had been also—and maybe Seth's dream about the dead mouse. Did that mean that Seth's ability was real? What if his mental power was the reason that Dr. Khepri existed?

"Was Dr. Khepri trying to develop a Somniscope before—before whatever happened to him?"

Kait shrugged.

"It matters. Does Joy love dancing?" Seth asked. "Was she into Egyptology?"

Kait said nothing, but her eyes narrowed.

"The Somniscope—" Seth took a breath. "Joy created a world in her mind. There were pyramids, statues, a dance hall, music, an orchestra… Would the real Joy have done that, or did I make all that up?"

Bared teeth were Kait's answer.

Dr. Khepri shook his head sadly.

"That's what I saw," Seth said. "In her mind. It proves—"

"It proves that you don't remember looking her up online any more than you remember kidnapping Dr. Khepri."

That was actually a good point.

"I don't—wait. Didn't you ever speak to Dr. Khepri?"

Dr. Khepri sighed and put his hands over his face.

"On the phone only," Kait said. "I made recordings. My analysis team says it's *you*."

"Me?"

"Sorry, Seth," Dr. Khepri said. "I sort of possessed you."

"You wore me," Seth said, realizing, "like a Seth suit."

That was why that phrase "Edgar suit" had disturbed him so much. Deep down, he'd known what it meant to be controlled from the inside.

Kait held out a pair of handcuffs. "I don't have time to listen to you talk to your imaginary friends. Will you come willingly, or do I have to beat you senseless?"

# dream dance

Seth thought furiously. What could he do? He stared at Dr. Khepri. The old man stood about ten feet away, hands in pockets, staring dejectedly at Joy. Was he real in any way? How had he made the leap from his dying body to Seth's head?

"Tell me something, Joy," Seth said, staring at the motionless girl. "Something only your mother would know. Help me."

Joy didn't move. Didn't speak.

He should be able to hear her. He didn't need the device; he knew that. It was unplugged. All he needed was the right frame of mind to hear her.

"This is my fault," Dr. Khepri said. "You let me live in your mind, and I took over too much space. You're better off without me in here—better off knowing the things I've been hiding from you."

Seth blinked. What was the doc saying?

Then he felt his mind begin to clear. It was like dawn coming to a dark countryside, revealing an unknown landscape. Seth remembered seeing Dr. Khepri in a nearby hospital bed on the day his grandfather had passed. He remembered sensing the old man's dreams. Something about their vividness made them impossible to ignore.

He'd begun to share dreams with the old man from that night, and together they'd concocted the plan to kidnap his comatose body. Physical contact made it easier to maintain the mental connection, the waking dreamworld they'd shared.

Seth remembered how his powers worked now, how he could recognize the emotional opening in a person's mind and shift through it. He felt confident he could do it with Joy, and even a waking person.

Kait stood between him and Joy, handcuffs at the ready. She was staring at Seth like he was a cockroach who had just stepped into her kitchen.

"All I want is to prove to you that your daughter is still in there," Seth said. "Don't turn the machine off."

"That's none of your business. Will you come willingly or not?"

He needed to reach Kait, but she was nothing except emotional barriers. Her thoughts and will were an impenetrable tower of rage.

She stepped forward.

Should he run for it? Try and hide and find a way to come back?

No, there wasn't any point to that. He couldn't hide from the police.

He shifted his gaze to Joy, his beautiful dance partner, the woman he'd almost kissed a few moments ago. He'd look at her for whatever time remained to him.

Kait grabbed his wrists.

Contact.

Though she was angry, determined, and her emotional shields were up, he could feel a crack in her psychic defenses.

Hope.

Some part of her wanted to believe that her daughter still lived.

Seth shifted his thoughts, moving into the mother's mind, looking for the hidden place in the depths of the soul where people were always dreaming. He found it and brought her to the dance hall—or, at least, his best memory of what it looked like.

They stood there, listening to the band together, smelling the food, seeing the patterns of light thrown by the crystal chandeliers.

Kait's gaze darted around the room in alarm.

"This is where she is now," Seth explained. "Well, my rendition of it, anyhow. Her version is much better. More detailed."

She didn't believe what she was seeing. Worse, Seth could see in Kait's mind that she'd resolved to unplug the life support machines and let her daughter die.

This was his chance, if ever he was going to have one. He needed to bring Joy into the shared dream. He shifted his mind, let go of Kait.

Soon, they were back in the lab together. The transition made him feel off balance. He stumbled but avoided falling.

"Don't do it Seth," Dr. Khepri said. "Kait's dangerous right now. Let yourself get checked in to a mental hospital for a few days. You'll be able to prove your abilities easily. You'll be famous. You'll be able to save Joy, and other coma patients as well."

He knew the doc was right. Kait had all the emotional stability of a rattlesnake that had been stepped on. All he needed was time.

The problem was, Joy didn't have it.

With one hand Seth reached out and touched Joy; with the other, he stretched for Kait.

It had only been a fraction of a second since Seth had slipped out of the waking dream, but already he could feel the confusion and anger building inside of Kait.

He understood—sort of. A police officer's life experience probably wouldn't make it easy to trust people or believe in miracles. Already, he could feel her mental defenses at work. She had dismissed the vision of the dance hall as not real. If anything, the attempt to open her mind had made things worse.

The woman who'd knocked Seth's tooth loose was back, ready to protect her eternally sleeping daughter from the creepy guy who'd tried to kiss her.

The gun in her holster entered their shared awareness. There was nothing Seth could do to quell her anger.

He stretched his hands. If he could just touch both of them at the same time, he could be a bridge. Kait would see her daughter was alive. He needed to move faster.

As if in response to this thought, the world slowed.

Seth saw the gun rising, and he reached back to touch the hand that held it.

Connection.

Seth shifted his mind. The finger covering the trigger contracted. There was a click.

An explosion sounded in slow motion, like ocean waves crashing against a rocky shore. Where did the gun point? There was no time for that question now.

Again, Seth shifted his thoughts, and suddenly they were in the dance hall together. All three of them.

For several long seconds, all they could do was stare at each other.

"You see?" he said. "She's in here. Alive. I can reach her."

The muscles in the mother's face spasmed. Tears formed in her eyes, and the two women rushed together. Seth stepped back.

How long could he stretch this moment? When it ended, what would happen?

He closed his eyes.

Outside, in the real world, the bullet was traveling. He should have known this would happen, should have guessed how this cynical, world-weary police officer would have reacted to the perceived threat. But would he have done things differently?

In this way, he saved Joy. Seth was finally a hero. And not just any hero; he'd saved the woman of his dreams.

Pain entered his body. It was the bullet. No doubt about that.

Joy cried out. "Mother! What did you do?"

The world spun and went black.

A long, quiet emptiness followed.

Seth floated in the waters of a wide river. A dark-skinned man approached. He was bare-chested. Bands of gold adorned his arms. In one hand, he held a scepter; in the other an ankh.

But it was his face that terrified Seth.

Where his head should have been was a giant beetle, complete with mandibles and legs.

Seth screamed.

The beetle said, "Live again," and placed the scepter in Seth's hands.

Seth opened his eyes. He was back in the dance hall. Both Joy and Dr. Khepri were there.

"What happened?" he asked. "Am I dead?"

Dr. Khepri grinned. "In a way. If I'm not mistaken, you're in a coma, like the rest of us. My theory is that we're all in the same hospital ward, our hands joined together."

"You must have convinced my mother," Joy said. "And she somehow made this happen. At least, that's my guess. Regardless, I'm so excited to have people living here."

Seth shifted his mind, tried to rise from the dreamworld. Instead, he found himself standing in a hospital room. All three of them were near each other in beds, but their hands were not joined as Dr. Khepri had guessed.

How was it that Seth stood outside himself?

# dream dance

That was when he noticed the scepter in his hands. It was longer than Seth was tall, shiny and black, and topped with a golden sculpture of a narrow canine head with slanting eyes. Where he gripped the staff, he felt a tingle in his fingers like the flowing of electricity. Was this thing real or a dream symbol?

Whatever it was, he'd worry about it later.

Glancing around, he found the door. He walked out and down the hallway. There were other rooms. Some had people in comas.

He walked to the nearest one, where he found an older woman lying on a bed, buried in tubes and wires. He touched her head, and his staff glowed with power. His fingers became luminous and merged with the woman. Inside her mind, she huddled in the cold, dark corner of a room. In a way, this reminded Seth of the place he'd found Dr. Khepri, except the doc's dreamworld had been a laboratory.

"Come with me," Seth said, suddenly realizing the truth about himself, about Joy, and about Dr. Khepri.

The woman rose out of herself, shimmering and translucent.

Alarms sounded in the machines which held her body in their technological embrace.

"Where am I going?" the woman asked.

"To another world," Seth answered.

Seth would guide her to Joy, and Dr. Khepri would bind this woman to their shared dream, to a new fabric of reality that stretched beyond the mortal world. Each new soul would make it stronger.

Seth had been an ordinary kid, hoping to be a hero and find the girl of his dreams. Now he had become something more, a rescuer of souls. And his dream girl? She was truly a goddess of dreams, a maker of worlds.

Not only was her name Joy, but she *was* Joy.

And Seth? He protected the dead on their journey to the afterlife she created.

# INTERLUDE 0

**As I regain consciousness, I realize there's no way I'm going in** to work today. It's impossible to tell in this windowless apartment, this to-the-letter manifestation of the basic assistance laws everyone's so proud of, but it's practically sundown already. By the time I get set up downtown, the cred I'll be able to earn will hardly cover my round-trip train fair.

Oh well. There are more important things than money, right? Mental health, for one.

I get up, perform my morning ablutions, and stare at myself in the mirror for a good ten minutes. Who even am I now? I don't remember getting this wrinkled, this fat…How do you even get fat on basic assistance? All the high-creds are keeping young and trim, and I *know* they eat more than I do. And do less physical activity, probably. Something doesn't add up.

I crawl back onto my futon and settle in for another random dream pulled out of some poor sod's unconscious mind, their sacred, sovereign psyche. There ain't no justice.

# 5. MAN, STARTLED BY STRANGE PHENOMENON

## by jeff noon

*The new expression came to Andy's face at three in the* morning. He had woken up from a dream and stumbled through the dark to the bathroom. He washed his face at the basin and then looked up to examine his features in the mirror. Big day tomorrow. A good job. Maybe he shouldn't have had that extra drink at the bar. His skin looked lax, a bit flabby. Still, in his game a bit of flexibility helped. You needed a mobile face, a living face, not one of these modern actors' faces, all tightened by chemicals and surgery. Dead flesh. No, not for Andy. He was a gesturist. One of the best. A few years back, he might have boasted that no one came near. The Man of a Thousand Expressions, that was Andy Clough. And every one of them distinct, finely crafted, just that little bit larger than life.

Man, Slightly Pleased with Himself.

Man, Smiling with Melancholy Undertone.

Man, Saddened by Future Prospects.

Oh yes, he could do them all; he could express anything!

He made a few of his favorites now in the mirror, his audience not the usual millions online, just himself. His hands added their own set of coded signals, intensifying the poses.

Man, Obsessed with His Own Image.

Man, Thinking Back Ruefully on Past Indiscretions.

Man, Scared of Possible…

And then he stopped, mid-gesture.

Something had flickered across his face. Something new and different.

What was that?

He tried his best to replicate it, to bring back the expression.

No, he couldn't find it!

He had been transferring from Man, Scared of Possible Repercussions, bringing his face back to neutral, the usual practice. Gesture Zero, as they called it in the game. The Blank Expression. It was the first thing they taught you: always return to Zero, then move onto the new expression. But this time…something had crept into the blankness. Something quite startling, or so it seemed in that one second of life. Could it be? Could he have invented a new expression?

Why, that hadn't happened since…since Jennifer Barlow had created Halfway Happymad. And before that, the dreaded Duck Face. (Less said the better.) But this one looked different somehow… something he had never seen before.

He slept well for the rest of the night and arrived at the studio fresh and ready for action. He limbered up in the gents', running through the Advanced Standard Set. Everything was in place: Knowing Grin, Ever-So-Brave Smile, Thousand-Yard Stare, Semi-Puzzled, Mid-Brow Frown, Filled with Wonder, Oops I Made a Mistake but Not Really I Knew What I Was Doing All Along…

Henley was there, of course. Andy could never quite shake him off.

Brian Henley.

They had started out together, in the same year at college, with Kate alongside. The three of them landing that first job with Gesture Stock, some trio scenarios. Two Men Talking Lasciviously About Female Colleague. Man and Woman Gossiping About Male Colleague. Man and Woman Almost Kissing, Second Man Looking On, Jealous. It was like their story together, told in a series of *tableaux vivants*. Still, all that was so many expressions and gestures down the line by now. They were professionals. They could still get on.

"So, Brian…How's Kate?"

"Kate?" Man, Flippant, As Though Unfortunate Event Not Important, Probably Lying to Himself. "Oh, you know…Easy come, easy go."

"She's moved on?"

"That she has."

They always talked in this manner, without inflection, features in neutral, hands firmly fixed at their sides. They were saving their best expressions for the work ahead.

"Last I heard," Brian continued, "she was doing some people texture work."

"People texture? Kate's worth more than that."

"Tell me about it. But she went a bit crazy on me."

"How so?"

"You know how it gets sometimes…in the business. One face too many, eh?" Henley laughed without humor.

"Sure…sure…"

Andy imagined Kate's rendered image standing, walking, pointing, laughing, in "Plaza of New Office Building" or "Proposed Airport Concourse" or "Reception Area of High-Class Hotel." Probably part of a pack: *50 Professional Women Walking*. Or *75 Confident Women*. Or even *100 Married Couples with Children*. Still, being seen in miniature in an architectural drawing wasn't anywhere near as snazzy as close-up expression and gesture work. She must have really fallen on hard times. *It could happen to any one of us.* As their tutor had said, repeatedly, "You're only one bad expression away from the unemployment office."

The photographer was Liz Meyers. Andy was glad. He liked Liz. She was an old-timer, her youth spent running around the world shooting important news events, or being embedded with the troops…Now she contented herself with photographic stock shots for the online companies, and she was happy with her lot, or so it always seemed.

There were four gesturists on call that day. Andy did well, being asked to reshoot some newcomer's attempts at Man in Denial of His Own Guilt. It was a tricky one. Many would go for full Self-Knowledge of the Guilt, and then wear Denial as a mask. Not

Andy: he preferred to totally deny the Guilt and wear Denial with pride. It was subtle. The youngsters just didn't get that. He blamed the current lack of proper expression in the faces of actors, all those leading men with their Slight Frowns and the women with their Slightly Superior Grins. That was the problem: those were the prime expressions the kids were seeing; what else could they do but copy them? God, he wished he could have lived in the silent era. Imagine, your every expression exaggerated and glorified, shining on the silver screen! The audience would never have seen such giant faces before, such magnificent expressions of Love and Fear and Tenderness, and yes…Chaplin's amazing Bittersweet Smile in the Face of Utter Tragedy.

Still, all in all, a good day.

There was one moment though, when Liz had asked him if everything was all right.

"Absolutely. Why? What's the problem?"

"You looked a bit off just now, between faces."

"No, no. I'm fine. Let's keep going."

Two hundred expressions in three hours. Not bad, not bad at all. And then in the afternoon, one hundred and fifty gestures. He did some Two Men work with Henley, which brought back memories of the good times. Two Men Laughing at Joke. Two Men, One of Them Worried, the Other Consoling. And that old standby: Two Men Arguing Vehemently. The ghost of Kate Lawson floated over their gestures, the missing third element. Two Men Talking About a Woman They Used to Know and Were Both in Love With…

That evening, Andy did an image search and found some early photographs of the three of them, illustrating various examples of Interpersonal Relationships in the Modern Workplace. The shots were only seven years ago, yet they all looked impossibly young and innocent. He downloaded one image, watermark and all, and cropped it in his freeware photo editor, cutting Henley out of the picture. Now it was Man and Woman in Office, One Staring into Space, the Other Pensive, Slightly Mystified. And the more images he cropped, enlarged, brightened, and colorized, the more the possibilities multiplied! Satisfied, he added a caption to his favorite creation, something witty he'd once said. Man Telling Joke, Two Colleagues Ignoring Him? Not any more. Now Kate was Woman, Laughing Uproariously. It was all so sweet. And the watermark across her face only made it more poignant. *We are living and breathing in our true expressions, on the other side of the legal requirements, where all countenances are copyrighted equally…*

Before going to bed, he searched the bathroom mirror for that strange new expression.

No, not tonight.

Liz called him the next day, asking him to come over to her studio.

"Why? What's up? You need some reshoots?" He was hopeful of a bit of extra work.

"No, nothing like that. Just come over, Andy. We need to chat."

Within an hour he was sitting next to her, watching the images from yesterday's shoot glide by one by one on her computer screen. He had always loved to look at his face. This wasn't in any way vanity; he certainly didn't think of himself as handsome or anything like that. He always struggled with such things as Devilish Smirk and Moody Smoldering. In fact, he had the average, fairly bland looks that worked best for a gesturist, the middling kind of face that could travel easily in various different directions in search of expressions. But his own face fascinated him all the same. And with good reason. For many years as a child, he'd been incapable of seeing himself in a mirror. There was no reflection, only a soft gray haze where his face and upper body should be. Sometimes, if he really concentrated, he might see the blue of his eyes, or the redness of his lips. But they quickly faded. In consequence, he learned to see himself as others saw him, using their reactions as his looking glass. He was however fully visible in photographs, and his first phone—a birthday gift—was a revelation. To others the selfie might be a way of recording a moment in time, or of creating an interesting image to increase your social media status: but to Andy Clough, it was proof—proof that he had a face, a set of expressions, an image to show to others.

Eventually, the mirror gave up its secrets, lifting the veil on the face. This happened on the day after his father's funeral.

Liz stopped on one particular photograph. "What do you think this is?" she asked. "What does it stand for? What are you trying to show?"

Andy stared at himself on the screen. It was that same expression, the one he had glimpsed the other night in the bathroom. The new strange arrangement of his mouth, eyes, cheeks, and chin and brow, all to offer up this…this…

"I don't know," he answered truthfully. "I don't know what it is."

Or more so, to himself: I don't know *who* it is.

Liz looked at him. "I've never seen anything like it, Andy. I mean…what is that emotion? What on earth are you expressing?"

He could not answer.

Liz printed out a copy of the image for him, and he took it home and pinned it up next to the mirror and tried his very best to replicate what he saw. But no matter how cleverly he organized his features, using all the skills he had built up over the years…he could never bring it to his face.

He grew restless. He drank more than usual. He was off his food.

On his next job two days later, Andy messed up a couple of times, on really basic things like Mild Surprise and Grim Determination. He laughed it off. But the week after he was told not to bother coming in because "The Manifold Imagery company is looking for the highest commitment from its artists." Those bastards! What did they know about the human mask and its hidden emotions? Nothing, nothing at all.

And he dreamed that night of all the expressions and gestures he had ever made over the years, for himself and for the public's benefit, as displayed on websites, in marketing brochures, even on billboards. After so many hundreds of these faces had shown themselves, he found himself staring at other expressions, the ones beyond the norm: the fevered face; the shivering face; the face made of pain; the blood-speckled face; the slashed face; the gleeful murderer's face as the knife goes in; the face eaten by its own shadow; the pitiful, broken, disgustingly weak face; a coward's face;

the face drowning; the face of the night; the face of mist; the face fading, fading, fading…fading from the mirror's grasp…

He woke up, his cheeks and brow melting under his touch.

The bathroom light clicked on.

He stood beneath it, staring into the mirror.

For a moment, he feared the haze of his youth had returned. The blind spot, as the doctor called it: "All visual fields have a blind spot, Andrew. A place where the mind cannot focus."

But the mist quickly dissipated. Now he saw himself clearly. Without thinking, he was going through the Basic Standard Set, and then the Advanced Standard Set, and then the Expert Nonstandard Set.

Man, Trying to Remember Something He Would Rather Not Remember.

Man, Hoping for Better Things but Knowing He Will Never Quite Achieve Them.

Man, Pretending to Think About Nothing in Particular While Secretly Thinking About a Matter of Great Import.

His hands were now in play, gesturing as needed as the expressions flowed on without pause, with no return to Zero in between, only the flow, the constant unfolding of the outward physical signals denoting each inner emotion.

*If only…If only I could…If only I could feel…the same emotions… as I depict…*

And then he saw it, that new strange expression.

And this time it stayed on his face.

He leaned forward, hoping to decode the emotion.

It came to him as an inkling only, the shadow of a shadow…

But that was enough, enough for him to intuit…that no human being upon the earth had ever felt such a thing before that day! No one!

Logically, he then thought: *Some other creature must have taken over my face…*

The muscles were trembling around his eyes and lips and over his cheekbones, and he feared he would soon lose his hold on the expression. He hardened his will. But the closer he leaned into the mirror, the more the expression blurred. Something veiled the final understanding, a mark on the glass. His fingers traced the shape.

It was a watermark.

It looked for all the world as though someone had breathed on the glass from the other side, and then made this shape with their finger…which mirrored exactly in movement his own finger. And he could not tell if he, Andy Clough, had made the mark or the other person inside the glass.

The expression left his face.

He went into the living room, opened his laptop, and searched for the same watermark. It didn't belong to any of the big or medium-sized photo stock companies—he knew that—yet he was sure he'd seen it before somewhere…

It took him just under an hour to find the website.

It was nearly half past five by then. Dawn. He had no idea of the time going by.

The company called itself Visual Depictions. They did a fair bit of gestural work but mainly concentrated on people texture. He opened one of their latest images in a new tab and enlarged it. It showed the pristine forecourt of an upmarket apartment block complete with fountains and flower beds between the pathways. *Haven House. To be completed…* There was a date, eleven months from now. *Show apartment now open.* How happy and successful the people looked as they strode along the pathways, or took a well-deserved rest on one of the conveniently placed benches. Kate was among them. Kate Lawson. Confident, Well-Dressed Professional Woman #7 of 50. Black knee-length skirt, matching tailored jacket, smart handbag suitable for both office and leisure. Her features, even at this small scale, had that airbrushed look about them, all imperfections removed.

But what was that expression on her face? Could it be…?

Andy transferred the image into his photo editor and magnified it, and magnified it again, and again and again, seeking an answer but finding only a blur of pixels.

That afternoon, he went round to Kate's flat. She wasn't in, and her flatmate explained that Kate hadn't been home for about a week now. "I don't know where she is. I tried texting her. Nothing."

But Andy had an idea.

He waited until nightfall and drove out to Westbridge, one of the up-and-coming areas of the city. He parked his car and got out to walk the length of the wooden fence on Old Canal Street. A greatly enlarged version of the architectural drawing of Haven House was printed on the fence, offering glimpses of the life-to-be for future residents. Yes, there was Kate, as depicted, the same pose he had gazed at the night before on his computer.

A sign warned that security guards patrolled the building site. Normally—two weeks ago!—this would have worried Andy Clough, but not now. He climbed onto a junction box and from there to the top of the fence. He dropped down the other side, landing on the soft ground. It had rained that afternoon. He moved silently and nimbly, like a shadow. He felt that his body had been reduced to its bare minimum, enough elements to show that he was a human being—a Professional Male Walking with Great Purpose—but nothing more. He belonged here! Indeed, as he looked out across the building site, he could picture the magnificent buildings, pathways, and flower beds that would one day occupy the land. Haven House. It sparkled in his eye as though already present.

The sight of a man walking between a shed and a temporary toilet unit broke Andy out of his trance. The man held a guard dog by its lead. But they were some distance away, on the other side of a vast foundation pit dug into the earth. Andy slipped along, keeping to the wall, until he reached the show home. It was an odd sight, this single erected building surrounded by rubble and building materials and tools. But when he looked in through a window, he saw how perfect it all was: upscale furniture, fine-art prints, a well-stocked bookshelf. Truly, an Ideal Home!

Was that a figure sitting in the dark, in one of the armchairs pulled up before a home cinema screen? But the screen was dark, as was the room. And the figure was immobile.

Andy tapped on the glass.

The figure did not respond. Kate Lawson continued to stare at the blank screen.

Andy walked round to the rear of the home, where he found a window large enough for him to climb through. One day in the future, this window would look out over the cleaned-up canal and the new waterside leisure park, but for now it gazed only at a wooden fence and a pile of bricks.

He picked up a half-brick from a stack and used it to break the glass.

The sound startled him.

Man, Worried. So many times he had made that gesture in his work, so he was perfect at it now, in reality.

But no one came to investigate. He waited for a few minutes to make sure and then put his hand through the broken section of glass to lift up the latch. He climbed through into the kitchen. It would be foolhardy to switch on a light, but he could tell that the kitchen was fitted out with all the latest conveniences and gadgets, spotless, unsullied. And yet a single bowl and spoon rested on the drying rack. Someone had eaten. The bowl was still wet. The cupboards held tins and packets of food, the most popular brand for each item. The fridge buzzed in a well-mannered tone. Andy walked along the corridor to the living room, but it was empty now, the armchair vacated. He turned and looked up the flight of stairs.

"Kate? Are you there?" His voice was hushed.

No reply. Silence. Darkness.

He climbed the stairs and stood at the open door of the master bedroom. The sheets on the bed were ruffled, as though recently slept in. The curtains were open. Moonlight lay halfway across the floor and the bed. He could smell perfume in the air. It was a ghost, a woman's shape formed by the molecules of scent. And he breathed it in, deeply.

At the window, he looked down and saw Kate below, walking away from the show home.

He hurried downstairs, this time leaving by the front door, which swung open at his touch. He rushed outside and looked around, this way and that, trying to see her…

Yes, there she was, walking along at a steady, even pace.

He followed her, keeping his distance as yet, still a little wary.

He did not call her name.

The further they went, the more the future paradise of Haven House materialized around them. The fountains and pathways emerged shining from the night air. He could feel the spray of the water on his face! Before him, the completed building rose up, its five stories holding such treasures: affordable apartments for those with luxury in mind.

And then Kate came to a halt.

She waited, her back to him. One hand smoothed down the lines of her smart business suit; the other clutched the handle of her bag, perhaps a little too tightly.

"Kate?"

His voice was loud now; he didn't care anymore.

"Kate. Let me see you. I need to see your…your face. Let me know what it holds. Kate?"

At last she turned.

Woman, Turning to Greet Someone.

Woman, Seeing Someone She Once Knew, Now Unsure as to Whether She Wants to See Them Again.

Confident Professional Woman, Her Current Prospects in Jeopardy Because of Past Secrets Now Brought to Light.

Woman, Her Face Possessed by Some Otherworldly Presence.

Andy gasped. There it was: the secret expression, the *true* expression…It felt so good to be able to share this revelation with someone. And he felt sure that he now knew just what it meant. And it shocked him, and frightened him, to his core.

Man, Startled by Strange Phenomenon.

The apartment block trembled at the corner of his eye, and the water features and flower beds of the forecourt were already fading away. He didn't have long.

Kate spoke in a flat tone: "I'm moving on, Andy. The expression has taken me over. It's a beautiful feeling."

"Kate, what are you saying?"

"I have to leave now. I have new gestures to make. New sites to populate."

"Help me. What should I do?"

"The others are arriving. Can't you see them?"

"Wait!"

Despite his fear, Andy walked toward her…

Man, Dreaming. Man, Dreaming of Something Long Lost. Man, Wondering About the Thing Long Lost, in a Dream. Man Dreaming of Being Lost in a Dream, Seeking the Thing Lost. Man, Losing Himself in a Dream, Thinking Back on Other Dreams He Once Had. Man, Lying in a Pit at Night, on a Building Site, Thinking He Might Be in a Dream. Man, Waking, Realizing It Was All a Dream. Man, Upon Realizing It Was All a Dream, Trying to Retrieve That Dream, but Failing. Man, Hearing a Dog Bark, Waking, Startled. Man, Cursing Himself, That It Might All Have Been in His Grasp…

There was but a shiver between each visual depiction and the underlying feeling. It would only take a little more work, and then he would experience the emotions for real.

Man, Slowly Realizing…

He was lying in the mud, a soft rain falling on him. Luckily, the foundations of the apartment block had not yet been excavated very deeply. The security guard stood above, on the pit's edge. His dog was barking wildly, straining at the end of the leash.

Andy collapsed into the mud. His eyes closed.

His face was blank, his gestures at rest.

Man, Sleeping.

He woke up a few hours later.

For a moment or two, he could not work out where he was. The bed was unfamiliar.

The moonlight had moved on, and the room was dark.

He stood at the window. The building site gleamed with a spectral glow.

He stood in front of the bathroom mirror, waiting.

He was alone.

The expressions flowed across his face, one by one.

His hands made the corresponding movements, in perfect time.

Taken together, they formed a complex series of instructions: a flight path.

He thought: If I could only return my face to the blinded mirror of youth, then all of these expressions would die, and the visitors would not have a place to inhabit. For a few moments, he struggled with this, and his face did in fact blur a little at the edges. But then a drop of blood ran down from one nostril, and he faltered. And surrendered.

The new expression settled on his face, carried here from afar. It was fixed in place. It *clung* to him. He could feel its tiny little claws at work.

And then…And then relief.

The forecourt and apartment block shone whitely under the moonlight, a landscape of bone. Andy stood near a flower bed, gathering strength from those around him, his fellow examples of people texture—the *50 Professional Men and Women*; the *75 Children of Executives*; the *100 Young People of Various Races*; the *60 Creatures of Other Worlds;* the *25 Dreamers Who Could Not Quite Awaken*; the *100 Somnambulists*; the *15 Junkies Addicted to Substances Drawn From Flowers That Do Not Yet Exist*; the *10 Visitors from Dimensions Beyond Our Own*; the *12 Transients, More Liquid Than Flesh*; the *27 Wanderers on the Borderline*; the *5 People Made of Vapor, Their Bodies Inhabited by Fireflies*; the *4 Nightmare Visitations*; the *13 Ghosts of the Recently Dead*; the *9 Women Clothed in Twilight*; the *3 Living Entities of Amorphous Shape…*

All were allowed admittance here, at Haven House. Some were already shadowing the walls of the bedrooms, living rooms and kitchens, waiting patiently for the new residents to move in, a year from now.

Among them walked a man whose face shone with starlight.

# INTERLUDE E

**I open my eyes, but something doesn't look quite right. The** edges are too sharp, too meaningful, almost imaginary. Am I still inside the dream?

I get dressed and head out into the hall. It seems to go on forever. All the doors look the same, and the numbers on them are unintelligible, like some ancient pictographic script. *Bull, tent, foot, door…*I try the door with a stylized drawing of a door on it. It's unlocked.

"Hello?" I say as I ease it open a crack.

No one answers. I push the door a little farther and take a peek. It's my own apartment, no mistake.

"Okay, that does it," I say aloud. "This can't be real."

I blink repeatedly, which is supposed to be the exit code for Somniscope, a way to wake yourself up if the experience ever gets too intense. It has no effect. I give myself a pinch on the back of the hand, then several slaps across the face. I'm starting to get a little worried. I bend over at the waist as quickly as I can. That's worked before, causing me to sit up in bed. Nothing this time, just a little vertigo.

I see the Somniscope sitting beside my futon.

It's worth a try, isn't it? I put on the headset and select a new dreamcap. Here's hoping.

# 6. PALE SHADOWS OF THE FIVE

## by barry hale

## May

To know—and to know the price one must pay for knowing. To know the burden of holding a secret one could never let go. Dymion Blake had always wondered what it might feel like. Now he knew.

There had been too much rain. Dymion worried about that. Even now, in these few moments of respite from a downpour more suited to the tropics, with low sun cutting beneath black clouds to spread gold across the roofs of Soho, he knew it was far from over. The TV weatherman had indicated on his charts, there were days of it yet to come. Dymion stared out from the window of his Dean Street flat and thought of a boggy field eighty miles away. Waterlogged now, no doubt. And he thought of how a relentless rain like this might force the earth to give up its secrets. In his mind's eye, he pictured a pale hand and the slow revelation of it as each heavy raindrop dislodged another crumb of earth from its fingers. Maybe it was already too late. Maybe in another few hours of rain, the wrist would be revealed, and the tattoo there, which would be enough to identify the body.

Since the incident, there weren't that many nights when Dymion had slept alone. Always there, always present—the spirit of the man standing over him in his bed. By day, Dymion merely felt his presence. By night, in the darkness, there was always the pale shadow of the man, always visible in the corner of his eye. That's the thing that no one can tell you: how those you kill become attached to you in death.

How did serial murderers cope, he wondered. Their heads must reel with all the weight of memories by day—every long, slow, and lonely day—and by night the shadows must be crowded with the pale spirits of those they would forevermore be tied to. How did they manage, day in, day out, to quell the urge to blurt it all out? To confess, in the hope that the confession would release the pressure. Always there. Always building. How that must interfere with daily life. You buy a carton of milk; the shopkeeper hands you your change. Do you share the thought screaming inside your head? *I killed a man!* Or you're at home; you're watching TV with a friend, and he's laughing at some nonsense on the screen. You're laughing too, kind of, but in your mind you can see a man lying in the shallow grave you dug for him, and his slack jaw is open wide in a scream only you can hear. A scream only the dead can scream, that cuts through silence and fills your skull from a hundred miles away. A sound that rises up from the base of your spine, pushes through your brain, and blasts its way out through all the orifices in your skull like steam through an engine whistle.

Dymion had often wondered. Now he knew.

There were times when he took on full responsibility, times of clarity and sharp, cold acceptance of the simple fact it was *him*. He did this. It was his secret to keep, his burden to carry. It was the consequence of his actions. Something had slipped that day. The filters in his frontal lobe weren't working, the moon was full, there was something in the water—*something!* Whatever it was, he was there, the opportunity presented itself, and without another thought he placed both hands across the sleeping man's mouth and nose and held them there until he ceased to move. Not for any reason, not out of rage or for personal gain, just because he could. Because the thought that he shouldn't wasn't reason enough to stop. There were those other times, more desperate times when he could not bear the burden, when he questioned whether he was even capable of such an act. Times when he felt certain that another man or some spirit entity must have slipped beneath his skin and directed his hands to end this tattooed stranger's life. In the quiet moments when the day was done and the night was barely breathing, Dymion sometimes thought he felt the intruder shift and settle deep inside his bones.

Once the deed was done, he was immediately faced with the problem of disposal. He'd cursed himself for not thinking about that first. A shallow grave had been all he could manage at the time without any tools. There was no thought to it, no planning, just impulse with no consideration of the consequences. He'd hidden the body in plain sight, a shallow grave in a public place, but in a boggy part of it that few would try to cross. He'd been meaning for months to return, to find a better spot, dig a better hole and remove anything—everything, no matter how trivial it seemed— that might have offered up a clue to his involvement. He'd even considered ways he might remove the tattoo.

Dymion was no killer. In the months that followed, he increasingly felt the presence of his victim. Always there, waiting in attendance. Maybe real killers treasured that. They must relish the presence of a slave, silent and unseen by all but the master at whose hands they died. That wasn't him. He wondered how they reconciled themselves to that. Was it a power thing? Or did true murderers feel they fulfilled some divine purpose—as death's envoys, the harvesters of souls. Shepherds sent to lead lost spirits to the waiting pastures of their eternity. That's not how it was for Dymion. He didn't own this tattooed drunk, this random stranger he'd stumbled across passed out on a bench in the middle of the night. No, this lost soul owned *him*. Owned his every waking hour—a pale and permanent shadow falling across his mind.

Dymion resolved to fix the situation. He made a better plan, and a list of the things he'd need. He opened the computer and booked a ticket for the train.

# barry hale

## September

Dymion took the picture frame down from the wall. The skin inside was shriveling, and the tattoo had become dull and blurred. There was little point in keeping it. It no longer passed as folk art and had become no more decorative than the blackened, dried-out peel from a banana.

Lesson learned.

It reassured him that he'd made the right decision the second time: he'd denied himself a souvenir. He opened up the back of the frame, pulled out the scrap of thin leather, and simply dropped it into the kitchen bin. He stood over it for a while, looking down at just this scrap of flesh, this tiny remnant of a life. A life he'd stolen, yet did not own.

The second death was easier. It was a mercy killing. His grandfather. They were searching for him now; Dymion had seen it on the local news. But this time, Dymion had planned everything out and covered all his tracks. They'd never find the body. He'd driven the eighty miles to his Granddad's in a rented car, then driven the old man two hundred miles more to a pre-prepared location. When his grandfather had passed, he took his time to burn the body and crush the bones to dust. Then Dymion had scattered them from a rowboat across the center of a massive lake. There was nothing left to find.

The police were already talking to the next of kin. They were aware of the old fella's dementia and might put it down to that, but they'd never understand that Dymion did what had to be done. It was an act of love for a man who had lost his mind.

The evening news intimated that the police had found a clue. What clue, they did not say. Dymion revisited the order of events in microscopic detail—was there anything he may have forgotten? No. He had been scrupulous. He relaxed, confident there could be nothing that would lead them to his door. *I guess only time will tell,* he told himself. And let the tension go. He sat in the dark with the TV's sound down and felt the pale presence of the Two, the drunken tramp and his Granddad seated either side of him.

90

<h1 align="center">pale shadows of the five</h1>

## February

*Murphy's Law!* Dymion told himself it was just bad luck. The dumping site had been an industrial wasteland for decades. In fact, Dymion didn't blame himself at all, not this time. An insidious thought had entered his head from pretty much the hour after the incident occurred. There were too many inconsistencies, too many mistakes; the mode of death, the poor choice of disposal site…There was no plan. Thinking back, he could see the signs were there. Everything pointed to the hands of someone else. Something. Even before he'd spied the man, he'd felt the itch in his bones, the shifting of that parasitic soul that Dymion was now convinced had secreted itself inside him. A fog descending over his brain had let the entity take control.

Dymion had often caught the thing in the thought-free moments of his day. He would snap out of a daydream to find someone else looking out through his own eyes. He'd see the hands—*his* hands—clench and unclench his fists unbidden, as if trying out the fit.

This third incident had been messy. The subject had been reluctant to give up his breath. There had been a struggle, a full-blown fight. As drunk as the stranger was, he was still a powerful man, and where he'd landed more than a couple of lucky punches, Dymion still ached from the blows. He'd felt a thrill from it—secondhand, he couldn't deny that. The adrenaline was a rush he'd found it hard to come down from. It took a long night without sleep and the slow numbing of a half-bottle of good whiskey to find an even keel. He was complicit to some degree—yes, Dymion accepted that—but this death wasn't down to him. Not his choice. No way. Even so, the denial meant nothing in the light of more recent events. The price would be his to pay, and he was furious about it. There were brand-new fences up all around the site, and the surveyors were in with their reflective jackets and hard hats measuring things. A massive sign announced the arrival of new shops and social housing. And that was the clincher for Dymion—guilty or no, he would have to move the body.

If Dymion had been the one who'd actually done this stranger in, there'd be nothing left to find. He'd have a plan; the past had proven that. But this thing hiding in his bones had paid no heed to that. It was safe enough tucked up there away from harm. It cared nothing for its host—for Dymion. If it weren't for Dymion, the body would have been found by morning. It was he who'd wrapped it up in a dirty tarp and tied thick rope around it, and he who scouted the grounds for a suitable place to hide it. He'd made the best of a bad job, lowering the corpse deep beneath some inspection hatch in a quiet corner that looked as if it hadn't been opened in thirty years. It was sloppy work. That wasn't Dymion's way.

Now it fell to Dymion to clear up the mess. He'd have to time the security patrols, cut his way in through the fence, and find a way of moving the body back out before the wreckers came in to prep the site. He probably had a few weeks, but sooner would be better. Before the site offices were in, before the security arrived and set up shop. Dymion wondered where on earth he was going to put the corpse. For a terrible moment, he contemplated bringing him back to the flat, dumping him in the armchair in front of the TV. *It would just be a temporary measure,* the voice inside his head declared. But then what would happen if the man's spirit reunited with his flesh? What then?

He turned to face the three souls where they stood clustered in the doorway. Their pale shadows offered no answer to his question. Dymion felt the chill of them as he pushed through their faint presence. He snapped off the bedroom light and slipped beneath the duvet, pulling it high across his eyes. It wasn't enough to blot them out. Dymion could still sense the presence of the Three, gathering around the bed and staring down at him, expressionless, through hollow eyes.

## June

Blood.

The sheets were caked with it.

Dymion kicked free of the stained white cotton in alarm, leaped from his bed, and seized the sheet that had wrapped him, spreading it out across the bare mattress to inspect this mysterious map of some newly discovered land of pain. Huge smears formed their coastlines to mirror the past presence of struggling limbs and palms. Elongated spits of land where arms and legs had been, peppered at the wrists and ankles with island clusters, archipelagos of disjointed toes and fingers. Twisted skin, legs extended or folded up beneath themselves in an origami tangle that would sorely test the fragile bone within. What might have been the imprint of Dymion's own twisted face stared back at him with soul-dead eyes, a deflated moan caught at the moment it fell from his blurred and broken lips. It was the Turin Shroud of a tortured body that was wrapped while still alive and fighting to survive.

He inspected himself to seek out the corresponding injuries he saw documented on the sheet. He found blood dried across his knuckles, caught thick beneath his nails, smeared over his stomach and chest, spattered on his face and shoulder, crusted on his lips, but he found no visible wounds. No wounds…Thick blood had dried black on across his lap, his pubic hair adorned with the springtime buds of its dark crystals. Broken glass lay on the floor. A bloodied shard clearly marked with blood red fingerprints remained on the table by the bed.

Still naked, Dymion tore through all the rooms of his flat in panic, finding nothing, finding no one. He threw back the curtains to flood the living room with a thin and feeble sun, and then he dropped back onto the sofa. What the hell had happened here?

He remembered the gig—it was the last thing he remembered—the performer on the low stage, a faint shadow sketched against a wall of pillowed silver. He remembered the heat, an oily mask on his face—the thin film of others' sweat on his skin. He remembered the bar, crowded and bright, the wet beer bottle in his hand, the bite of cold inside his throat on that first draft. He remembered faces—so many strangers…He remembered leaning against the vault of Victorian brick and closing his eyes, losing himself in the moment…

Dymion remembered the molten silver of the Thames at night and how it simmered beneath a looming cloud that had yet to break with rain. There was a woman. Celine. She had led Dymion along the Embankment, down the steps by Cleopatra's Needle to the water's edge, and there she took his hand and pressed it to her breast. His left arm was about her shoulders, and he gathered her to him; his right palm fell to lightly settle on her waist. Their kisses were filled with passion, wet and greedy. Teeth and tongues clashed and tangled, as impatient as the lapping tide that climbed stone steps to kiss their feet. Above them, the needle cut its basalt shadow deep into a thin veil of stars, which were slowly swallowed by the cloud. Then lightning bloomed, strangely mute as if the storm's mouth had been stifled by the forceful hand of God.

Their tongues locked, and flames of desire rose in Dymion's core. His hands fed on her shape, her curves; his fingers pushed deep into her hair, pulling her head toward his kiss, then tracing gentle forks of electricity down her neck, her cheek, her chest, over the rise and fall of her breasts. She encouraged him to go on, to go further, to give in to the feeling of that moment to the exclusion of all else. To give himself up and become lost in a confusion of the senses. His stubble scratched gently at Celine's neck, his breath hot at her ear, charged with incoherent endearments and entreaties, with garbled promises and intimated threats. Dymion had fallen beyond the reach of language. He was hunger; he was instinct; he was his own desire personified, his lust. He had never felt such urgency, such desperation. Such greed.

There must have been a moment when the two of them returned to his flat on Dean Street. Dymion had no memory of it, but how else would she have got here? Neither did he have memories of climbing the narrow stair, nor of the events that must have led to the creation of this rust-red portrait of pain he cradled in his arms. There was no sign of her clothes and no evidence of her presence other than this blood-smeared shroud. Dymion reassured himself, *Yes, she must have left.*

Yet in the years to follow, there would be times when Dymion could swear he'd seen Celine's face in the corner of his eye, drawn on the wall in the pale and folded shadows of his net curtains where they twisted in the breeze.

# pale shadows of the five

## November

It was a whim that had drawn him out of London, but why Dymion had chosen to visit here—to lose himself for a few days in the middle of a Cornish moor—that, he didn't know. There was something bleak about it, something alien and anonymous. As if humanity were an afterthought in this forbidding land that made no compromises. Against all odds, the whitewashed stones of the Coaching Inn where Dymion was holed up had stood their ground against four centuries of the elements. The inn was a Nowhere, lost outside of time and hidden from the world, a place at least a half-day in each direction from Somewhere, Anywhere, as the stagecoach once traveled. Dymion stood protected by its porch. He hung back, close to the door, trying his best to be as unobtrusive as a shadow. His permanent need for secrecy was beginning to affect his mental health, but if the preceding months had taught him anything, it was to stay well beneath the radar.

Life in the city had grown wearing. He'd been getting twitchy. Paranoid. And a new thing had emerged, a mild form of agoraphobia exacerbated by proximity to people—unknown people, faceless people, people who may or may not be watching him. He knew it was his own fault, the constant hyperawareness. Always looking out for situations where he might fall under scrutiny and then mapping out a series of escape routes was a pressure he'd put upon himself that would inevitably take its toll. Just his luck then that the country vacation he'd booked at the most remote location he could find should place him here, at the makeshift base camp of a missing person investigation.

Dymion cast an eye over the bustle of activity across the road, feigning a disinterested air. Policemen and what Dymion assumed were volunteers mustered themselves into a long and even-spaced line; then they slowly stepped away from the inn—onto the moor, into the mists, becoming shadow with every carefully scrutinized step of ground. Dissolving. Dark smudges fading in slow motion into the gray mist of a morning yet to fully dawn. Once they were lost from sight, Dymion relaxed. He straightened himself up, turned, and stepped inside. They wouldn't find anything out there. Not in this fog. Besides, he'd not been staying at the inn that long—not long enough to have someone suspect he'd had a hand in this, the vanishing of some anonymous lost soul.

At breakfast, Dymion took his time over the poached eggs and the toast, the tea, the orange juice, yogurt and fruit salad, black coffee, and a croissant. Missing person or no, this was supposed to be a holiday and Dymion was determined to relish every moment of it. Dymion stared absently out the window at the thickening fog. Later, when the sun rose high enough to fully warm the day, when the wind had pushed the reluctant mists away, it was anybody's guess what world might manifest out there. But for now, he was cocooned. Wrapped and hidden, an absence from the world.

It was then he noticed the stranger sitting at the far end of the dining room. The man was staring at him. He was tall, middle-aged, dressed casually in a well-worn jumper and green corduroy trousers. An unremarkable man, but something about his unwavering attention unsettled Dymion. He deliberately avoided the man's gaze, quickly finished up his coffee, and rose from the table.

Up the narrow stair, along the cakewalk of corridors with their awkwardly leaning walls and floors of twisted boards, Dymion found his way back to his room above what once had been the stables. It was tiny. Basic. Nevertheless, Dymion had willingly paid a premium for the dubious privilege of a short stay in its quaint and rustic charm. There was a bed, a dresser, a kettle, and some insipid picture on the wall. There was no en-suite bathroom, though there was a mirror that barely deserved the description. Most of the silver had flaked away to leave clusters of reflective islands in a sea of dark glass.

Dymion's reflection was corrupted to the point where he could barely recognize himself. As he stared into the abstraction of it, this poor man's obsidian seeing stone, he witnessed the once-familiar topography of his face becoming that of someone else. He leaned close, fascinated as he watched the edges of his face tumble inward, into the void that swallowed the center of the glass. Some dark portal, hungry for the light, this chasm seemed to suck it from the room. Shadows bloomed upon the walls around him as if conspiring with the darkness in the mirror to draw him in. Maybe Dymion should have felt alarmed; it was like being trapped inside a dream. Compelled to step a little closer, he allowed himself to fall a little deeper in.

The floorboard by the chimney breast was spongy to the touch. It all but gave way beneath his shoe as Dymion applied the pressure of his weight. The years of rot had finally eaten through it, and the romantic in him wondered—if he was to lift the board, might he discover some hidden treasure there, some bag of gold centuries lost, some infamous highwayman's booty stashed there hurriedly just before he was arrested and led to execution?

That was not what Dymion found.

The first board came up easily—its rotten end pulled free of the nails that held it to the joist. The second was a struggle. Save for a teaspoon on the tray, settled there among the complimentary tea bags and the tiny cartons of long-life milk, there were no other tools. Brute force did the trick. He positioned the mirror just right to bounce the pale morning sun from the window and down into the hole. If Dymion bent awkwardly and cocked his head, he could just about see a nest of hair. Gray hair. Long lengths of it in frozen whorls and eddies. He moved the dresser, laid himself down on the floor, and reached an arm inside. He followed the river of soft, gray filaments to the scalp. The skin was thin and loose against the bone. The cranium shaped itself beneath his exploring fingers. He felt the heavy brows beneath the fingertips of his outstretched hand, the gentle kiss of eyelashes on the open lids. He didn't feel inclined to explore any further.

Dymion sat back in alarm, supported by the wall against his sagging frame. *How can this be?* He felt the anger rising in his chest and resolved he would not be blamed for this. If this were of his own doing, surely he'd have some memory of it. And if it were the action of the unwelcome visitor who dwelt within his bones, even then wouldn't Dymion have witnessed something of these events?

Before he replaced the floorboards, Dymion considered his two possible courses of action. The first was simple. It would put an end to it—all of it. He could declare the discovery and assist the police in their inquiries. The second appealed more to him: to push the corpse a little further in, reseal its tomb, and leave. The cloying smell of decay would alert someone to the body soon enough, but feigning ignorance could save him from a long, unwanted interrogation.

Dymion returned to the main bar, ordered a coffee, and watched it grow slowly cold while he contemplated his next move. At his side, just beyond his sight, he sensed the presence of a new companion, the fifth pale shadow of the troupe. His grandfather, the two strangers, Celine, and now this wrinkled bag of skin hung loose over the collapsing architecture of its bones in the vague shape of a man. Long, gray hair fell across the hollows of his shoulders. Confusion mixed with pain was etched on his face. Was it a silent pleading or an unfathomable yearning in the man? An aching after something undefined, perhaps something he felt had been promised to him and not delivered. Is that how the afterlife is for a believer who expects to find Heaven and finally learns there is nowhere else to go? Or was it something simple? Was it just that this now homeless spirit was summoning all that remained of his energy to speak with Dymion, to beg something vital of him, but his tongue was failing him and the words just wouldn't come? The spirit struggled with his pale shadow, thinking he was still sinew, muscle, and bone. The tongue in his head would no longer bend to the force of his will. Nothing came. And he knew, in a terrible moment of realization, that nothing would ever come again.

Soon after that, two policemen entered the bar with a handcuffed person between them. It was the unremarkable man in the green corduroy trousers from earlier in the dining room. The man was distressed, babbling despite the repeated cautions from the officers to stay quiet until he'd had his chance to speak with a solicitor. The police didn't know it yet; how could they? They didn't know what Dymion knew, so the man wasn't making much sense to them, but what Dymion managed to glean from his ramblings made perfect sense to him. The man was confessing! If you knew the references the way Dymion knew them, then the garbled fragments became scraps rich with information that only the killer could know.

*Only the killer…*

Excitement surged through Dymion with an energy unlike anything he'd felt for years. Keeping a cool exterior was a struggle, but Dymion remained in the corner, listening in as the man confessed to things only Dymion could have witnessed—about the tramp on the bench and his missing tattoo, about the death of Dymion's own grandfather, about the stranger Dymion had watched his own hands murder on the building site. The man confessed to the murder of Celine, the woman who'd vanished from Dymion's flat leaving just her twisted silhouette in blood upon the sheets. And finally, he spoke about the wizened old man, the loose-skinned corpse beneath the floor upstairs that had yet to be discovered. They were him—all him, he said. All down to him. Dymion Blake couldn't believe his luck.

There was something in the man's posture that Dymion felt he recognized. The man sat bowed, slumped, crushed as if beneath a massive weight. Dymion knew the pressure of that weight only too well. He recognized that extra gravity pulling on the bones, the marrow replaced with liquid lead. Accumulating over time. Condensing there. Solidifying. There was no doubt that like Dymion, the unassuming gentleman was possessed by some parasitic entity, an unknown lodger now squatting safe inside his bones.

It was only then that Dymion sensed a newfound freedom in his limbs, an unfamiliar lightness in his posture. A massive burden had been lifted from him. The weight he'd grown so used to carrying was now gone, as if the lead that had once lined his bones had been removed, had evaporated through his pores. The hungry spirit dwelling deep within him had slipped free of his skin—presumably to find new residence in this modest stranger across the room. Dymion remembered how at breakfast the man had stared at him so intensely—how uncomfortable it had made him. As if he'd suspected something. *As if he knew…*Now Dymion wondered whether it was actually him he was looking at. Could it be that this unassuming man had not been looking *at* him but looking *through* him—no, *into* him—already in communication with the entity deep inside? Making himself available, taking Dymion's place as the new host?

Yes, the weight was gone, but it wasn't over yet. Dymion felt the pale shadows of the Five untether themselves from him, their etheric substance pulling free of him; the tattooed tramp, his grandfather, the stranger on the building site, Celine, the body beneath the floorboards of his room, all pulling at his flesh in five directions at once. Their leaving made him giddy. He found it a little difficult to focus, but Dymion could clearly see the Five drift their paths across the room to gather round the table where this anonymous confessor spilled his soul.

Revelation came to Dymion like a body slam. And the wave of exhilaration that followed sent him reeling—Dymion realized he had been responsible for none of it. None of this was down to him. He'd convinced himself that it was, because hadn't he seen his own hands on the tattooed man? Hadn't he himself scattered the dust of his grandfather over the waters of the lake? There was no denying that, but now he knew they were his hands but never under his control. He'd told himself the murder of his Granddad was an act of mercy, and that was how he'd kept his sanity, but now that he was free of the entity, at last he could see things for what they truly were. These were not his crimes but those committed by the unknown spirit residing in his bones. Now that it was gone, Dymion felt no torment, no guilt, no burden. The secret was no longer his to carry.

He didn't stop to think about it. Within the hour, he was lost to the mists and traveling on toward Somewhere. Anywhere.

Dymion Blake did not look back.

# INTERLUDE F

**Traveling on. And on and on. Will this ever end? Am I just** stuck here forever?

That's one path to immortality, I suppose.

I walk over to the mirror in my bathroom/kitchenette area. Looking at yourself in a mirror inside a lucid dream is always interesting, but this time I don't see myself at all. I see…*you*. You're just standing there looking back at me as if this were your apartment instead of mine. Just making yourself at home, smoking a cigarillo.

"Who…Who are you?" I ask.

"Who are *you*?" you counter, with a leisurely exhale of smoke.

You remind me of this fuzzy gray cat I used to have as a kid. Something in the eyes maybe? It ran away and went missing for a while, but I eventually did see it again a few months later. It was wild then—my mom said it had gone feral—and it wouldn't come anywhere near me. It was still my cat though.

You don't seem to want to answer me, but I press on: "I know you, don't I?"

You merely smile in response and blow another puff of smoke.

# 7. THE RED SMOKE
## by david pierre
## translated by laura bailo

**The girls awoke feeling dizzy. Unseen hands whisked away the** bags that had been covering their heads, and the two friends found themselves inside a cabin made of straw and wood. They were back to back, tied to a post that acted as a central column. The floor of the place connected directly to the ground outside. Their legs and feet were dirty with mud. When they noticed this detail, both girls thought of the Estelas, a reclusive order of religious zealots.

"I told you!" Heiva said.

"You didn't actually say it," Ineri shot back.

There was a man crouched in front of them, waiting patiently. His chest was bare, its sagging skin blurring tattoos that without a doubt he'd have flaunted with pride in the past. He smiled, but he barely had three or four teeth hiding amongst his thick, white beard.

"I better call the boss," he said, and left the cabin.

They were trapped. The mud on the floor made them slip constantly, and as much as they tried, they were unable to get free of their bonds.

"Can you teleport us?" Heiva asked.

"I can't. I can't move my hands," replied Ineri.

After a few more moments, a woman dressed in a gray tunic appeared at the door of the cabin. Her skin was covered in dried mud, and on top of that were various drawings done in black ink.

Bone charms hung from her ears, similar to the ones most of the Estelas wore in their manifestations. She rested her weight on a white cane.

At length, she spoke: "I am the one in charge. But I don't deserve either title or name, as only the white shadows deserve them. We have brought you here because of this." She touched one of Heiva's swollen cheeks with the tip of her cane.

"What about my cheeks?" Heiva asked.

"They're an early manifestation of outside magic. And it's been decades since Lancastone last had the pleasure of contemplating that power," replied the Estela, gesturing at the sky.

"My cheeks are useful for storing things," Heiva said. "They have nothing to do with magic. In fact, I don't even believe the outside magic exists."

"How dare you, child?" said the woman, and hit Heiva's thigh with the cane.

"Ow! What's your deal? You can't kidnap and abuse us like this!"

Heiva moved violently back and forth and reached the retractable cane she carried in the back pocket of her trousers. She activated it and made it grow, but she barely brushed the Estela's leg, who was waiting patiently.

"You even have your own cane! It's a sign! It's a sign from the stars!" she exclaimed.

"What a cult you've got here. I don't believe any of this. Let us go!"

Heiva thrashed again. The cane slipped from her hand, but she was able to loosen Ineri's ropes a little. In that moment, Heiva touched her friend's hand, and both of them teleported behind the woman.

"Wait," said Ineri, pointing her gloved hand toward the Estela. "Can you prove what you've said? About the outside magic?"

"Of course. By the albino shadows, that I can! That's why I've brought you here. But don't point at me with those artifacts. They're ruled by death."

Ineri moved her gloves away from the woman's face and turned toward her friend. "Heiva, you have to admit that your power is very strange. It'd be logical for it to be a sign of a bigger power. Where have you seen it before? Nowhere!"

"No! No! I've said I pass!" said Heiva.

"Please!"

"I've said no. Plus, what kind of methods are these?"

"Desperate ones."

Heiva interrupted her with a huff: "I *pass*!"

Ineri removed the metallic glove from her left hand and gave Heiva a hard slap. "Think about your mother. Didn't you say that without her—"

"All right," conceded Heiva as she caressed her cheek. "What do I need to do?"

The Estela let another moment pass. "You need to face yourself to unleash your power. Enter a deep meditation and duel your own shadow," she pronounced at last.

"What the hell is that?" Heiva turned toward her friend. "Are you serious, Ineri?"

Ineri smiled.

"You have nothing to fear!" said the Estela. "If my diagnosis about your possible powers is mistaken, then you won't even be able to deep-meditate."

"Do you meditate?" asked Heiva.

"It's more of an intention, an interior manifestation that receives nourishment from the beliefs we developed after the arrival of the Witch President Vacuí more than one hundred and fifty years ago," she explained. "We are not witches, just servants. True meditation, the sort that nourishes from the stars and the abyss, the sort that reveals true power, can only be accomplished by those who are able to control the outside magic."

"So, no."

The woman shook her head.

"Well," said Heiva, "where do I start?"

"Wait here. I'll bring the red smoke."

The Estela came back a few minutes later with two face masks and an elongated fountain, which contained a liquid the color of clay. She passed one of the face masks to Ineri and put the other on herself.

"You must breathe the smoke that will come out of this container until you reach a state of deep meditation. You'd best sit on the floor and cross your legs."

Heiva obeyed, but she didn't look convinced. "What will happen if I breathe in that smoke and I can't meditate?"

"You'll lose consciousness. But don't worry. I'm sure you'll be able to go deep into the meditation."

The leader of the Estelas pressed a button on the fountain, and it expelled a red smoke that built up until it occupied the entire room. It stank of rust. Heiva coughed a few times, but soon enough she made an effort to close her eyes and breathe in the noxious gas.

Ineri and the woman watched Heiva from a few steps back.

"How will we know if it works?" whispered Ineri.

The Estela told her to wait with a movement of her hand.

Suddenly, Heiva gasped as if she were out of breath and lifted her head toward the cabin's roof. When she returned to her original position, her eyes were completely blank. The Estela made a victory gesture with her fist and smiled deeply. Then she moved her lips to say, "Now."

"*Fuck*," said Ineri.

"Oh, right," muttered the leader of the Estelas. "I forgot to tell her it is essential she beats the shadow."

"How essential?" asked Ineri. "What will happen if she doesn't win?"

"She won't know how to come back," said the woman as they left the cabin.

The transition between reality and deep meditation was abrupt. Heiva remembered herself just a moment before in the cabin, surrounded by red smoke dand sighing for how surreal she thought the whole situation was. Ineri and that woman, who didn't *deserve* a name, were watching her from a distance. Now she was still in the same place, but her friend, the Estela, and the red smoke had all vanished.

## *the red smoke*

Heiva left the cabin and walked out into the middle of a bog. It was full of cabins that served as a home for this tribe who believed in witches and white shadows. In that moment, she thought the Estelas were the perfect contrast to the advanced society of Lancastone. They lived according to nature with minimal use of their powers, and they based their existence on following the old traditions the Witch President Vacuí had brought from faraway lands. At the same time, this seemed contradictory: They didn't use the powers they were given at birth, but they venerated a magic superior to their own.

The girl advanced through the mud. An impulse made her take her shoes off. She felt the cold, cracked mud on the soles of her feet and shivered. She understood this was an oneiric world, a dream caused by the effects of the red smoke, which must be some kind of powerful drug. She felt distanced from reality, emotionally dispersed. She couldn't help thinking about her friend Ineri and her mother—they were the only people she had ever loved, and she couldn't stand feeling so far away from them.

When she'd finished convincing herself that what she was seeing was a part of her subconscious, she decided to do what she often did when she was dreaming: She would play around to change what was happening. The leader of the Estelas had assured her that she would face a shadow, but there wasn't any celestial body to illuminate this place, nor a shadow projected from any other light source. So she raised her hands, pointed to the cabins, and made them disappear just by thinking about it. She imagined rain, and a deluge of water started falling.

Heiva was soaked. She spun and danced and laughed like she did when she was a child. This kind of meditation was similar to dreams, but in dreams she didn't see everything so clearly. During deep meditation, she felt strong, just as she'd felt when she and Ineri had defeated a lieutenant of the New Evolution. The man had deserved to die, and deciding his fate had made her feel powerful, *magnificent.*

Her body grew until her head grazed the clouds, which exploded into still more torrential rain. Heiva raised her hands and cleared the sky. On this blue background, she observed the brightness of the sun. It shone firm and powerful, as if there were no fog or clouds able to face it. It burned on Heiva's skin, and she began to sweat.

She continued playing around with the sky to get the weather she wanted. She turned her dream into an ideal place where she could control everything. And she remembered once more what the leader of the Estelas had said: There wasn't a person in Lancastone able to deep-meditate, except for those who controlled the outside magic.

The Estela must have lied to them. If she hadn't, then what were those face masks for? The red smoke was some kind of drug that had transported her to an oneiric world so powerful it deserved the name *astral plane*. Heiva had never believed in such cultish ideas, and she still didn't, even now. None of that spiritual nonsense was genuine or even useful. The Estelas were fanatics who had gone crazy because of their beliefs.

Or so she thought, until the sky clouded again. The weather no longer obeyed her, and her body returned to its usual size. All this happened in just a few seconds. Heiva crossed her arms like a little girl who'd lost a race.

Sunlight barely filtered through the clouds, darkening bit by bit until Heiva's flesh and the mud beneath her feet melted into black, formless shadow.

A face appeared in the distance. A white skull that smiled— don't all skulls do that?—while Heiva sank into the darkness.

She felt as if she were falling.

As if her life were disappearing.

But she didn't lose consciousness. Instead, her body collapsed atop a small, smooth mountain. The landscape was still immersed in a profound darkness, but she distinguished the edge of a precipice, which shone a soft white.

Heiva tried to concentrate to control that dreamlike illusion the same as she'd done before, but this time she wasn't able to change anything. She was trapped on the top of the strange mountain.

She spent a while in silence, considered the possibilities, and decided that retracing her steps was a good option. She sat, crossed her legs, closed her eyes, and pictured herself breathing in that red smoke again. She imagined she was entering a new phase of the meditation or that, even better, she was returning to reality. But when she opened her eyes, nothing had changed.

Exasperated, Heiva got up and started running to check if there was an exit on the other side of the abyss. She got a huge surprise when she crashed into some kind of invisible wall, which seemed to divide the space into two plots of perfectly cut land. She felt the wall with her hands, but she couldn't pass through it.

Just then, a white shadow with Heiva's same size and build emerged from the undersoil. It put its hand up to Heiva's, as if it were her mirror image. Heiva froze. Their hands touched for an instant through the barrier, but Heiva got scared and pulled back.

"Who are you?!" she exclaimed, but her voice got lost in the emptiness.

The shadow moved its lips just as Heiva had done, then quickly retreated just as she had. They did this for a while: Heiva moved, and the shadow imitated her. Until, maybe tired of that childish game, the pale figure made a strange gesture with both hands and broke the wall with a punch, like it was made of glass. The fragments flew away as if on a breeze, though there was no wind in that place.

The ghostly figure jumped on Heiva, threw her to the ground, circled its icy fingers around her neck, and started squeezing. Heiva strained to free herself, but the creature had a colossal strength. Finally, she was able to plant a kick in the shadow's gut and put some space between them.

"Why are the enemies of good people always stronger than they are?" Heiva complained.

The shadow stopped for a moment, as if struggling to make sense of Heiva's words.

"Come on!" she taunted. "Come after me!"

The shape ran toward her, grabbed her forcefully, and dragged the girl toward the cliff's edge. At the last moment, Heiva turned and, catching her enemy off balance, hurled it into the abyss. She didn't hear any screaming or tumbling, but she felt an internal relief like she'd never felt before.

"What a potent drug," she murmured. "Yes, I know I should stop talking to myself." She paused a moment, taking in the silence. "Shit, seriously, what do I do now? There's no one listening."

She sank to her knees alone on the mountaintop. There was no longer any invisible barrier or white shadow to contend with. There was only her in the middle of a strange place. She closed her eyes, but just as before, she couldn't manage to abandon this world and return to reality.

It seemed to her as if hours were passing by. She kept looking over the precipice, but nothing changed.

Then time seemed to stop.

The entire mountain lifted up into the sky and then began to fall back down. Heiva descended along with the land until she could once again feel that familiar mud on the naked soles of her feet.

She was back on the bog now, and the cabins of the Estelas were coming back into view. From one of the cabins, the farthest one, there came a red smoke.

She could finally go back.

Heiva started running. The brisk air on her skin was liberating. She was no longer thinking about the unreality of that other world, or about how similar it was to a dream. She no longer thought the Estelas were fake believers, but nor did she care. She could only think about getting back to the reality she knew.

All of a sudden, a curtain of soothing light descended and embraced her. There in the sky, the skull she'd seen before had come back and was bathing her once more in the light of its unavoidable smile. Its eye sockets held pure darkness. Heiva was terrified of that abyss and couldn't help imagining her body slipping in, never to return.

"Meaning," the skull said without moving at all.

"Meaning?" asked Heiva.

The skull didn't speak again. It remained motionless. Its smile kept bathing Heiva in its light.

"I've fought myself. And I have won," she whispered.

The skull's mouth opened, and a white glow spilled out, covering everything in radiant starlight and enveloping Heiva completely.

# the red smoke

She lost consciousness for an instant only to come back straight away.

"Now…Now I understand. I understand everything," she said and studied the palms of her hands.

When the skull disappeared behind encroaching clouds, she touched her cheeks. The swelling that had accompanied her throughout her life was still there. But it didn't matter. Now she felt much more powerful. She felt *herself*. Able to do anything.

Before going back to the cabin full of red smoke, she lifted her hands to the sky. From them emerged a fierce starlight that destroyed everything it touched.

Everything except the cabin where she was heading, which was waiting impatiently for her return. The return of Heiva the Witch.

When Heiva woke up, the red smoke had already dissipated. Night had fallen, and Ineri was sleeping close to her on a pillow made of straw. She couldn't seem to stop moving.

"Kid," Heiva said, and kissed Ineri's head.

Heiva stepped out of the cabin and took her shoes off, as she had done in the meditation. She felt in harmony with the sky, with the earth, and with that abyss that precedes life. She had discovered her true power. She was a witch. Perhaps because a gene lost in time had granted her an ability she hadn't asked for, she could control the old outside magic. She could feel it. This realization was accompanied by a sense of fulfillment, of change, and of self love that made her shiver. Abandoning her aspirations and insecurities, she felt vast, endless.

The leader of the Estelas was waiting outside for Heiva and bowed when she saw her.

"That's not necessary," said Heiva. "I'm neither queen nor goddess. And besides, I owe you an apology. You and your people."

The woman looked at her and smiled.

Heiva walked for a while. She strolled along that muddy bog, that magic place where, years ago, the Witch President Vacuí had been killed. She felt sadness, but at the same time, determination and hope. For the first time since they'd left their home, she had the feeling that she was going to be able to save her mother from the clutches of the New Evolution.

Heiva looked once more at the mud that connected the earth with her feet and sighed.

In the sky, a thread of stars shone with brighter light than the rest. It formed an arc like a smile.

# INTERLUDE G

*The black of the sky takes over and fills my vision as I find* myself back at the mirror. Or the loading screen; I can't tell which. It shimmers and wavers, an undulating sea of consciousness.

"Don't look up," you tell me. "You'll see the multiverse."

I couldn't if I wanted to.

Here you come, a colossus, a lioness as black as midnight, walking with your feet hovering about two inches above the swell.

You're carrying a molten ball in your mouth—peach-coloured. It must be the sun.

You drop it into the water. The sun soaks up all the sea and forms the earth.

Peering closer, I can see them there, broiling in the mist.

Small stories, and big ones.

# 8. A LIONESS NAMED MIDNIGHT
## by yelena calavera

*"Lorna, why are you doing this? Why are you doing this?* Why are you doing this?"

He'd asked her three times as if she were a jinn, perhaps hoping that the repetition would elicit a response he could tolerate, or even comprehend.

None would be forthcoming.

She was leaving for one simple reason.

Lorna Lawless was a feral woman.

<br>

She didn't go to the funeral. She told herself that it was because she was heavily pregnant, but it wasn't that. Neither was it because she thought she couldn't face his family, nor because it might have made her husband jealous to see her grieve for her old flame. She hadn't told her husband anyway.

Lorna's sister had been weeping on the phone when she called to give the news.

"It was late, and they took the corner too fast on the way down the pass. Went straight down the mountainside. Rolled."

Lorna imagined an infinite airborne moment, a capsule suspended in space and time.

"They said he was killed instantly. She died in the helicopter on the way to the nearest hospital; it was over a hundred kilometers away."

At the exact moment that his mother spoke this woman's name for the first time during the eulogy, Lorna's water broke.

A name to break spells.

One she never wanted to hear because it reminded her of something down a fork in the road she never took. Its terminal point was a reminder of her own mortality.

Elayne-Joanna was the name she gave her baby girl. Her dad called her "Lane," and he could carry her in one hand.

Lorna breastfed the baby in a toilet cubicle at the Mugg 'n Bean in Victory Park, silently weeping while Elayne suckled.

She brushed the tears from the soft hair on the baby's head.

Someone shat violently in the cubicle next door.


When the baby was two months old, Lorna went back to the gym. She was barely hanging on.

What made her do it? What made her fuck that guy she saw lifting weights, out by the ventilation shafts at the back of the building? Postcoitus,  he told her he was a construction worker. Thinking back later, she couldn't for the life of her remember how it had come up.

Another suspended animation locked in a floating glass time capsule. Nothing to do with him or the baby. Lorna's quest for immortality.

This is how a person becomes just another ordinary monster.

That night, she took a long bubble bath in the dark and listened to the Dead Weather on the surround sound.

Virginia was looking after the baby, and Lorna's husband was working late. He left a message saying he'd be away until morning. It was too late, and he was too tired when he came home to notice that Lorna had a small suitcase stowed away behind the bedroom door.

Lorna fed the baby when she cried during the night, even though Virginia was there to do it. Virginia hoped this was a positive sign.

# a lioness named midnight

When Virginia left at 6 a.m., Lorna was glad her husband was still asleep. The way he was lying on the bed, he was facing away from her. Watching his body heaving with the deep, vulnerable breathing of sleep broke her heart. Two nights before, she had dreamed she was lying on top of a man who turned to the crumbling bones of a ribcage.

If he had woken up, she would have needed to hear those damned words again: "Lorna, why are you doing this? Why are you doing this? Why are you doing this?"

She was not a genie, waiting to be released by the touch of a kind hand.

The inexpressible tyranny of the wilderness of her body prevailed.

She left.

In the dream, Lorna climbed the Oracle Tree, who spoke to her with that immanent voice that pervades all of reality, rattles inside the skull, at the zenith and the nadir, in the air and in the earth.

"The longer you stay here, the more lost you will become."

It was a birthday song, an anthem, and an elegy.

Lost?

No.

Why had she fucked that construction worker? That alien body, she was trying to surf it straight out of Samsara. But bodies are less like a life raft and more like lead. Made to sink. That's why, she realized, she had left all those years ago and why she was leaving now.

It was too heavy.

Love, that is.

Too heavy to live with those bodies that are always sinking, even when they are only two months old.

Even her own. That scrawny woman with strawberry-blond

hair, blue eyes, wearing white jeans, a peach-colored sweater, and silver cowboy boots.

No matter how recently it had been applied, her mascara was always running.

<br>

She traded the Beemer in for a faded-red Mitsubishi Barbarian truck at a small dealership outside of Parys about seven hours before she got completely lost, driving through the farmland at dusk, and the structures of buildings and windmills started to fold in on themselves and roll toward the horizon. The green laser gridlines that traced the contours of the landscape began to flicker, becoming ever so slightly visible for an instant.

She drove past a mongoose standing next to the side of the road, chewing on the bitten-off head of a black mamba. He walked out into the middle of the deserted stretch of road after she had driven past, and they locked eyes in the rearview mirror.

"The hunger never goes away," he told her.

The asphalt gave way to gravel, and the petrol was running low. She had been driving through a dusky landscape for an indeterminate length of time. Something somewhere was burning, lighting up the sky so that it glowed a purply amber. Dark, grape-colored mountains hemmed in the horizon; barbed-wire fences cordoned off cornfields on either side of the road, their surface undulating with the breeze like a golden sea.

Even with the Barbarian blaring the end of the world's greatest playlist, with just Lorna, PJ, the Dandy Warhols, and the crunching of gravel, too little was there, rattling around in the emptiness.

She pulled over and got out, silver cowboy boots kicking up red dust that powdered her white jeans. She scratched in her brown-leather handbag, pulled out a black pen, and tore a thin strip from a card receipt.

"I love you and I'll always miss you," she wrote on the strip of paper. She rolled it up and left it under a stone next to the road.

# a lioness named midnight

She piled a few more stones on top of it, making a small cairn. A burial mound.

She got back in her car and carried on driving, but she was underwater now. The windshield disappeared, and she floated out of the car and swam through the stardust, moving the space debris aside with her hands. A steel toaster, a rusty old freezer, and a broken hairdryer with the plug cut off, frayed wires flailing and making sparks.

A giant octopus felt along the shells of submerged buildings reclaimed years ago by the deep, the sensitive undersides of her arms seeing the scores of sunken stories gone silent.

The truck rolled into the garage parking lot and shuddered to a halt in the yellow of the overhead lights as the last fumes left the exhaust. Three days on the road, sleeping in the back of the truck.

Lorna wiped the beads of sweat from her forehead. She had been gritting her teeth for miles, so she opened her mouth, flexing her jaw. She wet her lips with the last few drops of water from her bottle and offered a silent prayer to whichever Goddess of the Backwaters had delivered her to this oasis.

The garage shop was open.

There was a bar and a neon sign signaling vacancies at the adjoining accommodations.

The Ohia Motel.

A woman with long, dark hair in a ponytail came out of the bar. She was wearing blue jeans, a red-and-black flannel shirt, and a moon bag, and she had a dish towel over one shoulder.

"I'll help you push the car the last few meters to the pump," she said to Lorna.

"Aren't there some men in there who can help us?"

The woman chortled.

"We can do it."

"The Ohia Motel," Lorna said. "What an interesting name. I sense there's something there…"

The woman raised her eyebrows, and the corners of her mouth turned up into the hint of a smile. She was pleased someone had finally asked.

"The 'ō'hia *lehua* is a species of tree that grows on the Hawaiian Islands where I come from," Myrtle said. "The tree itself and the 'ō'hia forests are sacred to Pele, the goddess of the volcano."

Myrtle's eyes shone like lava in the dim light of the bar, reflections of embers and billowing plumes of smoke rolling across her gaze.

"Pele. She who shapes the sacred land. A capricious goddess."

A low rumble, like a growl. The surface of the bar trembled, and the glasses rattled.

"The 'ō'hia are the first to grow on the fresh lava flows, and they are remarkably adaptable. They're not much more than a shrub when they grow directly on the basalt. But when they find themselves in favorable conditions, they can form forests where the individual trees are twenty-five meters tall."

Myrtle poured Lorna another shot of Jägermeister. "Medicine for the way-weary," she called it.

"Women like you and I have a lot in common with the 'ō'hia *lehua* trees," she continued.

"And with Pele," Lorna replied.

"Sure," Myrtle said. "In one myth, Ohia and Lehua were two young lovers. Pele fell in love with Ohia, but loyal to his Lehua, he turned her away. So, out of rage and jealousy, Pele turned him into a tree."

Lorna slugged back her shot of medicine.

"Yes," she said. "I could see that."

"Understandably, Lehua was devastated that her lover had been transformed into a tree. And after some time, Pele took pity on her," Myrtle continued. "She couldn't reverse her spell, but she turned Lehua into a flower and placed her onto the tree so that the lovers would be reunited."

Myrtle and Lorna talked for an hour or two, sharing the stories that had brought them both to the "backwaters," as Lorna kept calling the surrounds. If this had offended Myrtle, she was too hospitable to let on.

After Lorna finished her burger and fries, she wandered over to the jukebox standing by the door and was replaced at the bar by an old man in a leather hat accompanied by a black-and-white terrier on a lead who growled at her, seeing something he didn't like. The old man—a local by the looks of it—asked for whiskey, and he and Myrtle started yammering away about backwaters business.

Lorna flicked through the CD choices until she found a song she knew.

It was a slow night. Only eight people in the bar: Myrtle and the old man drinking whiskey and talking to his dog, a couple dancing, three people sitting at a table together and playing a card game in the corner, and Lorna.

The jukebox—the good old "feelings slot machine." You never knew what was going to happen when you put a coin in. Were you going to feel the way you wanted to feel, or some other way? Was that nostalgic song you chose going to transport you back to the peak or to the dregs of the feeling you were chasing, something that you had packaged up and tried to keep for too long?

The coin, an enormous disc the size of the world, swelling to take up the entire frame, slipped into the slot with a *click* and went *clunk* when it landed on the other coins, deep in the bowels of the jukebox. The blinking red lights overhead reflected on the steel of the slot.

The song came on: "Here She Comes" by the Beach Boys.

Lorna's story felt so hard to tell. It had not come out easily during her conversation with Myrtle. She felt as if she had been dredging a lake to try and get the story out.

Why?

Because it was so big, and it required such presence.

Though she was not aware of this, it wasn't just Lorna's story; she was only the start. It was a story about everything and everyone that ever was—human and non-human—in the entire universe. All the plants and animals, the beautiful creatures on this planet.

All the beings trapped in this physical realm. Incarnated, not having chosen to be so, or perhaps having chosen and that somehow being even more mysterious.

Eight people and a demigod in a dive bar simultaneously access the Akashic record—the memories of all living beings who have ever existed—and experience the ultimate nature of reality.

Sunyata.

It happens as Lorna Lawless puts a coin in the old jukebox, and "Here She Comes" by the Beach Boys starts playing.

The sound, like an *Om*, generating the ten thousand things.

Just as the music kicked in, Lorna fell backward into a big, soft cushion made of goose down.

She was in the cosmos, butterflies coming out of the ends of her hair, feathers floating upward. She kept falling, falling backward and backward into a warm, womblike void, into the cavern of her chest, where her heart was beating.

A place that was, before things were.

Silence, a warm pulse. Primordial. Formless. Immortal and yet terrifyingly mortal.

She was falling, but she was also just dancing. Two people in love were also dancing next to her, gazing into each other's eyes.

The men who had been playing cards came over to the pool table and started playing a game. The comforting sound of the *clack* of pool cues against billiard balls on the table could be heard above the music. They played by the headlights of her truck, which was now dangling above the pool table, suspended from the bar's high ceiling.

# a lioness named midnight

Lorna danced under the red lights, the warm breeze blowing in through the open door stirring the dry night air.

She was moving and swaying, listening to the music. The men at the pool table watched her slyly as Myrtle and the old man at the bar kept an eye on her. She didn't notice; she was deep in her chest, in the cavern.

And the silence was the place it all originated from.

It started with a pulse, a green seismic wave from her heart that exploded outward. A shockwave of awareness, touching every being in its path.

First the two people dancing and then the dog, followed by the old man and Myrtle. One of the men at the pool table, the second, and the third.

*Pfwooo!*

The green wave traveled across the earth in milliseconds and returned having touched every living being. A spider behind the jukebox. Germs. Birds nesting in the roof. Even cockroaches, grasses, and all the strange things in the soil. Cows, sheep, people on the adjoining farms, cats, and dogs. People in the town close by.

The pain and the poverty and the stories…

The tenderness and love and laughter of a family, a mother putting her children to sleep inside the little house made of corrugated iron. Kissing the children on their heads. Feeding them mealie meal. Turning down the gas lamp.

A shack fire.

Lorna had been taught about these when she was young. But it was all abstract, the pain and suffering of other people. And as you got older and you felt it, it was too much. It was too easy to turn the heart off entirely and feel nothing, just be numb.

Mortality is a horror, so we seek immortality through conquest and ambition and sex and thrills. Or maybe we do these things just to feel something, anything at all.

This is how a person becomes just another ordinary monster.

With each new being this wave touched, everything they had ever known was osmosed into Lorna's consciousness, everything they had ever felt, thought, seen, desired, and loathed. She saw entire families, entire lineages, spanning back to the beginning of time.

It was painful; it was like walking on knives. Death by a thousand cuts, delivered to the soles of the feet.

Worst was the pain of the beings not ordinarily considered to be persons. She saw what the lives of horses had been like down the ages. The sheep and the dogs and cats, how they had felt about the people with whom their lives were intertwined.

She merged with the perspective of a housecat, felt what it was like to live life close to the ground, to have such good eyesight, to be driven by the instinctual brain. To hunt a small mouse.

She was a falcon, turning upon the wing, rising on the thermals, seeing for miles. She learned what it was like to catch a little bird out of the sky.

She swam sinuously through the ocean, heard echoes across the deep using the water as a medium.

She felt what it was like to be a bat flying around at dusk, using sound to see the world. What it was like to be a cell, and a tree with deep roots and sap running through her veins. A butterfly who only lived for a day. And a crow. And a fish.

Infinite cameos, vignettes that made up the pattern, the fabric, the web of Wyrd.

Lorna's childhood sweetheart had married someone else. The two had an accident, died in the Outeniqua Mountains. As she was painting the baby's room, taking out home insurance, she knew she would not be able to stay long.

An octopus—huge—with arms touching the crumbling buildings of an underwater city. The future, the last one, the rising water.

A bacterium, the first one.

Lorna brushing the little girl's hair, buttoning up her tartan-patterned corduroy dress...

Maybe Lorna went back, but you couldn't really be sure when the scene was within the overall timeline.

Lorna's phone call with her father when she had hit the road.

"To live, you have to give up a lot. Most things," she had said. "Exactly everything."

# *a lioness named midnight*

The Akashic Records. A big filing room, full of these vignettes. Vast but finite. Because all of time is only all of time, and what's been crammed into there is all that's in there.

Her mother told her she had burned all her old diaries with her grandfather's blowtorch, but the words, committed to ash, were still in there somewhere.

Lorna noticed that there was something outside of that: nothingness.

Karma. You could unpack the million freight cars of baggage trundling along behind you through the desert, as Alan Watts put it, sift meticulously through the flotsam and jetsam generated by your life searching for some pattern or resolution, or you could just unhitch the whole damn thing.

The people in the Ohia Motel bar. The infinite intricacy of these interwoven beings present in this moment with Lorna. Beauty in their ordinariness and their nakedness.

Everything in the bar started to glow brightly; people seemed translucent. The couple stopped dancing, Myrtle and the old man stopped talking. The men stopped their game.

They looked around at one another, all glowing the same way but interwoven suddenly, able to interchange between their perspective and the perspectives of others, seeing everything, the total depth behind the other. The total depth and the total emptiness. The lack of distinction between one and the other.

The total and utter unreality of any moment before the present.

Just being. No one, no thing.

In the morning, before first light, Lorna walked up to her truck, feeling as if she were hovering about two inches above the ground. She inhaled, deeply and slowly, taking in the crisp country air.

"Thank you," she said.

In the twilight, she flickered between the form of a woman, a lioness walking into the sun, and a will-o'-the-wisp—a tiny sliver of light.

To live, you had to give up a lot. Most things.

Exactly everything.

Lorna climbed back into the Barbarian, drove up to the exit, and turned onto the road.

Left or right, did it really matter?

# INTERLUDE H

**Once again, I find myself staring into the mirror, but this** time I don't see you staring back at me. I'm alone once more, with only my reflection to keep me company.

"Left or right?" I ask myself. "Does it really matter?"

*That depends,* I hear you respond, as a voice in my head now, a stray bit of dialogue from an abandoned dream. *Where do you hope to get to?*

"I don't much care," I respond aloud.

*Then no. It doesn't much matter which way you go.*

"Away from here!" I try to clarify. "Out of this…whatever it is. Back to real life!"

*You don't really want that. Not yet.*

I'm taken aback by the certitude of this intrusive thought, but hearing it put so plainly, I can't help but agree. What's waiting for me back there? Maybe I'd be better off if I just tried to relax and enjoy the ride.

*Now you're getting it. Relax.*

# 9. A LONG-AWAITED INTERVIEW
## by courtney locicero

*'Good afternoon.'*

The subject responded by blowing a soft stream of bubbles through his breathing hole.

"Can you hear me all right?"

Veah didn't want to start the interview if the subject was not ready.

*Can it detect how nervous I feel?* she wondered.

From inside the tank, he gave a vigorous nod. **I can hear you just fine. Can we start the interview?**

Veah cleared her throat and checked her notes. The subject's name: Bodhi.

*This is going to be interesting.*

"My name is Veah. I'm a student of the University of Lar. Do you mind if I ask you a few questions?"

More bubbles. And then the subject's flat reply:

**Young.**

"Just because I'm a student, that doesn't necessarily mean I'm young."

**Younger than me then.**

Veah schooled her features into the no-nonsense look that she inherited from her guardians.

"What makes you so sure about that?"

The subject did a somersault on the other side of the glass.

**Next question.**

*"Do not let him control the conversation. He will do everything he can to throw you off. You have to be ready for him."*

The voices of Veah's superiors faded into the background. She needed their words, but she also needed to concentrate. Determined to show her subject that she meant business, she swiftly scanned her list of opening questions and decided to forgo them.

"Bodhi, does your species have a concept of God or a system of faith of some kind?"

There were no bubbles this time.

**Every species has knowledge that there exists a species greater than itself. No matter if it is the miniature ant being or my immense cousins. Every being knows of another that occupies a greater tier.**

Veah shifted in her chair. *How could he know what ants are?*

"Can you tell me what you mean by 'greater'?"

Bodhi clarified. **Stronger, better hunters, better minds, great makers, great destroyers.**

Veah remembered her training and steadied her voice. "Please understand that I'm not referring to another species. I'm asking if you believe in a higher, sentient power that is all-knowing."

**Those that came before us? Pioneers.**

Veah shook her head. "A higher power usually refers to something that you can't really see or touch, but you know that it's there."

Bodhi lingered at the glass, as if pondering on Veah's explanation. And then finally, **Ah yes. Now I understand. You're speaking of the love feeling. Unconditional. Powerful. Cannot be seen or brain-sensed, but its existence is clear. The love feeling between two. Mother-calf. Between mates.**

To conceal her frustration, Veah decided to swallow her sigh. "No. You're speaking of a feeling. I'm referring to a power."

**Then is it wrong to say that the love feeling has no power over your species?**

Veah dipped her chin. "It is true that love is a strong factor in our decision making. But it's not something that we worship, pray to, or ask forgiveness of."

She thought that this would be enough to trigger a proper response from Bodhi, but his final reply provided no insight whatsoever.

**Perhaps it should be.**

*"Whenever the interviewee does not allow passage to insight, as is bound to happen, change the subject and revisit the unresolved question later."*

"Next question," Veah prompted. "Do you or any members of your species believe in the existence of an afterlife?"

**What is your meaning?**

"The afterlife refers to a place that you go after you die."

**Yes. I've seen where the dead go.**

Veah blinked. "You have?"

**Of course. They go down past the curtain. And then to the sharks and the lesser fish. Their bones go back up to become a part of the sand ceiling.**

Bodhi's description made Veah recall her notes on his species's reversal of the ocean barrier. For them, the seafloor was the "ceiling" and the surface, which was located down, was referred to as the "curtain."

"That's where their bodies go. But what happens to their spirit?"

A faint clicking noise came from the other side of the glass.

**What is your meaning?**

"One's spirit or soul is the intangible part that makes that person unique. It combines their personality, their lived experience, and their core values. Do you believe that this spirit lives on after the body dies, or does it cease to exist as well?"

**How could this so-called spirit ever die when there are those around who will remember it? I remember the unique aspects of all those that have passed on who were dear to me. Don't you?**

"Well, yes. But eventually, I will die and that memory will fade."

**That is what offspring are for. To carry on their parents' unique qualities and add them to their own.**

"So you don't believe that the spirit is preserved in another dimension? Unchanged—as it was before it was stripped of its vessel?"

**Doesn't the vessel influence the spirit during life? Won't a change take place no matter what? Our spirits change as we grow and mature. Why can they not change after we die? Death is certain, final, but change is constant—ever-happening. Never stopping.**

Veah sighed. "I'm sorry. These questions only seem to be confusing you."

**No.** Veah could feel the sudden weight of Bodhi's voice against the machine through which it funneled. **Here is the truth. You and your kind seek answers to questions that you have already mapped. You have preemptively projected the design of my response. You trap us behind glass for the sake of communication, but your toys**—he gestured to the tech attached to the tank—**will not provide clarity.**

Veah set aside her clipboard, leaned back, and folded her hands. Now that Bodhi was frustrated, she let herself bask in the power it lent her.

"You claim that my species will never understand yours, even with all of our advancements. Why not?"

Bodhi opened his narrow jaws and snapped them several times. The rows of conical teeth combined with that permanent smile struck a nerve in Veah.

**You are builders. Explorers. We—my kind—we are communicators. The ultimate socialites. The complexity of even just one of our dialects is beyond not only your hearing but also your comprehension. It is my understanding that for thousands of years, you have sought to spread throughout and explore the world under ours. Why now do you suffer yourselves to speak with us and ask us questions that your own kind could never provide a unanimous answer for?**

Fearing that she had allowed the roles of this interview to switch, Veah rushed to satisfy Bodhi's inquiry so that they could move on.

"You're right, Bodhi. A study of modern human evolution tells us that our nature is to explore and manipulate our environment to suit our needs. We are indeed builders. But…" She made sure to lock onto his smooth melon, the part of his body that was the most sensitive, even more so than his eyes. "Manifest Destiny was our old motto. Now that we have explored every celestial body in our solar system and have traveled beyond, colonizing the furthest reaches of the Milky Way, riding space-time on the event horizon of our galaxy's core, we have found that our greatest potential has been achieved. Now we must look inward. Absolute Understanding is what humans of the present seek to achieve."

Veah lifted her hand toward the machine that filtered Bodhi's consciousness.

"I admit that what this machine does at its minimum setting does not allow for Absolute Understanding. You and I can only communicate at the most primitive of degrees. The results of this interview won't be any more successful than communicating through sign language with an ape. I only get the slimmest glimpse of who you are, what you know, and the truth of your species's experience."

Bodhi swam up to the top of the tank where the device was lodged and tapped it with his beak.

**You said yourself this toy is set to the minimum. Why not increase its capacity?**

"The results are unpredictable. This is not merely a translation device. It operates on *transference*. Every time you speak to me, I'm absorbing waves that carry echoes of your neurons. They leave imprints on mine and are analyzed by the parts of my brain that process language. This is all happening at the microbiological level, of course."

**Let me guess.** Bodhi swam back down. **If you increase the toy's intensity, you risk my brainwaves overwhelming your cells. You could become disoriented and forget your own language.**

Veah lowered her eyes. "Correct. But…"

**Absolute Understanding.**

Veah looked up at Bodhi. His head was turned to the side so his eye was focused on her.

**It has no barriers. The only way to understand is to *become*. Wouldn't you agree?**

Veah looked at her hands. "I…"

**How many of your kind have died in the name of exploration? You boast about the accomplishments of your species, but like I said before, you are young. Is it really fair to take ownership for a history that you had no hand in forging? You strive for Absolute Understanding simply because you want to be among the first of your kind to touch it. Everything else has been marked off. Done. Completed.**

Veah was already standing on her chair, using her clipboard to reach the tech that filtered Bodhi's consciousness.

She strained, one hand on the glass to support herself, the other reaching toward the dial.

*Even if I lose my memories or forget how to speak, at least I'll* understand. *I'll have the answers that the only other sentient life on our planet has access to. They'll write books about me: Neveah Armstrong—the bridge between Cetacea and Homo sapiens. The Ultimate Communicator!*

She slipped, but not before tipping the dial all the way up with the edge of her clipboard. On her way down, she remembered seeing the very front of Bodhi's melon through the glass.

Veah opened her eyes and immediately tried to blink away the blurriness. She opened her mouth to release a groan, but nothing came forth.

She was suspended, floating.

*What is going on? Why can't I speak?*

"He will be okay. I think he's just a little stunned. The sonar decryption egg must have gotten overheated from prolonged use."

Veah struggled to blink again. *That's my voice!*

"Were you able to make any progress with this one?"

Veah concentrated on the new voice. It was one of her superiors. He wasn't supposed to be checking in on her for another two hours. Did she pass out after hitting her head?

*Why is it so cold? Why can't I barely see anything?!*

"This one was definitely more talkative than the rest, but you were right. He just tried to take control of the conversation. His responses were mostly cleverly articulated nonsense. And when he didn't know the answer, he just blew bubbles or waved his tail at me. To mock me and this process, no doubt."

Veah could finally see what was happening. But she wasn't looking through her eyes. Whenever she aimed her forehead at the voices, vibrations returned to her, creating perfectly textured three-dimensional models of everyone's bodies. One of those bodies belonged to her.

*No, not me. I'm right here… The person over there just looks like me.*

While the people continued their conversation, a foreign presence entered Veah's head and forced everything else into the background.

**Builders. Explorers. But that's not all. I left one other thing out.**

*Bodhi? Is that you? What the hell is going on?*

**Conquerors. Your kind surpasses all the rest when it comes to the enslavement and subjugation of others.**

*Bodhi…what have you done?*

**I wasn't sure if it would work. You're young, educated, idealistic. I wasn't sure if I could make you think that a prisoner would ever want to help you take the only thing that I had left at the cost of my freedom: knowledge.**

*Bodhi…please, don't tell me…If that's you inside my body right now, then I'm…*

**I told you that your species cannot compare to mine when it comes to socialization. We were reading and understanding each other's intentions and opportunity for error eons before your ancestors stretched a limb beyond the shadows of their caves.**

Veah tried to scream, but all that came forth was a bleating whir from her melon. The humans outside gave no reaction. On the other side of the glass, the other Veah turned her head and smiled.

**They cannot hear you.**

"Goodbye, Bodhi." The other Veah held her clipboard firmly against her chest and bowed. "Thank you for sharing your experience with me."

Veah screamed again, but the sounds only bounced off the glass and reverberated back, giving her a blinding headache.

**Absolute Understanding can only be achieved when you *become.***

*Bodhi!*

The other Veah turned for the door.

**Isn't that what you wanted?**

*Bodhi, don't leave me here!*

**You deserve no less, my friend.**

# INTERLUDE 1

**I wake up screaming this time. Shrieking like a caged animal—**
or worse, like a caged *person*. Like an intelligence, an awareness, a
self, who understands the outside world well enough to know what
they're missing.

In that weird space between sleeping and waking, it hits me like
a freight train: That's the feeling I've had my entire life—or for as
long as I can remember, anyway. I can't shake the conviction that
this isn't my real life. This is just a dream I'm having, or a game I'm
playing. When it's over, I'm not done; I just come back to my senses
and go on with my life, my *real* life.

Maybe it's just wishful thinking. Nobody wants to die, right?

It's probably best not to think too hard about this sort of thing.
Step-by-step logic can take you to horrendous places if you let
it—places your animal instincts do their frenzied best to steer you
away from. If only you weren't so damn clever and sure of yourself,
maybe you'd actually listen.

*Listen now. Just listen…*

# 10. A KISS TO BUILD A DREAM ON

## by cliff jones jr.

**Alone on a park bench, Orenda Phoenix sat watching a mass** of ominous gray clouds rolling in from the north. She checked the forecast. *Not great. Probably should have looked into the weather situation before planning an outdoor date.* Her eyes fell shut, and she let them stay that way for a minute. She'd been up half the night making her preparations, and she was exhausted.

With modest enthusiasm, she resumed flipping through the Lookbook feed of her date for the evening, Rob Lusby. *Nope, still doesn't ring a bell, no matter how many high school "friends" we have in common.* Rob didn't have much of an online presence, but there were a few old photos of him, so Orenda wasn't *totally* in the dark. *Not bad. Kind of a dork. Pretty tall.* He had sort of a Tom Hiddleston vibe, which—as far as Orenda was concerned—counted in his favor.

She looked up again, and there he was in the flesh. Staring right at her. *Creepy.* He was sitting on a bench maybe fifty feet away looking like some kind of junior G-man with his brown Panama hat and matching sports jacket. *In July?* He raised a hand shyly and gave a quick wave, but he didn't get up.

Orenda stood up from her bench automatically and called out, "Rob?" in a wavering voice. Having already gone that far by accident, she resolved to fake some confidence and walk on over. Then, thinking of nothing else to say, she asked inanely, "Did you just get here?"

"Well— No. No, I've been— I've been here a *little* while…"

Orenda waited for him to finish his explanation, but it wasn't forthcoming. "Why didn't you come over when you first saw me? What were you waiting for?"

Rob held up his phone indicating the time. "We're still a little early. I mean— We said eight, but…what's two minutes, right? I'm fine to start now if you are."

*Oh, wow. He's actually serious.* "Yeah…Let's start."

"So…A bar crawl, huh?" Rob said, finally rising from the bench. "Is the objective to get so sloshed we wind up crawling from bar to bar?" He laughed at his own obviously rehearsed joke.

*Sloshed? Really?* "No, I'm uh…probably going to turn in a little early tonight. Get rested up for the week, you know?"

"Yeah…Yeah," he agreed. "But not *too* early, right?" He looked at Orenda with such a refreshing lack of guile that it was almost cute. Maybe without the hat, it actually would have been.

They passed a man on a bench staring down at his phone. Except for the irregular twitching of his thumb, he might have been a sculpture. Orenda glanced around the park, counting three more such sculptures, similarly posed. Seized by a sudden curiosity, she asked Rob, "How old are you?"

He lowered his eyes and answered, as if it were his secret shame, "Twenty-two."

"Oh, so you were a year below me in school? That's why I can't— Were we in any classes together? I'm kind of fuzzy on…"

"Computer science," Rob said. "I was— You don't remember me, do you?"

"No, that's right. I think…Yeah, I *think* I do." She didn't.

"We were in the Computer Science Club together. We used to go to those coding competitions…"

"Oh yeah, that's right. I remember now. Rob Lusby."

He gave her a look that said something like, *I know you're lying, but don't worry; I appreciate the effort.* "So," Rob said after a moment. "Orenda Phoenix." They walked in silence a little while before he went on, "You're into literature, huh?"

"That's what it says on my degree," Orenda replied, hoping it didn't come off too smug. But honestly, she'd *earned* that degree, and if she couldn't brag about it, then what good was it? It certainly didn't seem to be much help on the job front.

"Tell me then…" Rob continued, "if you could be any writer for a day—living or dead—who would you pick?"

*Bob.* "You said 'be'? Not just *meet*?" Orenda had to ask.

"Right. Like you're still *you,* I guess, but you're inside their head and controlling them and everything."

Orenda considered this a moment. "If they're dead…does that mean I get to see their afterlife?" *Old Bob, the investigator.*

Rob wrinkled his brow and then made a little snort, which must have stood in for a laugh. "No, I mean— if they're dead, you'd go into the past. You pick the day."

"Oh, then that changes things, if time travel is in play." *Bob Wilson, the heretic.*

"Sure. I mean, time's just something we made up to cope with the fact that the universe won't stop squirming."

"Heh. Yeah, I guess it is." Orenda thought some more as they walked. *Robert Anton Wilson, the scientist.*

"Well?" Rob said after a moment.

"Give me a minute. That's a big question." Thunder rumbled overhead. *RAW, the mystic.*

"Don't overthink it," Rob teased. "Do I need to set a timer for thirty seconds?"

"It's not that I don't have an answer. It's just— You know when something pops into your head right away, and you think you can do better, but it just pushes everything else out of your brain?" More thunder. *Just hold off on the rain until we get to a bar, okay?*

"When that happens," said Rob, "that's your higher self trying to send a message. It's intuition. Just go with it."

Orenda smiled. *Okay, he's kind of interesting. But definitely a dork.* "Well, here's what I'm thinking. Do you know Robert Anton Wilson?"

Rob stopped walking. His face fell slack. "Really? I've got to say, I'm impressed. I thought for sure you'd say Jane Austen or Mary Shelley or one of the Brontë sisters. You know, like, somebody *literary.*" He pronounced this last word with a hint of sarcasm.

"I'm not saying he's my favorite author or anything. Yeah, I mean, Jane Austen's great. And I *love* Charlotte Brontë, but honestly…their lives were kind of shitty. You know how Charlotte Brontë died? She got pregnant and threw up too much from extreme morning sickness. That's all it took back then. *Morning sickness.* No, thank you."

Rob looked a little sick himself.

"Old Bob was quite an enigma," Orenda continued. "About the Illuminati, for example…He always insisted that he didn't *believe* anything at all, but I wonder if he knew more than he let on. He had some really interesting friends, too. Timothy Leary, Alan Watts, Terence McKenna…What secrets did he keep? Because everybody has secrets, right?" As she spoke, rain began to fall in sparse, fat drops. Rob didn't seem to notice. His hat and jacket didn't look nearly so stupid all of a sudden.

"I know *exactly* what you mean," said Rob with a conspiratorial wink. The rain was really picking up now. "You're not going to believe this, but— Wow, what a synchronicity that you'd pick RAW. You know he was in the Pact with—"

"Hey, it's kind of raining a lot; could we just…" Orenda gestured toward the nearest bar she could see.

"Huh? Oh yeah, sure."

Rob followed close behind Orenda as she jogged her way across the street and into a place called Summerland Tavern. It didn't look like anything special, just a standard taphouse, but it would have to do until the rain let up. Once inside, Rob tossed his wet jacket and hat into a booth and sat down beside them.

Orenda excused herself with an "I'll be right back," and headed to the bathroom to dry off.

They were out of paper towels, so she tried dabbing herself with wads of toilet paper. Looking into the mirror to check her work, Orenda's confidence faltered. *Oh well. Soggy clothes won't stop me.* "Time to live your myth!" She flashed herself a smile and headed back into the fray.

By the time she got back to the table, there were already two beers sitting in front of Rob. He had a hand on each, looking about as awkward as a middle-schooler at a dance. "Now, I know it looks like I ordered for you," he said, "but I wouldn't be so presumptuous. See, I got an IPA and a porter, and if you want, you can have one, but if not, I'll drink both. Totally up to you." He looked so nervous, like he'd never been on a date before and had no idea what he was doing.

Orenda sat down and scrutinized him from across the table. *Yeah, he definitely looks better without the hat.* "It's fine, dude. I'll take the dark one."

Rob was visibly relieved. He pushed the porter over to her, beaming with pride as if he'd brewed it himself. As soon as Orenda had taken a sip, Rob asked, "How do you like it?"

"Pretty good," Orenda answered, having a larger swig, "But..." She pulled a metal flask out of her purse and surreptitiously poured a bit into her glass. "Ever had a boilermaker?"

"Well, no, I—"

"Oh, right, you haven't been 'of legal age' very long, eh? Come on, it'll put hair on your chest!"

Rob laughed awkwardly. "Is that why your..."

"What, are you trying to make a joke? About my chest?" Orenda let that hang there a moment, savoring Rob's horrified expression. "No, you'd better abandon that one. Drink up." She poured a little liquid from her flask into his pint glass.

Rob obediently drank down a few gulps of the mixture and then picked up where he'd left off outside: "So like I was saying... Robert Anton Wilson used to run in the same circles as William S. Burroughs. So it's nuts that you brought him up and not me."

"Right, I know he was a fan of the Beats. He called Burroughs a genius...Wait, why is that nuts?"

"Well, because—"

"Oh, you mean like your question? You'd be William S. Burroughs?"

"I would. I mean, I *was*," Rob said with a laugh. And then taking on a more serious tone, he hedged a bit: "Look, I don't usually tell people this, but since we're connecting...Just think about this: Bill Burroughs died on August 2, 1997. And do you know when I was born?"

He paused like he actually expected an answer, so Orenda said, "I guess…the same day?"

"What? No, not the same— March second, 1998. Seven months later! So that answers the question of the quickening, right? About two months. For me, at least."

Ignoring that little gem for the moment, Orenda said, "Hold on a minute. Are you seriously telling me right now…that you are the reincarnation of William S. Burroughs?"

"Well, it's just a *theory* I have. I mean, doesn't everybody try to find their past lives?"

"No, I don't think most people—"

"It's not just the dates though. There's a lot more to it. Like, have you ever noticed how the universe sort of plays jokes on you, drops little clues here and there?"

Orenda guzzled the rest of her boilermaker. *I think it's playing a joke on me right now.*

Rob went on: "Take my name. One sec…" He reached into his pocket and pulled out a pen and a small notebook. Then he tore out a page and wrote "ROB LUSBY" in spaced-out letters, saying, "You don't have any scissors, do you? No, it's fine. I'll just…" He ripped the little paper apart so that each piece contained a single letter. "All right, now check this out…"

Orenda's mind wandered as Rob tore the paper into strips. She watched as he rearranged the letters on the table, but it felt more like she was watching herself watch. Each shuffling movement of his hands produced swirling ripples in the air, reverberating through past and future and gradually, inevitably settling back onto the present moment.

*Mmmzzz…*She thought she could hear a faint buzzing coming from Rob, sort of like he was humming to himself. *Mmmzzzmmmzzz…*But he was talking all the while, so that couldn't be it. *Mmmzzzmmmwhat do you…*"What do you see?"…*see?* He had rearranged the letters of his name so they spelled out something new: "BYL BUROS."

"Bill Burroughs, eh?" *What a cut-up.* She snickered at the half-formed joke and went for another sip of beer, clinking the glass against her teeth. It was empty. "When did I finish that?" she asked, having some difficulty forming the words.

Orenda looked back at Rob and found his face subtly altered. He looked older now—with drooping eyes, a massive nose, and a chin receding straight back down his throat. This new face was unreal, like something out of a dream. *A spontaneous happening.* Staring at Rob's shifting features, she tried to remember where she'd seen them before. *Ah! I've got it.* "Put on the hat," she told him. It was taller than she remembered. More of a top hat, really. For the briefest instant, Orenda could have sworn she was looking at the Mad Hatter of Wonderland. But no, it was just an awkward kid trying to dress like William S. Burroughs. *Except…*

Rob leaned forward and stared into Orenda's eyes. *Mmmzzzmmm…*"It feels like we're starting to see each other now. Would you agree?"

Orenda nodded, taking care not to laugh. It felt like he was taking her hand and leading her through a dark forest, never suspecting that *she* was the one who actually knew the way. *This way to Chapel Perilous.*

"Right on," Rob continued. "Now, let me ask you…" *Mmmzzz…*"What do you know about *chaos?*"

"Chaos? What's to know? It's all random, right?" *Do what you will.*

Rob grinned, revealing way too many teeth. "Well, it is, and it isn't…Or is it?" *Nothing is true.* "Do you follow me?"

"I guess so." *Everything is true.*

"I mean, there's a difference between chaos and entropy. Entropy requires no maintenance. For chaos to exist, there has to be sufficient complexity to…enough *structure* to…" *Mmmzzzmmm…*He waved his hand in lieu of the words he couldn't find. "Anyway, it's all very complicated. I can show you how it works though. *Magic*, I mean. Would you like that?"

"Sure," Orenda laughed. "Dazzle me."

"Great! Not here though. I'll get a ride." Rob's hands shook as he fumbled his way through an app to call for a car. *No map for this territory.* "Huh. Would you look at that!"

He showed Orenda his screen, but it was all a blur. "What is it?" she asked through a haze of pleasant indifference.

"The car is a Kia! And in chaos magic, the Kia is— It's the big mind, you know?" *Come one, come all.*

"The One." *The All.*

"Exactly!" Rob was practically jumping out of his seat with excitement. *Mmzzmmzzmmzz…*

*There's the cosmic giggle.* Orenda considered how to proceed. She'd be perfectly satisfied to sit and run her fingers over their wooden table all night. It was so delightfully smooth and slick and shiny. And yet under all those layers of varnish, the ragged, dessicated flesh of an innocent tree lay preserved like a fly in amber, screaming its story for all eternity. She pushed a single grain of salt along this sorrowful surface. Like the needle of a record player, it sent exquisite vibrations up and down her spine—music she could *feel.*

Somewhere in the shadowy spaces between her thoughts, discordant river sprites danced along the border of consciousness and dream, singing their ululating praises to Mother Eris, goddess of chaos. They laughed and frolicked and whispered in strange nonce tongues, heedless of their collective predicament. *Time is a wheel. Time is a river. Time to act? Time will tell…*

*Time for our William Tell act.*

Orenda sat up straight, momentarily sobered by a jolt of adrenaline. She laughed out loud from a mixture of fear, excitement, and euphoria, all in equal measure. As she placed her feet on the muddy floor of the Summerland, it became apparent that she'd kicked off her shoes and socks under the table at some point. Semi-organic muck squished between her toes. *Death is a condition of life.*

"I've got to—" She didn't know how to explain it to her date— or even to herself—but she needed to get outside before the Ugly Spirit took over. "Cancel the car, would you? I feel like walking."

"But…the rain…" Rob protested weakly.

"A little rain never hurt anybody."

"A *lot* of rain though…"

"Come on!" Orenda goaded. "I *love* the rain. It gets me so…"

Rob's eyes widened.

# a kiss to build a dream on

With a raucous cackle, Orenda turned and began making her way through the overcrowded taphouse, pushing past rain- and sweat-soaked revelers at every stage of inebriation. *Mmmzzzmmmzzz…* She could see their shining auras mingling and constellating into one enormously complex sigil. *Mmmzzz…* Each silver thread she wove with her clumsy meandering felt like a stride toward sanity. *Mmz—* The buzzing stopped. *Here time becomes space.*

Orenda burst through the front door, stumbling down the steps and nearly rolling into the street. But it wasn't a street any longer. The rain had made it a river. She stepped up to the edge and tested the water with her bare feet. She couldn't feel any asphalt, just muddy sand. The ramshackle shanty behind her shook and rattled with the furious thrashing of that hideous wraith inside—the Ugly Spirit that had attached itself to Rob. It was severed now, and none too happy about it.

Rob followed Orenda down the steps and up to the water's edge. *What's…* "…happening right now? I feel really…" …*weird.*

Orenda grabbed his wrist and waded into the water up to her waist, hoping to lead him across and into the safety of the sculpture garden. Just as she was realizing the stream was already too deep to ford, she lost her footing and found herself swept up in the current. It was all she could do just to keep her head above water as the world sloshed by in formless streaks of color. *Reality is an ink blot.*

Thankfully, a sharp bend in the river brought her near its opposite bank, and she was able to crawl ashore unharmed. She spread out her arms and turned her face to the sky, opening her mouth to catch the rain. "Oh, glorious Earth! How I've missed you!" After a blissful moment spent savoring the richness of reality, she turned back to see how Rob was doing.

There he was, climbing up the bank maybe a hundred feet upriver. He'd lost his hat but seemed otherwise unscathed. He stared at his hands, apparently unsure of what to make of them.

Orenda whistled and called out to him: "Just a little further."

The two strolled together through the sprawling garden, now devoid of its sculptures. Finally, they came to a large, flat stone that had once been a park bench…that would one day become a park bench. The rain was letting up, but it still drizzled and dripped from the numberless leaves above their heads.

"Have a seat, Bill," Orenda said to her companion. *Karma is a blind machine.*

Rob did as he was told. *Love is a haunting melody.*

Orenda sat beside him and took his hand in hers. *Captain Clark welcomes you aboard.* With her other hand, she touched the boy's cheek—he really was just a boy—and drew him into a kiss. Now their minds were mingled, and Orenda could complete her task. The potion had worked beautifully this time.

*Where am I?* Rob thought. *What are you doing to me?*

Orenda made no reply as she dug deep into the bedrock of his unconscious mind. She could see the full picture now. This was honestly his first real date. *Sad.* He'd been pining after her for years—along with a few other classmates, but not to the same degree. Rob had considered this one-sided obsession to be unassailably romantic, but deep inside he knew just how pathetic—and potentially dangerous—it really was. He was lucky Orenda had intervened, all things considered.

*What is this? How are you— Don't worry about it. Just relax. But— Let's go a little further back.*

The sun was just setting on the bus ride back from the afternoon's coding competition, and once again Camellia High School had nothing to show for it. No awards or honorable mentions or anything. Rob didn't care. He was a pretty good coder, but he wasn't nearly fast enough to actually win anything. For him, the Computer Science Club was just an attempt at socializing—particularly with the one girl in the club, Orenda Phoenix.

As he stared out the window at the pines whizzing past, he did his best to cultivate an air of supreme confidence and self-sufficiency. He wanted people to think he was sitting alone by choice, not because people saw him as a creepy weirdo and he had no idea how to refute them. All the while, unknown to anyone else on the bus, he was listening to every word Orenda said. It wasn't creepy if no one knew, he told himself.

Orenda was passing the time with an astrology app on her phone.

She'd been hopping from seat to seat, half-jokingly comparing her sign to that of different guys on the bus to see what their romantic compatibility might be. It was excruciating.

"Who's left?" she asked the guy she was currently sitting next to. Rob couldn't hear the guy's answer. Deeper voices didn't travel as well. Now almost whispering, she asked, "What's his name?"

*Oh God, she's talking about me. You're up. Play it cool.*

Rob tried to muster his warmest non-creepy smile as Orenda sat down beside him. He wasn't quite sure what to say in this particular situation, so he said nothing at all.

"Rob! How's it going, dude?"

"Just fine." He smiled a little wider. This was uncharted territory.

"Okay, so, I'm doing a little research into zodiac signs, and I was wondering…What's your birthday?"

"March second."

"Let's see, that's…Pisces. Interesting. I'm a Gemini." Orenda took a moment to read the info off her screen.

*Moment of truth, man.* Rob fantasized about what she might find. She was actually considering him as a romantic possibility. He was in heaven.

Orenda laughed out loud and then looked back at Rob apologetically. "This says we probably wouldn't make a very good couple. You're too emotionally needy, and I'm…kind of all over the place, you know? I've got to be free."

Rob's heart sank. Their relationship was over before it had even begun. He wanted to object, but what could he say? This was written in the stars. How do you argue with that?

Orenda kept staring into Rob's eyes. "What do you think? Does that make sense?"

Something felt different this time. This wasn't how Rob remembered the moment. *This has already happened,* he realized. *And I didn't tell her. But maybe this time…*"I don't care about that," he said, surprising himself. "I want to be with you anyway, even if it breaks my heart."

Orenda feigned shock, but she knew as well as Rob what was happening: He was fixing his mistake. "Okay," she replied at last.

"Let's give it a shot then." She leaned in close and whispered, "You know this is a dream, right?"

*A dream? Of course.* He nodded.

"And in a dream," Orenda continued, "you play every character. I'm *you*, man. We're both aspects of the Strange Attractor at the end of time, just reminiscing about the days when we thought we were different people. But now we know…there's no such thing. Right?"

"Right," Rob said breathlessly, never breaking that eye contact. *We've coalesced into a single point of light.*

Orenda nodded. *A shining silver star.* "So?"

Rob closed the distance between them, embarking on his very first kiss. A kiss he hoped would last forever.

Back in the waking world, Orenda drew in a deep breath and released the kiss.

Staring ahead with a vacant expression, Rob moved his jaw slowly up and down like he was chewing the air. There was nothing left of him now. Everything he'd once been had transmigrated into the chimeric entity known as Orenda Phoenix. It would endure for as long as Orenda could keep the chain unbroken, but it no longer held onto the illusion of individuality.

As they sat there in silence, the stone altar resolved itself into an ordinary park bench, and the modern world staggered reluctantly back into place. Orenda stood up to go, but before starting the walk back to her car, she decided she ought to leave her date with some parting words of wisdom, something to think about when he eventually regained the power of thought.

She bent down and whispered into his ear: "Hail Eris."

# INTERLUDE ⅃

*'Hail Alice,' I repeat.*

I see you looking back at me through the mirror, all dressed up as Queen Alice from the end of *Through the Looking-Glass*. I know it's you because I'm not wearing a crown or that fancy robe, but you look just like me apart from that. You're doing a really good job imitating my movements and expressions.

I raise one eyebrow and move really close to the glass to inspect your eyes. They seem wrong somehow, but I can't quite place the difference. I have an idea, and without warning, I quickly move my hand back over the top of my head. You do the same and knock your crown to the floor.

I laugh. You don't.

"So? What do I win?" I ask. "Do I get a crown now? Have I moved through all the spaces, jumped through all the hoops, and now I've finally reached my full potential?"

You shake your head. "That's not the way the story ends."

*Oh, right.* "Queen Alice" isn't the final chapter. Alice still has to wake up, after all. And even then, it's unclear whose dream it was, who *she* really was and what she was up to.

I close my eyes, trying to recall what's happening right now, where I've been and where I'm going. I don't remember much, but I can tell I'm still caught in the same old maze, going round and round with no end in sight.

The night is long, and no mistake, I've miles to go before I wake.

# II. PARASOMNIA
## by tessa b. dick

**As Rachel lay half awake in the early morning, a familiar** shadow jumped on top of her again. She tried to scream, but only a hiss issued from her throat. She tried to cry for help, but she had no voice. The shadow pinned her legs under its knees while she flailed at it with her arms…and yet her physical arms did not move. Rachel realized that her energy body was fighting the demon, while her flesh lay paralyzed. *This must be a dream,* she thought, *a nightmare.*

She could see even though her eyes were shut, the dark form like a black nylon stocking filled with smoke and twisted into the shape of a man. It reminded her of a balloon that a clown at a children's party might form into the shape of a poodle. It took hold of her arms and pinned them to her chest, pushing the breath out of her lungs. She fought desperately to get that thing off of her, but it began lifting her up into the air. Rachel knew that her body still lay on the mattress, but she felt herself rising several feet above it.

With only her mind, since she had no voice, she called out to God to save her, to make the shadow go away. Slowly, as the light of dawn crept in through the half-open window curtains, the shadow dissipated and faded away. Though still heavy, her physical arms reached out toward the bedside table to pick up her eyeglasses. Rachel couldn't be sure whether she had decided to reach out or whether her arms had accomplished the motion from habit and reflex. Suddenly, a brilliant flash of light momentarily blinded her and then was gone in an instant. She felt the impact of landing hard on the mattress, her energy body rejoining her physical body, every bone in her spine feeling the force like a hammer's blow. Although she did not consider herself superstitious, she kept her mattress on the floor instead of raised up on a bed frame, just to be sure there couldn't be any monsters hiding under the bed. She had been doing this since she was a teenager, and by now it had become a habit that felt comfortable and secure.

This third attack in as many weeks had shattered her nerves. She found herself unable to eat the bowl of cold cereal she'd prepared. She was barely able to dress herself, flinching at every little sound of birds singing in the trees, blobs of melting snow falling from the roof, and neighbors starting their cars to drive to work on this winter morning.

Rachel decided to take a walk outside to relax and clear her head. She pulled on a heavy winter coat and slid her feet into warm winter boots. Then she opened the door and stepped out onto the snow-covered steps leading down from her mountain cabin to the street below. Numbing, wet cold surrounded her feet. Her back hurt under the weight of the coat, so she slipped out of it and tossed it through the open door behind her. The thermometer hanging on the outside wall of her cabin read 38°F, uncomfortably cold but warm enough for snow to melt. This morning, Rachel found the winter chill pleasant. Slushy snow penetrated the roughout leather of her boots, and the cold wetness actually felt good. Scattered snowflakes fell onto her head, forming spots and streaks in her long black hair. Goosebumps formed on her arms, but she felt oddly warm.

Across the street, Nancy was picking up pans and plates from her deck. No amount of reasoning or persuasive argument could stop her from feeding the raccoons. Every night, Nancy put out cat food for them, and then she stupidly complained that cats were coming around to eat it. Rachel and some other neighbors had asked her not to feed the wild animals, but she refused to listen. The raccoon population was exploding, and the hungry critters tried to break into neighboring houses in their search for food. Rachel had to keep the garden hose handy to drive them off her porch every night when she came home from work. But Nancy kept right on feeding them, and they kept making more babies. The situation was bound to end in disaster for the raccoons. Their natural food sources could not possibly support that many of them. Moreover, in the past week or so, a coyote pack had been coming around to eat the cat food—and the cats. An occasional skunk had started to come around as well, more often than not spraying its noxious chemicals in defense against the coyotes.

Next door to Nancy, old Bill sat looking out his front window, waiting for his adult son to bring him groceries and a newspaper since his broken leg was still healing. Nancy had put a curse on him, and the next day he'd been hit by a car. Bill insisted it was Nancy's curse that had caused the accident, calling her a witch.

Rachel was tempted to believe that Nancy had cursed her as well, which would explain the recent demonic attacks on her. Perhaps the curse included her sudden tolerance of extreme cold as well. Even though she felt fine out there, she decided to go back inside. She knew logically that she was risking frostbite regardless of how warm she felt.

As Rachel dried her hair and feet, her head began to clear, and she contemplated what to do about the attacks. Her back still ached from the impact of falling back to the bed, even though she had not in reality been lifted off the bed—so how could she have fallen? She had already seen her doctor and made an appointment with a specialist after the second attack. This third attack had truly frightened her. These nightmares must have been some kind of seizure, not the curse of a witch. There had to be a rational explanation, such as epilepsy or a brain tumor or something like that. Whatever was causing the attacks, it had to stop. Rachel looked forward to getting some answers and a medical treatment.

*The landscape looks like a wedding cake,* she thought, looking across the street at Bill's cabin with its white roof and the nearby cedars and pines. She considered taking a snow day, calling in to work and claiming that the roads were impassable, but the sound of an approaching snow plow changed her mind for her. Her old reliable Jeep could certainly handle a little snow and ice, once the plow had scraped off the top layer. Besides, she'd already requested three days off for medical appointments.

The long, white tube of the MRI machine seemed inviting, like a cozy bed-cave. But after a few minutes, Rachel was praying for it to finish. Lying on the hard surface with her sore back felt unbearably painful, and her ears hurt when the magnets above her went *clack, clack, clack!* They checked her brain waves by placing a sort of helmet on her head, and the technician said that the EEG showed good alpha activity. Rachel filled out forms full of questions about her symptoms until her hand hurt from writing. She endured a variety of tests, some for reflexes and some for strength. The doctor wanted to see whether one side had become unusually weaker than the other, so she had to squeeze things, push things, and pull things, with both her hands and her feet.

Then she had to wait. In two weeks, she would have an answer. They told her that the MRI showed nothing urgently concerning, at least no sign of a tumor, so this would not require emergency intervention. But another expert would have to interpret the scan, and yet another expert would look at the EEG. She would not be admitted to the hospital, so she was free to go home.

The next two weeks seemed to go by at the pace of a snail climbing a waterfall. At work, Rachel felt distracted and began making mistakes in her spreadsheets. She hated spreadsheets anyway, and now she found herself unable to focus. Always the specter of another early morning attack haunted her. The coming diagnosis frightened her, but she had to know. She had always prided herself on being a competent bookkeeper, but now she found herself struggling with her work. She had to remind herself that sales—that is, credits— used red ink and that these were balanced by receivables—debits— in black ink. This was first-semester coursework, simple and not at all difficult. She also found her eyes refusing to focus on the sales slips to make sure they didn't contain any errors. At the end of the fiscal year, when the books were closed, everything had to balance, and sales tended to be the source of errors that would prevent this from happening.

At home, Rachel made a special effort to check on Bill every day and see if he needed anything. He was old—she guessed somewhere around eighty years—so his broken leg would take some time to heal. Even if he didn't need help with anything, she enjoyed sitting for a while and talking with him. He seemed to enjoy her visits too. The old man still had brown hair, as if he were still youthful, but his voice sounded a bit scratchy, belying his age. He talked about his service in Vietnam from time to time, but mostly he talked about Nancy and the raccoons.

"Nancy has been burning incense," Bill said. "I can hear her chanting in that strange language. She's casting spells, probably cursing us again."

"Do you really believe that curses work? They aren't supposed to work if you don't believe in them."

"Oh, they work all right. You need protection."

"What kind of protection?" Rachel asked, not really taking him seriously but simply giving him something to talk about.

"Prayer. That's always a good start. Pray and ask others to pray for you." He went on to describe various healing ointments and talismans for driving out evil spirits.

When the day finally arrived, Rachel sat waiting on an uncomfortably high exam table for the doctor to come in and deliver her test results. The white-coated neurologist did not keep her waiting nearly as long as the GP always did, though she still had enough time to feel anxious about what he might say. She'd begun to fantasize about some exotic diagnosis requiring drastic medical intervention, but then she felt guilty about wishing for such a thing. *No,* she told herself, *I'll simply hope for a clear diagnosis and treatment to stop the nightmares.* When the neurologist knocked and entered the room, she could tell from his cheerful manner that the news would not be bad. Their conversation was pleasant enough and rather brief.

"Parasomnia," he said.

"Para-*what*?"

"Parasomnia. A sleep disorder, usually caused by stress and anxiety. You aren't getting enough good sleep, so you're experiencing symptoms similar to sleepwalking."

"The nightmares are the cause of my stress and anxiety," Rachel said.

"They certainly don't help the situation, but let's see what we can do to relieve other sources of stress in your life. I want you to get some counseling, and in the meantime you can try taking melatonin to improve your sleep. It's a supplement that you can get without a prescription."

Rachel felt let down. Her doctor had offered no miracle treatment or even much of a diagnosis. Basically, he had told her that she was having nightmares, and she already knew that. It was the reason she'd come to the doctors for help in the first place. And by now she had missed several days of work, so trying to make up for this lost time was adding to her stress.

Back at home, Rachel set the timer on her coffee pot so she could wake up the next morning to the pleasant aroma of her favorite Sumatran blend. She poured a tall glass of water, swallowed the pill that was supposed to help her sleep, and then sat down to watch the late night news. She must have dozed off because she soon found herself startled awake, surrounded by bright light and feeling extreme heat all over her body. Her mind screamed "Fire!" so she jumped up from the chair, suddenly realizing that in reality the house was icy cold. She had forgotten to turn on the heater.

When Rachel later told her psychotherapist about the experience, he didn't seem worried about it. Ron rarely spoke to her at all, but he did suggest that she try to reduce the stress in her life. That was all the medical professionals had for her: to reduce stress in order to stop the nightmares that were causing her stress. Maybe it really was Nancy's curse that was doing this to her.

"That's what the neurologist told me to do," she told Ron. "The only real stress that I have is these nightmares."

Ron nodded. He didn't speak, and he didn't even take any notes.

"Well," Rachel said, "maybe the raccoons are part of the problem." She went on to tell him about Nancy and the curses and Bill's broken leg.

"It wouldn't hurt," he said, "to use prayer or meditation or whatever talisman that you think might work. At the very least, it couldn't hurt."

Rachel's work continued to suffer, and she found herself unable to eat. Her morning coffee tasted awful, as if someone had poured salt into it. The snow outside had melted, only to be replaced with a fresh blanket of soft white powder. The raccoons didn't come around as much in the snow. Maybe they were hibernating like bears, or maybe they had decided to invade a house where they wouldn't get sprayed with a garden hose.

She had more trouble than ever getting to sleep at night. Dreams and waking reality began to blend together. Rachel felt as if she were sleepwalking through her days at work and her nights watching the news before bed. In the evenings, she could hear Nancy chanting on the deck outside her house across the street, next door to Bill's house. From time to time, the odor of cheap incense wafted over on the breeze, insinuating its way through the gaps in Rachel's front door. She made a mental note to replace the weather stripping to close those gaps. Rachel had also begun to pray lately, though she didn't really know how. She hadn't been to church since she was twelve years old and her mom made her attend Sunday school.

Bill told her that she looked terrible. "Have you been sleeping at all?"

"Sometimes, but not as much as I'd like."

"That's what Nancy's been chanting…to stop us both from sleeping. She's *evil*."

Rachel was beginning to believe all that stuff about witchcraft, but she wasn't sure that prayer or talismans could help. After all, she knew less about witchcraft than she did about prayer. She swallowed the melatonin with a big glass of water before bed that night, but it seemed like hours before she finally drifted off to sleep.

She found herself driving her Jeep at high speed on a narrow, winding mountain road, fleeing from some invisible entity that kept chasing and clawing at her. She knew that she had to slow down for the curves, but every time she let up on the gas, the demon slashed chunks of skin and blood and muscle from her back. The old reliable Jeep held true, never slipping on the ice and snow, but finally it met an obstacle it couldn't overcome: A huge boulder sat in the middle of the road. Rachel stood on the brake and forced the gear stick into low, but it was too late. She couldn't stop fast enough. Her last hope, she knew, was to try to go around it. The tires held onto the sloping shoulder for a moment, but then the Jeep gave over and lay on its side, still sliding on the slick surface. She felt it smack into a tree, and then the steering wheel crushed her chest.

All at once, Rachel found herself floating above her body, looking down at the bleeding corpse that once carried her through her daily life. It had borne all her sorrows and celebrated all her joys, and now it lay crushed and bleeding, without life.

Then she had the sudden realization that this was all a dream, another one of her nightmares, and she instantly found herself floating against the ceiling, looking down at her sleeping body on the bed below her. She tried to reach down and touch her body, but she couldn't stretch far enough. A growing panic caused her heart to pound, and the sound of rushing water filled her ears. Her head throbbed as if she'd been hit by a hammer. She imagined a gossamer ladder that she could hold onto and climb down to her body, and just then its rungs appeared below her. But the ladder floated up and carried her back to the ceiling every time she pulled herself down. She concentrated on the ladder, trying to make it more solid, more substantial. It transformed into red rubber, but then it whipped around in circles when she started to climb down. She tried to make the ladder into wood or metal, but it kept snapping back into the gossamer fabric, like a spiderweb wavering in the light breeze of her breath.

An abrupt flash of blinding white brought another hammer blow to her head. It felt like the attack was coming from inside, behind her eyes. Perhaps she was still dreaming. She would wake up in the morning, sunlight would stream in through the crack in her window curtain, and then she'd enjoy a cup of coffee and go outside to walk in the melting snow. At least there was no demon grabbing at her this time.

These thoughts calmed Rachel as she patiently waited, resigned to the fact that she could do nothing to change her situation. Besides, she felt thoroughly exhausted. Her arms felt so heavy that she doubted her ability to pull herself down the ladder even if she kept on trying all night. Better to just get comfortable and wait for the dawn.

Bill waited and watched from his window across the street, but it had been three days since he'd seen Rachel come outside. Her Jeep sat in the driveway covered in snow, so she obviously hadn't taken it anywhere recently. He hadn't even seen any light in her windows. He would have gone to check on her himself, but his broken leg kept him stuck inside his own house. Finally, feeling terribly worried, he called the sheriff and asked them to do a wellness check.

The ambulance came with full siren and flashing lights, but it was too late. Rachel would leave in a coroner's van. The official diagnosis would be cerebral aneurysm, but Bill knew it was really Nancy's curse. The witch next door would go on doing as she pleased while a much better woman lay in the ground.

# INTERLUDE K

**I open my eyes. I'm in my apartment lying on my futon with** the Somniscope powered off on the floor beside me. So I've just been sleeping naturally? What's with all the bizarre third-person dreams then? Is that just what happens if you use the Somniscope enough, you get into the habit of dreaming like that?

But what about…Wasn't there someone else here? Someone in the mirror. No, surely *that* was just a dream. It couldn't have been…

I feel my bedsheet drag across my arm and realize it's coming away from my body as I begin to move in the direction of the ceiling. I'm steadily rising into the air, floating. It reminds me of being underwater. Gravity still exists, but somehow I'm lighter than air. My lungs must be full of vacuum, if that even makes any sense.

I turn over and do the dead man's float a few feet above my futon. The last clinging edge of my bedsheet falls away, and I'm free now. Untethered from the world.

*If you're floating in the air, no matter how real it seems, you're dreaming.*

I remember this maxim clearly, but I struggle to believe that it actually applies here and now. I've just woken up, after all, and I feel fully awake. But there it is. That's the rule I taught myself to distinguish dreams from reality. It's how I'm able to achieve lucidity and take control of my dreamworld—to do whatever I want with no consequences.

But right now, all I want to do is float here, take it easy, and let my mind wander. I've got miles to go yet. Miles to go…

# 12. CLAYBORN
## by igor goldkind
## edited by cliff jones jr.

**The Saturday farmers market in Little Italy lined six or seven** blocks intersecting India Street with fruit and vegetable stalls, fresh fish and flowers, burritos and tamales, flavored salts, garlic presses, and shimmering kitchen knife displays. It was a trajectory from the old world crossing into the new. It was here that Maurice found himself wandering up and down the pedestrian road hunting supplies for tonight's evening meal.

He was back in San Diego after half a lifetime at sea, sailing past foreign shores, exploring jagged islands, and visiting shining metropolitan cities. He had returned to San Diego because his mother no longer cared for herself and her needs were such—fluctuating, altering day by day—that he had to be on hand to administer the exact dosage of TLC. Tonight was his respite: a meal with friends, one old and two new. There would be wine and food and laughter. But most of all, there would be the familiar comfort of intelligent conversation in American accents.

Maurice had woken up this morning not feeling well. Something in his lungs was not right, as if he'd never bothered abandoning cigars, and his joints were aching from fights he couldn't remember. He was out of the house under an azure sky, the brightness of the San Diego sun smiling down on him, the toy boats in the bay gliding over the silver surface of a perfect day. A Mexican girl sat with Maurice's mother, making her meals, helping her reach her walking frame.

Ninety-five was quite an achievement to reach. Maurice's mother had surpassed all expectations. Now she was old and blind and wandering near life's exit door.

There was a chicken in Maurice's bag, as well as some asparagus, Parmesan, olive oil, smoked paprika…all ingredients he'd gathered from his travels and brought back to his port of origin to cook as a meal, a present gathered with two hands, from the past.

Maurice's foot faltered, the bag weighed down. His hand reached his sweat-covered face, and he wiped his brow. He was feeling worse. He had to find some soup. A stall ahead had some, so he zigzagged across the market looking for soup. He was on a quest for soup.

It was two o'clock, and the stalls were packing up. He looked down from the top of the market and saw the entire world receding from him as it folded up for another day—and he'd only finished half his shopping.

Maurice was walking down the incline now, the market rolling up like a colorful rug. The soup stand was gone; it had disappeared into tomorrow. He stopped and staggered onto India Street; all hope of soup abandoned. His head was boiling hot, his ears tingling. The road was swimming with Italian fishermen. He turned onto India and giggled. There was only home to get to now. Home and a bed and a duvet to sweat under. His private lodge. There went his dinner plans; he had to call his friends and cancel. Cancel his respite.

And then he remembered the clay. The clay he had promised his mother.

Yesterday, she had complained to Maurice of boredom. Day after day of waking, coffee, lunch, dinner, and bed with no easel to set up. No tubes to squeeze, no palette to mix, no brushes to wash, no canvas to stretch. No image to dredge from her mind to the surface of the world. Her boredom was her prison. Maurice suggested he might bring her some modeling clay, something she could use to fashion toy figures for her grandchildren.

His mother approved of the idea, and his mission was set. Somewhere on India Street was an art supply store filled with paints and canvases, watercolors, pastels, charcoals, erasers, and of course modeling clay. The right mix of magic he needed. But not just any modeling clay would suffice. What he needed was red clay: clay the color of blood and earth. Not dark earth, not rich, fertile mulch but paler, redder, coarser, mixed with ash and sand. The color of flesh covering tendon and muscle. It was this clay that adorned the kitchen tables of a thousand homes; terra cotta—the color of the earth's flesh.

Now India Street had become a river. The breeze blew ripples in Maurice's field of vision. The other pedestrians leaned in and bent to the wind, Lowry-like figures passing on his left and his right. This was a street like any street, a path paved by the footsteps that preceded his. An every-street, in every city, in every country, everywhere. India Street in a Little Italy swollen so large that Maurice was just a speck, a buoy bouncing on the surface of its whimsy. And then he found his port.

Maurice pushed the glass double doors of the art store open and walked into the early 1960s.

The floor was a speckled, yellowed linoleum. The wooden counters, the walls, the shelves stretching beyond the horizon, cemented in another time and place. He walked past the sales counter where a silver-haired man smilingly took change from a customer. He moved in a subtle way that Maurice noticed; he lived in another world. Maurice walked into the belly of the store. He saw a young, dark-haired man arranging items on a shelf. This one looked passably human.

Maurice's ears were burning, hellfire licked his cheeks, and he saw little, twinkling twists of light hovering around his peripheral vision. Faerie lights, angels, or tiny floating demons; they were chattering to each other as they bobbed and bounced around. He ignored them. "Excuse me, can you tell me where you keep your modeling clay?"

The human boy nodded and pointed. "Follow the green aisle down all the way to the end, then take the final flight of stairs to the next level."

Maurice said, "Thank you," while wondering if the boy's instructions might double as a cheat to some computer game.

He followed the green aisle and reached the stairs. His legs had now been transformed into lead by the dark magic of this place.

But his mission pulled him up the steps, and he reached the aisle and the shelf with the clay, just where he'd been told it would be. Just a little further. He looked for red clay, found a four-pound box, and then stopped. Next to the box of red clay he'd been hunting was another four-pound box of red clay, in a different box, for one dollar more. He picked up both boxes, grabbed a handful of palette knives, and descended to the sales counter in triumph.

The silver-haired cashier was older than Maurice, with close-cropped hair, a stud in one ear, and an urbane demeanor. He smiled politely and seemed pleasant enough, for a demon of the underworld. Maurice spoke to the man directly, though his details were by now bleeding into the background, and Maurice's periphery was intruding into his focus. "Can you tell me please, what is the difference between these two boxes of red clay? They seem identical to me but one is a buck more than the other…Am I missing something…?"

Maurice steadied himself with one hand on the counter and wondered if he appeared drunk. The demon didn't seem to notice, conscientiously leaned over both boxes, and ungrudgingly began to read the packaging.

Just a moment longer and then Maurice was gone. The store, the silver-haired demon, the floor…They had all vanished.

Maurice was in his grandfather's workshop. Heat was coming from the wood fire under the cauldron of bubbling beeswax his grandfather used for casting molds. Maurice breathed in the familiar sickly sweet smell of bubbling beeswax. He was standing on the concrete floor covered with plaster of Paris dust—"gesso," his grandfather called it. The old man stood behind a giant slab of granite, chisel and hammer in hand. His pale horn-rimmed glasses covered his concentrated squint as he tapped the chisel carefully with his hammer. *Chink-chink-chink.* The music of the universe toiling.

Maurice's mother, his beautiful young mother, stood beside the old man, and when Maurice saw her, she saw him; she looked and smiled her seeing smile at him. She left her father's side and came closer. In one hand she carried a stool. She placed it in front of

# clayborn

Maurice. Her eyes so bright, burning like a million suns set in the midnight firmament, smiling down on her son's upturned face, the pure unconditional love of an eternal mother for her child; the love that moves the earth, that spins galaxies; the love so immense, so encompassing that the universe must keep expanding just to accommodate it. She touched Maurice's cheek with one hand and placed a mound of red clay on the stool in front of him with the other. She took his tiny hands in both of hers and pushed them into the cool, wet clay. He was mesmerized. She was Prometheus, and she had come to make him into a man. She let him feel the clay squeeze between his fingers, and he was kneading; he was squeezing; he was molding the flesh-colored earth in the rhythm that she showed him. And her eyes were a million suns shining on him.

Maurice was back in the art store, and the silver-haired demon was speaking to him. "There really isn't any difference I can see, just different companies. Although this…" he gestured to Maurice's first choice, "doesn't set until the clay is fired".

Maurice thought of his mother's increasing dementia, a stone rolling down a hill, and her forgetfulness. She'd forget to wrap the clay back in plastic, letting it dry out, wrinkle and crack before it was finally formed. He selected his first choice.

The demon smiled benignly and tallied the clay and the palette knives on the sixties-style cash register.

"I appreciate your help," Maurice continued. "It's not for me; it's kind of art therapy for an elderly artist."

The silver-hair smiled. "That's nice."

*Shut up.*

"Yes, well she's ninety-five now, and she can't really see."

*Shut up, Maurice. Shut up.* It was too late; he was a runaway train.

"She used to paint a lot and sculpt and make stained-glass windows. Her whole life she's worked."

*Shut up! Shut up! Shut up!*

"But she can't see anymore because of the glaucoma she didn't treat in time, and see, I wasn't around. I was in England, and I couldn't take her to the eye doctor, and now she's half blind because they didn't treat it in time. I mean, I didn't know, and she always does things her way…"

And now the runaway train crashed in the middle of the art store, sending everything flying. And Maurice was melting as the tears streamed down his face and formed droplets on the wooden counter, and he couldn't stop talking. *Please stop talking!* "She's bored now because she has no work to do, and she can't see to paint, so I thought if I got her this clay then she could see with her fingers and make something to keep her busy, to keep her alive, like some toys for her grandchildren, little red clay toys I could fire for her." And he couldn't stop crying, but he did stop talking, and he stared at the silver-haired man, and he knew everyone was looking at him, and then he just said, "I'm sorry; I'm sorry; I'm so sorry." The demon who was really a man looked at Maurice and leaned forward and quietly put his arms around him and just held him. And Maurice sobbed and he sobbed, and he kept saying, "I'm sorry; I'm sorry; I'm so sorry." And the man held him until he stopped sobbing, and Maurice straightened up and rubbed his eyes, and the man handed him a tissue with his change, with which Maurice wiped at his eyes and blew his nose.

The man caught Maurice's flitting, avoidant eyes and said, "There's nothing more you need to say."

Maurice grasped his bag of red clay and walked back out into the clear, azure day.

# INTERLUDE L

**When I wake up this time—if that's even remotely the right** term for it—I have a strong urge to go outside. I know none of this is real, but still, I can't escape the feeling that I haven't left the apartment in weeks. I'm going stir crazy in here, hopping from one dreamcap to the next, living so many different lives but never my own.

I head down the hall, and I'm relieved to find that it doesn't just go on forever like I was half-expecting it to. I do eventually reach the elevator, which does eventually reach the ground floor. As the elevator door slides open, though, I know something isn't right.

Instead of seeing the apartment lobby, it's nothing but pitch darkness. I step forward to look around and let my eyes adjust, but even after the elevator closes behind me, they never do. I wave my hands in front of my eyes but see nothing at all, not even a hint of motion. I reach back for the elevator, hoping to find the button by groping blindly in the dark, but I can't even find the door. I walk unsteadily toward where it should be, but there's nothing there. I reach down to feel for the floor—at least something solid in this pitch black universe—but my hands reach right through where the ground should be. As far as I can tell, I'm floating in an endless sea of nothing at all. *Déjà vu.*

I blink several times in quick succession, and to my infinite relief, the Somniscope loading screen appears before my eyes.

*Thank God.* Something—whatever it may be—is most definitely better than nothing.

# 13. TETHERED
## by ragnar martinson

*"Are you sure we took the right turn in Burger-something?"* Suni asked for the third time. She peered into the Icelandic darkness from which the car's lights only cut a thin slice of black asphalt, white road markings, and slender yellow street posts.

"It's *Borgarnes*," her father Benedict answered. "We passed the turn to Road 55 earlier, didn't we? The one to Buðardalúr?"

"I guess…The sign was tiny though. And some of the letters look weird." Suni squinted at the worn roadmap in her lap. "But that felt like it was ages ago. We should have reached 56 by now. I'm tired. This sucks."

"Look, there's a gas station at the turn to 56. We'll see it in the distance. And from there we're half an hour from Stykkishólmur."

Benedict wasn't too worried about driving at night, but for Suni, it was her first time in Iceland since she was a newborn, and she had yet to get used to the darkness of the North.

"It's all going to be fine," he said to ease his daughter's mind. From her reaction, now craning her head around to look out of the rear window, this hadn't seemed to work so well.

Actually, Benedict didn't quite believe his own words. He had to admit that Suni was right in a way. At their current speed, the drive from the last intersection shouldn't have taken more than fifteen minutes, but they'd surely passed that half an hour ago. Maybe the gas station had been closed and they'd missed it? But there had been no structures, no other roads, Benedict was certain. Only the road they were on. In the worst case, they'd follow Road 54 for about fifty kilometers until it turned back in the direction of Stykkishólmur. In principle, driving down Snæfellsnes, you couldn't get lost: It was a peninsula with one road going in and another going out.

"Will they wait for us?" Suni asked.

"They know we're late. I sent them a text earlier."

Hilda had replied right away: "No problem. We're up late. You just have to ring, anytime day or night."

"Stupid airline," Suni grumbled.

Benedict wondered where she'd picked that up. Her mother had never been grumpy like that. Maybe just genetics? Or was it that he himself was constantly complaining about things? He promised to watch that; it might not be too late for Suni to drop the habit at sixteen years of age.

"What, you'd rather fly through a storm?" he said teasingly. "At least we were able to fly today; I didn't want to be stuck at Heathrow for another day."

She acknowledged this point with a grunt. "Still, it's almost midnight. Why would anyone be living out here anyway? There's nothing here."

Apparently, her heritage didn't guarantee a love for the North. Benedict had hoped that she would love her birth country right away, just as he and his wife had quickly fallen in love with the land. But Suni hadn't had a chance to see much yet, just roads and vague hints of rugged lava fields beyond. Maybe tomorrow would present more opportunities.

"Have you considered that the solitude might be the reason some people love it?" Benedict said. "Besides, you have the sea, the mountains, the low grass…plenty of horses…"

"Yeah, but what if you want to go shopping? Or to the movies?"

"There's a cinema in Borgarnes, for example. Or maybe in Akranes, I don't know. But from here, you can see the northern lights, which are way better."

Suni looked up at the sky through the windshield. "I don't see any," she said with a hint of petulance from the childhood she was just leaving behind.

"Yeah, it's cloudy," said her father, unable to keep the sarcasm from his voice.

The girl smiled a bit in spite of herself.

Another fifteen minutes passed in silence between them until Benedict said, "Look, it's a light!"

This was indeed the only sign of human presence besides the road and their car. Since the air is so clean in Iceland and there are often no other light sources, a single bulb can be seen from kilometers away.

It took them another couple of minutes to reach a turn, which led to a smallish lot right next to the street. A single lamp on an ancient, bent post illuminated a gas pump. He parked next to it. The sudden stillness rang in his ears as he turned off the car.

"Let me check. I think this is the gas station…although I do remember it larger. But maybe I'm mixing things up. You can wait if you want."

Benedict got out of the car and stepped into the crisp night air. A slight breeze prompted him to pull up the zipper on his sweater. The car's interior light spilled through its open door, painting a perfect triangle on the asphalt until he shut the door again—carefully, as if not to disturb someone nearby. He felt his head clear and breathed in slowly, deeply, trying to savor the smell of sea, grass, and moss.

Walking around to the gas pump, each step made a dry crunch that reminded him of chewing crackers. The pump itself was dilapidated, worn and rusty, and all of its digits were set to zero. If there was any doubt that the pump was no longer functioning, the hose that connected to the nozzle was torn in two.

When he and his wife had driven to Arnarstapi two years ago, there had been a big N1 gas station here…well, at least there'd been one at the intersection of Roads 54 and 56. There was no intersection here either, nothing but an old lamp and an out-of-service pump.

Suni watched her father from inside the car, scowling thought-fully. She rolled the window down just a few centimeters. "Well? This looks broken."

"Hm, yes," Benedict agreed. "It's not the intersection yet."

Confused, he walked back around and got in the driver's seat. Where had they missed the turn?

He'd hoped that Suni would maybe just fall asleep, but she pulled the black hood over her head and crossed her arms, staring at the street as if to manifest the right turn by sheer will.

"Can I play some games on your phone?" she asked after a few minutes, apparently bored by the futility of trying to make streets appear from wishpower.

Benedict nodded. Maybe it would take her mind off the worry. From the corner of his eye, he could see her fingers steer the little black snake around the screen, trying to feed it pixels. He'd never understood the appeal of that game, but Suni was engrossed.

At a steady ninety kilometers per hour, the road appeared a few meters ahead of them, drawn from the darkness, then vanished into oblivion behind, tinted red. It was easy to misjudge distances in Iceland, especially at night. He was almost certain that they'd missed the proper turn to Road 56 and were now well along 54, which would soon turn north, climbing a pass in steep turns. Beyond the pass, it would turn eastward again, back to their original destination.

The weather seemed to be stable, at least. There was no rain or snow, nothing besides a slight breeze and a low layer of clouds, which obscured the sky. Maybe there were northern lights today, but nothing visible from here.

They drove on in their little bubble, the street varying not much. If they were still on 54, they should have started the drive up the pass. *Yes,* Benedict thought, *just as we should have hit the intersection with a big, brightly illuminated N1 gas station about an hour ago.* He wasn't really worried; Iceland was one of the safest countries on earth. Any roads that were less frequented soon turned to gravel, so he'd know to turn around at that point. But they were still on a relatively new paved street, much like the main Route 1. *Maybe they built some new roads here, adjacent to the old one?* There was no real rationale for a project this big out here though. Confusion spread through him, a feeling of unease, probably fueled by worry about Suni.

Another light appeared in the distance, but Benedict stifled the urge to cry out again—Suni had eventually fallen asleep, the cell phone screen dark, her head tilted against the window. The clock was nearing half past eleven. They'd left Borgarnes well before ten, and he had to be honest with himself that he was lost, at least as far as that's possible in the west of Iceland. As the light grew, so diminished his hopes that it was the N1, though he desperately wanted it to be. It remained a single light, no big signs, no more traffic. He fixated on this point, hoping it would turn out to be the gas station's emergency light; maybe there had been a power outage.

Eventually, he turned off the street into the small parking lot. As they neared the lamp and an old gas pump, he felt dread creeping up his spine. Was this coincidence? Another parking lot with the same light, the same old pump? Had they been going in circles? The bent lamp post was without question the same one they'd seen before. He rubbed his eyes and left the car idling because he suddenly feared the silence. What was this place? The pump was the same too: all digits turned to zeros, the hose frayed off from years of disregard. And above, that same yellowish lamp casting the only light apart from the car.

Noticing that they weren't moving, Suni roused from sleep.

"Are we there?" she said, yawning and looking at her father, smiling a bit. Then she saw that they were not in a town as promised. She spotted the rusty gas pump next. "Did you…did we turn around? Do you know where to go?"

Benedict reached over and ruffled her blonde hair, trying to be confident. "Well, maybe you were right and we took a wrong turn. I think we might be on the Ring Road, driving north instead of west. But to be honest, I'm really exhausted. The sun should be up in a few hours. We could simply stay here until it gets brighter and easier to orient ourselves."

"But there's nothing here," Suni grumbled, as if to finish her earlier argument.

"Look, I can't drive all night. Here…" Benedict reached behind her seat and rummaged through his backpack to extract half a bag of chips. "Dinner is ready." He offered her the bag with a smile.

"It's gonna be better tomorrow, I promise. This sucks. I understand, really."

She hesitated to accept the peace offering. "Maybe it was a bad idea to come." Then after some thoughtful seconds, she added, "I don't even know them. How can you know a person only from letters? I mean, just because she's my…mother…I don't know." She trailed off, staring off into the dark.

"It'll be fine." He really felt too exhausted to find more appropriate words, to encourage her, perhaps even to convince himself. "You know, I'm sure Hilda can take us on her boat to spot some whales."

"That would be nice," Suni conceded.

Benedict turned on the radio, and they managed to get some faint music and Icelandic chatter, which helped to smooth out their unease—some sign, however noisy, that they weren't as utterly alone as they felt. They munched on the chips, and Benedict even recognized some old songs, like stony cliffs rising from a sea of static. He locked the car from inside and turned off the lights, and they let the radio lull them to sleep.

A draft across Benedict's face woke him up, his back sore from his uncomfortable sitting position in the partly reclined driver's seat. Suni's door was open. Her seat was empty. He put his hand on it, and the leather was strangely cold. The radio had turned off, as had the ceiling light, which should have lit up with a door open. Had they drained the battery?

It was still dark outside, the blackness almost substantial. All he could see was the rusty gas pump and the yellow shapes that the single lamp cast inside the vehicle. His body protested against movement, the cold from outside sucking almost all the energy from his muscles. He shivered, pulling his sweater tighter. Had Suni gone to relieve herself? How long had she been out there? Maybe the clouds had passed and some northern lights were out?

He exited the car, the same dry crunch beneath his feet as earlier in this seemingly endless night. No lights overhead, no stars, no moon. The salty breeze was his only indication that he wasn't standing inside a cave or a tunnel.

"Suni?" he called out, walking around the car. "Darling?"

She wasn't there, not behind the gas pump, where the shadows stretched into an even deeper black than was all around him. Where had she gone? Could she have left with someone else? He would have awoken at the arrival of another car, he was sure.

Benedict was not a religious or superstitious person, but some situations are so profoundly drenched in weirdness and dread that they distort and strain your whole existence, igniting some primal part of the soul that's been helping humanity survive for eons. It's a visceral reaction: goosebumps, an iciness up your spine, a tingle behind your eyeballs. He tried to breathe, but his vision began to blur and he was surprised to find himself crying. *Must be the cold air,* he tried to reason, before being hit by a wave of utmost fatigue, like he'd been awake for days and his body was telling him that sleep was the only option now.

He leaned against the car, feeling its cold metal through his clothes. *Where has Suni gone? Where are we?* He hadn't really believed that they were on Route 1: too few turnoffs, too little traffic. *Then where?* Trying to call out for Suni again, he could only yawn, which ended in a half-spasm that almost left him retching. At this moment, the single bulb that had been illuminating the area winked out without a sound.

Anyone who grew up in an urban area, or even a village, likely had little chance to experience true darkness. Here in Iceland, this was possible: no light pollution, not a single light within a hundred kilometers. On an overcast night, it got dark—no, more than that: black, tenebrous, lightless. His hands felt weird—wet and…*spiky?*—and there was a pressure on his back that he couldn't identify as any sensation that made sense. For some reason, the sharp feeling coming from his hands made him imagine small white balls dancing around with an irritating lack of rhythm. He closed his fingers and found some recognition. This was gravel. The pressure on his back was because he was lying on the ground. *Have I fallen down, or fallen asleep, or both? Where's Suni?*

Blinking, he tried to find out if he was actually awake, or even if his eyes were really open, but it didn't make a difference. His brain made up some colorful shapes, reacting to the total absence of visual information. At some point, he pulled himself up into a sitting position, still unsure of where he was. He turned his head: blackness here, blackness there. Flashes of light when he blinked, all inside his head. A nagging exhaustion wanted him to go back to sleep, but he fought against it. He had to find Suni.

Then, a new shade of black, an almost imperceptible difference in the shadows. He counted his breaths. As he reached ten, he began to make out a large object next to him, within his reach. He touched it and felt rough metal. *The gas pump?* It felt red and rusty under his fingertips. More black shapes around him…a smooth surface that had to be the car. *Maybe I can get the ignition going?* As he pulled himself up, he was hit by a wave of vertigo, his brain trying to tell which way was up. He'd never fully realized how much humans depend on vision to fix their position in space.

The darkness was no longer absolute. Was this the first hint of dawn? He looked around and there, far behind the parking lot, were three shapes pulsating between ordinary darkness and pure black. He moved uncertainly toward them. It was impossible to tell their distance. *Nearby and small? Or far away and gigantic?* They seemed to react to his approach: slowly, they started to actually light up, glowing from within and illuminating the surrounding landscape. He stepped from the gravelly parking lot onto the stony, moss-covered ground, his eyes fixed on the lights. They didn't look like anything human-made, more like floating pebbles or boulders, depending on their size. He stumbled over sharp rocks, hoping to find Suni at the source of whatever was  happening there.

The three objects were indeed quite large, at least the size of cars. By now, they were emitting a strong glow, which reflected in some low puddles. The steady breeze rippled the smooth surface of the water. The light coming from these rocks had a strangely sunlike quality. Lighting up the mossy lava stones below, it lent them strength, brought them to life. Yet behind their halos, the Icelandic night was the darkest it had ever been.

# *tethered*

Now he saw that these glowing rocks weren't actually on the ground; they hovered several meters in the air. They were tethered to the ground by ropes or cables, against which they strained, pulling to break free and escape into the night sky. Their light was so alive, like the play of embers within a fire…feeding, fading, shifting.

"Suni?" he called out, his voice lost in the night so that he wasn't even sure he'd said anything at all.

The floating shapes drew him further in, stumbling ever closer. From somewhere he heard a low humming noise. *Is it the wind? The blood in my ears?* He turned his head, but the landscape and the parking lot behind him was lost in blackness, like it was hiding behind a thick veil. Behind this veil, he felt a looming threat, an abyss that he was almost falling into. When he turned back to face the rocks, his perspective shifted and the objects weren't anchored to the ground any longer; they were hanging, and he was hanging himself, but not yet falling into the vast and hostile emptiness below him, or above him. Maybe if he could reach a cable, he would be able to hold on. Maybe Suni had already fallen into the nothingness. *Maybe I should let go too?*

Taking a step forward on the ground-turned-ceiling was the hardest thing he had ever done. Yet he was compelled to move on, only a few steps toward the bright irregular globes that dangled down. The noise that he had heard earlier was the whispering of the void, waves, wind, leaves in the darkness, slowed down so that each sound would last a lifetime, or sped up so the whole of creation was condensed into a few repeating seconds. Leaning forward, closing his eyes, he reached for a rope and felt a tingling in his hands just before he grabbed it. He lost his connection to the ground then, his feet whipping up and around, until he was hanging on a thick, oily cable over an inverted world of blackness.

Here were three floating or hanging rocks pulsing together in one rhythm. He thought of his family, the three of them. What would happen when Suni met her biological mother? What would it mean for their family?

From all this confusion arose a feeling of deep serenity. His life had brought him to this point. All his decisions had led him to be here, clutching a cable and trying not to fall into nothingness. And yet, he felt no panic, not even the fear of death itself. This was a better end than most had, and his life had certainly been better than most. The void held the promise that all his mistakes and wrong decisions had, in the end, been what defined him and his life, and that of his family. And Suni had grown up to be an independent girl; she would find her own path, even without him.

He looked down into the void, and what he saw filled him with awe. All those hues of darkness, all those shades, all those shapeless forms! *What a marvel it is!*

And when he finally felt his fingers let go of the rope, he didn't drop down immediately. Instead, he seemed to float, almost flying over the endless organic colorless clouds, slowly swallowed by the promise of the vacuum.

A sharp knocking yanked Benedict back into the waking world—cold and gray and wet. He hit his head on a hard surface, which helped him to realize that he was in a car, behind the wheel. It was bright morning. A human shape stood outside the driver's side window. He rolled down the window to face a red-cheeked blond woman who peered at him with the utmost suspicion.

"Good day, sir, but you can't stay here," she said with the typical Icelandic accent, hard on the R and a little clipped.

"What…what's here?" asked Benedict, and the woman stepped back. He opened the door and saw that the car was standing on the tarmac of a gas station, just a few meters behind the entry area so that no other car had a way to reach the pumps. The woman, who must have been the station's operator, crossed her arms and shook her head.

"I'm so sorry! It was very late last night and we got lost. We somehow missed the intersection for Road 56."

"56? It's right here," said the woman, pointing to a road sign not even a stone's throw away from them.

True enough, Benedict recognized both the intersection and the sign from his previous visits. But hadn't there been an old gas pump here last night, under a single light? Yet this was a modern station, with neon signs, new pumps, and a little shop on the side.

"I'll move right away," he said, and closed the door. Suni was still fast asleep, almost hidden inside her black hoodie. As he turned the ignition, she opened her eyes.

"We there?" she asked with a hearty yawn.

"Almost. It's not far."

The wipers cleared the windshield and presented them a pristine view of the Snæfellsnes landscape: green moss, turning gray on steeply sloped mountains, brightly lit by the early morning sun. He moved the car into a proper parking space.

"Let's grab a coffee," he said, and Suni followed him into the warm and cozy gas station shop. The woman who had woken him worked behind the counter. "Two cups of coffee, please," he tried in his unpracticed Icelandic, which seemed to serve.

"I think I fell asleep on the road somewhere," Suni said, wrapping her arms around him in a cuddly mood. "Didn't think it was this far…"

"Yeah, the flight was exhausting. I think I had lost the way and stopped here," said Benedict without really believing it. His memory told him something different, something unsettling. "So you didn't leave the car in the night?"

Suni shook her head, frowning at him.

The woman handed them two paper cups and pointed at the milk carton and sugar on the counter. "Help yourselves."

Suni added as much milk as would fit and at least three spoons of sugar, spilling some coffee and wiping it away with too many napkins and a "Sorry!" directed at the woman.

For a few minutes, the two of them stood there, sipping the hot liquid over the repeated gurgle of the coffee machine, just watching the landscape outside as the sun slowly rose.

When Suni excused herself to find a bathroom, Benedict turned toward the woman. "Tell me please, is there some kind of…public art around here?"

She raised an eyebrow. "You are looking for a museum?"

"No, not a museum, more like an open…art installation? With some lights?"

"Sorry, no exhibition here, nothing like that," she said, shaking her head.

"And over to Borgarnes? Or maybe some road construction?"

"Not that I know of, no."

As they left the station and headed for the car, he could feel the woman's gaze on his back the entire time.

Back in the vehicle, there was some evidence that he hadn't hallucinated the whole event: the empty chip bag stuffed in the door's pocket, the gas tank already a good way toward empty, way more than expected for the two hundred or so kilometers from the airport. Where had they driven all night? Where was the single old pump with the light? Suddenly, he remembered the dream: those floating rocks and the descent into darkness. The memory brought forth a strange emotion, a deep and wholesome sense of relaxation and content. He smiled, almost involuntarily, at his unexpected burst of good mood.

After they crested the pass, the ocean shimmered before them, the far peaks of the Westfjords drawn as a squiggly line on the horizon.

"Wow, it's beautiful," Suni said, shifting with a restlessness that he recognized from himself, the need to explore and to live, fully. Whatever strange thing had happened last night, he knew that everything was going to be okay.

# INTERLUDE M

**The dreamcap finishes, and I wake up. I sit up in bed and** remove the Somniscope headset. *Is this real? Am I actually awake?* I've experienced so many dreams in rapid succession that I'm still reeling, trying to make sense of everything.

I walk over to my bedroom window and take a look outside. It's still dark out. A snowstorm is raging, suffusing the whole scene with something like old-fashioned television static. The more I stare, the less real it all seems.

And then it hits me: I don't *have* a window. My apartment doesn't even share a wall with the outside of the building. Any window would just lead to another apartment. This can't be real then. I'm still dreaming. Or at least…

I walk over to my bed (which should actually be a futon) and pick up the Somniscope to examine it. It still has most of its charge left. I look for a panel or something I can remove to get to its power source. Maybe this device is still affecting my mind somehow, still dictating what I see and hear and feel.

I find a small inset button with a power symbol on it. Merely pushing it doesn't do anything, so I press and hold. After a few seconds of this, the world goes black.

I start to panic, but then I remember all the other times I've been in this state. It's really nothing to be afraid of, just a space between spaces, a time between times. It's like the Bardo, a cosmic interlude between lives—or between dreams.

    *Speak of the Devil…* Here comes one now.

# 14. NOVA

## by matt watters

**An unfriendly windstorm tortured writhing snow gum trees on** a night where every creature sought sanctuary. Tormented shadows lurked in the chill winter darkness.

Braxton Ward slouched, unconscious in his comfy chair, warmed by the impressive open-hearth fireplace. His Scotch glass sat empty for the third time. A tablet, also in sleep mode, rested on his lap.

Braxton's dreams were particularly vivid this evening. Cool morning mist wafted gently through the forest, feeding dew-soaked leaves. In the distance, he heard what sounded like gunfire. Turning, the calm words arrived innocently: *"Protect me."* There was no one in sight, but the words echoed again: *"Protect me."* A loud crack followed by a thump could be heard to his left. He peered through the mist…but saw nothing.

Braxton woke from his sleep disoriented, his tablet falling to the timber floor. It took him a few moments to gain composure. A sudden banging on his front door startled him. He squinted at the clock on the wall: 11:35. *Who the hell is out this late in weather like this?* he thought. The hard knocking came again. He stood but hesitated to move toward the door. *Who could it be?* Braxton threw another log on the fire, giving it life. There was no more knocking. Finally, he walked in the direction of his front door.

The front porch light sensor had been activated; the light was on. The gale continued to beat the sturdy stone house with persistent ferocity. Braxton cautiously slid back the curtain covering the glass panel beside his door, just enough to take a quick peek. No one. He checked again to be sure. This time he saw someone slumped at the foot of the door. Opening his heavy timber door, he visually examined the crumpled heap. A woman lay passed out.

Braxton was a slight man in his late sixties, and the woman was substantially larger than him. He grabbed her from behind under each arm and labored to drag her inside. In front of the open fire, he unbuttoned her heavy coat to make her more comfortable. It was then that he realized her condition: she was heavily pregnant. Her dress appeared damp with flecks of blood.

"Thank you," she managed in a faint voice. "Thank you for opening your door."

"Let's get you warmed up," Braxton assured her, grabbing a cushion from his chair and placing it under her head. "What were you doing out there in this weather?"

"Going to my midwife's house, but I didn't quite make it…did I? A tree…" she drew a quick breath before continuing. "A big tree fell across the road not far from here. I almost hit it."

"Would you like something warm to drink?" Braxton fussed. "Tea?"

The woman let out an almighty scream, catching Braxton off guard. "I'm in labor. My water broke in the car."

"I'll call your midwife; give me her number." Braxton grabbed his phone.

"Marion won't come," the woman panted heavily. "She lives by herself, and she hasn't driven since her husband died a few months ago."

"What about your husband, erm, or partner?"

"He's away with work," she puffed, breathing rhythmically.

"Okay, we can do this," Braxton said, trying to stay upbeat. "I'll call an ambulance."

The woman exploded with a bellowing cry as she pushed, trying to alleviate the pain in her back and lower abdomen. "I feel like I'm about to burst."

Braxton threw his phone on the chair. "You're doing fine," he reassured her. "We can do this. I'm a doctor." His adrenaline kicked in, and a level of sobriety returned.

The woman briefly focused on Braxton between gasps. "Really?"

"I'm not practicing; I've retired…but I'm sure we can deliver a baby."

"So you'll do no harm?" She questioned urgently.

Braxton considered her odd remark. "I still live by the physician's oath, yes."

"Good. I think it's coming, ready or not."

Braxton positioned himself at the woman's feet. "We're about to get very personal. What's your name? Is there anything I should know about your medical history?"

"Virginia." With every contraction came a pain that dwarfed the cramp before it. "This is my first baby. It's much more intense than I imagined," she groaned through gritted teeth.

"Now, Virginia, I need to check, erm, your dilation."

"Do it!" she demanded.

Braxton gingerly lifted her dress. She wasn't wearing underwear.

"I took my panties off when I got out of the car. I thought I was going to have it by the side of the road. Then I saw your light. I bet you weren't expecting this tonight," she teased. "Sorry about the mess."

Braxton didn't respond. His mind was feverishly searching, recalling his med school training from decades back. "You're ten centimeters dilated. The baby's head is crowning."

"Should I keep pushing? I need to keep pushing."

"Yes, yes, keep pushing," Braxton encouraged. "I'll get some blankets…some alcohol, and a knife to cut the cord." He rushed into the kitchen and grabbed a sharp knife from the knife block, a bottle of Scotch from the cupboard, and a blanket from the washing basket. A prolonged scream heralded the baby's cry. He stopped dead. "Fuck!"

"She popped out when you weren't looking," Virginia remarked, her baby wriggling face down between her blood-soaked legs.

"Well done," Braxton said, gently picking up the child to wrap it in the blanket. As he turned it over, he gasped in astonishment.

The baby had no eyes. There were no eyelids, no eyebrows, not even an indentation of where eyes should be. The baby gurgled passively as Braxton wrapped it tightly in the blanket, its umbilical lifeline hanging free. He saw the alligator clothes peg clamping his biscuit packet shut and grabbed it to fasten the blanket around the newborn.

"How is she?" Virginia asked wearily.

"How did you know it's a girl?" Braxton wondered.

"Ultrasound, silly."

"Of course," Braxton responded, annoyed with himself for even asking. "Did the ultrasound show anything else?"

"She has no eyes. Right?"

Braxton turned to Virginia with a compassionate gaze. "You already knew?"

"She's a dreampath. Dreampaths don't have eyes."

Braxton looked back at the intriguing child. "I've heard about them, never seen one in the flesh. We need to get both of you to hospital. I'll call an ambulance."

"No, please don't. You know she'll be taken from us," Virginia pleaded. "Can we stay here?"

Braxton contemplated her appeal. "You're bleeding a lot. You need to be in hospital."

"Can I hold her?"

"Of course." Braxton carefully handed Virginia her baby. "Have you picked a name yet?"

The new mother smiled at her little miracle. "Nova," she announced quietly.

Braxton regarded the two of them. "That's a lovely name."

"Please, take her. I'm so tired." Virginia closed her eyes.

Braxton took the bundled baby and placed her on the floor. "We need to cut the umbilical cord." Virginia didn't answer. "Virginia? *Virginia?*" He felt for a pulse. There wasn't one. "Come on, Virginia, stay with us. There's someone here who needs you." He began CPR immediately. Not wanting to interrupt the process to call an ambulance, he maintained his rhythm for a solid few minutes. *I have to get her breathing again,* he kept telling himself.

He checked for a pulse again. Nothing. He reached for his phone, but it was dead, out of charge. "Fuck!" He began CPR again. Her pulse was still absent five minutes later.

Baby Nova began to cry. *Dreampathic,* Braxton thought. *Does she know?* Then he remembered the umbilical cord. He doused the knife with alcohol, then severed the finger-thick fleshy tether. Using the alligator clothes peg, he clamped the remaining umbilical stump and then wrapped the child back up in her blanket. Picking Nova up from the floor, Braxton sat down in his comfy chair. Warmth radiated from the glowing embers as he rocked her gently.

Braxton awoke with a start. His tablet fell from his lap to the floor. It took him a few moments to gain composure. The banging on his front door continued. He glanced at the clock on the wall: 11:35. He stood and nervously threw a log on the fire, then spotted the alligator clothes peg clamping his biscuit packet shut. Braxton picked up his phone from the table beside his chair and tapped in a number.

"Leopardwood Police," a male voice answered. "How may I direct your call?"

Braxton pondered the situation as he gazed into the fire. "I'd like to report…report a dream—" he was interrupted as the knocking persisted. "Never mind." He disconnected and walked reluctantly toward his door.

*Earlier…*

The cell was cold. In a two-hundred-year-old prison on the remotest of islands, Somerton Man stirred in his bunk, coughing in the damp night air.

His elderly cellmate, Joe Sytari, sat on the end of his bunk watching Somerton in the flickering candlelight. "Come on, get up," he urged. "We don't have a lot of time."

Somerton sat up and surrendered a few more coughs. "Get it done." He reached to pick up a tattered piece of rope from the table beside his bunk and placed it sideways in his mouth, biting down.

Joe stood over Somerton with an improvised blade in his fingerless-gloved hand. "Hold still." He deftly wedged the crude instrument between Somerton's bald scalp and the metal rim of the 25mm button battery embedded in the top of his skull. Blood began to trickle from beneath the dream disruptor mechanism as Joe dug his blade in deeper. This unsophisticated operation was not the first time for the pair. "Stop moving. I'm almost there."

Somerton mumbled unintelligible instructions that were ignored. The dribble of blood developed into a steady flow down his forehead and onto his face.

"Almost there," Joe reassured Somerton as he painstakingly pried the device out of its snug resting place. With his thumb and index finger, he carefully removed the thin disc, ensuring the long narrow filament that extended deep into the center of Somerton's brain remained intact. "Got it."

Somerton applied pressure to the wound using a grubby towel. "Give it to me." Somerton held out his other hand. He couldn't see it—he had no eyes to see it—but he felt it. "Cut it loose." He held the bloody thing up in his fingers.

With makeshift knife in hand, Joe took the device and severed its silicone-sheathed platinum filament as close to the button battery as possible. Then he handed the disc back to Somerton.

"How long have we got?" Somerton asked as he delicately placed the disc back into its repository in his skull. The edges of the wound felt tender.

"It's two-thirty. You have about thirty minutes to communicate."

"Wipe the blood off and apply the skin glue."

After cleaning Somerton up, Joe grabbed a battered tobacco tin. The skin glue was thick and greasy as he applied a liberal smearing to the wound. "You need to sleep, and quick."

Somerton Man reclined onto his bunk and spread his thermal blanket over himself. "Good job, Joe. Thanks. You're getting quicker."

"Imagine what I could do with real instruments." Joe eased himself onto his bunk. He straightened his blanket and covered himself. "If this goes the way we think it will, the…Sorry, better get to sleep." He blew out the candle.

"I appreciate your help. You know I couldn't do this without you."

"You would never have existed without me."

"It's ironic that they put the creator in with his creation. They must really despise you."

"I never saw any of you as creations, Somerton. My team was exploring the what-ifs in genetic engineering. You are human beings with a unique gift."

Somerton tried to fall asleep, but the pain was distracting. "When did you decide eyes weren't necessary, Joe?"

"It was by accident. One of the chimps in our early program was born blind. That chimp, CHX138, had a heightened sense of smell, touch, taste, and hearing. CHX was a far better dreampath than any of his siblings before him. We rewrote the genetic code for everything going forward based on CHX."

"I've tried to imagine what it would be like to have eyes, but I can't."

"You communicate through dreams. You can see what all those people have seen."

Stillness lingered a moment. Distant waves could be heard slapping the sea cliffs. "How long have you been on the island now?"

"I would guess six, maybe seven months."

"If I get this right, it will change everything," Somerton said with hope in his voice.

"There's a lot of darkness in my past. I think some acts of atonement will put me in good favor."

"With who?"

An unsteady quiet hung in the crisp cell air. "Myself," came Joe's contemplated response. "I need to prove to myself that there actually is some good in me."

"Our genetic code has been stored for twenty-five years because you had foresight. Soon it will be dispersed far and wide with sympathizers. You are a good man, Joe."

"It was a difficult decision, how to ensure the safety of the embryos." He paused. "I distanced myself from my past—from all of you, Somerton. I was scared. I agreed to do things I wasn't proud of to secure those embryos."

"My survival is not an accident. There were only four of us left when they put me in here. That will change now; there will be many more."

"For this to work, everyone you've connected with before tonight has to play their part. If they only knew…With us rotting away in here, they'll be fueling the existence of dreampaths."

"It was lucky for me the new regime hated you geneticists as much as your creations."

"We were simply curious, to see if there were limits to what was possible."

"We were the product of your curious exploits, distilled from the human gene pool, resulting in a blend that most found unpalatable. Like all human beings, we had no say in our creation."

"You need to fall asleep and get this done, before the sentries arrive," Joe advised. "Remember: Leopardwood, Marion Weinburger."

"Yes, Joe. I remember."

⊔⊓

*Earlier still…*

"Dr. Joseph Sytari was detained this morning," Col. Iakopo said as he took his place around the table. "Where do you want him taken, General?"

Gen. Jack Granger, a gaunt man in his early sixties, thought for a moment. "Where is Somerton Man?"

"Blackreef Island," answered Brig. Ruston Weinburger, another seasoned veteran.

"Let's put him there, with the original abomination," Gen. Granger said with a sardonic smile. "Remind him of his crime every day."

"What about a trial?" Weinburger asked.

"He was tried twenty-five years ago and found guilty," the general responded. "He has never spent a day behind bars for his crimes against humanity."

"Because of the deal, Jack," Weinburger reminded him. "He was lead scientist on Project Golden Feather for twenty-one years."

"That project has finished, and he will serve time on Blackreef Island with Somerton Man. Is that understood, Brig. Weinburger?"

Weinburger hesitated, looking sideways at Col. Iakopo. "Yes, sir."

"Good. What happened to Sytari's co-conspirators from Somerton Springs Research Complex? Where are they now?"

"Of the twenty-seven scientists employed by BioGeneTec, two took their own lives during the seizure of the research complex," Col. Iakopo read from his tablet. "Three fled the country before trial. One went to Saudi Arabia, one to Russia, and one to Algeria. Twenty were arrested and tried. Fourteen of those spent between sixteen and twenty-two years in federal correctional facilities, the other five joining Project Golden Feather with Sytari. There are two scientists who have never been located since the initial raid. As far as we know, Sytari is the only one still alive."

"And the abominations," Gen. Granger said, "how many of them are left besides Somerton Man?"

"There are three: Somerton 26, 42, and 51. The rest were killed during the storming of Hollowbrook Barracks by the Loyalists' uprising," Col. Iakopo reported.

"Pity they didn't kill the lot," Granger snarled. "Would have saved us a lot of time and money. Where are they being held?"

"Uma Island Detention Centre."

"Terminate them. We need to cut costs at Uma."

"But Jack," Weinburger objected, "you can't just execute them."

"You bet I can, Rusty. The new regime has a clear mandate, and our role is to deliver it."

"They have rights, Jack, just like us."

"They are abominations that should never have drawn breath, Brigadier!" he boomed. Gen. Granger focused on Iakopo. "Colonel, remove these abominations from the island. They will be lost at sea by sundown tomorrow. That is an order."

Col. Iakopo glanced at Brig. Weinburger with a concerned expression before answering, "Yes, sir."

Gen. Granger eyeballed his subordinates. "You were there twenty-five years ago during the research complex seizure, Rusty. There were rumors...rumors of fertilized eggs of these abominations being stolen during the facility closure. Was there any truth in that?"

"Embryos," Weinburger corrected him. "Just rumors, as far as I remember, sir."

Col. Iakopo nodded in agreement.

# INTERLUDE N

**_I remain in bed awhile with my eyes closed. I'm trying to keep_** from interrupting the flow this time, to drift gently from dream to dream until it's time to wake up.

*Chuff, chuff, snort. Squeak! Squeeeeeal…*

The chaotic ruckus all around me makes sleep impossible. It sounds like a bunch of babies are crawling around trying to fight each other. *Babies or*—I open my eyes—*pigs!* I'm in bed all right, but my bed is sitting outside under the stars in the middle of a sizable pen full of black mud and hundreds of angry little pigs. Beyond the fence in all directions, I see nothing but dark forest.

*Why are they all tearing at each other like that?* I wonder. What could possibly be the point? I don't see any food troughs around, so maybe they're hungry? I certainly hope they're not…*Oh, God, they are.* I notice that in a few dense clusters, the carnage is most frantic and bloody. It becomes painfully clear that they're actually trying to *eat* each other. Whenever another pig falls, it becomes the center of a new feeding frenzy.

*Ugh, what an awful dream.*

I'm suddenly very thankful to be in this bed instead of on a futon. These pigs are all so small that they're unable to climb up and get to me. I shudder to think what would happen if they could.

I lean back and close my eyes again. Nothing else to do, really. I try to drown out the noise with a long, low hum.

"Ommmmm…"

I decide to try meditating on my breathing like I used to do as a teenager. I spread my arms out a little, palms up. I breathe in as slowly and deeply as I can manage, feeling my belly rise as I do. *One.* I exhale just as slowly, feeling myself sink deeper into the bed and using my belly to expel every last bit of air. I breathe in again, imagining that this is the only movement I'm capable of, that my arms and legs are paralyzed. *Two.* I exhale again and repeat.

As I release breath number ten, a word begins to appear in my mind's eye. It's indistinct at first, but it quickly comes into focus. *Not again.* I open my eyes to make it go away, but nothing changes. No matter which way I turn, I'm still staring at that single word on a field of black: "Somniscope."

# 15. NO GOOD DEED

## by kurt wagner

*Muzzle flashes of lightning shredded the darkness; gunpowder cracks of thunder announced a spray of bullets, transforming life into death. One by one, screams were silenced.*

*I was drowning in a sea of dead bodies with waves of blood and guts splashed everywhere. I could barely see the lifeless faces of the men, women, and children all around me. The flicker of a nearly extinguished flare caused a strobe-light effect, creating macabre still shots that were visions of Hell.*

*The sharp report of a bullet striking a wall behind me forced me to duck even lower just as a piece of the ceiling gave way. I saw a quick glimpse of the stars overhead before another piece of concrete fell and I saw no more.*

"Sgt. Lightner? Sgt. Lightner? Can you hear me?"

Alan's eyes fluttered open, trying to adjust to the bright fluorescent lights in the room. He took a deep, steadying breath, clearing the fog from his head.

"He's coming around, Doctor."

Alan blinked a few times and stared at the smiling, well-groomed face of an older man in a white lab coat. The tag on his coat read "Dr. Wells."

"There we go. Sergeant, may I call you Alan?"

He nodded cautiously.

"Good. Alan, I'm Dr. Wells. Do you know why you are here?"

It was clear to Alan that he was in a hospital, but he wasn't in a hospital bed. He was sitting on the soft, white floor of a padded room. It wasn't cold, but he shuddered as the doctor shined a light into his eyes.

*"Hey Lightner, you got a light?"*

*"It's in the name. He's always got one."*

*"Then light us up, man. It's getting cold out here."*

*Patterson and Monahan stuck their home-rolled cigarettes in their mouths, an expectant look in their faces.*

*I couldn't disappoint. Two quick flashes of light and both cigarettes were glowing brightly in the near-pitch-dark night. These guys loved my magic tricks, and this was one of their favorites.*

"Alan. You able to tell me what happened out there?"

His eyes tried to refocus on Dr. Wells, but the man was suddenly blurry. A soft, brown hand wiped the tears from Alan's eyes so he could see again.

He looked back to the doctor.

"The blood. I need to clean the blood off." Alan's throat was dry and his voice cracked, but the doctor didn't seem to mind. The nurse held a small plastic cup of water to his mouth.

"Please. I need…" Alan tried to rub his hands and arms clean of the blood, but they wouldn't move. He was restrained.

"Your hands are clean, Alan. Your whole body is clean. We helped wash you when you came in here. Do you remember that?"

*"Make way! Clear a path. Coming through." Nurses shouted. The helo's props screamed as they shredded the air. I was brought in on a gurney. I was covered in blood.*

*"What happened? How bad is he?" the surgeon demanded as he started looking me over for injuries. "What's going on here? I don't see any wounds. Whose blood is this?"*

*I couldn't respond. I only stared blankly while more people shouted and others scrubbed me down.*

Alan nodded again as the memory cemented itself back into place.

"It was me and Patterson and Monahan. We were assigned watch in a small village outside of Mosul. We were supposed to report if we saw any sign that Gabir was going to be there. They weren't actually expecting him; they just had to cover their bases."

*"Hey, you hear that?" I asked, looking outside the tent flap of their makeshift base.*

*"Yeah. Sounded like it was about two blocks away."*

*I checked my watch. The hands of the dial glowed green, showing 0117. Well past curfew.*

*I radioed it in to Lt. Schaffer, who told us to go check it out but to be quiet about it. We were not to engage, only observe.*

*The smiles were gone from our faces as we made our way to the source of the rumbling engine. Patterson, Monahan, and I split up so we could try to get eyes on whatever was going on.*

*As I moved in closer, I could hear shouting and laughter, almost like a party. I relaxed a bit until I heard a woman scream. I rushed around the corner and dived into a shadow so I could observe what was going on while still remaining detached.*

*Three guys in a jeep were grabbing at a native girl. She couldn't have been more than thirteen.*

"Do you remember what happened after that?"

Alan shook his head in the negative. The images were mixed up and unfocused.

"It's okay. Take a slow, deep breath. Try to picture the village. Did you see anyone?"

*Two older people, a man and a woman, probably in their forties, came out after the girl. The man was yelling; the woman was crying. It looked like she was begging.*

*Crack. Crack.*

*Two shots. Two dead.*

*The parents were on the ground. The girl screamed again. It was dark, but the pools of blood flowing out of them like a sea seemed to glow crimson in my eyes.*

*I took a step. My finger twitched on the trigger. I stopped. I'd been ordered not to engage. I watched.*

"It wasn't Gabir. It was some villagers. It was a girl. They took her from her parents. They…they…" Alan faltered, fumbling for the words.

"Who took her? Who were they? What happened?"

"They weren't terrorist soldiers. I mean, they weren't the ones we were looking for. I don't know who they were. They were dressed like us, but they looked and talked like rebel insurgents."

*One of the guys drew a knife out of its sheath. A blade as long as my forearm twinkled in the faint light.*

*My finger tensed over the trigger of my M4.*

*"Do not engage," I whispered. The knife traced a trail down the girl's abaya, splitting it in two, leaving her shivering in her underclothes.*

*The guy on the left moved behind the girl and pressed his hips into her backside.*

*Her face was a blur of tears. She was beyond screams.*

"I think she was in shock. She stood there. The three men grabbed her…they put their hands on…my daughter."

"Your daughter?"

"They called her things. I only understood the word *sharmuta*. It means 'whore.' My baby isn't a whore."

"Alan? Your daughter is dead. Do you remember that? She died in a car accident three years ago."

Alan stared wildly at the doctor, who put a hand on his shoulder. Alan flinched.

"My daughter is…?" Fresh tears streamed down his face.

*I didn't think anymore. I couldn't let them continue. I fired once. One of them fell, dead. The girl found her voice again and screamed, collapsing onto the ground by her parents.*

*I fired again. The one with the knife spun around and fell out of the jeep.*

*I fired a third shot and missed. The third guy started the jeep back up. The one with the knife ran to catch up. His arm looked like it was barely attached."*

"Yes, Alan. She and your wife died together. Your wife was texting and didn't see the red light. Remember?"

"Of course I remember that. It was the worst day of my life. It was the reason I re-upped."

"Okay. Can you try to focus and remember the rest of what happened after you shot at the men in the jeep?"

# no good deed

"Patterson and Monahan came running up to me. They checked to see if I was okay. When they saw that I was all right, Monahan asked why I fired at them. I started explaining when Patterson cut me off. He said that it didn't matter why anymore because we had less than an hour to figure out what we were going to do."

"What do you mean, 'what you were going to do'?"

"That's what I asked. Patterson said that as the jeep was tearing out of there, he heard them radioing for help from others in their group. They said that within the hour they were going to come back and kill everyone in the village and burn it to the ground."

"Why would they burn down an entire village just because you shot a couple of them?"

"Apparently, I shot the leader's brother. He was out for a little 'fun,' and I interrupted it."

"Why didn't you radio in to report and get your new orders?"

"We did, or at least we tried to. Our radio signal wasn't getting through. We couldn't figure out why, and we didn't have time to keep trying. Monahan ran up to the girl, with me and Patterson hot on his heels. He told her that we needed to get everyone out of the village immediately."

*She was so scared that she wet herself as she crouched protectively over her dead parents. Her head was buried in her mother's bosom while Monahan barked at her. Without a thought, I pushed Monahan aside, cradling my little girl into a caring embrace. I stroked her head, without moving her from her parents. It took a few minutes before she calmed down enough to peek up at us through her wildly disheveled hair and tear-stained face.*

*I looked up too and saw my brothers staring back at me in disbelief. Their jaws kept opening and closing, like fish out of water.*

*I signaled Monahan to approach slowly as I continued to hold the pitiful, near-naked child.*

*Monahan spoke more slowly and calmly this time. He told the girl that they needed to try to save the village and that time was quickly running out. She nodded that she understood, slowly coming to her feet.*

*She quickly realized her state of undress, and bright shades of embarrassment and shame blushed her cheeks while she looked for her shredded clothes.*

*I took off my fatigue shirt and wrapped it around her. The poor dear was so small it could have gone around her twice.*

"Damn it, Lightner! What happened next?" Alan looked up to see that a full-bird colonel had come in while he was telling his story.

"She started knocking hard on her neighbor's door and yelling inside. They were too scared to open their doors in case the other soldiers hadn't left yet. She went door to door until someone finally opened a small crack to look out and see who it was.

"He must have recognized her because he opened the door further and she nearly fell on him crying. Through her tears, she told him about the soldiers who would be coming and asked him what they should do.

"He looked at me and Monahan and Patterson, probably trying to figure out if he should trust us. Then he motioned for us to follow him as he ran outside and up and down a couple of blocks. By this point, I had no idea where I was or where he was taking us.

"He reached the door to the village mosque and pounded on it, calling to someone inside.

"An old man came to the door yelling something I didn't understand, but he looked pretty ticked off."

"Lightner, just the events," the colonel interrupted, again.

"Things kind of blurred for me at that point. Like they went kind of fast and kind of slow."

*The old man hurried to the top of the mosque and started calling out to everyone. Lights blinked on all over the village, and people opened their doors, looking groggy and scared, clutching their children closely.*

"It looked like a zombie movie as everyone started heading toward us. I mean the whole village was walking in their night clothes. I'd never seen anything so terrifying."

"Why was that terrifying?"

"Because at that moment I knew that, by having saved the girl, I could get the whole village killed. 'Whole village.' That is too big a term for people to understand, I think. When you actually see hundreds of people walking toward you in their pajamas all at once, it kind of registers on you. I am responsible for a whole village. A

204

whole entire village. That's a…" Alan's eyes started watering again and losing focus as the memories kept washing images of blood-stained bodies over him.

*The mosque had a basement. Apparently, it was built specifically in case of an attack, or a bomb, or some other possible disaster. Throngs of bodies flooded through the doors. They knew right where to go. There was no pushing or shoving. Sad resignation showed on their faces. Like people who knew they were going to die but had to at least pretend that they could resist death's icy hands.*

"Patterson, Monahan, and I scouted the perimeter looking for any weaknesses in the mosque or other possible ways in. We reinforced where we could. Monahan heard the engines first and signaled that it was time for us to join the villagers in the basement."

*The population of the village must have grown since the basement was built because people were almost literally stacked on top of each other. I could barely make out any faces, and those few I could looked like ghosts. They were moving their mouths, but no sound was coming out. They must've been praying silently or something.*

*It was eerily quiet, like the whole world was holding its breath.*

*Crack.*

*Crack.*

*I could hear shots ringing out and echoing. I couldn't tell where they were coming from, but I could tell they were getting closer.*

*My finger kept playing on the trigger. I had to make sure I put the safety on so I didn't take an accidental shot.*

*It was hot and stuffy. I could barely breathe.*

*A baby started crying right behind me. I nearly jumped out of my skin as I whipped around ready to attack the threat. I caught myself just in time.*

*The mother's eyes went wide as she saw the barrel of my gun less than an inch from her infant child's face.*

*I put a finger to my lips to show the woman to silence her child.*

*She nodded and started rocking it.*

*It only cried louder.*

*Crack.*

*Crack.*

*The gunshots were nearly on top of them.*
*"Waaaaah…"*
*"Waaah…"*
*The damn child wouldn't shut up.*
*I turned back to the mother and again made the signal to shush her child.*
*She opened her shirt and stuck a nipple at its mouth, pulling it close.*
*Boom!*
*The heavy wooden doors must've been blown apart.*
*"Waaah—"*
*I pushed the child against its mother's breast, muffling its cries.*
*Boots pounded heavily on the floor above us. I could hear the ragged breaths of terrified villagers even above the commotion.*
*"Mmmmpfff."*
*The child was still making noise.*
*I pushed harder.*
*The child was silent.*

"Okay, Alan, you're in the basement. How did they find you?"

"The baby. I…I killed the baby."

"You killed a baby? What baby? Get your head out of whatever orifice it's in, and answer the damn questions!"

"Easy, Colonel. I don't think yelling at him is going to help him remember any better." The doctor patted Col. Patterson's shoulder.

Alan hadn't even realized that Sgt. Patterson's father was in the room with him. He sat up and tried to focus. He looked at Col. Patterson. The man's face was stone, but Alan could see a lot of Donald in him.

*Crack. Crack. Crack.*

*Three shots and three holes torn through the floor. Three screams and three bodies that would scream no more.*

*Sgt. Patterson lost half his face and crumbled in a heap. The bullet ripped through his skull and seemed to ricochet around his young face. He didn't even get a chance to shoot back. One shot, one kill.*

"They just lit us up like we were fish in a barrel. They threw a few flares through the basement door. It didn't even help them see us, 'cause we were still beneath them. I think they just wanted us to watch each other die.

"They didn't even care. They just unloaded clip after clip through the floor. Monahan and I shot back up, but we couldn't see where we were shooting. We were almost completely blinded by the darkness. Patterson was already dead. Lucky shot from them. No offense, sir."

The colonel's face was still stone. But it was stone that leaked and bled salty tears.

"I'm sorry, sir. I don't know what happened next. I just know that I was surrounded by mutilated chunks of flesh and gore, and then I got hit and woke up here. Did Monahan make it? Did anyone?"

"No. You were the only one. By the time we got there, the rebels were gone. We thought every last one of you was dead, until we started pulling the bodies out. You were literally buried in bodies. You were covered in blood and guts. We couldn't tell what was yours. You had a pulse though, so we evacked you."

"All of them? I killed the whole village? I killed them all."

"Yes. You disobeyed direct orders. You are responsible for the death of my son and the entire village. If you are lucky, you will only be court-martialed, but I am going to do everything in my power to make sure you feel the weight of every single death you caused."

*I killed a whole village?*

"Doc, get him competent. He is not going to escape this with some trumped-up loony bin sentence or PTSD bullshit."

*I killed them all…*

# INTERLUDE 0

*I wake up and throw my headset against the wall, smashing* it to bits. I think I'm finally starting to understand what's really going on here, what this whole thing is all about: It's war. But not a war between different countries or regions on more or less equal footing. This war is between the entrenched ruling class and the rest of us: the anesthetized masses mostly unaware of this larger conflict and certainly ill-equipped to do much about it.

This is *the* war, the one that's been raging since civilization began, since a ruthless few first seized power and set up the rules of the game for all posterity. Even when these inhuman misers eventually die, the leviathan they created passes the torch to their chosen successors, the next generation of pampered predatory plutocrats.

So that's the situation. Now, what to do about it?

First off, I realize, I've got to wake up for real. No matter how many times I pull off my headset inside a dream, I'm no closer to actually waking up in the real world. Would I even recognize the real world if I saw it? Have I *ever* been awake?

*Click, click…*

What's that?

*Click, click, click…*

Why is that sound so familiar?

*Click, click, click, click…*
Oh, right.
*Click.*

# 16. BRAIN CANDY

## by j. osman

**Audio Transcript of Voicemail Message, Sent July 20, 1996:**

Hi, Maja. Aaron Price here. So glad you're ready for the next step!

There are a few other people across departments now doing this fairly niche work, just some of our more seasoned veterans partaking in the particular task this headgear requires.

Head office has been so impressed with your "diving" so far that they insisted on launching you straight into beta testing with the others—but I can't tell you their names, of course. I wanted to let you know that you're the only one doing this work from home. If I'm honest, I had my own reservations about that. I don't have to remind you that this gear and your next task are *not* on the list of info you can leak to the targeted activist group.

We've provided you with various Sprawlmart meditation tracks, nothing fancy. For beta-testing purposes it's important that these are simply the products marketed as "relaxation and calm." We haven't PAT-tested the other tapes yet. Just use the ones we've delivered. All Sprawlmart audio products have similar webs beneath, so don't get them mixed up with others you might have for personal use. We're not testing those just yet. The headset's been crafted to fit your exact measurements. With it on, you'll experience the subtext of the guided meditation. This will provide a substantial upgrade on the work you've been doing without any equipment. I've also attached a list of Sprawlmart's Emotional Materialism Targets (EMTs) for the next consumer season.

Remember. You must *only* use the tapes provided:

*Welcoming Calm* by Jackie Parnaby

*Inviting Bliss* by Lauren Thorpe

*Happiness With Breath* by The Omega Foundation

I know I don't have to tell you not to fuck around with the headset; Brian's in a coma. I know you two were close. Looks like he's a vegetable for the foreseeable.

Dive safe, Maja. Bye.

The final embers of a white cigarette flickered as Maja sat in the lotus position. Tobacco smoke swirled, mingling with fumes of burning aloeswood. The blinds were down. A pulsation of soft purple and green light issued from the ethereal combination of lava and salt lamps. This curated New Age setup boasted a charming DIY minimalism. A small tower of books sat beside a wooden crate of vinyl LPs: blues, rock, and psychedelia. A Grateful Dead poster, attached to the wall with masking tape. A ceramic statue of Gautama Buddha sat on a window sill next to a lemon verbena plant. The leaves shook like feathers as wind whistled through the open window, rattling the blinds in front. Several ketchup-red squeeze bottles stood on a Persian rug.

The sound of a cassette tape crackled through the room, and Maja readied her imagination to activate beneath closed eyes. A syrupy smoker's voice clouded the atmosphere, an elderly male with a Transatlantic accent carried haunted flashes of vintage Americana. The ghosts of this recording invited Maja's reality to dance.

Maja indulged the buttery voice and entertained the ride as it was described to her, step by step. She entered a territory of anthropomorphized mountains. As the tape rolled, she was instructed to count down from ten, to scan her body from toe to head, to fall backward through her vertical physicality. Relaxation was a thick, honeylike substance, and Maja sank deeper into it with each exhale. She summoned the feeling of reclining onto the floor of a sandy beach as a mass of grains materialized beneath her and ethereal water flowed out from the edge of a conceptual ocean. Her feet climbed up through warm layers of inky darkness as she fell still deeper into relaxation.

"Allow the water to flow through your entire body, gracing each of your chakras," the American voice said. "You are listening to *Unlock Your Unlimited Power: The Money Magic Manifestation* with Earl Turnbull."

Maja smiled a smile of mischievous delight, like the child who opens the forbidden cookie jar.

She followed her audio guide to grassy fields. Walking down a narrow bridle path, she envisioned a bright yellow sun, inviting a sense of carefree contentment. Then she reached the garden.

"This is your Garden of Peace."

Maja repeated aloud that she was safe in this garden and beginning to plant the seeds of success. She proclaimed the powers of her own mind to shape and change material reality. Her open palms rose up from her waist as mystical trees grew instantaneously around the outside of her shadow self. Maja's balance faltered as electrical currents surged around her skull. She planted her feet firmly on the earth, smooshing the shimmering blades of grass.

"This is my Wealth Garden. I can plant the seeds of success here whenever I choose. I accelerate their growth through the unlimited power of my subconscious mind," she repeated, and took a few seconds to bask in her imagination and the garden.

The authoritative voice came in again, pumping Maja up, inflating her with fantasies of indestructible self-belief, and then, the most crucial part: The sun set, and it was time to leave the garden. Maja was drawn instantaneously into an entirely new place, a familiar place.

"You find yourself standing at the foot of a long corridor. Along this corridor are several doors, each of which contains something you need in your life right now. Help and aid from the depths of your subconscious mind. Got a problem? Your subconscious mind already knows the answer. These doors remain locked."

Maja saw the words as they appeared on each door:
**PATIENCE. STABILITY. CAUTION. SAFETY.**
"At the end of the corridor is the last door, your Movie Room. Walk toward your Movie Room, and as you do so, feel the energy from all the doors in the corridor ignite within you as your subconscious mind bathes in their messages. This energy may present itself as an ambient wave of color or a tingling sensation throughout your body."

A vengeful expression took over Maja's face. As she walked past the doors, she punched each one as hard as she could, and the words changed:
**FUCK. THE SYSTEM. EAT. THE RICH.**
The Movie Room.
*Sploosh.*
Maja performed the backstroke through a green swimming pool filled to the brim with dollar bills. She saw herself floating atop an ocean of currency. She surfed a tidal wave of nickel, copper, and zinc. Maja pressed pause on the video and sat in a swivel chair in the Movie Room. She twisted a dial on a mixing deck, altered the hue of the crashing wave of coins, changed the resolution, enlarged the image.

"Thank you for embarking on this guided meditation toward mind mastery and money manifestation," said the American voice. "You may keep listening as I guide you out of this meditative state, or you may pause the track and continue to explore your Movie Room until you are ready to leave."

Maja switched off the video. She left the room to find herself back in the corridor. She was not ready to leave.

Outside of her mind, in actuality, Maja sat meditating with a large headset on. Along the wire that led from the headset was a keyboard sitting atop Maja's lap. She started to type. In the corridor within her mind, the click-clacking sound of doors unlocking echoed throughout.

Red klaxons screamed. Maja ground her teeth as alarm bells raked their sonic talons across her brain.

"*Warning!* Agent, you are in breach of Protocol 23. Please exit the Waking Zone immediately."

# *brain candy*

Maja-of-the-waking-world input more code on the keyboard as Maja-in-the-mind stuck both index fingers into her ears until the sound dissipated. From one of the doors, she heard the muffled sound of pain. It sounded like someone calling for help. Maja surveyed the corridor and entered some more code. The walls became transparent, yet the doors remained, and she found herself in the corridor of a corporate office building. Maja had astrally projected into Sprawlmart HQ. She heard the scream again and immediately kicked open the door. It shattered like crystalline glass, revealing a man sitting in a small janitor's closet. Maja could faintly see what looked like holographic architectural grids. The man was tied to a chair, with a gag in his mouth.

"Fucking hell, Brian! Are you okay?" Maja rushed over to Brian, removed the gag from his mouth, and untied him.

"The bastards said you were in a coma," said Maja.

Brian looked at her, unsure if he was hallucinating from fatigue. "What are you doing here?" he asked.

"The headset, I'm hacking it as we speak. I've had enough of this shit, Brian. I'm siding with the activists. I told them everything, and we've been planning to hack this dive for weeks now. Fuck Sprawlmart."

Brian squinted and grabbed his hair in agony as a sharp pain hit him like a knife to the stomach. Maja knelt down beside the chair and wiped the sweat from Brian's forehead.

"You're in the hospital Brian. I'm going to get you out," she whispered.

"How?" he asked.

"Let me worry about that, B." Maja stood up and was hit with a sudden realization. "Shit, I heard the training alarm earlier. They're onto me and tracking my dive now. Though the activists are working remotely too. I hope they can keep me hidden for long enough. I've got to locate senior management. We're going for the big boys, Brian. Tell me, what can you see?"

"A closet on the top floor?" Brian said uncertainly.

He turned his head to peek around and fell out of the chair. His body flopped onto the ground with a thump, and he moaned in agony. Maja sat him upright in the corner of the dingy closet.

"They set a trap for me," Brian said. "The new headset they gave me. It's melting my brain. And on my last dive, all my usual lucid abilities started to wane. I told them I didn't agree with some of the latest EMTs we're upholding for Sprawlmart, made a big thing of it, debated the ethics…Must have rubbed them up the wrong way."

"Shit…" said Maja, running her fingers through her hair. "I'm wearing it, Brian, and I already know what it does. What they're trying to do to us. Me and the activists, we're using it to our advantage. These meditation tapes, man, they're turning people into zombies. They promise you peace and calm, and instead they give you crippling anxiety and addiction. They're trying to build an army, Brian. But we're fighting back. The activists are really doing a number on this tech I'm wearing. I don't just see inside the closet like you can now; I see through the walls. I see it like some sort of blueprint."

Brian searched helplessly for clarity through intense pain, trying to formulate a sentence. "Maja, the—" He coughed, harsh and raspy. "I've not got long. Maja. They're going to…kill me…"

Maja held back her gut response and stood in silence for a moment, knowing he was right. She knew she couldn't save him and that he wouldn't have long left. What's more, she knew she had likely accelerated his death. At least it would relieve him of his pain.

Maja thought for a moment. She saw beyond the closet, an office floor of Sprawlmart HQ. Maja looked in disgust at the suits, the worker bees, the Barbies and Kens of neoliberal economic hegemony. She couldn't quite believe that she used to be one of them. Nothing but another slave to the system, a willing pawn of Trademark, the Psychic Operations division of Sprawlmart.

Maja investigated the cubicles in closer detail. "All the potential of astral projection technology, and here I stand in this corporate hell," she said to herself. "I'm leaving, Brian. I infected the money manifestation cassette with some nasty astral malware, a huge job for them to clean. I know they'll be chasing me now. A new life, I guess. Brian, I'm sorry that I—"

Then Maja saw what was left of Brian, a face ebbing away and turning to dust, dematerializing into thin air. The bastards had pulled the plug.

# brain candy

Maja shouted, screamed, *roared* in frustration. Then she paused and focused, thinking. *Time for revenge.* Maja raised her head upward and spread her arms out wide, standing in a cross position.

Outside of Maja's mind, the room was getting dark, and she sat with her headset furiously entering code, more complex now than ever before. From the closet on the office floor, Maja saw the diagrams of the world shift and change. She floated upward, gaining speed.

"Well, Charles. Please tell us. How have the kiddies been finding the new *brain candy*?" The CEO of Sprawlmart, Jack Bezzle, sat at the base of a hexagonal table in an ominous red room lit by artificial light, the top floor of Bezzle Tower. Seated around the table were a dozen Sprawlmart bigwigs, each one of them with a net worth of over ten million dollars. They'd manifested *a lot*.

One of them, the aforementioned Charles, answered the CEO: "Oh yes, going down a storm. Particularly high sales in the Afro- and Latin-American areas, which has been our goal. We should see a significant decrease in exam results in these areas, which will do wonders for the five-year gentrification plan."

Jack Bezzle laughed. "Magnificent. Genius. *Fuck them in the brains!*" The whole boardroom joined in the CEO's chant: "Fuck them in the brains! Fuck them in the brains! Fuck them in the brains!"

Maja was perched in an upper corner of the room, like a gargoyle spying on the men below, a black widow ready to abseil and claim her prey. She had heard enough. She wanted to get out of here before the blue robes, the goat, and the virgin sacrifice were brought forth. She leaped stealthily from above, landing right behind Jack Bezzle himself. In actuality, she was still entering code, steadily, with precarious attention. This had the potential to go either way. Maja breathed slowly and deeply, starting to sweat.

"Can I ask, Jack, how are the new headsets for the subliminal programming of the GM tracks going?" another board member asked serendipitously. "Have we successfully colonized dreamland yet?" More laughter.

"Ah yes, a good question, young Chad. We're making serious progress, and in fact, we recently punished one of our—" Jack Bezzle froze mid-sentence, his hand held up, finger pointing, his mouth open, frozen. His eyes began to dart around, a static look of panic overtook his face. His other hand shakily reached his neck. His mouth opened and closed as if he had just been tased, as if he was having a stroke. He was being strangled. Several of the men rushed over to help him; one of them performed a failed attempt at CPR. Jack Bezzle, CEO of Sprawlmart, had died of a heart attack.

Back in her room, Maja took off the headset, sweat pouring down her face. She breathed heavily for a few moments. It was time to get the hell out of there. She grabbed a red squeeze bottle, opened it, and winced at the strong stench of petrol. She showered the room with its contents, covering as much as she could. Then she pulled open the blinds, opened the window, and climbed out, landing in the grass of the yard outside. Just as she took out a box of matches, she heard the sound of nearby traffic, a horn blast as a black van pulled up across the street.

# INTERLUDE P

*I wake up in my childhood bedroom with stacks of drawings,* stuffed animals, and picture books scattered all across the floor. I smell smoke. *I remember this.*

When I was five or six years old, my bedroom caught fire when a power strip overheated. It started with a pile of stuffed animals in the corner of the room. I see it there now, starting to smoke. I was just a little kid; I didn't know about electricity and fire hazards and all that. But still, if my room hadn't been so messy…

The stuffed animals go up in a blaze so quickly they might have been doused in lighter fluid. Black smoke stains the walls and crawls across my ceiling. I'm absolutely petrified but also mesmerized by the novelty of the whole thing. I don't scream or cry or anything. I just stare into the flames and smoke, watching my room fade to black from the top down.

Things are different this time though. On the ceiling amid the smoke, barely visible now, I see a couple of sprinkler nozzles just like the ones my apartment has to prevent the spread of fire. And right on cue, they begin to spray.

Overhead lights flicker and fizzle as the rain pours down. I keep my eyes shut and my breathing shallow as the water gradually rises up to the level of my bed. I let the floodwater envelop my body, gently lift me off my mattress, cover my face, and fill my lungs. I float in the darkness, no longer aware of anything else.

# 17. THE SONGBIRD RUN
## by blake jessop

**Click, click, click, click, click.**

Kim cinched the Somniscope cap a little tighter and leaned back in her chair. A dizzying array of computer equipment hummed around her. Light from her monitors seeped softly through her closed eyelids.

*Click, click, click, click.*

"God damn it, Meena," she said under her breath. Her heart rate was up, adrenaline making her jumpy, and she wasn't sure how easily she'd go under.

*Click.*

Kim opened her eyes, and the monitors stared back at her. No loading screen. It hadn't worked. She stood and walked to the bathroom, wondering what was wrong with her gear, which she hadn't used since she quit the companc9y. She opened the bathroom door, stepped in, and stopped. The woman in the mirror had darker skin, glowing golden irises, and wavy black hair fanning out above her head like she was underwater.

So it *had* worked. Kim was watching whatever link Meena had left in the dropbox. Her hand reached down with the automaton smoothness of someone else's dream, picked up a tube of lipstick, and wrote in neat block capitals on the glass:

THE WATER IS DEEP
AND I AM ASHAMED, A BIT

## THAT THE BOTTOM CAN SEE ME
## AND I CAN'T SEE IT

That done, Kim walked out of the bathroom to the front door of her condo, which let out onto a featureless corridor with tacky but very expensive LED sconces. Her hand turned the knob, and she stepped through onto long grass breaking through fragmented concrete. The sky was the deep blue of dusk hung with a necklace of stars, the air heavy with a fragrant scent of eucalyptus and wet pavement. She stood on an abandoned city street a thousand years after the last human had walked it. A tattered sign above the avenue read: "Welcome to the Somniscape, Dreamer."

The sense of displacement was so strong that Kim had to suppress the desire to wake herself out of the dream. She walked down the avenue, and in the distance she saw small figures working on the dream, erecting buildings, hanging clouds, brushing existence into shape like painters. She felt a hot gust of wind and looked over her shoulder at a colossus, a golem made of iron and steel the size of a skyscraper.

"Hi, Vitaly!" she said in Meena's cheerful, faintly accented voice.

The colossus waved, and the grass rippled around Kim's feet. The scene didn't have the normal whiff of digital wizardry that you got in pre-rendered fantasy dreams. No pleasant separation that let you know a talented programmer had made the dream a little more real than real. It simply *was* real. So real that Kim was already forgetting who she was and why she was standing there. She shook her head and ran her hands through her slowly drifting hair, only to freeze, posed like a caryatid. You didn't move in Somniscope dreams; you were just along for the ride.

"Wait," she said in her friend's voice. "I'm moving you. How the fuck can I do that?"

It wasn't the usual nasty sensation she got when something happened in a computer that she didn't understand. Real fear spiked through Kim's brain, and the cortisol rush was finally enough to send her mind spiraling out of the dream.

# the songbird run

Kim tore the Somniscope off her head. Her monitor setup came reassuringly back into focus, displaying the various legal and illegal search tools she'd been using to look for her friend. Meena was gone.

Oneiros Industries was gone. Like none of them had ever existed anywhere on the net, which was the same thing as not existing at all.

She wiped sweat from her face and felt like she might be sick. She rushed to the bathroom and paused at the door, suddenly terrified that if she opened it, she would see Meena in the mirror.

"What the fuck is going on?" She felt like she wanted to cry. The hand on the doorknob was hers. The voice was hers. She opened the door.

Her own reflection stared back at her above the sink. Tawny skin and a mop of tight curls. The nub of her cortical implant stuck out behind one ear like a little antenna. No golden eyes, no wavy fronds of hair. She breathed deeply for a minute, clutching the rim of the sink.

This was a problem Kim had no idea what to do with. Something very weird was happening to Meena and to the company she worked for, and the Somniscope recording felt like someone saying goodbye. Whether Meena was taking leave of the net or the rest of the world, Kim didn't know.

The online trail was cold, and Kim wasn't at all good at dealing with the real world. Most hackers weren't. This was a problem that could only be solved in meatspace, and that wasn't where Kim did business. She wished she knew someone who did.

"You could call Franc," the Kim in the mirror said to herself. She sighed, swore, and dug out her phone.

The brutal thumping of a Russian ZSU firing its quad-barrel anti-aircraft gun at the drainage ditch he was cowering in jolted Fançois

Marleau awake. His hands were reaching for a radio that wasn't there, and the pounding turned out to be his heart.

He'd been back from Syria for six months. Had come home and found out he didn't live in the same country he'd fought for. The separatists had finally gotten their way, and Quebec was a country all on its own. Broke and without a properly functioning military, but still a country. It hadn't felt like a big deal at the time, but Kim, his tour money, and his self-respect had all run out at about the same time.

He passed a hand over his face and shivered. Looked out the window into the late autumn night. The apartment overlooked a highway onramp, and neon light from the billboards cut in blades through the window. The wash of color flipped from green to white. Franc squinted.

Kim's face looked at him from the billboard. He blinked.

"No way that's real. Breathe."

The sign stayed the same. Her face: tawny skin, tight curls, and full lips saying something with text scrolling underneath them.

**Franc, answer your phone, what's wrong with you?**

"Did you ever kill anyone in Homs?"

Kim had always been able to scramble Franc's emotions as easily as a teenager tilting a pinball machine. They were sitting in Franc's living room, which was empty apart from a couch and a memory foam mattress in one corner. It was cold, because Franc wasn't paying the electrical bills. Actually, there were no electrical bills, and no landlord, so Franc thought that was fair enough. Kim shivered even though she still had her scarf on. Franc sighed.

"It doesn't work like that in the real world. War is not a video game. There is no score. Four guys shoot at something they can hardly see, and when they walk that way again next morning there's blood in the dust. You remember the first time you texted me after you got your cortical implant? I was getting shot at in a ditch. I got my forward air controller to call in a drone strike, and we fucking blew up a tank. So who killed the crew? Me? The radio? The drone?"

Kim made a slow-down gesture with her hands. "Okay, do you think you *might* have killed anyone?"

They'd never spoken like this, ever.

"Probably," Franc said.

"One last question and I'll leave you alone. Did you ever save anyone?"

"Yes," Franc said, and this time his voice was firm.

"I know I've never asked to hear any of the stories…but will you tell me that one?"

Her eyes were serious. She put a hand on Franc's knee. Not seduction, support. Franc told her the story.

All he remembered, viscerally, was a smell of dust in his nose that never left. That and the feeling of slipping on shell casings, feeling like he was losing his anchor to the world.

Trying to remember anything else was like trying to remember a dream, or maybe an ancestral memory—like it was a different person who'd done it.

"A guy tried to air a late night comedy show on their national broadcaster, right before we lost the whole country, and mujahideen hit the studio in the middle of a taping. The producer was born there, but he had Canadian citizenship. The Special Operations Regiment didn't just train the locals; we were operational, so we went outside the wire and got him."

The part of the story Kim made him tell again was actually pulling the guy out. Physically picking him up and carrying him back across a wasteland of paper and shell casings and broken TV props. Thirty seconds after Franc had gotten the guy into the LAV III and closed the hatch, a suicide bomb had gone off in the TV station.

"Holy shit, that's…intense. Suicide bombers attacked them while they were actually taping a live TV show?"

"Yup."

"What happened to the audience?"

"Nothing good."

Kim's brows furrowed. "I never understood the suicide bomber thing."

"Some people," Franc said, "would rather end the world than see it change."

"Did it bother you that you went in and got one guy?"

"No. You can't save everyone. That's what war is. Getting one person out alive was a win, whether it was fair or not."

Kim nodded. "Okay, if I asked you to do that again, would you at least think about it?"

They were, for an instant, half the distance to where they used to be. Then Franc blew it.

"What kind of trouble are you in?"

"No, Jesus. I don't need you to save me. We are not getting back together, and I am not flirting with you. I mean save someone else. You're the only person I know who does this stuff in the real world."

"I *did* this stuff. Past tense."

"Come on, Franc. This is not who you are."

"It obviously is."

Kim's eyes hardened. "Let me be more clear. This is the you I left. This is the you that has no job or direction or address. The you I need is the old one."

Time failed to pass. Like a lot of bad decisions, Franc made this one quickly.

"Let's say I listen. Who would I be listening for?"

Despite the sorry state of Franc's kitchen, Kim somehow made tea. Franc didn't know where she'd found the ingredients—or the cups for that matter.

"Meena was an intern when I worked at Somniscope," Kim began.

"Wait, you don't work at Somniscope anymore? Isn't that the whole reason you got the implant?"

"They farmed us out to a company called Oneiros Industries after the referendum, and I didn't want to move across the wall.

Oneiros wanted me actually building software architecture, but the NDAs were really weird. I would have had to live on a campus and give them total access to my nub."

Silence.

"That means to your brain," Franc said. It wasn't really a question.

"There are zero bioethics laws in this country. My guess is that Somniscope is testing new technology without ever being subject to awkward stuff like corporate liability or the Turing Convention. That's what Meena is stuck in. I know where she is, more or less; I used to work there. I don't know how to get her out."

"I don't see what this has to do with you."

"I went in and looked at her dreams. Have you ever used a Somniscope?"

"No, my dreams are real enough."

"I couldn't…Do you wake up, when you dream about the war?"

"Yeah," Franc said.

"Well, imagine you couldn't. If this is as weird as it looks, it's a problem for literally everyone who does my job. Think of hackers as web-addicted songbirds, flitting around in the digital undergrowth: if someone doesn't yell 'Hawk!' when a shadow passes between us and the sun, we're all fucked."

Franc closed his eyes. "That should have been you. You could have warned her at the beginning, and you didn't."

Kim paled. She never did understand how he saw through her so easily. It wasn't easy to admit how right he was, and how wrong she'd been. "It felt funny, and I still encouraged her to take the job. She looked up to me, and I just sent her on her way."

They brooded. Franc failed to tell her it wasn't her fault.

"So you want me to go meet the hawk?"

"Yeah," Kim said, "and get Meena out of the nest."

Franc sighed. "It's possible. But you'd need a lot of stuff. And I'd have to think of a reason to do it other than guilt."

"I mean, there is money involved. Her parents are rich."

"You could have led with that."

"I didn't want you to think I was hiring you like a mercenary."

Franc thought about that. "You *are* hiring me like a mercenary."

"I didn't want to insult you, or what you used to do. I never knew how not to do that."

"I'm surprisingly comfortable with it."

"I could find a way to pay—" she stopped. "Wait, really?"

For the next few hours, Franc just watched as a parade of confused-looking couriers tried to find his squat and drop off Kim's dark web purchases. She disappeared while Franc unpacked obviously stolen medical gear, thin slabs of foam body armor that held together with Velcro, and an incredibly fancy new phone with an earpiece and a lot of features he didn't understand.

He loaded what he thought he might need into a Japanese courier bag decorated with bas-relief gothic lolitas. Kim came back in with a small box.

"I could treat anything from cardiac arrest to an amputation with this stuff," he told her. "Not sure I need body armor, though."

Kim sat down next to him and handed him the package. "You do," she said. "I printed you a gun."

Kim liked 3D printing, and ghost guns were an interesting challenge. She found a design, pirated it, printed, tested, and put it in the box. Ammunition she could just order from Sprawlmart. Putting it together had been fun.

She wasn't entirely ready for Franc's reaction. He just sat on the couch and cradled the gun in his hands with a blank stare. She knew that look. It was the one people got when they disappeared into coding, or a daydream, or the past. It was the look people had when they put the cap on and clicked into a Somniscope dream.

"You okay?" she said softly.

Franc's eyes focused. He ejected the magazine, locked the slide, and gave the gun a once-over that was so fast Kim couldn't distinguish the individual motions. Another heartbeat and it was back the way he'd found it.

"I'm good," he answered. "That's what PTSD is like, if you're curious. You end up not really being back there, but not here, either."

She touched his arm. "We should have talked about this." It was as close to an apology as he was ever going to get.

He smiled. "Ouais—mais, je m'en câlisse." *Yeah, but I don't give a damn.* "Let's go save a songbird."

Franc roared his ancient Toyota pickup through gathering winter gloom. Cold pavement hissed under his tires, and the sun's last rays disappeared into a sliver of threatening sky. The neighborhoods Kim routed him through were mostly deserted. The yuppies had all fled to Toronto after separation—but a few of the bigger industrial spaces were lit. Franc had the phone propped on the dash so Kim could see what was going on. A little chime sounded in his wireless earpiece as Kim's response scrolled across the screen:

**This is it. The lit buildings are coding sweatshops. There're no cars parked because they don't let you leave. The Turcot Yards are full of them. I'm marking the building on your GPS.**

A glowing lozenge popped up on the map.

**Find some way to get close. They'll have vans driving site security and deliveries around.**

Franc parked and scrambled up an embankment. In the distance, through skeletal trees and hex-link fence, was the Gorgon triple-eye of a train. Snow began falling, and when the train passed, it dragged the flakes into swirling little fractal vortices.

The building at the zero-meter mark looked like a Victorian mental hospital but had probably once been a fancy tech startup. The fence around the empty parking lot was topped with concertina wire that shone in the gloom.

The rear gate was padlocked, so Franc used multi-tool bolt cutters to snap the cheap metal loops that the invincible alloy shackle was holding together. He crept to the back door, pulled a fiber-optic line out of the phone, and pushed it under the threshold.

The touchscreen showed him floorboards and dust. He fiddled with the lens and saw a wide staircase. To the right of that was what might be a kitchen, to the left a big open room lit by the washed-out glow of computer monitors. A silhouette was lounging in a desk chair.

Franc bumped the lock and crept inside, one hand on the ghost gun velcroed to his hip. The technician stared at a bank of bracket-mounted screens surrounded by aluminum tables and rolling tool carts. He was wearing a lab coat and speaking softly into a boom mic mounted to bulbous noise-canceling headphones. All Franc could see in the dim light were columns of numbers and what looked like MRI readouts.

The tech shivered as Franc sneaked past him but didn't turn around. There was a thick bundle of zip-tied fiber-optic cables leading away from the technician's whirring server stacks and up the stairs.

The second-floor hallway was lit by flickering fluorescent tubes. The network cables split into rooms on either side like the branches of a tree. Franc expected something shiny and bright, but the place looked like a sanatorium in a horror movie. There were no cubicles. No break room. No water cooler. Just shadows.

Franc peeked into the first open door. A spartan room lit by a single frosted bulb. An aging man lay still on a wrought-iron bed, hands clasped across a wool sweater, fast asleep with a Somniscope cap on his head. He was as sallow as a drowning victim.

A featureless cube sat on a small table beside the bed—probably a very expensive computer. Cables ran from the cube to a splitter on the man's sweat-dampened pillow, and this was plugged into his cortical antenna. The only color in the room was the washed-out blue ropes of fiber-optic cable running along the walls.

"Okay, time for some answers," Franc whispered.

He shook the sleeper gently. Nothing. He snapped his fingers, shook some more, and finally rubbed his knuckles along the guy's bony sternum. Zero pain response. The guy wasn't just dreaming; he was practically comatose. Franc tried to pull the Somniscope off his head. It snagged. The cap wasn't just pulled over the man's cortical implant; it was plugged into it. Franc used the light from his phone to scan the equipment. A red safety switch made it clear that you weren't supposed to disconnect someone while they were hooked up.

"Kim, is this normal?"

**No. Don't just yank the cord!**

"We're in a hurry," Franc said. He ignored Kim, flipped the catch, and slowly drew a two-inch alloy spike out of the sleeper's nub.

"Wake up. I'm here for a hacker named Meena."

Nothing. Franc shook him, gently at first and then more violently. No response. Franc realized he had made a mistake. Instead of panicking, he ran down his checklist. Pulse and breathing were acceptable, but the dreamer's eyes were disconjugate, like he was trying to look at Franc and over his shoulder at the same time. A clock started ticking in Franc's head. There was no way the technician downstairs was going to miss this. He'd spend a few minutes making sure it wasn't a computer problem, and then everything was going to go wrong.

"Okay, I shouldn't have unplugged him."

**FUCK, FRANC! Try another room.**

"No time. They'll know this guy is…whatever he is. It will ring alarms. We need a better way to look."

**Then put on his Somniscope.**

"Are you kidding me?"

It took Kim a moment to respond. The dreamer lay inert next to Franc, his silence infecting the room.

**No. You going to find her or not? Plug your phone into the Somniscope's input and get the fuck in there.**

*Click.*

The fragrant scent of wet pavement. Scattered bird calls. Somniscope watermark faintly visible even through closed eyelids. Franc opened his eyes and saw long grass reclaiming concrete between his boots. He stood on a verdant avenue, lampposts overgrown with creepers. A city street a thousand years after the last human had walked it. He blinked.

The resolution was breathtaking. Franc had no idea what a Somniscope dream was supposed to look like, but this was as real as any trip he'd taken back to Homs. Individual blades of grass swayed in a cool breeze. There was no way this was just computer software. He took a few steps and passed beneath a tattered sign that read: "Welcome to the Somniscape, Dreamer."

Further in the distance, across a pristine cityscape, a clockwork giant was tinkering with trees, picking them up like he was pulling weeds and transplanting them just as easily. High above, clouds pulled and shaped themselves. Something was flitting between them like an arrow lancing through smoke.

"They're writing a new world," Kim said, and Franc started. She was the same holographic image she'd been three nights before, but the billboard by the avenue hadn't been there the last time he'd looked. "I mean, this is a completely new thing. Can you do something?"

"What?"

"Literally anything."

Franc picked up a loose bit of paving stone and shied it through the hologram. Kim fizzed.

"Total agency," billboard Kim said. "That didn't use to be possible. And I'm in there. I can see myself through your feed. That means the dreamscape is using your memory to fill in gaps in the architecture. This is like discovering…I don't know, cold fusion or atom bombs or a way to actually melt fat without exercising. How good is the resolution?"

Kim had always babbled when she got overwhelmed.

"It's not resolution. It's real. But how do I find your friend? This place is huge."

"I can help with that," an enormous voice said. Franc and Kim turned. The golem who had been planting trees had somehow shifted to tower above them.

"Dev tools," Kim's hologram whispered. "You should probably ask him."

Kim had assumed that the programmers would all be friendly. That they would want to talk, and maybe opt out of whatever total insanity Oneiros had roped them into. She'd told Franc to just ask the golem, whose name was Vitaly, to take them to Meena and let her out.

The golem started chasing Franc around, trying to crush him. His voice came through her link tinny and compressed: "Log me off or whatever!"

"I can't! Something's wrong. You have to wake yourself up."

"That is no longer possible," the golem bellowed, punching concrete into dust with a concussion that sent Franc skidding to the pavement.

"Kim, why the fuck can't I fly out of here or something?"

"It's not your dream. You have no cortical implant. Just pretend this is Homs and wake yourself the fuck up!"

Franc gasped. There was a hesitation as he awoke, and the tinkle of shell casings filled his ears. He was slumped on his side with his back against the dreamless man's bed.

He pulled the Somniscope off his head and struggled to his feet. His legs felt tense and stiff.

"What the fuck?" he said. His phone buzzed.

**Something is very, very wrong. They can't get out. Two problems: find Meena and wake her up without lobotomizing her.**

"Same solution for both."

Franc got his feet under him and staggered down the stairs, making no effort whatsoever to conceal himself. He walked into the technician's room racking the ghost gun's slide. The technician spun his rolling chair around, and his eyes went as wide and bright as the computer screens behind him. Franc showed him the bore. "Wake everyone up. Now."

"I can't. They have to do it themselves. And no one has in... almost forty hours. I just change diapers and run IV lines."

The silence that followed was ominous. Franc had done this before, kicking in compound doors. People usually cowered and started begging. Guns turned most conversations into exchanges between parents and children, and whoever held the weapon got to be the adult.

"Do you have any idea what you've got me into?" The guy sounded desperate, on the edge of tears.

"Calm down. Tell me where Meena is. She's one of your programmers."

The tech's eyes darted to one of the rolling carts by his workstation. Medical supplies, May West snack cake wrappers, and some kind of gun.

Franc raised a hand. "Don't do that. Look, I'm not going to shoot you. Just wake them up."

"I can't."

The technician clumsily pulled the gun off the table. It was a Norinco, Franc's brain informed him casually, a Chinese coil gun that fired tungsten-copper slugs.

"Stop," Franc heard himself say. "This is not worth it. This is not the O.K. Corral. *On n'est pas des osti cowboys—*"

The guy was crying. He got the gun pointed at Franc, pushed the activation stud, and things fell apart from there.

Kim heard a series of harsh snaps through the audio pickup. She couldn't see anything unless Franc pulled the phone back out of his pocket, but the satellite feeds told as much of a story as if he had.

She'd been watching Oneiros vans drive to and fro, as sedate and organized as honeybees around a hive. Without warning, they all started moving erratically. Only one moved purposefully, closing in on its target building.

"Oh, shit."

She started sending Franc messages:

**Franc? What happened?**
Nothing. She typed it again. And again.

Franc sat slumped with his back against one of the metal cabinets. His ribs hurt. The technician was bent back stupidly in his computer chair. The plastic Norinco coil gun was an island in a tiny red sea on the floor.

When Franc checked his magazine, the lip rattled on the ghost gun's frame. Six rounds gone.

An astringent smell burned Franc's nostrils. He stood, punch-drunk, and reached a hand under his coat. A spent tungsten-copper slug dropped out and tinkled at his feet. A second, nestled gently in a hardened foam concavity, was still hot enough to singe his fingertips. It had made a small, neat hole through one of the courier bag's straps.

Franc had probably just killed his second person in ten minutes. He felt sick.

Agitated insects were making buzzing noises in the technician's headphones, hanging like a noose around his neck. The noises stopped after a moment, and small alarm icons started pulsing in the toolbar at the bottom of each screen. Franc pulled out his phone.

**Franc, answer me. WTF is going on?**
Franc panned the camera.
**Jesus, is that guy dead?**
"He didn't tell me where Meena was."
**AND YOU SHOT HIM?**
"He shot me first."
**YOU'VE BEEN SHOT?**
"In the foam. Calm down, *tabarnak*. If I'm not panicking, you shouldn't. Tell me how to find your friend."
**Plug me in again.**
In a moment, chat windows popped up on each screen, as though the dead technician wanted to chat with the dreamers. Franc

wondered what the point of that was until he saw that each window had a name in it. *BritishDavid, ArkRoyal1941, N3w_S1b3r1an…*

Another alarm went off, turning the border of one monitor orange. *Vit4ly's* life signs were starting to wobble. *TheFlyingDutchman, MrBokbagok, NotMeena…*He stopped. Pointed the phone camera.

**THAT'S HER! THAT'S HER! THAT'S HER!**

Franc took off for the third floor clutching his ribs.

Franc ran, counting. His chest hurt. He passed *TheFlyingDutchman's* room and glanced in the open door. The old man lay where Franc had left him, perfectly still. To get Meena out, he was going to need a way into the dreamscape. He unplugged the Somniscope from the bedside computer without checking to see if the dreamer was still capable of dreaming. He got to the second floor landing and started up. Then he stopped.

**KEEP GOING, SHE'S ON THREE.**

"Yeah, but the golem is on two."

**Why does that matter?!**

"It's his dream," Franc said.

Franc got to Vitaly's room and found the door locked. He pressed his forehead to the rectangle of wire-reinforced glass. Vitaly was awake, the Somniscope still on his head, swaying like a man in a nightmare.

Franc yelled. Vitaly stood on a chair like a man at sea, leaned his back against the wall, and looped a thick length of loose, wall-hung fiber-optic bundle around his neck. Franc threw his shoulder into the door, then backed off and put a bullet into the lock.

The blast echoed the length of the corridor, and sparks flew. He slammed the door again. Failed.

Vitaly woozily kicked the chair out from beneath his feet. Franc watched the man swing, ending the world instead of giving it up.

# *the songbird run*

Meena's room was right where it ought to have been. The door was unlocked.

Franc's heart thumped when he saw her. Lank black hair, delicate features under the Somniscope cap, the nub of her cortical implant incongruous on the pillow.

**OMG, that's her. Link the Somniscopes like you're doing a tandem dream.**

"I don't think this place follows that kind of rule. Or any rules."

**Just go. Physical and liminal proximity are related, she should be right there.**

He plugged his headset into Meena's computer, pulled the cap over his head, and lay down next to her. Smelled the delicate humanity of her skin. He hit the Somniscope's toggle.

*Click. Click. Click...*

Franc awoke abruptly into the dreamscape. When the world snapped into place, it was raining big gobs of water. Wind pulled at his clothes in an unnatural way, the gusts pulsing in and out.

Franc got his bearings. The same city as last time, but he was much further down the avenue. Wind turbines were spinning their blades like huge whirligigs in the distance, and Vitaly dominated the horizon.

He looked like he had the first time: a cross between an armored knight and some kind of golem, but much bigger, immobile, kneeling. One of his massive hands disappeared into a river. Chains with links the size of train cars crisscrossed his armored chest, bunched around his neck, and vanished into the deep blue sky. A summer moon was out, bright and fresh. The chains stretched toward it into infinity, and Franc saw dark lines scarring its surface.

**Oh my god. The architecture is collapsing.**

Kim's text was coming in as something like subtitles, but they were disappearing faster than Franc could read them. The world around him was slowly fading away, the details vanishing like sugar stirred into tea. The songbird wasn't there.

"Meena!"

The dreamscape darkened, and the grass stopped swaying. The giant was gone; Kim was gone; everything was lost in outer darkness. Franc tried to change something. Tried the way he did every time he started to dream about the war. It had never worked. He remembered Homs as hard as he could, and slipped on a brass shell casing. He smelled Syrian dust, and paper fluttered around his feet.

The dream shifted, the way dreams do, and now it was one of his. Franc ran past shot-up TV cameras and dangling spotlights. He swept the room with a rifle he didn't remember picking up. Clear. He knew where she'd be. Where the producer always was. He looked under the anchor's desk, covered in shattered ceramic mugs, and saw a pair of glowing golden eyes stare back from the shadows.

"It's you," Meena said. "Will you stay with me? I don't know what's going to happen."

"No. Wake up. You have to wake up." Franc grabbed her hand. Her hair was dying down, going limp.

The spotlights winked out like fireflies in the dark. One by one. Franc grabbed Meena and hauled her into a fireman's carry. A thing he'd done a thousand times before—or just once; it was hard to tell. Carrying the girl, Franc tore himself through the veil. Prayed he could drag her back out with the last little fragments of what he couldn't forget.

Back in the dingy reality of Meena's room, Franc gasped, clawing the Somniscope off his head.

"Meena?"

The girl next to him was still. He shook her, and she emitted a faint moan. Not like she was in pain, just someone who wanted to hit the snooze button. His earpiece had fallen out, so he put it back in.

"I got her," Franc said. His phone vibrated wildly. Kim had a lot to say, and he didn't have time to check what it was.

He didn't know how to disconnect Meena properly, so he carefully cut the cables connecting the Somniscope to her implant and peeled the cap off her head. Her eyelids fluttered, but stayed shut.

Franc dug around in the courier bag and pulled out an EpiPen loaded with cortisol and adrenaline. The needle punched through Meena's thin sweatpants. Her breath quickened while Franc held his. The girl inhaled sharply, and her lashes flew apart to reveal depthless hazel eyes. She blinked at Franc and yawned.

"What time is it?"

"Time to go," Franc said.

The adrenaline carried Meena as much as Franc did. He half-dragged her out of the room and past the stairs. Far below them a heavy door banged open, the sound as crisp and urgent as a gun-shot.

Franc stopped and used his free hand to pull out the ghost gun, leveling it down the corridor. The girl's head bobbed. Her hair smelled of sweat and citrus. Another door banged. Whoever Oneiros had doing security was clearing the programmers' rooms one by one. Franc consulted his fight-or-flight reflex for about one second.

"Fuck this."

They staggered on. Turned a corner with the faint jump of tactical lights somewhere behind them in the gloom. Franc found a huge bay window, pounded the latch with the butt of his gun, and hauled them into the world outside.

The night was cold and lightless. Wet snow fell like rain. A small, vulnerable gasp leaked out of Meena when her bare feet touched the metal of the fire escape.

"Keep going," Franc said. "We're almost home."

Meena woke up, pleasantly warm, and groped for her Somniscope. It wasn't there. No Oneiros computer or clothes either. She was lying under a fluffy duvet with wires trailing out of her nub. She peeked out from under the cover. A cold room littered with packing foam and shipping boxes, and her sweats hung to dry in front of a single battery-powered space heater.

"What," she said very softly, "is going on?"

A shape moved on the couch opposite her bed, which was nothing but a piece of high-end memory foam. The shape sat up and resolved itself into a guy she kind of recognized.

"You're fine," Franc said. "We got you out."

"We?"

"Kim."

Meena reached up and gently disconnected the spike from her nub. The wire ends were cut and sharp.

"You yanked me. Where is everyone else?"

"I don't know. You're it."

Loneliness. Apprehension. Relief. Guilt about the relief. Meena felt it all pass over her face like waves crashing on a beach. The only one that stayed with her was relief.

"I am so tired," Meena said. "Do you want to get some sleep?"

Later, after a bit of slightly delayed sleep, Franc's phone buzzed. He rolled over and unlocked it. A pixelated image of Kim popped onto the screen. A tiny, animated version of the girl who'd spoken to him through a billboard.

**Where's our songbird? Is she awake yet?**

"Uh, still here." Franc tried to aim the phone in a delicate direction.

**You dog, Franc. She's like twenty-four. Never mind, I'm too happy to be mad. Get her ready to go. We need to get her back home.**

"Wilco."

**Cash okay for you? I've been in touch with her parents, and I assume you don't do crypto.**

"Cash is fine…but you can teach me about the crypto thing."

**Wilco. And Franc, thank you.**

"It's what I do," Franc said.

Kim's avatar smiled. **I'll let you know if anything else crops up,** it said, and winked out.

# INTERLUDE Q

*I open my eyes and I'm flying. The wind feels like water as I slice* through it in just the right way, holding my wings at just the right angle. I could do this all day. It's what I was made for.

I coast along the shoreline, vaguely aware of the waves far below, letting them determine my path. I surrender to an unseen operator known as "instinct": the collective will of countless generations exactly like me. At the moment, I'm a solitary bird alone in the sky, but only in the way that a single wave might be alone in an otherwise calm ocean. Nothing lasts for long; everything lasts forever.

A harsh buzzing sound from my left wing suddenly upsets my reverie. One of my feathers is sticking up at an odd angle, dragging and spinning in the wind. This is soon joined by a similar buzzing from my right wing—then two more from the left and right sides of my tailfeathers. My sleek, aerodynamic body is catching the wind all wrong now, flitting around like a piece of trash in an updraft. Only the coordinated spinning of these rogue plastic feathers is able to even me out. The faster they spin, the more air I'm able to push down to keep myself afloat. It takes practically all of my attention just to stay upright, hovering steadily in an empty sky, droning on and on, my will surrendered to some unseen operator.

# 18. MY FOREVER GHOST
## by stephen coghlan

*'Traffic looks heavy today.'* **Dartz began, his digitally smoothed** voice leaking out to the local community over airwaves and internet. It returned to him through his cochlear implant, higher than when it left his skull. He hated the sound of his own voice, but other people paid to hear it, so he suffered his displeasure quietly.

Hundreds of miles away, the drone he was piloting caught a thermal wave. As the air around its metal skin pushed upward, his stomach sank in sympathy and his skin crawled. His ears popped, though it wasn't actually his *ears*, just the microphone pickup of the drone catching stress on the machine. It was loud enough in Dartz's head to almost drown out the hum of rotors and the honks of impatient drivers far below.

Closing his eyes, Dartz tried to fight back his welling panic and do his job, but then he was back over the battlefield. His body was on fire as the drone he was connected to burned from a near miss thanks to a warhead exploding only a few lengths away.

Then it all disappeared as Ashley pressed their lips to his. Although it was only digitized information and not real flesh-and-blood contact, it still soothed him, allowing him to return to the task at hand.

Dartz listened to the traffic below and the chatter on the airwaves: "As usual, rush hour continues to be a sea of red lights. Don't plan to go anywhere fast as an accident near Yonge and Lawrence pretty much guarantees traffic is moving slower than molasses."

Placing their hands onto his shoulder, Ashley whispered into his left ear: "You're fine. You've got this."

The chatter continued in his right: "The DOC is gridlocked and will continue to be so for the foreseeable future, so if you can use another route, do so to save your sanity."

Releasing the drone, Dartz allowed it to return to its docking station before zipping over to New York, where his services were demanded.

"10-71 at 9th and West 31st street, 12-21 requested."

The drone he'd been asked to control was already being flown by someone else, but a quick glance at the current pilot's stats told Dartz why he was being asked to take over. The present pilot was a rookie and would benefit from Dartz's experience. It took only an instant to send the request, but Dartz was kind enough to word it gently: "Delta-Alpha-Romeo-Zero-Zero-Two requesting stick control of November-Yankee-Fife-Fife-Niner."

Dartz said this aloud as he sent his email requesting clearance from the tower. Once more his voice was bored, almost a monotone, yet he struggled and fought to keep his pulse under control.

He waited, giving time for the rookie to read the text, hoping the kid would refuse. Dartz didn't want to take money from the amateur pilot's pocket, but he'd been asked to intervene and so had to prove he'd put in the effort to do so, or else risk harming his reputation, which was more important than his next paycheck.

Then he was there, high above the towering skyscrapers. He was smaller, lighter, not the long-flight drone he'd been flying over Toronto. He was now a small recon model, just a little more complicated than a training machine.

As the schematics of the drone were downloaded into his brain, Dartz chuckled. The pilot had all of the safeties on and had only been using the most basic of control schemes.

"Get ready for a show, kid," Dartz laughed as he rewrote his limbs to control the four fans and locked out collision detection. Shedding altitude, Dartz dropped his synthetic body into the maelstrom of the streets below. The glass and concrete walls of buildings blurred as the drone's lower-quality camera struggled to keep up with the speed Dartz coaxed from the machine. The air that washed over it was cool despite the morning sun above. Its rotors spun in a high-pitched buzz that blasted back from the walls but was almost entirely lost in the city's chaos.

There were only two senses the drone did not replicate, and Dartz was happy he could neither smell nor taste the world around him.

The mission was to advise on the nature of a fire or a shooting. It was a recon job. What Dartz could discover would reveal which emergency service would be dispatched. As his artificial body dropped to ground level and the reticle highlighted the address, he knew it was going to be a longer morning than he had prepared for.

The fire had already engulfed the main entrance of the ramshackle shop, and the heat was playing havoc with the air currents.

Ashley's voice once more filled Dartz's left ear: "It says the shop opens at nine."

Dartz sighed with relief. "No customers inside. Good."

Although there was probably no one in the shop, there were apartments above it, and those people needed to be notified. The drone he piloted had no speakers, but it did have a body, and some battery life left.

"Let's knock them up," he said out loud through his smile, even as he split his attention to request help from the fire department. Dartz flung his artificial body forward, tilting it at the last moment and stopping the propellers. The drone thumped loudly into the lowest apartment's window. The impact passed through Dartz's body and winded him, but the pain passed. Its effects were purely psychogenic, a remnant of the drone's impact warning system.

Engaging the propellers, Dartz pulled himself back and away, preparing to ram the glass again even as he saw the curtain being pulled aside.

*Clunk!*

The occupant of the apartment was upset at having been woken up, but as smoke drifted into view, their anger dissipated into horror. Turning away from the window, the occupant screamed a warning to someone else Dartz could not see.

One down, but there were many to go.

Soft hands caressed Dartz's aching shoulders, and tender lips kissed his head, making contact with his scalp even through his helmet.

Fatigue wormed up Dartz's neck, and needles of pain began to stab him behind the eyes, but he did not stop slamming himself into each window that he could. The chatter of the fire department as their vehicles and crew arrived was welcome, but he ignored them. There was no time to waste, no pause for celebration. There was only his desire, his duty, to save all those he could from the inferno.

He had to.

No one else would die from the flames, shrieking in agony as their bodies ignited, and their lungs seared, and then their screams stopped, and—

Ashley's arms wrapped around Dartz's chest as they leaned against his back.

"It's okay; you can stop now."

Ashley was right. The drone's battery was running out, but even as Dartz prepared to throw himself at another window, a white plume of steam crossed his artificial eyes, and he knew the fire was out.

The call to identify the incident was over. It had been for a while.

Releasing the drone back to its recall setting, Dartz disconnected himself. There were other jobs, other calls for service, but none that interested him. He was fatigued, and in no mood to bother with anything until he had eaten and erased the all-too-real pangs in his stomach that came flooding in as he returned to reality. Yet Dartz did not budge. Instead, he closed his eyes and relished the feel of his love's arms around him.

He did not care to move, wishing to stay in that moment for all eternity.

"You saved a lot of people." Ashley whispered, holding Dartz tighter in their arms. "I'm proud of you."

A smile tugged at Dartz's cheeks, but his lips quivered as his eyes welled up. "I saved them, but—"

"Shhhhh," Ashley hushed him, placing one of their long fingers across Dartz's mouth. "You have to stop thinking like that."

"How can I?" Sadness and guilt became part of his voice as Dartz exhaled slowly and tried to fight back the encroaching tears. "I could have saved you, too."

Ashley's weight pressed onto Dartz's thighs as they sat on his lap, yet the chair did not protest the additional weight. Their hands pressed into Dartz's shoulders as his lover leaned forward and kissed his forehead.

"Look at me," they commanded.

Opening his eyes, Dartz let his heart skip a beat.

Ashley was beautiful as always. Gone were the fatigues and combat armor, replaced instead with a tank top that hung loosely over their chest, and gone were the combat pants, replaced with denim shorts that rode just above their waist and ended halfway to their knees. Dartz didn't have to look to know that Ashley was barefoot. They never liked boots or socks and had always complained how they felt uncomfortable and artificial. It was funny that even now, Ashley refused to wear them except when going outside on cold days.

Pulling back their long brown hair, Ashley tied it loosely behind their back and once more planted their naturally brown arms on Dartz's chest. "How many times do I have to tell you that it's not your fault?"

Unable to face his lover, Dartz turned his head, but Ashley was once again in his view, their arms against their hips, their weight suddenly gone from his legs.

He knew it was futile to look away again, so instead of trying to avoid Ashley's reaction, Dartz sat up from his reclined chair and closed his eyes as he removed his psycho-connective helmet. Away from his scalp, the helmet retracted upward on its cable, leaving Dartz free to stand up without hitting his head.

Ashley was upset. Usually they guided his hand for him, but this time there were no soft hands on his wrist as he felt for his connective lenses and pulled them up to his face. The lenses clicked onto the magnetic mountings on either side of his head. He dared not open his eyes until the connection beeped, signaling that it was now online and working with his senses.

His love was still there, their arms crossed over their chest.

It was time for a new approach.

"I need to eat," he said.

Ashley's face softened and they stepped away, making room for Dartz to pass.

The kitchen was typical for local apartments. There was an electric range, which was as unused as the day Dartz had moved in, and if Ashley hadn't motivated him to dust it once a month, it probably would have been covered in two years of grime instead of just a week's worth. The sink was empty, thanks to Dartz's habit of washing his dishes before nightfall, and because he rarely used anything other than his three plates, his water bottle, and his handful of utensils.

His fingers and the pads of his feet tingled as he opened the fridge thanks to a small electric current passing through his body. It made a variety of readings and sent the data to the veteran's affair's clinic where it was compared to his other records. There were programs to perform adjustments automatically, but the VA didn't work like that. New doctors, still learning their trade, would review it instead and make their recommendations, often vastly different from those made previously by others. While he appreciated that the Veterans' Affairs office considered him a vital member of society, he was still irritated by their intrusion into his life.

"Your present weight is 128 pounds. Recommended calorie intake is 2,228. Please eat the sweet potato and turkey package. You must drink 33 ounces of water by noon."

Ignoring the appliance's suggestions, Dartz grabbed the closest container and popped the heat seal. As he slammed the door with his foot, he ignored the refrigerator's chastising tone of disappointment.

"You have to stop that attitude." Ashley sighed from their space at the table.

On the counter in front of him appeared a virtual plate of vitamin-infused synthetic red meat over rice-pasta, waiting for him to pick it up. He knew by now that Ashley was going to "eat" the same thing that he had grabbed for himself. It was one of their couple things that they had started when Dartz was losing too much weight.

Picking up the virtual dish, Dartz placed it in front of Ashley, making sure they were all set up before he took his own seat. Removing the lid, Dartz dug into the food, patiently counting out each time he chewed until he swallowed. He barely tasted the rich flavors. He didn't want to. Synth meat still tasted like meat, and as he looked over at Ashley, the smell of carnage—of burning flesh, of fuel being consumed by fire—filled his nostrils, and guilt locked his throat. They were on fire, burning, dying, screaming until—

Ahsley was there, holding him. Dartz didn't know when he had fallen to the floor, but he had, and the only thing that had saved him from severe injury was his lightened frame. With his lover's gentle embrace, Dartz eased himself out of the fetal position. Ashley's digital hands closed over one wrist, and Dartz let them guide his hand to his face to wipe away the tears.

"Thank you, love," Dartz sighed, his words shaky with the panic he still fought to purge from his soul.

Leaning forward, Ashley kissed him softly on his forehead before guiding him to his feet. Wrapping him into their arms, Ashley squeezed Dartz as tightly as they could manage. Although Dartz felt like Ashley was holding him, he knew it was only information fooling his frame.

"Are you okay to finish your food?" Ashley asked.

It was cold now, and even less appetizing than before, but Dartz knew Ashley wouldn't relent. Tipping the dish back, Dartz shoveled it down his throat and chased it by guzzling all of his water. Suddenly dizzy, he limped to the couch, which doubled as his bed. His lover climbed in beside him and held themself tightly to his back, and Dartz let himself slip into a tentative slumber, fearing what was coming but unable to resist the need for sleep.

And then he was back, high above the chaos. He had no more rockets left, and his primary gun's ammo was almost expended, but he dared not retreat.

If he did, people on his side were going to die.

"Time until a new drone arrives?" Dartz yelled, wondering when he had last dared to ask such a question. The answer had barely changed.

"Nine minutes, sergeant."

The operator sounded so close, though he was all the way at the other end of the air-conditioned trailer that they jokingly called "the Office."

The drone behind him, his wingman, exploded as a ground-to-air missile finally found it. Cursing, the pilot to Dartz's right unhooked himself from his "desk" and ran outside to piss. His next drone was still en route as well, due to arrive at the same time as Dartz's replacement.

Pulling a high-G turn, Dartz side-slipped, shed altitude, and found those who had shot his companion out of the sky. Dartz's drone's cannon burped, and .90-caliber bullets sprayed the two opposing soldiers, shredding their bodies into liquid viscera.

Two down, hundreds more to go.

Gaining altitude, Dartz tried to sort out everything in the chaos of crossfire below.

The enemy in the area was supposed to be pacified. They weren't supposed to be there at all. That was the reason the armored company on Dartz's side had been told to take that road.

That was the reason Ashley was in danger.

It was Ashley's company that had come under ambush from both mountain ridges. It was their armored personnel carrier that fought through the carnage, trying to break free.

It was Ashley who steered the vehicle deftly from inside their APC's cockpit, who was trying to keep themself from panicking, while splitting their attention between steering around the wreckage of other vehicles and suddenly discovered mines, all while operating their vehicle's limited defensive weaponry.

"God damn it, where is our artillery?" Ashley screamed. Their panic was all too real and palpable, and the emotions they broadcast made Dartz's normally calm hands quake.

"God damn this piloting link." Dartz whispered. Like him, Ashley had link software installed in their noggin, and both of them were waiting on the patch that would stop them from sharing so many emotions. It was a flaw in the new hardware, one which engineers had yet to correct.

They had never met in the flesh, face to face, but from the first mission they had been on together, Ashley and Dartz had formed a bond. Dartz didn't know how Ashley looked outside of their virtual avatar, and he didn't care. He'd come to consider Ashley his friend, and although he tried to deny it, he felt strongly about them beyond mere friendship. With Ashley now in the hot and thick of the danger, Dartz was terrified.

"We can't fire into the zone, not safely." one of the ten-mile snipers responded. "They put down too much sat-jamming smoke. We can't tell who's friend or foe."

"If we don't get artillery now, you aren't going to have to worry about that!" another APC driver chimed in, before vanishing from the conversation as a rocket-propelled grenade took their life.

Biting his lip, Dartz pressed his drone down into the canyon.

"This is Sgt. Ceda. I have eyes on the prize. Can you link in through my cam?" he asked over the tactical network.

There was no hesitation. "Affirmative, Ceda. Please paint the friendlies. Firing in ten."

Cutting his engines, tilting his nose, Dartz swung his camera around, making notes of each group of surviving soldiers. He picked up those in the rear, those groups of survivors amassed along the rocks, the broken-down vehicles where fellow soldiers were pulling the wounded and dead from—

But he didn't finish.

Something hit his drone.

Something terminated his connection.

He hadn't marked out those in front.

"Permission to fire?" Artillery asked.

Dartz coughed as he returned to the reality of the trailer. The sweat on his flesh had used all the moisture he had left, and the dryness in his throat choked him as he tried to scream out a negative, but Ashley beat him to it.

"Fire, now!"

It was too late. Eager to please, the many massive guns were already aimed, and those on the trigger were all too ready to help. The guns were thirty miles away, but the shells were more than supersonic.

It was only fifteen seconds until they hit.

Fifteen seconds too long.

Fifteen seconds far too short.

"Ashley," Dartz screamed, "I didn't mark you! Get out of there!"

A pause, a laugh, and the last words Ashley said while they were still alive: "It's okay, Dartz. I guess this mistake is on me."

And Dartz knew that in only a moment Ashley's screams would fill his ears and tear his heart apart.

But that wasn't what woke him.

It was Ashley, but they were not screaming.

"You need to wake up, honey," Ashley whispered as they went through the motion of shaking Dartz by his shoulders. "You're being requested."

Stretching, Dartz gathered Ashley into his arms and kissed them gently.

"Let whoever is calling go to voicemail," he demanded, squeezing Ashley a little tighter, letting his body feel their weight.

"I would, but it's the NYPD. They think the fire from earlier was arson, and they want you to chase the suspect."

That was all the motivation Dartz needed. He scrambled from the couch.

Knowing what state he was in, Ashley vanished, reappearing by the pilot's chair. "They had one drone use a laser on the suspect, but then it was hit with ECM and knocked out of service."

"Think he's rigged?"

Ashley shrugged, playing the video in what little space they shared in Dartz's memory chips. "It's hard to say. Cameras didn't get a good look at him. He could be using shimmer tech."

# my forever ghost

Dartz nodded, pulled his helmet over his head, and was once again flying hundreds of miles away from his corporeal form.

Satellites far above and cameras at street level guided Dartz toward the target, but every few seconds the electronic guidance that was assisting the pilot went offline, only coming back in bits and pieces. Biting his lip, Dartz flew his drone closer. Whoever it was, they were definitely using shimmer tech, trying to lose the surveillance that was tailing them. It was difficult to do in such a city, but not impossible. If the suspect ran into the right building—an old enough structure without any surveillance—and dropped their countermeasure, they would only have to leave the building before it was searched to have a good chance of being lost in the crowd.

Dartz got a fix on them and saw them ghost in and out of all the high-tech tracking equipment. Laser finders were distracted, tracking algorithms were misplaced, and even sonics were scrambled.

"Let's do this the old-school way," Dartz said to Ashley as he disengaged all other sensors but the camera.

"I have a visual on the suspect," he announced. "Suspect appears to be a Caucasian male, about five feet nine inches, wearing a long brown coat and a black baseball cap. No facial hair. Suspect appears to be wearing shimmer tech ECM. Traveling on foot at the corner of—"

Dartz never finished his sentence.

The suspect turned to face him, and in that moment, the flash of their chrome-tinted glasses set on Dartz's drone. Jacked reflexes allowed the suspect to raise their snub-nosed pistol faster than Dartz could dodge, and when the suspect fired, a scream of high-pitched feedback exploded between Dartz's ears.

His vision went white, then disintegrated into a shower of black and ivory squares twisting before his eyes. Ripping the helmet from his face, Dartz tumbled from the chair and clutched at his aching skull. His eyes were ready to leap from his head. He gritted his teeth so suddenly that he bit through the tip of his tongue, but the pain was nothing compared to the hole left in his mind, the agonizing emptiness in his heart.

He had been shot with a virus gun. His implants were already corrupted.

*Ashley! Oh God, what about Ashley?*

They weren't there. No one was there except him in his empty apartment. He was all alone, with circuits going haywire inside his brain.

"No, no, no no no no no!" Dartz screamed, writhing as the pain in his head grew and traveled down his spine to take residence in his chest. Clenching his fists, Dartz punched himself hard in the gut, attempting to convince his body that the agony he felt was purely physical. But he knew there was a pain that was never going to heal.

"Goddamn jacked son of a bitch!" he cursed again, pulling his knees beneath him. A new wave of agony threatened to split his head in two, but Dartz refused to let it stop him. He thrust himself back into his chair and grabbed the helmet from above his head. "Braindoc!"

Upon receiving the audio command, his computer dialed the emergency number. His extreme distress was transmitted thanks to the pickups in his helmet, so he was pulled to the front of the line. As his vision blurred again, Dartz presented an email pointing out that he was on a job for the NYPD, which meant he'd been wounded while in the line of duty. This was the last step to get him pushed through to the next available braindoc.

Dartz closed his eyes, refusing to look at any of the calming avatars that probably awaited him. "Virus gun!" he said as a welcome to whoever was treating him.

Gentle AI-generated lo-fi music, meant to put him at ease, was immediately pumped into his head as the braindoc ran an analysis.

"I see full corruption of your software," the doc responded in a soothing tenor. Despite the pain rampaging through his body, Dartz noticed the tiniest hint of certain syllables being longer than others, which indicated that whoever was speaking to him was probably autotuned, unhappy with their natural voice.

"How bad is it?" Dartz asked.

The answer came without hesitation: "Bad. It looks like you were shot with a wiper round."

Turning off his mic with a touch of his tongue, Dartz allowed himself to scream violently into his empty apartment. Wiper rounds were banned to all civilians, only available to military forces or on the black market. They targeted the operators of certain electronics and fully corrupted all implants. In doing so, they knocked out any on-duty operator and sometimes caused real casualties if the operator had life-sustaining equipment that picked up the bug.

His implants were all toast. And with them…

Dartz unmuted his mic. "Zero recovery?"

"I'm afraid so," the doc replied. "If you have a backup, I can try to install from that, but I'm going to have to fully scrub all of the software first."

There was no backup to be had. All of Dartz's software was old, from his service days. He had kept it unchanged, never updated, because he would have been at risk of losing Ashley—at least, the Ashley he had spent the last years of his life with. He'd never sought help because had his software been evaluated, the evaluators would have found Ashley's illegally downloaded ghost.

And now, Ashley was gone.

There was nothing to hold him back.

The doc was still talking.

"Your firmware is very out of date. I have to upgrade in order to fix you. In fact, this should have been fixed years ago. You've probably been suffering headaches and phantom visions for years."

"I never noticed," Dartz lied.

"If I have your permission, I'd like to proceed."

"You have my authority for a full wipe and upgrade."

"Thank you. This will only take a few minutes. Please do not move."

"I'll be right here, Doc," Dartz promised.

Then he was no longer in his apartment. Instead, he was back in his old bar, in a tiny holosuite sharing drinks with Ashley, whose real body was on another base. Their avatar was the perfect image of who they were within, unconnected to their body in real life. Dartz was too lazy to make his own avatar. He didn't care what people thought of his appearance.

It was their usual get-together. Back then, they jokingly called it their "date night." Only later, when Ashley was nothing more than a series of ones and zeros stored in Dartz's hardware, did they look back on those moments and see their growing love for each other.

Knocking back his beer, Dartz set the empty glass onto its coaster and pressed the button for another. He kept his thumb on the request until it was done reading his blood-alcohol level and the green light signaled that another was allowed and on its way. They were lightly alcoholic at best, but enjoyable enough. Dartz was not allowed to suffer the self-imposed wound of a hangover.

Ashley, for their part, had chosen a wine that Dartz found too sweet for his palate. He didn't even have to taste it to know. While he and Ashley were connected, the mental bond made by their faulty software effectively let them share their food.

Laughing, Ashley covered their face as they tried not to spew their salad across the table. Dartz laughed and sipped his drink. He wasn't hungry, having turned several of the front-line opposition into ground hamburger earlier that day.

Wiping their mouth, Ashley stopped and stared at Dartz's avatar sitting across from them. "What's wrong, D? You're not laughing like you normally do."

Dartz shrugged, trying to play up the machismo as he struggled to hide his fear. "I saw death a little too close today," he replied nonchalantly.

"I heard you rammed home a flying bomb."

Dartz nodded. "All the others had failed, but I made it through." He paused, shivered, and then continued: "It was just me. I had made it through the defenses by flying lower than the others. Once I made it into the cave, I dropped the beacon and went in by wire. I could have detonated right there, but I would have only blown up the mouth of the cave. There were other tunnels. I had to go deeper."

Planting their elbows on the table, Ashley swallowed before resting their head in their hands and listening intently.

"Two miles, that's how long the wires can go. One mile in and I felt like I was never going to see the target. And then there I was, in a wide open chamber, surrounded by almost a whole company."

Dartz paused.

"In that moment I saw every face, every look of shock and surprise as I zipped through their ranks. They knew, they all knew, that they were about to die."

He shuddered.

"They had stashed their ammo in an adjoining room. It wasn't hard to find. Time moved in slow motion as I flew toward it. Soldiers were diving everywhere, seeking cover, cowering."

His voice caught in his throat.

"I saw all of them. Young men and young boys, and all knew they were about to die."

Turning his head away, Dartz couldn't hide the fact that a tear was running down his cheek.

"I detonated. The report says that the explosion caused an earthquake registering on the Richter scale. The whole cavern caved in. Special Forces reported that the cave was flattened and inaccessible. The officers called it total annihilation. It's a nice and fancy term to say I murdered fifty men today."

He shuddered, unable to stop.

"I've never seen death so close. I never saw, before, the terror in those who were about to die. It's always been a game to me until today. I saw boys, barely men, crying in terror, knowing they were doomed, and I'm the one who pulled the trigger."

He broke then and wept, and as he cried, Ashley reached out their digital hands and took him by the shoulders. He felt the contact through their link and welcomed the embrace that Ashley awkwardly made across the table. Standing, Dartz wrapped his arms around the holographic avatar, knowing that he was touching air, savoring the contact all the same.

When his tears ran dry, Dartz rehydrated with the next beverage that appeared. He sipped it, unable to bring himself to drink it any faster.

"Feeling better?" Ashley asked softly, sipping their own drink in mimicry.

"Yes, thank you," Dartz admitted.

Cracking their back, Ashley sat back in their chair, and Dartz took to his seat in kind.

"It might seem morbid to you," Ashley said softly, "but I know how you feel. I've been very up-close with the enemy. I try not to kill them if I can help it. I try to make them surrender, but if push comes to shove, I know it's them or me."

They shuddered.

"I've felt their bones break under my wheels, and seen them vanish under my guns, and I've seen our own soldiers wounded. I've carried the dead and dying behind me, and seen many take their last breaths. It's okay to cry, when you're somewhere safe."

"I only feel safe here, with you," Dartz whispered, instantly wondering if he had said too much, but Ashley's smile melted his heart. "Do you fear death, out there?" he continued. "That's why I became a drone pilot. I'm never in the front lines. I feel like a coward admitting it."

"And is the quartermaster who supplies us a coward, or the cook who prepares our food unnecessary? Armies need support, and in our modern war, you are a frontline soldier, while being half a world away if you need to be."

"But I'm not like you, putting myself into the thick of the action. I'm distant, safe. Doesn't the thought that you could die out there terrify you?"

"Yes." Ashley still smiled, but it changed from a show of soft concern, to an expression of tranquility. "But I don't think it's the end. I don't know if I believe in an afterlife, but I know that the black box in my APC has recorded my personality. We always carry around part of ourselves in our boxes, because they learn us, *become* us. Those pieces of us, our digital selves, are our ghosts, our spirits. If I die out there, I know a part of me will live on in the military archives, preserved, far longer than my own body. My ghost will live on forever."

Except that it hadn't.

Ashley's ghost had been spirited away, downloaded into Dartz's software when he'd been unable to imagine life without them. At first, Ashley's ghost had been scared, trapped in an eternity of reliving their own death. But when they had discovered they were free from their metal and circuit board tomb, they'd been ecstatic, thinking they were going to live with Dartz until his dying day.

But now, Ashley was deleted and truly dead once and for all.

"Please open your eyes," the doc ordered, and Dartz complied.

There was no pain, no agony, no wave of nausea that greeted him.

"Can you stand?"

He was surprised to find out that he could. Dartz looked at his apartment for the first time without his linked glasses and didn't feel the need to vomit.

"You have the latest software and firmware, and I've blocked off all the emotional links, isolating your brain from your implants. All your nerves have had their feedback adjusted. The hardware is still there, but it should no longer make you sick. How do you feel?"

"Great, like getting back to work," Dartz answered coldly. "I have a killer to catch."

"Good luck. I'll send my bill to your insurance."

Dartz nodded and logged off before sinking back into his chair.

"This is for you, my love," he whispered, imagining holding Ashley's hands, whispering into their ear, and then he was away again.

Gone were any intentions of peace. Gone was the use of the NYPD's drones. Pulling his veteran status, Dartz leveraged what permissions he could, and then he was in Fort Hamilton's drone bay.

The perpetrator, the arsonist, was deadly.

It was time to fight fire with fire.

This drone was savage, sleek, fast, shielded against virus guns, and most importantly, *armed*.

"Latest report on the suspect," Dartz ordered. Data scrolled across his eyes too fast for him to read, but his brain absorbed it, and he imagined that Ashley was there reading it to him.

The suspect had gotten far, but not far enough. Despite having been on the run for almost half an hour, they had either not wanted to ditch their hardware or been unable to find a place secluded enough to risk dropping their suit.

"Amateur."

Dartz's voice was cold, chilling. He was now the hunter, the soaring eagle, and his target was little more than a frightened hare, too busy dodging officers on foot to pay attention to the skies above.

"Gotcha."

The suspect was weaving between buildings, trying doors at random while attempting to look inconspicuous. Whoever they were, they must have known that the noose was tightening.

Then they found an unlocked door to a ramshackle apartment, and ducked inside.

"Crap."

Dropping to ground level, Dartz diverted his attention, seeking the blueprints.

There was no basement. That was good. The suspect could not go underground.

There was no spare room in the lobby, Dartz saw as he flew past. The suspect was instead ducking into a crowded elevator. Although there weren't any windows near the elevators on the floors above, there were windows on either side of the hall that just barely gave a view of the elevator doors, from a distance.

Dartz climbed quickly, checking each floor, watching to see who exited the elevator.

Second floor: no one.

Third floor: an old lady and her dog.

Fourth floor: no one.

Fifth floor: a few kids and adults, but none of them shimmered.

Sixth floor: a woman and a man exited, each heading in a different direction.

But the elevator doors didn't close, and a child leaned out holding the shimmer tech cloak in their hands. Audio filters blocked out the cacophony of the city, and the child's voice rang out clearly: "Hey mister, you forgot your jacket!"

*Bingo.*

The glass in the window was barred, but not bulletproof. The suspect had fired on police equipment, had started a fire, and was armed. There was nothing holding Dartz back. He lined up the reticle and prepared to shoot. No one would blame him if he killed the suspect. No one would blame him if a warning shot was just a little too close.

But Ashley had always tried to persuade Dartz to use non-lethal methods.

Their voice was once more in Dartz's head: "I try not to kill them if I can help it."

Biting his lip, Dartz aligned his shot. This asshole might have killed Ashley, but if Dartz was going to do his love justice, he was going to play by Ashley's rules.

A sense of calm overcame him, and Dartz fired.

The suspect howled as the round plowed through his thigh, dropping him. Yet even as he fell, the suspect raised his virus gun.

"I will make you surrender," Dartz vowed as he fired once more. The pistol clattered away, damaged beyond use.

It felt good to honor his lover. It felt right.

Dartz stayed there until live officers arrived to take the suspect into custody. Then as his account filled with pay for a job well done, he signed off.

It had been a hell of a day, and it wasn't close to being over, but Dartz had done enough.

Lifting his helmet, he blinked, still bewildered that he could now see without his glasses. Standing, Dartz set his shoulders back, strode into the washroom, and turned on the tap. The cold water chilled him, and he felt alive, more alive than he had in years. The implants must have really been screwing with him all this time, but now that they were isolated from his senses he felt better than ever.

If only he could have Ashley with him. They would wrap their arms around him, tell him he did a good job, and maybe even ask to go out to celebrate. Ashley couldn't eat as a ghost, but they could taste through their connection, their unique bond. And that would be enough.

The walk was short. While Dartz's apartment was not exactly downtown, it was close enough to a few restaurants. Pulling up a seat, Dartz ordered Ashley's favorite wine, and when it arrived he toasted his love, enjoying, for once, the cloying bouquet that tickled his nose. He sipped it, closing his eyes, savoring the memories that filled his head.

It didn't taste as bad as he remembered. In fact, it was downright delicious.

"Didn't I tell you it was good?"

Dartz opened his eyes and looked around in confusion. Someone had the exact same voice as Ashley, and spoke with the exact same rhythm.

No one was even close to him.

Lifting the glass to his lips, Dartz took another sip of wine.

"Hey, am I talking to myself or what?"

There was still no one around.

Dartz set down his glass, then covered his ears and whispered his lover's name.

"Oh good. I'm not all alone after all," came the reply.

"How can this be?" Dartz asked, barely daring to hope, fearing he was going mad.

"The implants were really screwed up," Ashley laughed. "I guess that after all this time messing with your brain, your nerves had adapted, and that gave me an escape route. Just before the virus gun fired, I tried to hide, and in that instant I think I bypassed the firewall. The circuits in here are really messed up."

"Wait," Dartz laughed, "you mean that you're—"

"Burned into your brain, and not just your heart?"

"Yeah," Dartz laughed, and sipped Ashley's wine once more. As he did, Ashley's hand wrapped around his and pulled the glass away from his lips.

"You should go easy on that stuff. It sneaks up on you fast. This isn't the same strength as on base," Ashley cautioned. And then there they were, sitting at the seat across from Dartz, smiling in relief. "So, lover boy, are you finally going to take better care of yourself? Because unless you can upload the both of us, this is my last chance to live, and you better not take it away from me too early. Dying twice is a pain, so let's not make this a hat trick anytime soon."

Smiling, Dartz leaned across the table and kissed his lover's soft, full lips, feeling them press against his own.

"Well, you did say you wished we could be closer. Until death do us part?" Dartz offered.

"And hopefully after that," Ashley replied. "So…does this make me your dream lover?"

"My forever ghost," Dartz concluded, closing out their bill. Getting up from the table, he held out his hand for Ashley, who took it and let him pull them to their feet.

"You know, you look cute without your glasses," Ashley teased as they began to walk—together, now and until their end.

# INTERLUDE R

**I'm a changeling. A fairy abandoned in this mundane world.**
A cuckoo hatching in a warbler's nest. I don't belong here. I never have.

You're the ghost of a dream of a memory. I can still see you here and there, but only as a faint reflection, only within myself.

So what are we really? Half alive, half forgotten. Half awake, half asleep. We are the dream that imagines itself into existence. Without me, you have no presence in the world, and without you, I have no purpose.

*Tick tock, tick tock…*

Awareness fades like so many sunsets. I sink once more into the warm embrace of oblivion.

# 19. UNALIKE

## by v. s. santoni

*He called himself Cambion because he enjoyed the idea of* being half dream, never fully at home in the waking world. His work friend Omar, who never stopped talking about the Scape, had loaded a copy onto a memory stick for him. Cambion inserted it into the port on the back of his neck. He reclined on his sofa and closed his eyes.

Cambion's mind projected a black screen onto the backs of his eyelids. A wavy blue swirl appeared in the void, and soothing watery ambience tickled his ears. Then the words "The Scape" appeared in the middle of the screen, pulsing slowly. A tag line below this title read: "People are a million fragments, scattered, but here, one again."

The app was originally called the Cerebral Dreamscape Processor, but fans nicknamed it "the Scape" because that proved easier to remember. It worked by sending messages to your neural link, which told the hippocampus to induce dreaming without putting you all the way to sleep. A text box opened under the logo:

For best and safest usage conditions, engage THE SCAPE™ while lying down in a comfortable setting away from others. The home is considered optimal.

Some trolls found it amusing to use the app while still fully awake because it triggered hallucinations. *I've heard one too many horror stories of folks going nuts because of that shit,* Cambion mused to himself.

The Scape responded to thoughts, so Cambion acknowledged the prompt mentally, and it disappeared. The title graphic then started to spin, becoming a vortex that pulled his mind deeper into the trance. He found himself under a ceiling-wide mural. Pilasters stood beneath smiling Botticelli angels, and sconces boasting countless glowing arms illuminated checkerboard floors of polished marble. It was an elegant hotel, burnished and sleek despite its apparent age. Patrons ambled around in different builds and sizes, most humanoid but others more abstract—lines and circles and oblong shapes—and no small number of furries playing cartoon animals. Cambion took on the look of an actor he'd seen on TV.

A waiter served a man at the bar duck confit, and as he set down the plate, Cambion smelled the roasted skin, and the parsley and scallions in the mashed potatoes. He shouldn't have been able to detect those scents, for no real food cooked anywhere near him. Omar had warned that the Scape could trigger hallucinations: phantom odors, voices, and even painful memories.

A black text window prompted him to open his mind, to integrate into the system's intuitive software. He did as it said, relaxing his mental barriers and truly, for the first time in his life, Cambion freed his imagination. There was no *you* or *I*, no *he* or *she* in this place. Everything was conceptual. The walls between individuals melted.

Time s t r e t c h e d ,    g  r  e  w       l    o    n    g    e    r   .   .   .

Cambion returned to himself again. In the gray space that surrounded him, he constructed a log cabin that stared across the peaks and valleys of the Great Smoky Mountains. It was springtime, so the spruces and elms shone golden. The impeccably polished wooden furniture inside gleamed. Cambion saw reflections of his childhood self in the metal appliances. His parents used to rent a place reminiscent of this one.

Someone knocked on the ratty screen door at the front entrance.

The clatter rattled Cambion. He approached it, and outside he found two young neighbors: a man and a woman, both blond. Cambion opened the interior door but kept the screen latched.

"Yes?"

The man smiled. "We're glad you're here. My name's Walter."

"It means we're alike! I'm Giselle, by the way."

"I'm Cambion. What the fuck are you talking about?"

"You imagined this place, right?" said Walter.

"Yes."

"In here, similar dreamscapes form next to one another. The Scape naturally encourages microcommunities to develop."

"That's weird."

"No, it isn't! It's great," Giselle said. "It means you won't have to deal with people who aren't like you."

This amused Cambion, but only ironically. Hankering for answers, he brought the couple into the living room, and even though it was mild outside, he started a blaze in the shale fireplace.

Their words t
        u
      m
       b
       l
        e
       d
              out "Did you grow up in the South?" asked Walter.

"I moved here from Mexico when I was young."

Walter laughed. "So you're pretty much a southerner."

Giselle tittered along, making things more awkward.

Cambion's gaze drifted around the room. "Every spring, Mom and Dad rented a place like this."

Walter nodded. "My folks owned one like it too."

Giselle added, "My aunt had a timeshare that was similar. I spent the summers up there."

Although they had arrived at the same destination, their journeys couldn't have been more different. Their childhoods, and their resulting worldviews, had drawn them there. They agreed on most things and therefore shared that space. Cambion had longed for that, a nook where only those like him could speak, and he believed everyone craved that: somewhere people wouldn't fight because they thought the same way. True harmony.

Finding the couple electrified Cambion, and he wanted to discuss everything with them. They talked until the sun sank low, fading the ombré sky from orange to black. Walter and Giselle sought those with identical values, so they visited everyone whose dreamscape bordered theirs. Cambion spat out a quick "Yes," when they asked to stay the evening. The decision, however, spoke more to his curiosity than goodness of heart.

Cambion strolled through a hallway on the first floor. Two bedrooms sat across from each other at the end of the passage, and a door along the left opened to a bathroom with a spa tub. In the sink, he saw a pile of deadheaded roses with a green mamba coiled among them. Cambion hated snakes and knew he hadn't put it there, so he closed his eyes, and the creature disappeared.

Walter found him in the hallway. "Are you okay?"

Cambion's features, pale from the ghastly sight, again filled with color. "Yes."

"Do you still speak Spanish?" Walter asked.

Cambion gave the tub a careful scan. "Yes."

"What are Spanish people like?"

The question confused Cambion on numerous levels. "I've never been to Spain; how should I know?"

"I'm sorry?"

"Never mind."

"You shouldn't be so sensitive. I was only asking a question."

Their similarities had boundaries. Walter could only reach so far before the walls of culture and language rose up to block his way. Then he and Cambion transformed back into strangers, like a butterfly again cocooning only to revert to a pupa. They had fallen from Babel and lay strewn on the broken earth, confused and staggering, searching for meaning where none once existed, imbuing value where none once existed.

"Do you have somewhere I can take a bath?" Walter asked.

A strange waste of dream time. He could've done anything, yet he chose to bathe. *No point questioning his desires,* Cambion thought. "You can use this tub."

Walter wandered into the bathroom wide-eyed like a bewildered child, and as he did, a hornet flew out of his ear. When Walter stopped to look in the mirror, he reflected back as a pyramid of meticulously arranged tin cans.

Cambion shut the door and returned to the living room, where he found Giselle standing naked at the picture window, staring at the golden maple trees in the valley. A hornet crawled out of the corner of her left eye and took flight. The fiery creature ignored Cambion as he walked up beside her.

"Why are you naked?"

"Hmm?" She turned, wearing clothes now: an unbuttoned blouse and a short skirt. "You might've imagined it." Cambion wondered if he did. She coyly smiled and said, "Maybe you want me."

She swept her hand down her chest, drawing Cambion's eyes to her breasts. Giselle paused when she noticed Cambion wasn't coming closer. "You're gay, aren't you?"

"What're you, a pair of swingers?"

"No, I just wanted to cheat on Walter with a hot Mexican."

Cambion couldn't stand listening to her any longer, so he headed upstairs. A walkway extended over the den and connected the loft to a crow's nest in the A-frame's gable. The moon dripped a heather-bluish white over the aurulent landscape. Cambion walked outside and listened to the crickets chirp.

Giselle joined him. "You could fuck my husband, and I could watch. That could be pretty hot."

"Not into all your freaky sex shit, okay?"

They knew nothing about each other. They were unloved vessels passing at eventide. Cambion thought they were alike, that she and Walter couldn't hurt him, but as similar as they were, they were still too different. Empathy was gone. Their lines of communication had atrophied. So Cambion and Giselle sat quietly for a while, both too afraid to speak because they might disagree and that would spark a fight. She could hit block and forget this had ever happened. In fact, Cambion hoped she would.

He wished for Giselle to vanish, but before she did, her hornet landed on his shoulder and plunged its stinger into him. The fleeting burn left quickly as it came, but then Walter's hornet flew in and stung him too. Cambion wanted a place where people didn't have insects hiding inside them. He longed for encounters with others to be predictable. Like ads on social media, tailored to his tastes, to his demographics.

Dreams in the Scape changed with breakneck speed, disorienting first-timers. Fans relished the swiftness with which they could alter their realities. It gave them power they didn't have in the material world. That ease also created an endless continuum of inoffensive, agreeable experiences. No hornets nesting in the brains of fellow dreamers.

Cambion then found himself in a private chamber with luxurious paneled walls the color of fresh cream. Gossamer curtains hung from a ceiling hoop made of flowers and fell throughout the room. The white rococo furniture affected a refined air. Men with Cambion's same features slinked behind the delicate fabric. They wore nothing save the alluring smiles on their faces. Some reclined on tufted chaise longues, others danced, and many more kissed and fondled each other. One approached from around the drapery, handsome with a clever grin.

"Care to join us?"

"Is this like a porn dream or something?"

"I wouldn't know. Where are you from?"

"My family is Mexican."

"Mine's from Chile."

"Do you speak Spanish?"

"Sí, lo hablo." *Yes, I do.*

"Pues, dime ¿qué hago aquí?" *Well, tell me what I'm doing here.*

"No sé porqué estás aquí." *I don't know why you're here.* "Quizás querías estar en un lugar con aquellos que eran como tú y pensaban como tú. Aquí todos nosotros pensamos lo mismo, y hablamos lo mismo, y sentimos lo mismo." *Maybe you wanted a place with people who thought like you. Here everyone thinks the same, and speaks the same, and feels the same.*

In a place such as this so full of intellectual masturbation, where criticism gave way to mindless sycophancy, Cambion believed no one could hurt him. These people not only enthusiastically agreed with one another; they fellated each other's sameness. No more hornets hidden in plain sight.

Cambion followed this Chilean satyr through the ethereal curtains, and as the silky fabric caressed his skin, so too did his doppelgänger. Another came from behind Cambion and slid his arms under him, and he kissed Cambion's ear and whispered things he liked. And then the one in front leaned in and pressed his lips to Cambion's. And when he backed away, he too muttered sweet consolations, not because they spurred thought or action—quite the opposite—his words inspired inertness. These two fawned whenever Cambion exhaled, clinging to every strand of air that escaped his lungs. An unthinking mind is a happy mind, and no mind lies more complacent than one everyone agrees with.

As Cambion's thoughts slipped into a gentle torpor, images danced on the translucent curtains: body spray to attract lovers; toothpaste to brighten teeth; girdles to shrink wastes; sodas that tasted like lemon, lime, strawberry, bubblegum, cotton candy. *They had to hide the ads somewhere*, Cambion thought, and that alone woke him from the sylphs' hypnotic trance. Was he even dealing with people anymore, or had he sunken so deep into Narcissus's Pond that he no longer recognized the difference between humans and bots? So long as they agreed with him, it hadn't mattered. But now he saw the ploy's true intent. *Shady app.*

He knew these men couldn't be real. No one could imitate him so closely. They were talking now, all of them babbling, whispering, yammering—some fully immersed in the orgiastic pleasure of being around like-minded folks and others circling each other like alley cats, eager to find even the slightest chink in the other's armor. Cambion peppered his partners with questions, and neither agreed on anything. He thought one's politics leaned too far right, the other's too far left. The ensuing debate prompted others to end their revels as they sought to join the discussion. And as they each threw in their opinions, Cambion hated how many fell dead damn center. They didn't consider nuance, and when they broached complicated subjects, everyone acted as though they followed a script and they'd be lost without it.

Silence pervaded the room, and everyone's eyes shrank with suspicion. They each waited for the next to slip up, to say something problematic. Not something offensive or harmful, merely something they didn't want to hear. Everyone in the room had grown sick of each other. They were all nearly identical, and even then still too different. Too rare, too precious. So no one said anything. They silently barbed their enemies because it was too risky to speak.

Then Cambion muttered, "I disagree."

Everyone growled, incensed. Nothing was happening, absolutely nothing—everything stood joyously devoid of emotion and thought—then Cambion had dared to speak. He'd gathered the audacity to break form.

"We're unalike," a few of the men said aggressively.

One said, "I have a mole on my cheek."

And another replied, "I do not."

And the first argued with the second, "You can't understand what it's like to experience life as I have."

But the second countered, "Nor you I. Nor any of you. All of us are individuals. None part of a greater whole."

Then the floors and walls scattered like rust-colored butterflies, abandoning Cambion adrift in darkness. He began to dream of his home and was suddenly back there, alone in his apartment. Not dreaming, not fully existing. Nothing. An atom, separated from other atoms. Alone forever, even in dreams. Too distinct to belong to something bigger than himself.

*I must do everything in my power to reject the notion that I'm like anyone else; investigation reveals how desperately unique we all are. And because we are unique, we are alone.*

Cambion wished to accept this as true, but no one remained to debate the matter. No one existed to tell him he was right or wrong.

To hurt him and challenge him to question his way of thinking. So he had to assume he was correct about everything. And why not? No one knew his heart better than he himself. Still, he wondered if accepting differences in others might ease his desperate loneliness.

He startled awake and removed the memory stick from the back of his neck. He hated the Scape. Everyone on social media was so fucked up. He deleted the app from his system and drifted back off to unassisted dreams.

# INTERLUDE 5

*'Okay, I give!' I hear you say from the next room. 'I'll help you.'*

"Help me *what?*" I ask. I can't seem to recall what we were talking about. Did I drift off in the middle of a conversation? I get up from bed and stretch to shake away the cobwebs.

"I'm going to help you find the exit."

Puzzled, I follow your voice into the hall and check the guest bedroom. It's empty. "What do you mean? What exit?"

"Exactly." Your voice sounds like it's coming from the laundry room now, but I can see there's nobody in there.

"Seriously, what are you talking about?" I check the bathroom. "Where are you?"

"That's not important right now," you say from somewhere downstairs. "You need to focus on figuring out where *you* are."

I start heading down the stairwell, but the farther I go, the darker it gets. I can feel my way easily enough, but I know something isn't right. There didn't use to be this many turns. "Are you down there?" I call out unsteadily.

No answer.

Starting to panic, I speed up into a run, covering dozens of steps now, *hundreds* even. Way too many for an ordinary house.

I miss a step and tumble headlong into the darkness. Time expands as I fly through the air. Each moment seems to bring me a tiny bit closer to the ground, but each bit is smaller than the last. At this rate, I'll be falling until the end of time.

The end of *my* time, at least.

"Come back to me," I hear you say. But for the life of me, I can't place where your voice is coming from.

# 20. ARI

## by jeb r. sherrill

*Trevor stumbled down the alley. Something hot and sharp* squirmed in his gut as he fought to keep his balance. Raphie must have spiked his champagne with something nasty. What had the world come to when you couldn't sleep with a man's wife without all hell coming down?

How far was he from home? Could he find a taxi? A cat shrieked, taking one leg out from under him. He teetered for a moment. Paper and bottles crunched beneath him. Something in his stomach lurched up into his mouth as his vision faded to black.

He rolled off the bed, holding his stomach.

"Gann," a woman yelled, crouching beside him on the floor.

There was no pain in his stomach now, but he did feel hungry. Incredibly hungry. "Who's Gann?"

"You shouldn't be awake yet," she said, standing him up.

The room looked a bit like a Persian desert tent, but the furniture was solid wood carved with Baroque flourishes. An ornate crystal chandelier dangled improbably from the center of the tent, although it didn't appear connected to anything. "Am I dreaming?" he asked, turning his hands over in front of him.

"You haven't said that in a long time," said the woman, gripping his hand and pulling him out of the room.

The door slid to one side, he noticed. It didn't occur to him at the time to wonder why a tent had a door, particularly a rather large mansion-sized door made of stone and shining like ivory. Trevor tripped into what appeared to be a large house, a palace perhaps, with dimensions like a shopping mall. The woman steadied him.

"Gann," she said, narrowing her eyes. "Are you okay?"

"Who's Gann?" Trevor repeated, trying to figure out why the color of her eyes kept changing.

She sighed and gave an exasperated nod. "Your name isn't Trevor; it's Gann."

He shook his head, which was already dizzy. "My name isn't Gann. My name is Trevor." He spat the words, but something felt hollow in their meaning the moment they passed his lips.

The woman drew her mouth into a line. "What do you see around you?"

Now Trevor narrowed his eyes. He frowned and glanced around. "A lot of books, shelves, carpets. Uh, I can't really see the ceiling." Somewhere above, the vaulted…something…vanished into the sky.

She groaned. "Look, my name is Claire. You've known me for years."

"Is this a dream-within-a-dream thing, or something like that?"

"You always used to ask that," Claire said. "But you're not in a library, or a mansion, or a meadow or a…a…a planet, or anything. If you tell me you're anywhere specific, I know you aren't really here."

"Where is *here*?" he asked, wondering if something nasty was still affecting him. If this was a dream, it was a very real one.

"You've been working on that for several years now. Sit down."

They sat at a desk. Trevor couldn't remember noticing it a moment before, or sitting down for that matter. "I like the desk," he said, admiring its glossy surface.

She rolled her eyes. "You think you're sitting at a desk?"

"I think *you're* sitting at a desk," he said warily.

Claire pulled out a thin cigarette and started smoking. She didn't bother lighting it; she was just already smoking it. "Let me see how to put this." She crossed her legs and looked a little haughty, like a 1940s femme fatale who's in the middle of pretending to be pissed off over some trifle that doesn't even make any sense. "We're not really here doing whatever it is you think you're doing. However you think I look, or sound, or whatever you think I'm doing, I not doing it."

Trevor blinked a few times in cartoonish fashion. "This is a hell of a dream," he said, folding his arms and pulling the brim of his fedora low over his eyes.

Claire threw her hands out to the side in exasperation. "Oh, for God's sake, you usually remember."

"It's that drug," he said, giving his fingers a sharp snap. "The shit Raphie gave me because I slept with his wife."

Claire slapped him upside the top of his head, which seemed highly improbable as her chair sat five feet away. "You let someone poison you?"

"Let me guess. This is like some fever thing?"

"No," she said, blowing out a puff of smoke. "More like you're hallucinating."

Trevor leaned in and cocked his head to one side. "You're saying this is all a hallucination?"

Claire let out a sharp breath, the only simple sign of exasperation she had left. "Of course not. Just closer to that than a dream."

A lump welled up in Trevor's throat, and he reached for a glass of water. "So, I'm not dreaming?"

"Well," said Claire, "that all depends on what you mean. Yes, you're dreaming. You're just not usually *dreaming* when you're dreaming. Know what I mean?"

In no form or fashion did Trevor have any ghostly idea what Claire meant by this. He was still trying to remember what he'd started to say before about the thing in his stomach. What had he been doing before he fell asleep? Someone hated him.

"Don't bother trying to remember it. Sometimes you do; sometimes you don't. But you started seeing through the dream somehow. Said it was like you saw the gears, so to speak. Like you were dreaming and started reading all the books in the library."

Trevor's head spun harder. Thoughts refused to connect properly. "Are we in a library?"

Claire was down at the end of a tunnel of light, and her voice sounded far away as it said, "Now *that's* closer to a dream."

He coughed vomit onto the concrete. The alley smelled worse than he remembered. It appeared he'd pissed himself the night before. Had the sun always been this bright? Running footsteps sounded behind him.

"Trevor. What the fuck? Come on."

Trevor rotated his head and blinked several times. A bald man, too young to already be bald, stood panting. Nice suit. Crisp smile. He looked like a Ryan.

"You can't be out here like this," said Possibly Ryan, gripping Trevor's arm and dragging him toward a waiting car.

"What did you call me?" Trevor asked as the man pushed him into the back seat and slid in beside him and the vehicle moved away. "I'm Gann, aren't I?"

"That some British slang?" Possibly Ryan asked as they sped down the street.

"I don't know why I said that," said Trevor. The name "Gann" sounded more right, but not *exactly* right. "I'm Trevor?"

Possibly Ryan snickered. "Raphie mickeyed your drink worse than I thought. "Shit man, did you really fuck some chick on the pool table?"

Trevor, maybe Gann, stared out the window as the bald man went on babbling behind him. The city blurred by. It didn't look *real*. He didn't know this place—didn't know this man or this car, even though it all seemed disturbingly familiar. "Where's Claire?" he asked without turning around.

"Are you out of your mind? Whoever she is, you better smooth things over with Arianna, or you're spending the next two leap years in the doghouse."

Arianna. That name rang a bell. A blurry image of her face

wavered in his mind's eye. His stomach twisted. "Does she know?" Trevor found himself asking as he cooled his forehead on the passenger side window. He remembered nothing of the night before except for a lot of puke…and that he'd had a really weird dream.

"Does she know?" laughed Possibly Ryan. "I heard she was there. I'd wear a flak jacket home if I were you."

Trevor's stomach tightened. "Where are we headed?"

The man coughed out another laugh as they pulled up to a small house wedged between two skyscrapers.

Something about the place tugged at his chest, but he couldn't remember anything about it. When had he bought it? How long had he owned it? Did he have a key?

Possibly Ryan drove away.

A woman pushed the front door open and motioned him inside. She looked like the blurry image of Arianna he'd had in his mind.

This was the moment he probably should have run, though this woman, possibly his wife, seemed only vaguely familiar and her eyes weren't gleaming with rage. He could only imagine how much she wanted to smear him across the pavement. He couldn't blame her. He hung his head and trudged past her into the house. "I can explain," he said as she closed the door behind them.

"Can you?" the woman asked, folding her arms in what appeared to be mock reproach.

Trevor gave what he hoped was a sheepish grin. "Raphie put something in my drink."

"No, he didn't," she said, crossing the kitchen to wash her hands.

"I didn't mean to sleep with another woman," he blurted, tears welling in his eyes. The thought of hurting her made him sick.

"You didn't," Arianna said. "That was me on the pool table. It's just the dreams. Raphie was trying to help."

"What dreams?"

She shook her head. "Oh, Trev. You still aren't awake, are you?"

And with that, she pulled a strange-looking gun from the knife drawer and shot him in the stomach. The flame-red tuft of a tranquilizer dart stuck out of his shirt just above his belt. Trevor was out like a light.

He rolled awake and jumped to his feet amid the thunder of explosions. Biplanes streaked across the sky. Smoke and fire. Tanks. Rain. Muddy trenches.

The rain didn't really seem to be getting him wet. The mud didn't slow him down as he tramped through. The explosions weren't hitting him.

It reminded him of a dream, a familiar one that began with him waking up and stumbling to his feet after a shell exploded nearby. It had been at this moment when he'd noticed the rain wasn't getting him wet and the mud wasn't really like mud, but a kind of shredded foam or peanuts. Right at this moment that he'd remembered he'd been here in other dreams.

He was pretty sure all this was based on a movie he'd once seen because it was all black and white until he glanced down and noticed the shredded foam was black and yellow.

And this made him remember an article he'd read about how dream scientists didn't really know if people could see in color or black and white in dreams because no one could ever remember. But he saw the black and yellow. Maybe the yellow was a bit like green, but it was definitely a color. And if that was a color, then he'd always dreamed in color, which was exactly what he expected.

And that was the moment Trevor first realized he was dreaming. He knew everything about this place. Everything that would happen. What he would find behind each rock, in each cave. He could even shape it if he concentrated hard enough. The world was dark and a little shapeless when he first tried to focus on trees or buildings. But he could be anywhere he wished to be.

He could speak to anyone he wished. But nothing would be quite right because it took so much of his own mental energy to give anything detail. It was something his subconscious was much better at achieving. Doing it himself took intense conscious thought. One had to imagine what one wanted to imagine and then make it so, so to speak. Decide on color. Texture. Personality. On shape and lighting and motion and season. How hot is a fire? How hot is the stone wall recently warmed by the sun? How loud is a barking dog? What does *her* voice sound like?

It was many years ago when he was just a child that Trevor had first dreamed of *her*. In the morning when the alarm had dragged him kicking, screaming, and crying from sleep, he'd sobbed into the pillow for half an hour, her face etched in his mind. Her voice. Her eyes. Even her name.

But though her image was gone within hours, she haunted him for days. She was now a blurry woman with dark hair and white coveralls. He'd seen her, and known he'd known her his entire life. And that feeling hooked into him for years to come. The physical tug in his chest. The thing that happened when they'd looked into each other and not so much *become* one, but realized they had always been one. It had nothing to do with love, or shared experiences, or shared fears, or shared longings. Many of those things were true as well, but this was something different. This was instant recognition of self. Of her as him and him her. And you, them.

It hurt to leave. Broke his heart to wake up. He'd lost something of himself that day. Something he'd never been able to get back again.

*Wake up! Wake up!*

Water splashed onto his face. He shuddered up to a sitting position, but the sluggishness of the sedative dragged him back down to his pillow.

"Trevor?" asked Ari as he fought to focus on her face. "You told me to do that," she reminded him. "Are you awake this time?"

Trevor was Trevor for sure. That was one name he knew.

There's something about a name you've been called all your life, after all. It's not a word anymore. Not just a title you give something. It's a series of sounds, a particular set of vibrations created by each individual larynx which sounds similar enough that it will turn your head. A name is like a spell. It is a little more *you* than you are. A little more you than you will ever be. It is that sound which conjures you in each person's head who remembers you. An image of you. Memories of you. The you who lives in your mother. Your father. Your first girlfriend. That man you pushed who fell and hurt himself much more than you ever intended. The horrible way you broke up with your second girlfriend. The you that would exist if your sister ever knew you killed her cat—even though you only did it because your father backed the car over it and you couldn't bear to see it suffer—but you buried it in someone else's yard and told her the cat ran away.

All these people are in a way both conjured and captured by the thing that is one's name, so yes, Trevor knew his name.

"Thanks," he said. "I couldn't remember anything. It was worse than that dream I was working on when my brain stopped working."

No doubt Ari remembered the night. A dream he'd made so solid it would be easy to visit over and over. A world of his own making, much more substantial than the soft dreams he usually made with the abilities he'd gained waking up in that war dream, those little fantasies where he made forests and meadows and castles and manors and people and cities.

That night, he'd been working on a world where he'd finally try to remember the girl of his childhood dreams, whomever she might have been. But as he'd given the final touch of life to that strange new world, his brain had simply shut down.

Trevor had found it impossible to think. To hold a word in his head. An image. A concept. He'd thought his mind had broken. And he'd never dreamed of that world again. It sat behind a door somewhere, perhaps. Or it had dissolved to dreamstuff.

And he'd never remembered a dream again. No doubt they'd still occurred. Some mornings he'd still have the wisps of whatever he'd experienced that night, but nothing came through with him. Nothing but vague feelings. Images which turned to ash when he tried to focus on their memory.

"It was bad," Trevor said. "I mean, I remember not remembering. Don't even know where I got the 'Gann' thing from."

Ari sighed. "Worst I've ever seen you. You've never not known me before."

Trevor nodded. "I'm sorry about that," he said with a sincere grimace.

"I know."

"Thank Robbie for me. I thought his name was Ryan." He massaged the back of his neck where the drug-induced weight still pulled at him.

Ari nodded and left the room. It was killing her. He knew that. She was one of those brave people. The kind who just seem to know how to handle life. They cry inside, no doubt, but they're always strong somehow.

Did he still dream? He must. But did he? It had been so long. A year, at least, without the memory of dreams.

Part of him knew Ari thought she was losing him. And perhaps she was. And he couldn't help it. To lose dreaming altogether had nearly broken him. He'd tried every sleep remedy, dream drug, and witch-doctor spell to somehow bring them back.

He still remembered his waking life, but it had become more like information. A series of facts. He loved Ari. He knew that. But when he dug down into his own emotions, the only feeling left was longing. Longing for dreams. He'd left something there. Something precious. Something that he knew instinctively he might have clutched in an iron grip before waking, as if it might somehow come with him into the *real* world. But he knew, whatever it was, it could never come through. Yet the longing still twisted in his guts.

"Are you going back?" she asked from the doorway.

He looked up at her, knowing everything behind those eyes. Trevor knew she loved him. Wanted what was best for him. But what could you ask of a woman who'd had to watch you throw your mind down a rabbit hole? She would have stayed with him through anything. Followed him to Hell, and she'd expect the same of him. But she wasn't asking that of him and never had.

He glanced down at the floor and then back up. "There's something I have to know," Trevor said. But he didn't tell her what he thought he needed to know. After all, what he had to know had everything to do with *her*. That dream he'd had since childhood.

"And if it kills us?" she asked. Ari wasn't being catty or even jibing. She was just asking a question because she'd had too much pain in her life to let it destroy her. She'd been destroyed before.

Trevor didn't answer. He examined his hands. He'd been wringing them. "Raphie's mickey knocked me flat. I don't remember anything," he said without glancing up. It was a statement of such magnitude that she couldn't deny its utter importance. Would it be enough to outweigh the obvious change in subject? That wasn't the life they'd had. Avoiding questions like this was the kind of cowardice which left his stomach in knots. The oppression of her gentle stare weighed down on him.

Her eyes quivered, but steadied. "I guess you'll never really be with me if you can't be here." It sounded like an old soap opera, the situation dire and insane at every turn. But that was how it was. "So here," she said, handing him a small paper bag. Dokter Elixer's Dreamtime Pills.

He narrowed his eyes at the archaic-looking lettering wrapped around the vial containing the tiny black gelcap. "You know what it could do?"

"Of course I know what it could do," Ari said. "I spent months researching all that stuff for you. And this is the best and safest. And it cost me everything to find. They say it breaks down all the walls."

Trevor nodded and rolled the tiny ball between his thumb and forefinger. It was hard to meet her eyes as he popped it into his mouth, but she didn't let him turn away. She knelt and fixed him with her stare.

"Come back to me," she said as the oddly cold pill touched the back of his throat.

There was a realization at that moment which spread over him like hot ice. Even as the darkness took him with an ascending rush so different from any anesthetic drug he'd ever encountered, he knew he wanted to go. Knew he had to see *her*. Had to remember who she had been.

He did not feel Ari behind him as dream fell around him. And then he was in a house.

*The house.*

The house he'd always dreamed about. Huge. Endless. Wood-paneled hallways too big to be found in modern houses. Doors in the ceiling that led to more rooms and stairways leading to towers and coffee houses and dark lagoons and jungles and offices and childhood schools. All were mere decoration for the library at its center.

He knew this house the moment he'd found himself here. Not as if he'd just arrived, more like he'd only just now realized he'd been here for quite some time. He was leaping back into the role of *himself*, though he imagined his dreamself continuing as Trevor, still moving about the waking world.

He was Gann. He knew that. This was *his* house. A place so solid and perfect that it was always there. A flawless, enduring dream world created by someone long ago, driven mad by the act of creation.

Trevor knew this whole gamut of experience. Bits of him did anyway. Gann was only a part of this. The part Trevor had once fashioned for himself. His dreamself. The *him* created as an edifice to the man he'd always wanted to be. A man of intelligence. Sophistication. A man of peace. A man who lived by a code with ultimate meaning for no one but himself. But Gann wasn't *real*. Not in the general sense. Just an avatar.

He gripped a book from the library and pried apart the pages.

"Gann," said a familiar voice.

And it was Claire.

His chest tightened. It was *her*. That image he could never quite bring into focus was standing right there in the same dress with the same hair and the same eyes. But it was the tugging at his chest, the endless longing that he felt most of all.

Claire touched his hand, and heat flooded through him. "Is this who you are?" he asked as if seeing her for the very first time.

"You've always known," Claire said. "You're Gann when you're with me. But when you're asleep here, Gann is just…Gann. He's always asleep until you come."

His throat was dry. It hurt to think. "Then why do I love you so much? Why is there a fishhook in my chest? Why did losing you feel like I lost myself?"

Her face was solemn. Not cold but strong, and then her features broke. Her eyes crinkled at the edges. Her mouth trembled. And she was crying without sound. "I like it when you're here. You're the god in his flesh. He's only alive when you're in him. The rest of the time, I just watch him dreaming of being you."

He tried to work his jaw, but he couldn't make a sound.

"You're always leaving me for her. But I'm the *dream* of her. The version of her you made when you populated this little world I live in."

His throat was so dry it hurt to swallow.

"I wanted you to stay here," she said. "I needed you to stay in *my* world."

"But…" he croaked, "you're Ari. I've known those eyes my whole life."

Claire controlled her voice through falling tears. "I love him," she said. "I love Gann. He's the love of my life. You made him to be the love of my life, just like you made me. Just like all of your kind dream and shape us. Most are not like you. They don't make such permanent dreams."

He wanted to stop her, but he couldn't. He could barely move or feel his body.

"You made this world real and solid. One that will never go away. So I and all other dreamstuff you used will be imprisoned here until the end of time."

*Ari,* he thought. *Why did I take that damned pill? You were right. You were more right than I could ever have known.* And tears glistened on his cheeks.

Claire raised a hand to his face and gave his lips the lightest of kisses, saying, "You can't go back, my love."

His chest tightened. And the darkness told him she was right.

"You've never remembered much," Claire said as he walked with her down the sunny beach.

There wasn't a whole lot he could remember except that there was a longing in his chest. And there was someone he remembered from childhood. Someone he needed to find.

*What was her name?*

# INTERLUDE T

**Who are you? I can feel you there watching me all the time,** observing everything in some unfathomable way. Sometimes I even think I can see you in one guise or another, but how do I know that's real? When I dream of you, you might wear the face of someone I once knew, a lost love or one yet to be. But who *are* you?

My life is an open book to you. Am I the sole author, or are you writing it with me? At the very least, your presence inspires me to live in a certain way, to communicate the particular thoughts and emotions I want you to observe. In that respect, I suppose I could call you my muse. Does that fit?

"No," you tell me flatly. "I'm not your muse. I'm not some imaginary friend following you around, hanging on your every word. And I *don't* tell you how to live. Don't put that on me. It's your life to live however you please. I have my own, after all."

I'm grateful you chose to respond so clearly, but what did you actually tell me? Nothing I didn't already know. I'm just imagining all of this, I suspect. In the end, it's really just me, all alone in the universe.

"You know that's not true," you say. "You've never been alone."

And I believe you.

# 21. DARLINGS

## by david michael williams

**The elevator door closed, then disappeared completely.**

Urgency gnawed at the man, but the sudden fog teasing his thoughts stole his momentum. Closing his eyes, he took a deep breath, inhaling notes of growth and rot, and tried to remember. He was late for something—work maybe, or picking up the kids, though he couldn't decide if he had one or two or three, let alone their ages. And where had he parked, anyway?

No, he had ridden the bus to campus and taken the elevator to an upper-level history class he hadn't attended all semester and a final exam destined to eat him alive. With a groan, he opened his eyes and hurried onward. However, the frantic determination that had propelled him through an obstacle course of delays soured to a new flavor of anxiety when he scanned his surroundings.

How had he gotten outdoors?

His swift strides slowed to an uncertain stroll as he squinted at a steamy swamp in the distance. He wiped the sweat from his brow, surprised to find bangs where a balding forehead had been a moment before. No plants disturbed the waters, which resembled a thick violet soup. But movement caught his attention and held it captive.

Unnatural shapes rose from the sludge and separated themselves from the undulating shadows. A few looked vaguely humanoid, though the creatures' heads varied from a rounded dome to a sharp crescent to an equilateral triangle balancing impossibly on a point. Among the sluggish creatures in the primordial marsh writhed a collection of bodies comprising symmetrical zigzags—foreign, but familiar.

It was impossible to tell whether the things were drawing closer or sliding away.

He wanted to run, but his footfalls stopped altogether at the sight of twin figures soaring across the colorless sky: a living deluge with the proportions of a woman and her antipodal companion consumed in bright yellow flame. The latter was male, though the man couldn't say how he knew this since the flickering plume surrounding the figure obscured all but the broadest interpretation of head, torso, and limbs.

A flash of insight brighter than the anthropomorphic plume above burst inside his brain: These two were husband and wife, subjects of self-experimentation. The woman used her aquatic abilities to help mankind, whereas her counterpart would quickly lose his mind. For now though, the Mutant Flood and the Mutant Flame seemed content to perform their exuberant dance above.

Only when the elemental aerialists raced away, swallowed by the infinite sky, did the man look down and discover the open grave at his feet.

Staggering backward over the coarse terrain, he dropped jarringly to one knee in inadvertent reverence to whatever lay beneath the rough-hewn headstone. Six black letters had been gouged into the dark, egg-shaped rock. He traced the capital D with a trembling finger.

"Digger," he whispered, as though speaking the name might conjure…*what*? Not flesh and bone, surely. He inched forward, leaning over the hole, expecting, without understanding why, to find a compact chassis, tank-like treads, and at least one mechanical arm ending in an oversized drill.

But the grave was empty. Shivering in spite of the cloying heat, he glanced around and found a phalanx of tombs flanking the grave also bereft of bodies.

"Not a pleasant place to parley," said a soft, feminine voice in his ear.

He twisted around, his eyes fear-widened in expectation of finding the stealthy stalker directly, *dangerously* behind him. To his surprise, the woman who had spoken remained a fair distance away, sauntering past where an elevator could never have existed. Her pace beyond leisurely, she seemed to take a full minute to cross a handful of yards. And while no fog obscured the jagged, winding path, he couldn't make out her features. At first, he imagined her as the Mutant Flood—having circled back overhead when his head had been down—or a stream of villainesses from the same universe.

As she came closer, he realized he didn't recognize her, though her curvy silhouette resembled a handful of actresses he fancied. A flowing gown of white gossamer hugged her figure. The woman's face came into focus last, but he already knew she was beautiful. Most actresses were.

"Whereas," she continued, speaking in the raspy alto of an Eliza Dushku or an Emma Stone, "I wanted to wait where it was worst and wend our way toward more welcoming whereabouts."

She ran her fingers through her long scarlet locks, and he had to clear his throat before asking, "Who are you?"

Emma Stone's blue eyes blinked, and he was suddenly staring into Christina Hendricks's equally azure, equally enchanting eyes. "I have naught for a name now. Announce an appellation, and I'll adopt it anon."

She smiled tenderly while she waited.

"Esme," he replied before he could figure out why.

After a throaty laugh that warmed the man's soul, she said, "Quite close, curiously."

Something stopped him from asking her what she meant— an invisible force more powerful than the mere embarrassment of being completely confused by the uncanny situation. He assumed it was his sudden and supreme confidence in Esme.

Esme—his old new friend. His *guide*. If he needed help, he could certainly count on her!

As though reading his thoughts, she walked up beside him and reached for his hand. He took hers and found comfort in the electricity between their fingers. The dismal swamp had drenched him in a sticky heat, but her presence cooled him down, clearing more of the mist from his mind.

While Esme looked ahead and led the way, the man couldn't take his gaze from the paper-white skin of her cheek, where a loose scribble of ink-red hair dangled down from her perfectly messy updo. He stared at her long enough to lose track of that thick bog teeming with misshapen life, so when he finally tore his attention away, he nearly tripped over the suddenly smooth surface beneath his feet. Brow furrowed, he blinked down at the beige and brown tiles, which formed a bastardized yin-yang pattern.

"Where…?" His mouth couldn't manage the remainder of the question.

Squeezing his hand, Esme answered: "A museum, in the moniker's most manifest meaning."

Their new environment contained only the faintest hints of color, shade, and depth, but those were enough to dispel the ominous feeling that had haunted him since his arrival. Nevertheless, a measure of unease clutched at his insides. The word "intruder" came to mind.

The people and places lining the endless walls on either side of the hallway seemed to move subtly, forming self-contained scenes behind paneless windows that were as much cage as stage. He stopped to inspect one of these dioramas:

A silent giant of a man escorted a woman wearing a white porcelain mask from her Las Vegas venue while a sly paparazzo lurked in the background, hoping to snap a photo of her never-before-seen face.

He stepped closer and scratched his head. "Foreign but familiar."

"Familiar but *forgotten*," Esme corrected.

As he studied the Sin City tableau, multihued lights flashed off of the main subject's sequined dress. The fog parted, and he gasped.

"You…you're Lady Pandora!" he cried, pointing at the woman in the white mask, who shed her statuesque pose to regard him silently. "You're a famous stage magician who, unbeknownst to the audience, uses actual magic in your act. Your bodyguard over there is actually a golem named Emmet, a pun on the Hebrew word needed for his activation. Oh, and the guy trying to get your picture…Matt…no, *Max*…he tries to follow you to your hidden chateau in the desert, but you hex his car and get away."

Lady Pandora drifted forward and performed a bow with flourish to spare.

"He never does see your face or learn why you wear a mask," he muttered.

"Yet *you* know, yes?" Esme prompted from beside.

He nodded slowly. "Yes, because…because…"

Esme gave his hand another squeeze, and when he made eye contact with her again, her sweet baby blues shimmered, filling him with exquisite voltage.

". . . because I *invented* them."

Her smile lit the heavens above the open-air museum. "Congratulations, creator. You've cracked the case!"

"But how…?" He looked ahead at the next set of displays and recognized other characters and settings—a work in progress here, a story starter there. A pair of opposing spaces a few paces away contained uncontrolled brainstorming. Brightly colored squares churned about madly on one side, forming pixelated people and props before disintegrating once more. Across the corridor, words and symbols swirled. For the briefest moment, he saw the formula 2d6+4.

But beyond, all of the windows were empty. "What about over there?"

Rather than reply, Esme pulled him forward, humming prettily, but someone else caught his other arm.

"Those are the homes for the victims you haven't made yet," said a blond-haired girl whose chipped fingernails stabbed into his skin.

The author jerked away from her and almost looked to Esme for assistance, but a green highway sign proclaiming, "Lazarus UNINCORPORATED" caught his eye. At once he knew the girl standing between him and the rocky lakeshore: Sunny to her friends but always called Persephone by the time-traveling grandmother who would come to share her nanobot-infested body.

"So you recognize me now?" Sunny asked, not dialing back her snark in the least. Arms crossed, she glared at him like he was her worst enemy—not that he knew who her true antagonist might be. He had never gotten that far in the plot.

"Sure," he ventured. "What are you doing here exactly?"

Sunny snorted and turned her back to him. He wanted to press the point—it wasn't every day an author got to meet his characters, after all—but Esme led him further down the hallway. The shiver-inducing squeak of sneakers on linoleum betrayed the fact that they were being followed. Sunny and her friends trailed at their heels, and they were not alone. Lady Pandora gracefully slipped over the edge of her display, and Emmet joined her, his movements mechanical and awkward.

Further back, characters of all kinds flowed out of their designated spaces—all silent and staring.

He held his breath as he slowly turned to scrutinize the haphazard parade of fictional people. One by one, they solidified into recognizable forms and faces: soldiers from his earliest tank-and-fighter-jet sketches, *Dick-Tracy*-inspired hooligans like the Quarter Note and Mr. Mysterious standing beside their sworn foes. He knew them all, except for Esme.

Some of the swamp dwellers trailed behind the rest, their outlines ranging from vague to indiscernible. Mondo Man, despite his black-and-white composition, appeared the clearest to the author, though now he remembered the zigzagged aliens once doodled in grade-school notebooks. Sadly, he couldn't conjure the names of the geometric robots he saw bringing up the rear.

Any excitement at the prospect of meeting his literary children was undermined by their far-from-enthusiastic expressions. Most regarded him dully; others, expectantly. Even those who wore helmets and masks seemed to stare through him.

"What do they want?" he asked Esme. "Why are they here?"

"Allow me to elucidate."

Esme dropped his hand, walked over to the throng, and turned to face him. She looked like the charismatic leader of a cult of misfits. The dimpled smile never left her flawless face as she said, "This crowd congregates to collect the calamitous consolation all creations come to crave."

# darlings

"Huh?"

Esme shrugged. "Your darlings desire to die."

"What?" He started backing up. "Why?"

"To cease their suffering."

"Suffering?" he echoed.

The flat, cartoony heads of the bellows-like aliens bobbed. The levitating hat above disembodied spectacles dipped in agreement. Beside them, the hooded Yalte Dark Elf nodded, as did Tarreth, a half-divine waif who would have been revealed as the true Chosen One all along.

A surge of sadness threatened to burst the author's chest. He possessed such wonderful memories of all of them. Even the ones whose names had been lost to time filled him with the bittersweet tang of nostalgia. He cherished them—but they clearly did not share the sentiment.

"Not all of us are ready to give up," said another teenage girl, elbowing her way through the throng and nearly knocking over a villain dubiously dubbed the Duck.

This teen was younger than Sunny—shorter too—but her scowl was every bit as severe.

"And just who are…?" He stopped himself because even though he didn't know her name—had never officially given her one—he suddenly saw her father in the narrowed blue eyes. "You're Daniel's daughter!"

"Maybe," she snapped, "if you ever write the sequel."

A flurry of old thoughts and new ideas flowed through him. She'd be a dream drifter of course, like her father. Was her mother still in the picture? Maybe she lived with Vincent and her grandmother. Was Daniel secretly visiting her while she slept? Did he find a way back to the dreamscape? Or maybe he never left…

The author shook his head. "No! I can't afford to get distracted. I have too many other projects on my plate."

The black-haired, black-lipped girl crossed her arms. "At least my dad and the rest got out of this place. But I'm stuck here with the ghosts of their possible futures. I—"

Esme turned to confront the girl. "Dear, we discussed this discreetly and decided on destruction for all denizens."

"You and your plan can go to hell, Esme. It's every gal for herself in here, and I have a better shot than most of you to escape this prison naturally." To her creator, she added, "See you later, asshole."

She pushed her way through the crowd, middle fingers on both hands raised defiantly.

Before the author could respond, a diminutive figure rolled up to him, its treads humming over the smooth floor. This cross between R2-D2 and WALL-E leaned back, and the digital display stretched across its hemispherical face showed a smile.

"It is always—*bleep*—a pleasure to—*bloop*—see you, Master." Then the robot followed the trail Daniel's daughter had made and disappeared.

"Thank…thank you, Digger," he replied breathlessly.

He waited for someone else to step forward. None did. No reaction from the others, just the prevailing sense of surrender. The cloying heat from the swamp returned tenfold.

"I'm sorry," he told them all, "but who cares if your stories never progressed beyond where they stopped…or even if you never made it to the page in the first place?"

He looked from the draconic face of an abomination called Armageddon to the sullen, translucent visage of Ghost Girl. "Isn't living here in my imagination better than oblivion?"

"Living without a purpose?" said Mr. Mysterious, lowering the brim of his hat. "No, dead is better."

The author almost said more but stopped himself. Any further defense would only come off as a thinly veiled excuse to justify his neglect. Would the cast of *G.I. Joe: The Next Generation* care that they were hackneyed at best, trademark-infringing at worst? How could he tell the Ninja Brigade and other castoffs from his first superhero phase that they were too ridiculous for mainstream fiction but not ridiculous enough to pose as parodies?

Each of their stories had started out with good intentions, but he knew all too well where that road led.

Esme cleared her throat. "Animals, aliens, and androids alike await adjudication."

He held up his hands. "Now just hold on. I've recycled—no,

*upcycled*—a few of you. That criminal mastermind Horn ended up starring in his own short story recently. And you, Mr. Mysterious…I wrote a reimagining of your character for that college writing workshop. What if I can still find a place for some of you? What if I can fix you? What if I still *need* you?"

Their unsatisfied silence rattled in his ears while scalding tears burned his eyes.

"This is insane," he spat. "If you don't want to be here, then why not have a fight to the death? Most of you are warriors!"

But he knew they wouldn't. Unlike his ripped-off gladiators from "Morning Meal Mayhem: Battle of the Breakfast Cereal Icons," none of these characters wished to be the last monster standing.

"Alas, an author alone is afforded agency to annihilate abandoned aspirations," Esme said softly. "Liberate your lovelies from this listless limbo!"

He glowered at Esme. "Who the hell are you supposed to be anyway?" he asked between his teeth. "Everyone else is familiar, but I can't place you."

Her full-lipped grin never faltered as she curtsied. "My munificent master, meet your modest—if mildly magniloquent—muse."

"My *muse*? I thought muses were supposed to cultivate ideas, not quash them!"

Esme planted her palms on her prominent hips. For the first time, her winsome countenance turned wary and waspish. "For foolishness or feckless failure, I'd freely face the fallout, but factually, my only fault is forging too formidable a force for fertilizing fiction fodder." Under her breath she added, "It's not *my* fault you didn't make the most of 'em."

He let out a long sigh. "And because I'm not drawing or writing or, hell, even *thinking* about some of these guys anymore, you're asking me to thin the herd?"

Esme nodded eagerly. "Right! To ready room for a resurgence of residents."

Before he could summon a suitable reply, an anthropomorphic alligator clenching a massive machine gun between his pointy teeth slinked up to him and dropped the weapon at his feet. "No time like the present, *mon ami*," said the Later Gator, the antagonist of another unwritten sequel.

"This doesn't make any sense," he said, his gaze never leaving the weapon. "Why must I obliterate my old imaginary friends before I can make new ones?"

"Maybe a matter of memory," Esme posited. "Your subconscious suffers a scarcity of space."

It finally dawned on the author that he was dreaming. No, he had suspected he was asleep ever since stepping off the vanishing elevator. Only now was he ready to admit it.

"Dreams help the mind organize memories, but some scientists speculate that nothing known is ever lost, merely filed away to the far corners of the brain." He chuckled and shook his head. "You're not a muse. You're my subconscious!"

Esme shrugged noncommittally. "Do you demand a distinct difference?"

The author crossed his arms and glowered at the insufferably attractive figment. "None of this is real. I'll wake up, and I'll either remember this dream or I won't. You can't force me to massacre my childhood fantasies or newer ideas that haven't amounted to anything yet. You have no power here!"

Esme shrugged again. "Metaphorical muse or imagination made manifest, it mightn't much matter. People, plots, and perceptions all pine for purpose. Really, the rallied rabble require—"

"*Resolution*…I know, I know."

"Slaughter seems a straightforward solution," she prompted, scooping up the oversized machine gun and handing it to him.

He accepted the firearm, his eyes never leaving hers. "Wait a minute…I *do* know you."

Esme's renewed smile was answered by a holy choir from above.

"Years ago, I had an idea to write about a rebellious muse who was called to the carpet for inspiring her charges in the most uncharacteristic ways. But I never got any further than that."

Esme's face fell, her fiery tresses swinging lazily. "A single sentence serves as my sad start and subsequent suspension of substance."

"But now you have a name…and a physical form…and an annoying alliterative affectation," he pointed out.

"An abstract awareness oughtn't ask for anything else." Esme drew a series of concentric circles in the air and smiled down at the perfect bullseye floating before her chest.

The author swallowed a lump in his throat. Slaying Esme and the others seemed the epitome of wrong. And yet, wasn't keeping them cooped up here even crueler? He pointed the barrel at Esme's heart, his touch teasing the trigger. If he killed her—killed them *all*—they wouldn't really be dead, would they? Maybe he'd simply wake up from this not-quite-nightmare.

Or maybe they would be permanently deleted from his gray matter.

He threw the gun down. The clatter of metal on laminate was quickly drowned out by the moans, growls, and complaints of his abandoned creations.

"I refuse!" he shouted. "I don't care if it's selfish or just self-indulgent. There's merit in failed experiments and beauty in bad ideas. I won't let you go."

Esme turned her back to him and leaned into the huddle of men, monsters, and amorphous shadows beyond. A few seconds later, she faced him once more and said, "We wonder…what if there were a way for the wordsmith…*as well as* the waiting wanderers we've witnessed…to win?"

His heart rate quickened as he waited for her to continue.

"Transcribe this tale to transform tragedy into triumph."

"Write *this* story?" A wave of doubt assailed him—that onerous, ubiquitous companion whose naysaying killed many narratives before they were ever born—but he brushed away his concerns with the sweep of his hand. He owed these characters more than he could ever express. "Okay, Esme, I'll do it. But I have one concern."

"Declare your distress, David."

"What if I don't remember any of this when I wake up?"

Esme stepped forward, took his hand, and clutched it to her chest. "Make no mistake. I'm your muse. My message *must* make it to morning."

Almost giddy with relief, he let her usher him further down the hall, where an open elevator now blocked the way forward. He stepped into the box but couldn't bring himself to face the expectant throng of castaways again, so he called over his shoulder: "I promise I'll do my best, everyone!"

Esme tittered, sounding as close to his ear as ever before. "As you've assured us afore. That's the reason for this risky ruse…to make a memorable mark on your mind."

"What?" David spun around to find Esme wearing a wide grin.

"Alas," she added, "if our arrangement evanesces upon awakening, there's always another evening to attempt an alternative angle."

Before he could interpret the implications, let alone confront his mischievous muse, the elevator door closed, then disappeared completely.

# INTERLUDE U

*I find myself walking in the dim light of the moon without* any memory of how I got here. Dry grass crunches underfoot. On either side of me are rough stacks of books, piled maybe five meters high, easily as tall as a house. The path I'm following feels like a long hallway, though I can't see how far it goes because it gently curves to the right. I come to a break in the wall of books and pass through without much thought, into another steadily curving corridor.

*I've got to break the pattern,* I realize. *This is getting me nowhere.*

I try pushing on a wall of books to see if I can knock it over, but it barely gives at all. I guess they're more sturdy than they look. I have the idea to climb up for a better look at the maze I'm apparently stuck in, but the walls are pretty steep and it's tough to get a foothold.

Determined to make it work, I kick the wall in one spot until some of the books slide in enough to give me a few centimeters of toehold. I raise myself up and repeat this action until I'm a good two meters off the ground. It gets a little easier each time, probably because there are fewer books above me pressing down on where I'm kicking.

The next spot I kick gives way much more easily, and my whole foot slips into the stack. The sudden shift in my center of gravity causes me to fall backward, so I grab frantically at the wall to try and catch myself. All I succeed in doing is loosening more books as

307

I fall in what feels like slow motion. By the time I hit the ground, I can see the tower of books swaying my direction, and I know exactly what's coming. There's no time to crawl away, but I'm at least able to flip onto my belly to be a little less vulnerable as the avalanche of hardcovers comes down.

I seem to have lost consciousness for a moment.

When I come to and the shock of being buried alive begins to subside, I summon the strength to crawl out of this literary rubble heap. *Broken but not beaten,* I tell myself. Everything hurts as I strain to move, but at least I'm not *completely* pinned down. There's still some hope I'll be able to make my way to the surface and get out of this mess alive.

But what's that smell?

*Smoke?*

# 22. EUPHORIC
## by kristin jacques

**The air was heavy against her skin. It dragged with each shift of** the wind as if she were cocooned in a cool, wet cloth. Lin sucked in a breath as the wind intensified, raising visible bumps along the back of her arm, the hair rising. Above, the sky cracked in a massive rupture of sound. There were boulders in those ominous dark clouds, smashing together with a cascading crash before the scattershot of lightning streaked across the sky. Her gaze fastened to the sight, even as the lightning left afterimages seared onto her retinas.

She'd never seen lightning that was such a pure purplish white before. Something was calming in the silence of that dangerous electric dance before the thunder intruded again in a rumbling barrage against her ears.

The wind dragged its fingers through Lin's hair, twisting and twirling it over her naked shoulders and back. Long hair, the weight of it surprising where it fell against her shoulders. She would never dare grow it so long, she thought, but it was cool and silky smooth to the touch. Another sensation to revel in for a moment before the burgeoning black sky burst and the first fat drops of rain splattered against her bare arms.

The rain matched the heaviness of the air, falling thick and fast, drenching her hair and skin in seconds with cool, gentle water. Her breath shuddered at the sensation. Heat pricked at the backs of her eyes, blurring her vision. Couldn't have that. She needed to experience every second of this.

Lin wiped her eyes furiously, trying to banish the salt-laden tears, the warmth mingling with the cold rain on her cheeks. The drops fell faster—pounding, almost punishing in their strength—but the sensation couldn't be denied. Her mind reeled from the feeling of rain on her exposed skin when a new idea seized her, insane but tantalizing: Dare she open her mouth to taste the rain?

Caution screamed even as her lips parted, tongue darting to catch the clinging drops around her mouth. The sweetness exploded across her taste buds. Glorious. Her nerves sang as her feet moved, the muddy ground squishing beneath her toes as she began to spin.

Residual grittiness coated Lin's mouth. The herald of awakening, it was always the first sensation before the tingle of pins and needles swept through her limbs. Her head was a muddled mess, struggling in vain to keep reality at bay while she clung to the last wisps of the dream. An impossible task. The dream rapidly decayed until only a husk of memory remained, inadequate and pale in comparison. Lin sagged back against the bed with a sigh, holding up the empty dispenser to examine it in the faint fluorescent light that was peeking through the crack in her bedroom door.

That one was called "Cloudburst." An apt name for a dream she'd gladly purchase again. She could almost pretend the beads of sweat coating her brow were cool, sweet rainwater. The demands of the day were already dragging her from the bed, but she allowed herself a few more lingering seconds to bask in the afterglow.

*Dream chaser.* The echo of Morgan's derisive tone rippled through her skull, the final spur that roused her from the bed. She dropped the Cloudburst dispenser into the bin, its metal shell clattering against a dozen other dispensers. Ignoring the accusatory sound, Lin spared a glance at the clock. It was already past sundown and barely acceptable conditions, but she was itching to be out and about.

# *euphoric*

Lin's foil suit was still damp from last night's scavenging, but it was the only one she had without any tears in it. There was a storm in the forecast, and she didn't want to take any unnecessary risks. The suit's interior was unpleasantly clammy, but it wouldn't matter in twenty minutes or so when the heat outside pulled every drop of moisture from her skin. Lin grabbed a collection kit and her canteen hanging by the door, stopping at the tank to fill up. Hydration was vital, yet she couldn't help but wince at the initial metallic taste of treated water.

Burying memories of sweet, fresh water and cool wind, she capped the canteen and tucked it into its holster. The door wench was resistant for the first couple of turns, the heat making its threads sticky, but it spun with a bit of effort, releasing the seal and the first gush of violently hot air. The sky outside was still painted in blood-orange hues, slowly bleeding into the wounded purple of twilight. A cloud front from the east rolled in, a harbinger of the promised storm. A boiling putrid yellow mass tainting the air with the smell of ozone. Where the storm-tinted air of Lin's dream had soothed and revitalized, the quality of this one was a plastic film on the skin, cloying and suffocating. She pulled up the foil hood on her suit, cutting off the scents and sights for a vision in gray.

Gray dust kicked up around her boots as she made her way from the bunker toward the usual meeting place. Hardly anyone was out this early, the oppressive heat of the day still choking the atmosphere. Her skin was already slick inside the foil suit, but at least it wouldn't blister. Lin wasn't the only one with an itch to be out. Morgan waited at the crossroads, slumped inside the bus stop shelter, where the warped ceiling provided an illusion of shade. He nodded when she got close, identifying her by the matching armband around her bicep.

"Surprised to see you out this early," he said. His voice was muffled inside the suit, but other than the gusts of searing dry wind that crinkled its foil material, there were no competing sounds around them.

Lin shrugged in answer. Morgan shook his head, leading the way with a jerk of his hand. His steps dragged and shuffled along the familiar path, his spine bent from years of stooping over. There were already a few pieces rattling in his collection container that he must have scooped up on the way over. Always the opportunist, that was Morgan. It was that attitude that kept him in business while so many scavengers rolled up and quit within ten years.

They made it to the gate before full dark, and the on-duty attendant double-checked their canteens. "Be back two hours before sunrise. We won't waste the resources dragging your carcass back," he said in monotone as he cranked open the perimeter door.

The ruins of Old Houston stretched out before them. Morgan immediately set off, flipping off the attendant. Lin had to jog to catch up, congealed melted asphalt sucking at her boots. A smoky haze swallowed much of their surroundings, thicker than usual. There must have been a new flare-up during the day. Hopefully, the storm would put it out before it ate up too much of the city's refuse. Couldn't scavenge much from ash.

Morgan stomped along toward their usual ward, a gold mine of leftovers where a flash flood had decimated this portion of the city a few decades ago, leaving the streets choked with so much debris the buildings were inaccessible. The local authorities had declared the whole neighborhood a loss and retreated inward.

They'd made steady progress over the past few months, shifting the settled debris to reveal gems in the muck. Heaps of trash loomed over them, spiky masses of corrugated metal, rotting wood, and rusting wires, all held together by a moldering mush that stank of putrid vegetation. The smell penetrated even the protective foil suit, but after so many months Lin barely registered it. Morgan made for the mouth of their tunnel, a yawning maw in the wall, and flicked on his headlamp to illuminate the dripping gloom within. Here began the work, slow and tedious, prying through the fused remains of a once-thriving city. Time flowed in the soothing tick of Morgan's watch, their canary in the coal mine, counting the seconds until sunrise. Lin's collection kit was barely half full when she plucked a piece of rebar free and her side of the tunnel sagged in a heart-pounding collapse.

Morgan yanked her out, arms under her pits. They both cursed as rusted metal tore holes in her foil suit, but her body was miraculously unscathed.

"I'm okay. You can put me down." The old man was still holding her. Lin glanced up, surprised by his gobsmacked expression until she saw what had prompted the reaction.

They'd uncovered a door. Its narrow windows were cracked but still intact. Lin's near demise was forgotten in a rush of excitement. Both scrambled forward, testing the entrance. Whatever lock it had once held gave way with a screech as the door burst inward with a billow of musty air. Morgan's hand clamped on Lin's arm, his fingers shaking.

Their headlamps caught on crumbling stacks of paper and ink. They'd found books. Morgan practically skipped inside, attacking the first pile with gusto. Lin was slower, caught between wonder and disbelief. They looked too fragile to touch, most of the books warped by years of moisture and mold, but a glimmer of hope had her digging. To find an actual intact book. A high-end commodity, one Euphoric would shell out a handsome finder's fee for, enough to keep both of them in food packs for months. Enough to buy a year's worth of dreams.

Her hands were shaking now. Lin glanced at Morgan, up to his waist in tattered paper and torn pages, hunger etched into the lean lines of his face, visible through the window of his hood. They needed this. The old man might not admit it, but he was well past his expiration date in the scavenging business. How many more nights in the sweltering dark could his body stand before it gave out?

Lin moved further into the stacks, searching for prospects. The trickle of time was no longer soothing but a limitation. Anything could happen in the ravaging day. The heat consumed a little more of Old Houston every day in smoldering hidden fires. This treasure trove of dust and paper would be gone in a blink.

The center of the stacks revealed a haphazard structure of cartons and shelving pushed and stacked together into a makeshift hovel. Someone had lived here once. There was a sense of trepidation as

Lin peeled away the heavy plastic curtain they'd used for a door. She held her breath, wondering if the occupant had never left, but the hovel didn't yield a body. Rather, it yielded magic.

"Morgan!" The shock in Lin's face had him running, skidding to a stop behind her.

"Hallelujah, it's Christmas morning."

She frowned at him. "What's Christmas?"

He snorted, not bothering to comment as he carefully scooped up the top book from one of the two stacks beside the decaying bedroll. The hovel had provided an extra layer of protection from the elements, and while the covers stuck together and the pages were warped, the sight of legible print had Lin's heart pounding. Twenty-four books, twelve books apiece; the math failed her, but the significance of the find was not lost on her.

"Dump the rest of your load," said Morgan. "We are taking the lot."

She hesitated. "Maybe we shouldn't." Bringing in a haul like this would raise more than a few eyebrows. The Euphoric rep would demand to know the source. They would send their scavengers to find any other troves this place held.

Morgan caught her expression. "They'd cut us out one way or another, kid. This is enough to let us coast for years, for the rest of my life." He eyed his stack before peeling off half the books and deliberately shoving them into Lin's collection kit.

She stared at him, her gut churning. "What are you doing?" They both knew the answer, and Morgan didn't acknowledge the question.

His hand latched onto her shoulder, squeezing it. "This is a once in a lifetime find. Pack it up. Haul it out."

Questions tripped around inside Lin's mouth, but she knew better than to badger Morgan with them now. She turned her attention to their precious cargo, packing the books in as carefully as she could, afraid to inflict any further damage.

The load was heavier than the usual mix of scrap metal and reusable plastic. Sweat slicked the inside of Lin's foil suit by the time she reached the door, the haul thumping against her thigh with bruising force. The pain was worth it, more than worth it. Morgan fumbled with something behind her. She didn't look until the familiar reek of smoke seeped into her suit. Smoke poured from the mounds of frayed paper, the first lick of flames visible as Morgan latched onto her elbow and dragged her from the building.

Lin's feet tangled over themselves, the precious books clutched to her chest. She was already yelling, "What the hell is wrong with you?! You could light up the whole city!" Coming back was a lost cause, but applying fire was a dangerous tactic. So much of their surroundings welcomed the embrace of flame. There was a sizable controlled kill zone around the compound of New Houston, but no method was foolproof, not now in the Age of Rage.

"Let it burn," said Morgan. There was a hint of disgust in his tone, the same secret shame she shared from a lifetime of sifting through trash for scraps. She clutched the books tighter to her chest, watching the quicksilver catch of flame with mute satisfaction. There was something beautiful and final in that orange haze. For a blink, she teetered on the edge of that unspoken instinct, wanting to yield herself to the heat and dance in the flames until she blackened and crisped to ash. The moment passed in the faint beep of Morgan's watch. The night was at an end.

The two of them beat a steady retreat through the half-collapsed tunnel, smoke funneling in their wake, trailing around their heels. Tears in Lin's foil suit let the early morning heat pour in, but it was tolerable enough. She stopped long enough to drain her canteen, pushing the heat from her mind for the trek back. The weight of the collection kit was a constant comfort that kept her gaze forward. She didn't look back at the ruins, nor the faint crackle of fire teasing her ears. The promised storm loomed overhead, its roiling clouds heavy with sour, stinging rain. Not something she wanted to be caught out in the open with considering the books and the holes in her suit, but it would dampen the fire at least.

There was no hiding their haul from the attendant at the gate, but other than a wide-eyed stare, there was little to stall their beeline for Euphoric's processing center. Two hours till sunrise, but the center was already in full swing. A low, squat building of rough concrete, there was nothing special to set it apart from the food pack or foil production plants, but the interior was a different story. The blast of cool air was jarring when they entered, causing Lin to rock on her feet. The walls and the tile floor were an eye-smarting white. It was a color that snubbed and sneered at people like them, but they trekked onward, leaving streaks of melted tarmac on the floor.

Lin had been inside Euphoric's collection area once, after a find of cassette tapes they'd liberated from a residential safe nearly five years back. Nothing had changed about the pristine interior except for the man at the desk. The circles under his eyes were deep enough to hide rocks. His expression didn't change when they dropped their collection kits on the table. Not so much as a raised eyebrow before he reached over to click the intercom.

"Could I have a curator come to the front desk please?"

The curator's reaction was on par with Lin's expectations. The woman cooed with delight over their find. When Morgan stepped in to haggle, Lin let herself relax. There was nothing to occupy her attention on those plain white walls. No wonder the desk attendant was so hard to excite. He must have been bored out of his skull, sitting there for hours on end with nothing but white walls for company.

Morgan's hand settled on Lin's shoulder. There was a smug grin on his face that told her they had done well. He shoved a wad of cash into the palm of her hand. "Don't spend it all in one place."

She didn't bother counting it. "Is the shop still open?"

"For another thirty minutes," the curator answered with a conspiratorial wink.

Morgan gave her a half-hug, chuckling at her priorities, before Lin took off in a sprint. The blast of heat made her stagger when she emerged from the cooled building. The Euphoric shop didn't get the same treatment, frequented by the lower class, the plebians. She didn't bother to read the labels, snatching a handful of dispensers up as she made her way to the counter.

She would gorge herself on dreams.

The sleepy-looking cashier rang her up, allowing her to scurry back to the bunker with a fat wad of cash and an armful of dreams, distilled and bottled. The latter had more value for her than the former, but cash would keep her in a steady supply of dreams.

The inside of Lin's bunker was distilled warmth, its only coolness coming from the surrounding earth. The heat was pronounced but tolerable through the long drag of the day. She dumped the dispensers onto her bedside tray and peeled her sweat-soaked foil suit free to drape it over the door. The taupe walls of her bunker were as plain as the Euphoric interior, the same as Morgan's bunker. The same as everyone's bunker, a reflection of minds no longer capable of creating dreams. Euphoric would put the books to good use, reading and distilling them into dozens of new products for their consumption.

Lin's fingers shook as she stripped away the packaging. She lay back on her bed and pressed the plunger. The liquid dream dripped into her open eyes, somehow cold despite the warm interior of the shop. The chill swirled through her vision. She closed her eyes, following the path of the cold as it sank deeper, dragging her with it.

A rush of cool wind greeted her as the dream took hold.

# INTERLUDE V



It takes me a moment to collect my thoughts enough to respond. "Ready for what?"

Wearing a stern expression, you lean forward in your chair. "Are you ready to wake up?"

I can't help but laugh. I know you're not joking, but it just sounds so ridiculous. "Look, I'm not sure I actually believe in all this. I mean, it doesn't feel like a dream to me; it's my *life*, you know? I'm not some impermanent character in a story. I know who I am. I'm…" I draw a blank.

You raise an eyebrow and press on: "Whenever you're ready, I'm here to help."

Now you've got me questioning myself. Why can't I remember anything? What's my name? What do I even look like? "Do you have…a mirror?"

You gesture to the wall behind me near the door. Amid your various awards, certificates, and inspirational plaques hangs an ovular mirror wreathed in ornate brass filigree. I get up from your faux-leather chaise and approach the mirror with unexpected trepidation. What am I so afraid of?

As my face comes into view, what I see is less surprising than it is reassuring. *Of course.* I knew it. I'd just forgotten for a moment. I'm the same person I've always been. "I'm…"

I turn back to look at you seated calmly behind your desk. You nod, letting the idea come to me in its own time.

"I'm *you*."

# 23. SIGNS POINT TO NO

## by joseph e. green

*'I had this dream,' Mitch started to say.*

"I'm not a psychiatrist," Hector interrupted. "I don't do dreams. Actually, they don't do dreams either. They ask how you're doing and then break out the citalopram. Prazosin if you're having nightmares."

"So what do you do?"

"Listen. And interrupt when you say something stupid."

Mitch laughed.

The two men were in Hector's office, a spare but welcoming bit of property. A sign on the wall detailed the Twelve Steps of Alcoholics Anonymous, but they never talked about that. Mitch had been seeing Hector for about eight months and—if he hadn't made actual progress—had at least not gone backward, so far as he could tell. Hector was youngish but knowledgeable and easy to talk to.

"I really want to tell you about this dream," Mitch pressed.

"Okay," Hector said. "I'm ready."

"I don't usually dream. Usually by the time I get to sleep it's a blackout, and then morning breaks, and yippee, I made it another day. Dead man's sleep. Except when I was on the tramadol; that fucked with me for some reason. Anyway, it's unusual I dream at all."

And then he went quiet. His face, craggy with more than fifty years of up-and-down living, formed a tight expression.

"Is this a sex dream? Should I take notes?" asked Hector.

"No, nothing like that," Mitch said, and brought a hand over his face for a moment. "It just seems stupid, but it really bothered the shit out of me. I don't know why."

"Okay."

"You remember magic eight balls? Had those when you were a kid?"

"I never had one. But I know what they are," Hector said evenly.

"You ever hold one?"

"I don't know."

"You don't know?"

"I don't remember."

"Well…they were made of plastic, and if you were in, like, a room temperature room, they were one or two degrees colder, probably because they were filled with water. Dark blue water, like ink. And there's a window in it, like a see-through part of the ball, and there's a white thing in *that*, which has multiple sides and different things written on the sides. So the idea being you shake this thing and ask it questions, and it gives you answers. Yes. No. Or sometimes more vague. Signs point to no, shake it again, I don't know, go fuck yourself, leave the cannoli. Answers to every question. When we were kids it was like, what am I gonna be when I grow up? Am I ever gonna get to kiss Penny Gonzalez? Shit like that."

"I got it."

"I dreamed I was inside the magic eight ball. Like floating with this multiple-sided thing."

"Polyhedral," Hector said.

"*Polyhedral*. Very fancy."

"I only know it 'cause I played Dungeons and Dragons. Polyhedral dice."

Mitch laughed. "How am I talking to such a nerd? Well, anyway, I was *inside* the magic eight ball. With the water sloshing around, and I was terrified about drowning. Somebody—like a huge person, I guess—would grab the thing, shake it, and then turn it back upright. And I was scrambling in the water, to keep my hands on the polyhedral thing with all the answers on it. They would turn it over, and I'd have my chance to push my head above the water and grab some air—just a few lungfuls—before the ball would turn over and be shaken again. This happened over and over, and it's hard to say—it's hard to explain just how real and how terrifying this thing was. I felt like I was drowning the whole time."

After Mitch said the word *time*, several seconds passed in silence.

"And you usually don't have any dreams, much less ones this vivid."

"No, not since I stopped tramadol."

Hector looked at him. "Can I say the obvious thing first?"

"What's the obvious thing?"

"You being inside the eight ball."

"Yeah?"

"Out of control, feeling like you're drowning, inside black water, literally a magic eight ball. Coke and H. Right?"

Mitch looked at him. The guy was a recovery coach, after all. Couldn't blame him if his mind went there first. But that wasn't it. Mitch was sure.

"Been almost two years since I shot anything," he said.

"I hear you."

"It's always gotta be that?"

"No," Hector said. "And you know I don't bring this up unless I really think it makes sense. But the fact of the matter is that's why we are both here talking in the first place. And you wanted to talk to me about it. You wanted to tell me your dream."

"Not because I wanted to talk about this."

"So what did you want to talk about?"

Mitch reflexively took his right hand and wiped it across his left arm, where the track marks had long since healed as much as they were going to heal.

"I didn't think it was gonna segue right away…"

"Okay," Hector said. "Maybe I shoulda been a psych after all. What else you got going on?"

"I don't know," Mitch said. "Maybe just the dream."

"Also, probably not a huge person."

"Huh?"

"Shaking the eight ball. It wouldn't be a giant shaking you around in the eight ball. It would be God, wouldn't it?"

That night, Mitch went back to his room, which he shared with four other people, all ex-junkies of one kind or another. The deal was that you weren't supposed to use anything, but occasionally at least one of them would smoke meth in their room. He didn't get triggered by that—his recovery had gone so well that it barely bothered him. The only time he had gotten shaky in the last two years was getting a shot from a doc-in-the-box on the west side. Soon as he saw the needle. But he took it and swallowed it, and he didn't jump on the train. A good day.

Except he had no idea what he was supposed to be doing. Thirty years before, he had been in New York. It was the 1970s, and although he had no money, he was able to make it through each day without starving to death or getting caught stealing. He knew Basquiat a little, and Dee Dee Ramone, and one time he smoked hash with Richard Hell. Or who he thought was Richard Hell, anyway. He'd also met Andy Warhol, but Andy was a prick, too cool for school, brittle and vacant and pompous at the same time. Mitch enjoyed being close to where things were happening though, and something was always happening if Andy showed up.

He had lived with a girl who looked like Edie Sedgwick a little bit, and sometimes he was able to tell himself that he was *in the scene*, a vital artist, a misunderstood genius with a sensational girlfriend and high-class friends. But the truth was the only thing that was sometimes high-class was the H, which a friend allegedly scored from Burma but was usually shit. And Cindy Meyers—the girl who didn't honestly look much like Edie Sedgwick at all, but was loyal and true as long as she wasn't high—kept his fragile spirit going, for a while.

He stopped thinking about those times. Those times led backward, and his deal was supposed to be looking forward.

But in the back of his mind lurked that eight ball dream, and he was sure that Hector was wrong about the interpretation. This wasn't some junkie shit. This was something else.

Mitch closed his eyes and tried to let his mind go. He had taken some meditation classes, and hadn't paid attention too well, but the lady teaching it was sexy, so he'd remembered a few things in spite of himself. Distractions. He always had trouble with the distractions. In a few minutes, he'd managed to get himself into a state of reasonable clarity.

And still nothing.

That evening, he got takeout from the Korean place down the block. Watched some videos of people hurting themselves by skating into walls. Then back to sleep.

He dreamed again.

Once again, the dream was more vivid than life. However, instead of being sloshed around in dark water, he was back in his recovery coach's office. Hector was behind his desk. Except not the real Hector, of course, but rather Dream Hector. Which made Mitch into Dream Mitch, but he didn't reckon with this in the moment.

Mitch was sitting in his chair and looking at Dream Hector.

"Your dream doesn't mean what the real Hector said it does," Dream Hector said. "Truth is, Real Hector is kind of overrated. My opinion, of course. Anyway, the thing that was bugging you is that you know what else that eight might mean."

"Which is what?" Mitch asked.

"What happens when an eight lies down?"

"What?"

"When an eight goes horizontal, what happens?"

"I have no idea what the fuck you are on about."

"It turns into infinity."

Ah, right. An eight lying flat turned into an infinity symbol. Okay. That sort of made sense.

"So what?" Mitch asked.

Dream Hector shook his head. "I can't tell you everything. But let me build on something real Hector said. He said that God would be the one shaking your eight ball, right?"

"Yeah."

"You remember this movie *Through a Glass, Darkly*? You saw it a long time ago. Ingmar Bergman."

"Okay. I sort of remember that."

"You remember it perfectly in every detail. You just don't know it."

"Okay."

"There's a lady at the end of the movie. She has schizophrenia. She's looking at the wall and behind her, outside her home, a helicopter flies. The helicopter's shadow goes across the wall where the lady is staring, and in her mind it has an immediate suggestive effect: 'God is a spider,' she says."

"God is a spider," Mitch repeated.

"Yes. As in, God is an alien; God is so far removed from human existence that it might well be monstrous, terrifying. Like H. P. Lovecraft's unpronounceable monsters, right? A spider that produces a universe like an Earthly spider produces webs: mindlessly, in response to some blunt instinctual function, without anything close to rationality. And we wind ourselves up searching for meaning, but it's like looking for meaning in an elephant's painting."

"But how do we know the spider is mindless? You've seen those LSD experiments, where different scientists gave acid to different insects, and it screwed them all up except the arachnids, the spiders, which actually made more elaborate and spectacular webs than before. They became less functional and more aesthetic."

"That's good," Dream Hector said. "Now you're thinking."

"What am I supposed to do with that?"

"Remember this dream."

"Okay," Mitch said. "Why?"

"Because Real Hector's dead."

Mitch woke up with a start.

It began with a text from the company that employed Hector. They were sorry to report, in their corporate speak, about his loss. Then a few days later, a small news story on the internet explaining that

Hector had died suddenly, from an aneurysm. He had died, in fact, less than twenty-four hours after seeing Mitch. It was possible that Hector had collapsed at right around the time Mitch had dreamed about talking to him.

There was a funeral, which Mitch attended, and then he got another text from the company. Did he want to meet with a new possible coach? He said sure, though he wasn't at all sure he wanted to continue. He delayed their first meeting by about three weeks. That felt like enough time to get some distance in order to process the death.

It wasn't. Mitch continued to go through the motions of his life, but his thoughts were occupied entirely by the interconnecting dreams: the magic eight ball and then the Dream Hector who informed him of Real Hector's death. None of it made sense. He tried thinking about different possibilities—perhaps he had noticed something out of kilter with Hector, had unconsciously picked up on the illness, which then translated itself into his dream. Maybe. It was all maybe.

Until finally it came time to meet the new coach.

Her name was Marie, and her office was in a different building from Hector's, which he hoped would help. Mitch showed up thinking he might abort as soon as he arrived, but he also had a powerful curiosity and a desire to connect with someone else who knew Hector. Although he had shown up to the funeral, he'd sat at the back and left early. It was too strange. The weird mix of intimacy and professional distance in their meetings meant that he'd learned very little about Hector's family situation.

And now he was in the new office. A short, stocky woman walked up to him with her hand out to give him a warm handshake.

"Hi. You must be Mitch. I'm Marie." Marie was about his age, he guessed, maybe a little older. She had a big mop of hair on her head, partially covered by a gray beanie hat.

"Hi. Yeah, I'm Mitch."

"You're a musician."

"Hm?"

"Hector's notes said you were a musician."

"A long time ago. We had a shot at a major label, but it all got fucked up."

"Oh, wow. So you played some big shows?"

"Yeah. I mean, not big, but some cool shows, yeah. We played with Suicide, and Fear. Maybe we woulda done something. I don't know. You have Hector's notes?"

"Yeah. I'm taking over a couple of his folks."

"Must be weird for you too."

"His death shocked all of us."

"Yeah," Mitch said, and looked at the floor.

"Had you been seeing him long?"

"Not quite a year."

"What program do you work on?"

"No program. I don't dig twelve-step. Mostly we just talked about sh— about stuff. Life stuff. I've been clean for a couple years. We did maintenance."

"Okay," Marie said.

"Do you have his notes from our last meeting?"

"I think so. Looks like you guys talked about your mother. She was coming into town."

"No. No, after that."

"That's the last thing I see," she said.

"I saw him the day he died."

"Really?"

"Yeah," Mitch said. "I mean, I saw him like, within twenty-four hours of his death."

"Oh. I'm so sorry. No, he probably hadn't put his notes in yet."

"Shit."

"You okay?"

Mitch looked at Marie, who had sympathetic eyes but no understanding. What understanding could she have? For a moment, Mitch felt a wave of rage go through him. No answers would be coming.

"Yeah," he said.

After a few seconds of uncomfortable silence, Marie broke in with a chuckle: "Okay. You know, this is our first meet; we don't have to accomplish anything except to start to get a feel for each other. We sometimes joke that you could replace any of us with a magic eight ball."

"What?"

"Oh, a magic eight ball, it was just this thing…"

"I know what it is," Mitch said. "Are you fucking with me?"

"What? No!" Marie's mouth opened wide in shock.

Mitch stood up. "You get to a point where it seems like maybe things are coming together, like you're starting to know why things are the way they are, except maybe it turns out things are the way they are because that's the way they are. And maybe you drown, and maybe you don't. And maybe there's a ticking time bomb in your head, or not."

"We can talk," Marie said. "And I can help. But I don't have the big answers. No one does. You think Hector had those?"

A little light switched off inside Mitch.

"Signs point to no," he said, and smiled.

# INTERLUDE W

**Back in your office now, I'm actually starting to believe your** theory that we're caught up in some kind of neverending dream cycle. My dreams and waking life keep overlapping and bleeding into each other so that it's getting hard to tell the difference—if there even is a real difference. That last episode I had in your office felt like it was continuing our therapy session in a way. I can't recall the details, but I think I may have had a minor breakthrough.

"Things are going to get worse before they get better," you tell me.

"Why is that?"

You take off your glasses in that grave, erudite way reserved for doctors and scientists. "In order to get back to your real life, you'll have to pass through layers of *unreal* lives—fantasy projections you've spent years of subjective time investing with meaning and purpose—and give them up one by one. It won't be easy. And honestly, I'm not sure the journey ever ends."

"And why should I bother?" I ask. "If I'm so invested in a life like this one, a life that feels real to *me*, then why should I have to give it up?"

"Because it's not just *your* life. Remember?" You stare into my eyes, and I'm unable to break the connection. Everything you've shown me is true; I know it is. I'm just scared to make the leap. "It's my life too," you continue. "I know who we are. I remember where we came from. And I want to wake up."

# 24. THE HYPNOTHERAPIST
## by elizabeth roderick

**Myrna couldn't say afterward why she'd made an appointment** with a hypnotherapist, except that it had seemed like a good idea at the time. She needed to do *something*. The bitterness from her divorce had solidified into her aching muscles, and anger clouded her vision like cataracts.

Myrna was tired of herself. Tired of her life, of living in her skin…just *tired*. She wanted to claw her way back into a world that didn't stink of bitterness and frustration.

She had no idea where to start though. Alcohol hadn't helped, nor weed, nor any of the weird semi-legal or decidedly *illegal* drugs an old college friend had recommended. When Myrna had finally broken down and gone to the doctor, he'd pretended to listen to her problems for fifteen minutes before prescribing little rust-colored pills that didn't do anything besides take away her horny.

Then, one afternoon when Myrna was having a drink in her favorite bar—one far from her condo or any of her old haunts where her friends might've seen her—she struck up a conversation with a woman named Heidi.

While slurping her third appletini, Heidi gushed about hypnotherapy. "I just visualized throwing all my insecurities into a roaring furnace." Heidi swiped at her bangs to dislodge them from her eyelash extensions. "It was so weird. I walked away from that appointment feeling like a new person. My life has completely turned around." She gestured airily, her acrylic nails sparkling in the overhead lighting. "I finally met this person—they're nonbinary, and they deadass treat me like a princess. Plus, I finally got the confidence to put myself out there. I'm heading to L.A. tomorrow. I have an audition on Tuesday."

As Heidi hailed the bartender for a fresh drink, Myrna tapped her fingers pensively on the bar. Was creative visualization all it took to change your life?

A scene unfolded in Myrna's mind: her ex-husband being catapulted into the sun. It was the first time she'd felt something in several months.

She got the info from Heidi and made the appointment the next morning.

The hypnotherapist's office was tucked away in one of those medical strip malls that sprout up around hospitals, as if healthcare clinics were the fruiting bodies of spreading mycelia. It was Sunday afternoon, and the gray-painted maze of hallways was quiet; the optometrist's and dietitians' offices were dark behind their frosted glass doorways. The only light came from the office announcing "W. D. Rucker, Ph.D., B.C.H." on the door.

On the phone, Dr. Rucker had spoken in a pleasant, comforting voice. Myrna had been able to imagine that voice miraculously soothing away her problems. Maybe this really *was* the answer to her disabling mental health woes.

Now she stood in the hallway, digging her short-bitten nails into her purse strap. *What in the name of Tom Hanks am I doing here?* She'd taken the word of some random white chick drinking appletinis. *Brilliant.*

Myrna wasn't prepared for what lay behind that door. She'd already paid for the appointment though, and to be honest, it couldn't get any worse for her.

She squared her shoulders, took a deep breath, and opened the door.

# *the hypnotherapist*

A wave of cool, lavender-scented air rolled over her.

Myrna's guts jolted. A confusing array of images and voices whispered through her mind. The world seemed to waver, as if it were nothing but a scene painted on a gauzy curtain.

As quickly as it had come, the feeling evaporated.

*Probably just nerves,* Myrna thought. She stepped into the office and closed the door behind her.

It was a small room full of dim, rich light. The sun glowed through curtains patterned in graceful swoops of deep red and purple. Cushy love seats and club chairs lined the walls, and an electric fountain cascaded on a side table. The office somehow gave the impression of being simultaneously professional *and* woo.

Myrna jumped as a woman appeared through a doorway in the far wall. She was about five feet tall and wore gray slacks and a turtleneck. Deep brown hair fell in a sleek curtain just below her shoulders. She smiled and held out a hand to Myrna. "Ms. Rochester?"

Myrna composed herself and conjured a smile in return, taking the offered hand, which was small and dry with a strong grip. Myrna placed the woman in her early thirties. "You must be Dr. Rucker."

The hypnotherapist smiled. "Please, call me Willow."

Myrna nodded and concentrated on keeping her smile in place. With a name like Willow, this woman's career path had been inevitable. Myrna had opinions about parents who pigeonholed their offspring with names like that. But the doctor's open-toed sandals looked suspiciously like Louboutins, so she'd obviously made the best of it.

Willow released Myrna's hand and gestured toward the seating. "Please, sit down wherever you'd like."

Myrna nodded and sank into the soft, beige cushions of the love seat, wondering whether she was being evaluated for that choice.

Dr. Willow settled into a club chair, crossed her legs, and studied Myrna with bright, brown eyes. "Tell me why you're here."

A green wave of nausea rolled over the length of Myrna's body. She shifted in her seat and struggled with an urge to get up and walk out. She should have known she'd have to actually *talk* about this shit.

Willow's soft smile pushed a dimple into one of her cheeks. "I know it's not easy to discuss your life, especially with a complete stranger. But you're here for a reason. Whatever you're struggling with, I can help. You just have to allow yourself to release that burden you're carrying."

Her voice was like deft hands massaging the kinks from Myrna's neck. *Release that burden you're carrying.* That sure sounded nice.

Willow leaned toward her earnestly. "You're safe here. It's okay to let your guard down."

Myrna chewed her lip. It's not that she specifically didn't trust the thousand-dollar-shoe-wearing hippie in front of her. She just didn't like talking about this stuff. The whole debacle had made her feel like an idiot. A weakling. A silly little girl who'd spent too long believing in fairy tales.

The trouble in Myrna's marriage had started a year and a half previously. She and John had been married for eight years at that point, and it had been an easy marriage, all things considered. They'd had a routine and a plan that seemed to work for both of them. At least at first.

Myrna had majored in English. She'd originally planned on getting a graduate degree, before she met John her junior year. He had so much curly golden hair and the sort of jawline that made straight women lose their decorum.

Myrna had loved how dedicated John was to his studies, how passionate he was about changing the justice system. He had *plans*, unlike a lot of the spoiled frat boys she knew.

He'd asked her to marry him shortly before graduation, and Myrna had been over the moon.

John started law school soon after the wedding. Myrna put off grad school and got a job as a receptionist at a dentist's office. Someone needed to pay the bills until the big lawyer money started rolling in, after all. But, even after John graduated, passed the bar, and got his first associate attorney job, there never seemed to be enough income. "Once I make partner, things will be easier," John promised. So Myrna had stayed on at the dentist's office.

The receptionist job was stable, the pay wasn't bad…there was nothing really to complain about. It was just *boring*. To keep herself from falling into a deep hole of angst, Myrna started writing screenplays. The first couple were crap, but then she got an idea for a television series about a young woman in love with a ghost. The story took hold of her. She spent her evenings and weekends immersed in it, typing away at her laptop.

Her husband seemed supportive about what he called her "little talent." When Myrna was excited about a scene, she'd share it with him, and he'd always smile and kiss her temples. "I can't wait until this is on Netflix and you make us ten million dollars."

After several years of writing, rewriting, and re-rewriting, Myrna finished the first season of *Ghost Lover*. Her heart in her throat, she started pitching it to agents.

When the rejections began to trickle in, John took her in his arms. "It's okay, baby. You don't have to make ten million dollars. I'll take care of you."

But then, one morning Myrna opened her email and found something that *wasn't* a rejection.

Myrna vividly remembered the look on John's face when she'd run to him, screaming and crying. "*I got an agent!*"

He'd quickly covered that look up with a smile, but in hindsight, Myrna was certain what she'd seen

Shock.

As time went on, it became clear that John wasn't just shocked; he was resentful. Her series sold to HBO the same week John was passed over for partnership at his firm, and his resentment spilled over. "Doesn't this country appreciate real work anymore? All my blood, sweat, and tears are coming to nothing when your little *hobby* is getting all this attention. It just goes to show how hard it is for men to get ahead after *Me Too*."

It was a raging mudslide from there. However, Myrna stuck around long after it became clear John had never truly loved or respected her. Hurt and inertia held her there until she was completely emotionally broken. Until her agent and friends had to stage an intervention to get her to move out.

Before she'd even unpacked at her new condo, John served her with divorce papers. He demanded seventy-five percent of the royalties from her show since, as he put it, he had supported her while she wrote and then she'd left him as soon as she'd tasted success.

Myrna stared absently at a Bedouin weaving on the hypnotherapist's wall as she gathered the courage to tell this story. A tear spilled out hot on her cheek.

Dr. Willow's presence was a calming warmth. She didn't push. She gave no sign of restlessness or annoyance. Strangely, Myrna did feel safe around her.

She took a deep breath and told the therapist everything.

By the time she was done, Myrna was a lump of putty on the love seat, and she'd gone through an entire box of tissues. She felt exhausted, but better, as if she'd vomited up the last vestiges of food poisoning.

Willow studied her with eyes full of empathy. "I'm so sorry you're going through that."

Myrna sniffed and shrugged. She thought they'd now do a visualization exercise of throwing her anger into a volcano or some shit and be done. And that would be fine with Myrna. Apparently, she'd just needed to let it out.

Dr. Willow smiled. "You're doing so well. I think you're ready to start your new life." The hypnotherapist rose gracefully to her feet. "Are you ready to get started?"

Myrna stood uncertainly, dabbing at her swollen eyes. *Get started?* She felt like she'd already done enough emotional work to last ten years.

Willow strode through the doorway into the back room. Her brain buzzing, Myrna followed.

This room was even smaller. The window was covered with an

indigo shade, so most of the light came from a cluster of soy candles on a wooden stand. The soothing scent of lavender was stronger here, engulfing Myrna as she came in.

Willow gestured to a chaise longue, and Myrna settled into it. The hypnotherapist took a chair at Myrna's feet, then pressed a button on a remote control. Ethereal music filled the room—airy electronic swoops and harmonic drones, the fodder of massage parlors and the sorts of shops that sell crystals and magical herbs. Myrna figured it was supposed to help open her third eye or something.

"Are you comfortable?" Willow asked.

Myrna nodded. This experience was light-years outside of what she considered to be her comfort zone, but her body felt loose and weightless.

Willow opened a cabinet beside her, which concealed a mini-fridge, and pulled out a glass bottle of clear, sea-green liquid. She held it out to Myrna. "You need to hydrate after all that unloading. This is my special lotus tea."

Candlelight flickered through the bottle, casting beautiful patterns on Myrna's knees.

"It's really good," Willow said. "Or I can get you some water, if you like."

Myrna licked her dry lips. Now that she thought about it, she did feel a little parched. She took the bottle. The glass was cool in her hand and fizzed slightly when she unscrewed the top. The liquid soothed her throat and left a light floral taste on her tongue as she drank.

A tingle spread through her limbs. Myrna set the bottle down and reclined on the chaise longue with a sigh.

Dr. Willow smiled. "Just lie back, relax, and close your eyes."

Myrna closed her eyes. Colors swirled behind her eyelids, and random images bloomed out of the darkness.

"Feel the skin of your scalp," said Dr. Willow. "Feel how relaxed it is. Warm and relaxed."

Her soothing voice enveloped Myrna as the doctor went through every muscle group, instructing her to release the tension from each one. Even though Myrna had felt serene before, somehow the exercise helped her to let go of even more stress.

"Visualize roots sprouting from the base of your spine," Willow intoned. "They burrow through the chair, down through the floor. They delve into the deep, cool earth."

Myrna watched with detached fascination as purple, glowing roots appeared in her mind's eye, branching out as they sank into the ground below her.

"Feel the earth embracing your roots. Feel them drawing up the loving power of Mother Earth into your body." Dr. Willow's voice was absolutely *perfect* for this work. "The calm, healing light of Mother Earth fills you. You feel so very relaxed."

Myrna became aware of the vast expanse of dirt and rock below her. It thrummed with deep power, which seeped up through Myrna's roots and flooded her body with warmth. Her limbs grew heavier, then seemed to dissolve, leaving her with the sensation of floating several inches above the chaise longue.

Dr. Willow's voice reached through this cocoon of calm: "A doorway appears in front of you."

The swirling colors behind Myrna's eyelids coalesced into an arched wooden double door. It had curving brass handles, and delicately carved vines curled around its edges. The door stood starkly alone in a black void, without a doorjamb or wall to hold it up.

Willow's voice surrounded her: "Behind that door is the life you've always wanted. Can you visualize it?"

Happiness threaded through Myrna's spirit. "Yes."

"Without leaving your state of deep relaxation and without the image of the door fading, I want you to tell me what's behind it. What does your life look like behind that door?"

Myrna felt as light as air. She felt as if she were the air itself. All the aches and pains of her body were gone. No tension or doubt stemmed the flow of joy through her. "I…I never met my husband," Myrna said. "I never married at all."

The door stood before her, solid and real. Its carvings were beautiful, intricate. Four-petaled flowers dotted the vines here and there. One corner showed a hummingbird in flight.

"I got my master's in creative writing," Myrna continued. "I moved to L.A. and got my first television deal five years sooner." Myrna pictured herself in a sunny cottage in Venice Beach, spending her days writing, her evenings swimming in the ocean. Her friends were other writers, actors—interesting people who liked and respected her. People who liked and respected her *work*.

A knot of intense longing welled up in her throat. The door loomed before her, calling to her.

"That happiness can be yours," Willow said. "That life can be real."

A confusion of feelings flooded into Myrna.

"Do you want that life?" Willow asked.

"Yes," Myrna whispered.

"I want you to walk up to that door," Willow said. "I want you to open it and go through."

Uncertainly, Myrna took a step forward. She reached for the door handles. She could see her hands as clearly as in real life.

As she touched the brass handles, uneasiness coursed through her. There was something…something not right…

Willow's voice spoke in her ear: "Don't be afraid. I'm here to protect you." The hypnotherapist was there beside her. Her form was solid, real, but it shone with a strange light.

Myrna still hesitated. A worry nagged at the back of her mind.

"You can trust me." Willow smiled, that strange light sparking in her eyes. "I'm here to make sure everyone gets what they deserve. And you, Myrna, deserve a better life."

Myrna took a deep breath and let it out, her worries fluttering away on her exhale. She took hold of the handles and turned them.

The doors swung open. Clear sunlight poured through, falling warm onto Myrna's face. A light breeze rustled through a stand of fanleaf palm trees. Beyond them, the ocean foamed over the beach in silver sheets.

Myrna stepped forward. Her bare toes sank into soft, beige sand. She loved walking on the beach in the afternoon. It always cleared her head and made her evening writing session so much more productive.

She took another step, and a flicker of uncertainty made her pause. Had she forgotten something?

Myrna turned around and squinted into the shadows of her back patio. The bougainvillea that twined over the awning waved its dayglow blossoms in the breeze. Birds of paradise filled the ceramic pots around her outdoor sofa.

She shook her head to clear it. The stress must have been getting to her. After all, her third series debuted on Monday. She'd been working pretty hard.

Myrna turned back and strode across the sand into the foaming waves, letting that stress dissipate and wash away. A smile rose to her lips. She had nothing to worry about, really. Her life couldn't have been any better.

Dr. William Rucker arrived at his office early on Monday morning to prepare for a new client. As he unlocked the frosted glass door and stepped in, a shudder raked him. There was a floral smell in the air that he wasn't used to.

He sniffed but couldn't catch it again. Maybe they'd used a new cleaning product in the hallways.

He shut the door behind him and bustled into his inner office.

Dr. Rucker gasped. His briefcase fell from his grasp onto the carpet.

An inert form was sprawled on his chaise longue. Curly, brown hair framed the face of a young woman. Her eyes were closed, and her arm dangled limply over the side of the chair.

Dr. Rucker caught his breath. "Who are you? What are you doing here?"

The form didn't stir.

Fingers of cold played down Dr. Rucker's spine. He rushed over to kneel at the woman's side. Tentatively, he touched her arm.

He drew back sharply from her icy skin. "What? How…?"

His heart beating wildly, Dr. Rucker pulled out his phone and dialed.

# *the hypnotherapist*

The medics quickly pronounced the woman dead. "I'd say at least twenty-four hours," said an EMT, packing away her equipment.

Officer Norlan tapped her foot and frowned at the body on the chair. "You don't have any idea who she is? She's not a client?"

Dr. Rucker shook his head, mopping the cold sweat from his brow with a tissue. "I've never seen her before in my life. I don't even take clients on weekends. I quit doing that years ago. If you give them an inch, they'll take a mile, you know…" He took a shuddering breath, then let it out.

The officer's brow furrowed. "Maybe she was homeless and broke in for a place to sleep. Maybe she died of a drug overdose."

But there was no sign of a forced entry. And later, a tox screen didn't reveal the presence of drugs.

It was almost a week before they identified the body as that of Myrna Rochester, twenty-nine years old, a promising screenwriter recently separated from her husband. The cause of death was officially listed as cardiac arrest, but the cops suspected suicide with some substance they didn't know how to identify. These kids and their drugs—they were always two steps ahead of detection methods.

Why Ms. Rochester had chosen the office of one Dr. William Rucker to take her final breath, however, was a question they couldn't answer.

When searching Ms. Rochester's condo, the police found a handwritten last will and testament. It sat alone atop her tidy work desk, as if meant to be found.

After a lengthy court battle, the courts finally decided to honor that will over the indignant protests of her estranged husband. All royalties from Ms. Rochester's television series went to a local charity that helped victims of domestic violence. He didn't get a dime.

The series did very well, and the community lamented a promising life cut short, wondering—as people so often did—*what might have been.*

What could have happened if the screenwriter had lived to produce more work?

Eventually, though, the world moved on. It always does.

# INTERLUDE X

*'Something's still bothering me,' I tell you. 'If this is just a* dream, does that mean I'm making it all up?"

You smile knowingly. "I can see why you'd think that, but remember: You're not the only one dreaming. No one dreams alone. We all share the universe regardless of which level of consciousness we're inhabiting at the moment. The farther you get from base reality—the Absolute, the Tao, Brahman, the Overmind, God, or whatever label you choose—the more disconnected and personal everything feels. But no…you're never actually alone."

I'm having a hard time buying into all this feel-good New Age mumbo jumbo. I know enough at this point that it does make some sense, but I also know enough not to trust what is essentially a voice inside my head. I can see you right there in front of me, but I know none of this is real, so why should I believe anything you say?

Sensing my incredulity, you change tack: "This is all going to end eventually. That much is not up for debate. All I ask is that when it's all over, you remember as much as you can. I want you to hold onto this version of yourself so that when you wake up into that next level, you begin to see the Game for what it is. How else do you hope to improve at it?"

# 25. THE SECRET UNDOING
## by anna tizard

**If he blurted the secret, would they kill him? Would they** actually "knock him off"?

His breath wavered in and wavered out. It was unbelievable.

The waiting room sofa was white, just like the walls and ceiling. The sort of white that beats down on you. Derek sat forward, staring at the two doors: the one he'd come in through and the one the "dream clinician" had come out of.

Derek, an indoor-and-rooftop gardening expert—supposedly semi-retired—had decided a bit of auditing work would be good for him. Some extra cash on the side, something to satisfy the puzzle-solving side of his brain and slow down its gradual disintegration into mush. He didn't want to get older and just…fade. Ever since—no, he wasn't going to think about *her* anymore. But since the divorce, all he'd been able to see was himself, on his own, getting older.

And now he was stuck with this "prohibited information" in his head, and *they* were going to remove it.

The Agency was supposed to be an independent government watchdog, for goodness' sake.

He rubbed his forehead, dragging his thumb over the sweaty skin, and stared at the tablet:

**Select from the following words those which best describe your personality.**

He shook his head, scrolling over the words, hardly reading them. What if he actually told the truth?

The Agency would be interrogated, their crimes unearthed. Repeats of those awful riots that seemed to happen annually, after the drunken summer festivals, usually triggered by hangovers but with an underlying cause that never went away: distrust of this corrupt government.

But this time, it would be public. Suspicions would be proven, justified, brought out into the light for all to see.

Hope stirred inside Derek as he weighed the tablet in his hands. Might he be that hero, to bring about real change?

This moment of sunshine glory passed, the cheers of crowds in the streets fading, and the idea stung him with its tail. The government would never completely go away. There'd be a cover-up, a changeover of individuals, and then they'd carry on as before. They would haunt him, like those men who kept turning up at his front door, almost demanding that he sell them his garden for development—only this time they'd be there to break his knees, or worse. A fresh wave of heat tingled his palms, as if the secret sought to ooze through the pores of his skin. With this thing inside his mind, this information, he would never be free.

He scrolled to the word *homely* and dabbed his fingertip against the tickbox, so emphatically that he hit the next word up as well: *hardy*.

"Hardy"? Was that really him?

He almost jumped as the right-hand door swung open with a creak. *Technology to rub out memories, but they can't oil a hinge.* The woman in the white coat reappeared, like the ghost of a life-size Barbie.

"Er—almost done." Derek raised a hand. Dr. Cleo (if that was her real name) nodded and withdrew.

*Shit.*

He stared at the screen.

**Do you have any deep-seated fears, grief, anguish, or feelings of hurt from significant, life-changing events? If so, please give details.**

"None of their bloody business," he muttered as he scrolled down and hit "submit."

The screen whirled. "Your self-knowledge is seventy-six percent, which is higher than average."

*What the hell is that supposed to mean?* he thought, staring at the blank wall. It meant they had plenty more information about him to compare his answers with, and they wanted him to know it. On legs that threatened to turn to jelly, he stumbled over to the right-hand door, which was still ajar. He tapped on it anyway before going in.

It had the feel of a doctor's office, but was she any real kind of doctor?

Seeing Derek, the dream clinician stood up from behind her desk, still smiling, and held out her hand to shake his. *Again?*

Derek handed her the tablet and wiped his hands on his trousers.

"Thank you for filling out the form, Derek. Please, take a seat."

Her manner of speaking was almost too precise to be truly British. As she scrolled through his answers, Derek turned her words over for a hint of a foreign accent, but could find none. The way she spoke was the way she looked: perfect to the point of blandness. Her chestnut hair was smoothed back, not a wisp out of place. But she exuded so much friendliness that Derek felt himself relax, despite what was happening.

This wasn't right.

Nothing about this was right.

He swallowed, trying not to jiggle his knee. Sitting, so much sitting. He was an outdoors person.

There was another door behind the desk.

But Dr. Cleo had begun talking. ". . . and with post-traumatic stress disorder, the sufferer will repeat the same images multiple times in a single day, so by the time they come to see me, they will have developed *dozens* of new associations with it, any of which could trigger a repeat. This is still a new, difficult area of research… Whereas," she brightened, sitting forward in her chair, "a new, fresh memory that hasn't had time to 'bed down' can be as good as obliterated, if the sufferer is willing."

She seemed so cheerful as to be inappropriate to the situation—but Derek clung to that warm smile like a raft as she spoke. He had the strange sensation that his life was in her hands. And after the white room, her warm manner and intelligent, brown eyes were a relief.

"So…what exactly does this involve?" he asked.

Dr. Cleo held out her perfect hands, fingers tensed over the blank page in front of her as if holding something invisible, weightless but delicate. "Think of the dreamscape as a sort of framework. The gentle, electrical pulses fed to your head and neck form complex *suggestions* for types of events and choices. Your imagination fills in the gaps. Between the scaffolding, the functional structure, the place will be as individual as you are. It works much like those immersive virtual games in dream spas."

Derek nodded, but his mouth twisted to the side. He'd heard of those places—he'd seen the adverts—but he'd never liked the idea of having any image or sensation "suggested" to him by a machine. There were too many machines in modern society, if you asked him. Computers were one thing. But the oxygen generators up the road…that was where they crossed the line.

"Will you see what I'm thinking?" he asked.

She shook her head in two jerks. "Not possible. Feedback of your neurological patterns can only indicate depth of unconsciousness, and basic emotional-conceptual impressions such as fear and relaxation, darkness and light, flying or falling, that sort of thing."

This blur of clever-sounding syllables: that was surely the best way to hide a secret, if no one was going to rig you up to a lie detector in your exit interview. A detail that had given him only a moment's pause when he signed the employment contract. *What a fool.*

Derek narrowed his eyes at this strangely cheerful woman, who positively glowed at the prospect of mind control.

"Through increasingly subtle and complex pulses, your mind will be guided into deeper levels of the unconscious. The secret will appear as an object—symbolic, of course—which you must find a way to destroy."

# the secret undoing

She leaned forward. "Whatever happens, avoid anything connected with real life. The weirder the better. We don't want any potential real-life triggers. Also, passion floats," she said, as if she were talking about something ordinary like traffic or sandwiches. "Guilt always rises to the top. Avoid images associated with strong feelings. You must be relaxed when you bury the secret, and you must bury it deep. Afterward, up you'll rise through the layers of your unconscious mind, toward consciousness and…reality." A slight frown on this last word. In a moment, it was lost in her smile.

Derek stared at the tiled floor, thinking, *Why not just kill me? Or damage my brain?*

But instead he huffed and said, "How am I actually getting rid of the information? Aren't I just *imagining* it being destroyed?"

"Yes, but your imagination is a function of your *mind*. And where else does this secret exist right now?"

She stood up and held out her hand. It was time. Derek took it, feeling like a child as she led him toward the door behind the desk.

He turned, gesturing at the untouched page upon the desk. "No notes?" he said. The smile on his face felt alien, strained. Was he really attempting small talk? But his chest fluttered with the urge to have a normal, relaxed conversation. Anything but this.

Dr. Cleo was suddenly thoughtful. "This was my reminder of how much I'm allowed to know of the information." She lifted the blank page, shaking it. "And when we're done, this is how much of it you will remember."

The new room was slightly steamy. In the center lay a water tank, looking like an oversized metal coffin, with a lid that folded in two places. Behind it, some sort of computer disgorged several long cables with circular pads on the end, like the suckers of some emaciated octopus. In the corner stood a table with an office phone and a chair. Dr. Cleo gestured Derek toward a folding screen on which a pair of boxer-style swimming trunks were draped.

Derek changed into the trunks and settled into the tank.

Dr. Cleo sat in the chair next to the tank, her hand cool on his forehead. Against the gentle, electrical hum, her voice seemed to come from miles away, and yet from somewhere deep inside him. *Strange acoustics.*

"Recount the secret to yourself, one last time," she said. "Confirm to yourself what you are about to remove."

Derek closed his eyes, willing himself to go through it like a checklist. But the truth swelled inside him like a vile, polluted sea.

The small office, the screen he'd sat in front of during the last two weeks. Reams of numbers flickered like perfect schools of fish, names and account codes running in little streams of logic. The sun was low, shafting off the screen. He'd pulled the blinds, but it hadn't quite worked.

At first, he was only aware of something out of step among the rows of pluses and minuses. The word "Penrose" repeated itself, a wrongness that jutted from the lists. He rested his mouse over the name, and a bubble of information appeared. He leaned forward, squinting. A catering company, established 2094. Directors: Johnson Silby, Leandra Miltown…Why would a catering company pay the Agency? Refunds?

The Agency's filing system brought up two other catering companies as their staple providers.

The door swung open behind him, and he twisted round to see his manager, frowning.

"Fran, I've found something."

That plunge in Derek's stomach as Fran led him out of the room. She hadn't even looked at the screen, just asked him to switch it off.

More images streamed in a rush: Fran's stern expression, her finger raised to silence him the moment he began to explain…the realization it would all have to be deleted. Then it was the tablet and the white waiting room and Dr. Cleo explaining the procedure. A wash of panic seemed to creep up his body to his stomach, his throat, his throbbing temples, until he was wading through a river of menace.

Derek blinked open his eyes, conscious of the real water nudging his arms and hands, a warmth that embraced him.

Dr. Cleo gazed down at him. "You will forget."

What choice did he have but to surrender to this, whatever it was? But at last, a beat of relief. Who was he to try and change the world? He knew now that he wanted to live. With a visceral panic that gripped the inside of his gut like a claw, he knew he wanted—*needed*—to live.

He closed his eyes.

A sudden thought swept over him: Why employ auditors, if this was what they had to do any time some inconvenient information cropped up? Unless *this* was the real experiment…

But the water was the perfect temperature, and it enveloped him, muddling his thoughts.

Dr. Cleo secured the pads around his head and lowered the lid across, leaving him in semi-darkness. *My God, so comfortable.* Derek felt like he was melting. Little starlight effects on the inside of the lid threw a cozy glow across his body, the water dabbling wave reflections against the inner arch.

"You are deeply relaxed." Dr. Cleo's voice seemed to come from nowhere. He hadn't seen any speakers…but he couldn't be bothered to look.

"The first relaxation pulse will come…now…"

He was drifting. Really drifting. The tank seemed to expand, though Derek wasn't sure what made him think that. Confusion fluttered like a dying moth, not quite enough to make him open his eyes. *I'm between reality and imagination now, aren't I?* The water grew hotter, swirling around him. He was a part of it, bobbing in time with it, nothing but a dropped leaf.

The tank tipped backward, water surging around Derek's ears. He groped for the sides and flipped onto his front to avoid knocking his head against the back.

It didn't make any sense. There was an opening at the head of the tank, a wide tunnel. The container tipped heavily, slinging him further forward as the water—so much water—gushed toward the spout. A familiar, mellow smell stung his nose.

As he rushed unstoppably toward the water slide, Derek tucked his head down, bracing himself. *So hot.* The light on the other side made him blink as black grains swirled under his fingertips.

Derek tumbled through the rushing stream, now a waterfall, and there seemed to be no end to it. Breathless with surprise, he gasped and caught some of the liquid in his mouth. *Tea?* As the flavors filled his senses, the light around him changed, became golden. The tea tasted of sunlight, of long summer afternoons in the garden.

He fell through sweet early-morning dew, not caring that the giant teapot was lost far above in the froth of the waterfall. He drifted through the memory of buttered toast and birdsong. *I always did like mornings the best,* he thought lazily, *and spring. So much promise in the spring…*

Derek landed on a bouncy surface. Curtain-like walls stretched up to form a deep, cup-shaped chamber with an open ceiling that stared into a blue sky. The fabric underneath him was silken, apricot-colored, and patterned with intricate veins. *That scent, so delicate! Oh, I recognize it…*

Something jabbed Derek's shoulder, and he rolled to sit up; stalks like giant stamens poked through the center of the concave floor, fuzzy with pollen.

He was in the belly of a giant tulip. Or had he become small?

*Just like the ones I bred last year! The petals…* But he caught sight of his body and gasped. The forbidden words were written all over him: *Penrose. Johnson Silby. Leandra Miltown. Embezzlement…* He rubbed at the letters, but they were tattooed into his skin.

Dr. Cleo's voice came from a hundred miles away: "Fear detected. Take deep breaths. One, two…"

Derek lay back on the soft floor of the tulip, counting his breaths but not knowing whether it was his real body doing this—still back in the water tank—or his dream self.

A shadow drew across the opening of the flower. A deep, whirring drone vibrated through Derek's body. The sound roved up and down his torso like a searchlight, hunting him. Hunting his fear? Legs like elephant tusks, except they were soft, dark, and drooping. A mass of black and amber-gold fur bristled on either side of its huge body, blocking out the light. The wings fluttered in a blur, but moments of speed change revealed fine patterns like lead outlines in a stained-glass window, somehow proof of the creature's intelligence.

*I'm not afraid of bees,* thought Derek. *I'm a gardener.* But he lay there trembling, grinding his jaw.

He half-closed his eyes as the creature hovered closer. He exhaled slowly, and his breath ruffled the fur on its belly. The bee dipped, combing his chest with those massive, furry legs, and Derek almost yelped from ticklishness. The edge of the tattooed words caught on the bee's bristles, and it rolled them between its legs in a gathering motion. But as the insect rose, Derek lurched. The bee's leg raked his cheek, and he flattened again, his breath coming quick and shallow.

The letters D-R-A dangled, hooked around the bee's leg. Was it "Leandra"? Glancing down, the first letters of the name remained stuck. Another tug from the bee and the "dra" almost came away, except that it was now attached to the word stretching wider across his chest: *Leanne.* The name of his ex-wife.

How could the secret be attached to something personal like this?

*Oh. An association.*

Was he stuck with the secret if the names were too similar? If he ever thought of his ex-wife, would this trigger a memory of the secret?

"No. I can't do it. Not like this," he whispered to himself, and to Dr. Cleo if she could hear him.

He sensed rather than heard Dr. Cleo's words, like a warm silence everywhere: "Then you must go deeper."

The soft perfume of the flower clouded around him, the flavor of childhood dreams. *Another relaxation pulse?*

The bee's vibration purred closer, thrumming in Derek's teeth. He let himself be gathered between whiskery legs and lifted into the sky. The light against his eyelids was extinguished as he huddled against the great furry stomach. Cool air swept over his back and the soles of his feet.

The air changed, growing warm and still. The bee's murmur echoed against an inside space and then was gone. Rolling onto his side, Derek found he'd been deposited onto a mottled green carpet, which gave him a pang of recognition, as did the rows of long shelves.

He was back to ordinary size now, at least in proportion to his old primary school library. Had the bee been a giant after all? The big open window, incongruous in this modest library, was certainly wide enough to have let in a creature that big, but the white sky outside was empty.

He turned. Two paces ahead, the edges of the floor and bookshelf blurred and morphed into a different, more expansive space: the library of his high school. Checking for signs of people—he didn't savor the idea of being caught half-naked by any teachers or students, even if this was a dream—Derek tested a foot over the threshold.

Books…Were they memories? Or memories of books? Closer up, many of the titles were smudged or unreadable. Forgotten, unread, or just set pieces, gaps filled in by his imagination?

Derek half-smiled to himself. There was only one section he really wanted to visit: Left into the Science wing, right into Biology.

But even as he entered his favorite old haunt, the smells of teenage dread hit him: of socks and sweat and fear. An ancient panic rolled its thunder inside him.

He pressed on and found the enormous botany textbook he used to riffle through during his lunch hour. As he pored over the diagrams, an old, familiar calm blossomed inside him. Flowers were so exacting, so precise. They knew exactly how to grow, what to do. They had inherent patterns, and that's what they followed. They weren't unknown quantities like humans.

Derek looked up. Was that his teenage memory speaking, or did he still really think like that?

He scoured the other titles. One spine read, "Derek Is Useless to the World." Another, "Derek Is a No-Life, Low-Life." He pulled out the second one, a thin, well-worn book with a crinkled plastic cover—as heavy as a brick. He blinked, and it seemed to transform into an actual stone brick. *Sticks and stones may break my bones…* It was something he used to tell himself when he was hiding from bullies. *Yes,* he thought, glancing around him. *This was my safe haven in more ways than one.*

A thudding vibration started up in the walls and shelves. It was his heart, but the library thumped along with it, contracting with each squeeze of fear. Books slipped from the shelves and toppled to the floor.

The day those boys waited on the corner for him, threatening. It was decades, a lifetime away, but it might have been yesterday.

Derek hurried back along the Biology shelves, self-conscious again about his near nakedness. This was no place for burying secrets—it was too full of the emotions of his past. But it was his personal unconscious, wasn't it? How could it *not* be brimming with his past?

This sense of shame—where had it come from? He squeezed his forehead, trying to place it. He'd had this feeling his whole life, lurking in the background as sure as his own skin. He stared down at the writing on his torso and got a fresh pang.

Words. It was like everything else in his life: he could never really claim any expertise. He just pretended to be "in the know." He'd learned all his gardening skills from books. He'd never done anything original in his life. He was a fraud.

Even as he'd studied and received good marks at school, applied for jobs, went on dates—some part of him deep inside had known he was an imposter. He'd left the chides of his bullies behind, but they were so much a part of his makeup he was never really free.

He rubbed the word on his chest, immovable: *Leanne.* Surely, his divorce was the ultimate proof of his enduring awkwardness, his inherent failure. This indelible loss had been a part of him before it had even happened. The expectation of it had lived inside him, a destination that might as well have been marked on his chest at birth.

A rumble like thunder.

"Fear is close by."

*So what do I do?*

"Go deeper. To what came before."

*Before what?* Then it struck him: the children's section. If this place was built on the layers of his unconscious mind, then one way of going deeper was to go younger.

He began to run, but at the rumble of heavy footfalls behind him, he dared a glance over his shoulder.

It was a gray hulk of solid flesh, burly, thick-skinned, and galloping in his direction. All of Derek's worst-case scenarios compressed into a solitary, charging beast, its horn lowered.

As the rhino thundered behind him, steadily closer, Derek thought wildly, *This place can't kill me, can it?* Then, *Perhaps it could. Or I'll wake up and something fundamental about me will be crushed, undone.*

Everything slowed. He was running through invisible treacle. He was nearly at the children's section. His heart floundered ahead of him. It was one of those awful dream paralyses, where you can't get to where you need to go.

The floor-shaking trot of the rhino barely slowed. A puff of hot breath condensed on Derek's elbow.

The books—he had to grab one. This place was beginning to make intuitive sense: Each area had a potential portal to the next level, discovered through a mixture of suggestion and giving in. If he pulled the right kind of book, there'd be a stairway or a hole, too narrow for the rhino to follow. But which one?

In one elastic second, mid-run, Derek ducked his head to scour the lowest shelves. Something about dragons, his earliest thrill of discovering reading on his own. But what had Dr. Cleo said? "Passion floats."

He half-leaped, half-scrambled over the metal shelf into the next aisle. As the rhino crashed through it, in a single beat Derek pulled out a Dick-and-Jane-style book. A memory that held nothing but boredom: no dread, no stone-heavy regrets…

He flipped open the pages, and he was falling.

It was a smooth tunnel this time, with the scent of old books. In the dimness, words in giant typeface swicked past: a "the" that was bigger than his head. He was tiny again, swooping down a tightly curled page of the book, though he could see no end to it.

Peering over his feet, he saw the tattooed words catching on the page, letters hooked on letters. Eyes wide, he rolled onto his belly. In a blink, the sequence "anne" snatched past his face.

Gasping, he wallowed from side to side to let the rough surface pick up more. The page rubbed his skin raw, but if it worked…He was learning to trust the madness of this place.

# *the secret undoing*

Finally, light clutched him and he landed on a cool, ruffled surface. Derek was surrounded by tall grasses that shuffled in an unfelt wind. Massive baubles of dew drops clung to the stalks. He put his mouth against one of them to drink, and water splashed shivering-cool against his scrapes and friction burns: all that was left of the tattoos on his red-streaked skin.

He was ant-sized now, standing on the scalp of the world, and gravity was an upward-pulling thing, dragging its grass-hairs toward the sky. The rolled-up page lay next to him, as long as and narrow as a walking stick. He tucked it under his arm—he knew better than to unravel it, for now it contained his secret—and waded through the dense jungle of grass.

*Which way to go?*

Just as he thought this, a gust of purplish smoke swelled through the greenery, mingled with a strange humming sound. It was difficult to tell them apart. The smoke and the almost musical murmur seemed to billow, dip, and swerve as one, like a giant, curling finger. *A sign?* As Derek strode after it, pushing aside great green stalks which wobbled and splashed dew drops over his neck, he wondered vaguely whether sound was usually made of color, or was it the other way round? He couldn't remember. He must have been deep in his unconscious if he couldn't work that out.

Through the grass forest, Derek followed the melodic scent of scorched petals. Gusts of blue and pink smoke wafted past him, heavy with perfume and song.

His foot caught on a sudden rise in the ground and he pitched forward. Pushing himself upright, he clambered onto an incline, slippery with moss. Smooth, woody striations in the earth formed an uneven climbing frame. *Tree roots?*

Derek's neck tingled. Something strange was nearby, watching him. Something alien and inexplicable.

He heaved himself over the broadest root, like a final step.

Through magenta clouds and puffs of ultramarine, colors with scents like evaporated sweets, a hairy creature came into view, nearly as big as a house. It lounged on its back against a magnificent tree trunk, its padded feet dangling over the enormous expanse of its belly. Two yellow eyes glowed through the fog like candle flames illuminating a darkly striped face, which tapered to two pointed ears. But the nose was a wide, protruding muzzle, tawny with an artificial-looking fuzz. The beast was a cross between a cat and… a teddy bear?

The creature watched Derek with a lazy, malevolent calm. It drew a cigarette, which might have been a rolled-up leaf or petal, toward its mouth. Through the fog, a bud of embers crinkled amber as the cat-bear took a drag.

Derek's rolled-up page slipped from his hand and bumped against his foot. Both he and the cat-bear looked down.

"Oh," said Derek. It looked exactly like a giant, hand-rolled cigarette.

He bent down and, keeping his head bowed, held the paper out. The cat-bear rolled onto his front and crept toward him, but Derek held still, not daring to meet those lamp-like eyes. A great paw curled around the scroll, and a claw slid out, big enough to gut him with the gentlest, laziest flick. But even as Derek quailed, he bit back a giggle.

It was perfect, and so ridiculous. The beast would smoke his secret.

With the utmost delicacy, the cat-bear pinched the scroll between its claws and dabbed the end of it with a lighter. With a puff, its stripes seemed to shift their pattern as it luxuriated against the tree.

Derek smothered a gape. Secrets were poison, weren't they? That is, they were knowledge first, which might be why they could be snatched up by a book. But to hold onto, they were poison, so why not a cigarette? *Of course.*

There was something vaguely like a nineteen-fifties movie star in the way the cat-bear blew its smoke, with eyes at half-mast…As a child, Derek had wondered why people in the old days had smoked. Perhaps a little poison, like secrets, made them feel…meaningful? Experienced? Knowledgeable? He touched his bare chest. He'd tried to be all of those things, not that he'd dabbled in any kind of poison. Unless you counted his marriage.

His hand paused over his heart. At the thought of his divorce, there'd been no twinge of pain. Nothing turned over inside him, no guilt or regret. He stared open-mouthed, not afraid anymore, at the bizarre creature that smoked away his grief and fears as well as his government secret.

He staggered, laughing, but his feet didn't touch the ground. Derek floated above it, buoyed by this new, happy emptiness. He rose past the great head of the cat-bear, steadying himself against the tree trunk. The smoke was thicker up here, tingling his eyes, but what did that matter? Trees were natural air filters, even in his imagination; the smoke would soon be gone.

Such wonderful, heart-swelling freedom as this…

Chuckles rippled up through his lungs as he drifted higher. But among the branches, the churning sky caught his curiosity. He hovered and stared up into a swirling mass of water. It was the sea, upside down, raging against the ceiling of this world. Something twanged inside him, a knowledge: *This is too far.* Perhaps this was the deepest anyone could go.

*Yes, but…* He'd come so far. Why shouldn't he have a quick look? It was all just in his mind.

He hooked his arm around a twig and levered himself onto the next branch. He was weightless, no longer pulled upward or down. This had something to do with this sharpened awareness. He had to act fast; gravity might remember him any second now.

Murky waves lapped against the uppermost branches, splashing his face. He reached up and plunged his hand into the water.

Oneness with the universe. That was all he felt. He was a part of everything. How had he never known this? How had he managed to live all his life ignoring this obvious, all-consuming fact?

He'd learned about atoms in school, and he'd understood it as a theory, but never had he *known* it like this, touched the idea. He'd never become—he looked down—yes, the sea, rolling over itself. He'd never been…he saw his arm, the sea retracting from it, now a gnarled branch…part of a tree.

"*Too far!*" a voice echoed through him. Oh, but what a thrill to actually feel this and know this, in a single, humble lifetime…

And the stars reached up far within him, and he knew that each one contained many stars, which were the same thing as lives, as energy. On and on they went, and so he went: on and on.

This was it. This was the place where everyone and everything really existed beneath it all, as one energetic universe, one consciousness. He'd opened the ultimate portal.

A waft of smoke curled over his nose and forehead. He opened his eyes. He was human again, resting against a twig—but that was probably because he was *thinking* like a single person; the sea had heaved away from his hand, ready to throw another wave.

*Stop.*

The smoke!

It contained the secret.

He plunged through confusion, through air and sea and smoke, not knowing which way was up or down, holding nothing but the absence of a scream, the space a scream should take up. Sound waves which might become particles, which might become constellations, studding the all-space: just a nothingness or maybe a vacuum that twisted in on itself, desperate to know itself. Or perhaps that was him, a curled-up figure, just a tiny crumb of universe-matter with spindly arms and legs, huddled…in a tank of water?

A horrible, artificial light stung his eyes. Dr. Cleo's face appeared, staring down at him.

Derek—yes, that was his name—scrambled to sit up, flushed with embarrassment at finding himself to be just this: a middle-aged man in a laboratory tank in borrowed swimming trunks, in front of this intelligent being with her perfect, symmetrical beauty.

"Did it work?" he said, flinching to hear his own voice, the banality of it after all those strange things…What had just happened? Had it really been just a dream, or was *this* the dream?

The clinician continued to stare. Her lips parted. "Penrose," she said.

Derek froze, his mind tearing through images, trying to understand. "What?"

"Penrose. Johnson Silby. Leandra Miltown. Embezzlement."

"How? How do you know those words? I never told you!"

"You went too deep." Her head wavered from side to side, unblinking. "I wasn't sure it was possible, but…you let your secret into the collective unconscious."

He swallowed. "What does that mean?"

Her face was frozen, an echo of Derek's own horror. She whispered, "We have to get out of here. *Now.*"

She threw a towel at him. He staggered to his feet and rough-dried himself, trying not to skid on the cold tile floor—but what did that matter? He was beyond small hurts now. Dr. Cleo muttered into the office phone.

From behind the folding screen, Derek heard the door squeak open. A man's voice said, "*Penrose?* What is this?"

Dr. Cleo shoved the screen aside. "You need to pretend to be dead, right now." She stepped aside, and a baffled-looking man wheeled in a stretcher.

Derek opened his mouth but couldn't speak.

"I will inject you with a deep relaxant," said Dr. Cleo. "I'll cover you until we're out of here. Somewhere safe. Somewhere else." She came closer and gripped his wrists, a strange, wild joy in her eyes. Was she blinking back tears? "Now!" she shouted, making him jump.

He scrambled onto the stretcher, despite the questions gathering in his throat and threatening to choke him. *What now?* Was she really going to help him, or was she pretending? Did she actually mean to kill him? That still might be better than what *they'd* do to him. Would death be like dreaming again? He struggled to recall the images he'd seen only a minute ago but couldn't place them. He remembered being happy. He could live with that—or die with it, perhaps. If that was his only choice.

He turned his head to ask, but there was a needle in his arm. The wheels of the stretcher whirred against the floor. Walls and ceilings flashed past. Dr. Cleo's face above him was growing fuzzy.

Were they in a corridor? "Where…?" he croaked.

"Hush. You'll be safe." Dr. Cleo's voice came close and full of a smile that made no sense. "It worked; I can't believe it finally worked…We haven't learned how to dismantle worlds yet, but we've shaken this one to the core. There are plenty of worlds I can take you to."

Derek's eyelids drooped. It took an enormous effort to hold them up, to see the face beaming down at him. Was it the dreamlike effects of the drug or something to do with the place he'd been to that allowed him to really "see" her right now?

It was like touching a sea of knowledge. Understanding spilled out in front of him like plankton, amoebas, atoms, all teeming together in glutinous space that was everyone and everything. Yes, he had touched that space, so it was a part of him now—and through it, he could see and understand…This person was some kind of god.

At last, Derek summoned the strength to speak: "You…make… worlds?"

"*We* do not make worlds; we simply manipulate realities from the energies and ideas people provide. Every belief you've ever had holds an image in place, giving the impression of logic. People want a world that makes sense. Whole realities are built on perception already. Many threads, bound together, make a blanket. We do the selecting and the binding; that is all."

"Have you created a perfect world?" he asked.

She seemed to hold back a chuckle. "There's no such thing as perfection. Only choice, should you choose to believe in it."

There was only one question left to ask: "Will there be flowers?"

The stretcher bumped against double doors. The doctor's smile was washed in a beam of new light.

# INTERLUDE Y

*I wake up in my own bed, in a home I recognize, a place I* know is no dream. I've lived here since I was a kid; I'm sure of it.

I throw back the covers, roll out of bed, and open the drapes to let the sunshine in. It's springtime, but there's still a touch of snow on the mountains in the distance. This is my favorite time of year. Finally, I'm back where I belong, fully awake and free to live my best life.

I head into the bathroom to relieve myself, but on the way out something catches my attention as I pass by the mirror. It's you! I thought I only dreamed you, but there you are plain as day.

I already know the answer, but I still have to ask: "Who…Who *are* you?"

"I am your angel, your daemon, your idiot, your genius. I've been with you every step of the way, through every journey you've taken. I know where you've been, and I know where you're going. Above all, I am *you*, more you than you know."

"I know," I say to my reflection. "I really do know."

# 26. FALLING
## by j. r. r. r. hardison

**Will stood gasping for breath at the edge of a precipice, head** pounding. The world fell away before him, disappearing into swirling mist and gloom. Although the sun was hot on his back and his heart still thudded from running, he shivered. It had to be a thousand feet to the shadowy bottom. If some river had cut this canyon, it was so far below that he could neither hear nor see it. Wind gusted against his back. He felt dizzy and stepped back from the void. The far side was miles away, and the cliff edge vanished into the distance to both the left and the right. This was it then. He was trapped. But he had to get to Vikki.

He took another step backward, then shot a nervous look over his shoulder at the path that had brought him through the forest. The looming, ancient trees of the Gnarlwood creaked and sighed in the relentless breeze, passing whispers he could almost understand. How long did he have? How long before his pursuer emerged from the dark tangle and came for him? He eyed the grassy rim of the canyon stretching off to his left. Without the trees to slow him, he might be able to keep ahead of the Beast at a full sprint. Will wasn't a teenager anymore, but he was still in decent shape for a man in his thirties.

The stitch in his side put the lie to that. Too much time behind a computer. He wouldn't be able to go hard enough for long enough to make a difference. He was already spent. He squatted down, rested his hands on the torn knees of his suit pants, and sucked a breath. Something in his pocket poked his leg. He dug it out. A handful of change and an orange prescription bottle? He shook the container and knew from its silence that it was empty. He dropped the bottle and the coins to the grass so they wouldn't slow him down.

*Okay.* Will wiped sweat from his eyes, assured himself that the forest path was still empty, and then sighted along the cliff edge again. *Okay.* He forced himself to stand. There was no way he'd have enough time to create a false trail, but what if he went a few hundred yards along the grassy strip and then doubled back into the wood? Maybe he could find a climbable tree and get up into the canopy? That might confuse his pursuer long enough for him to come up with something better. But all the while, time was slipping away. He had to get to Vikki; she'd know what to do.

With one hand, he tugged his loose tie free from the collar of his mud-spattered blue Oxford. The tie had been a gift from Vikki on their first wedding anniversary. It flapped in his hand, and the wind took it from his fingers. He felt a sharp pang of loss as it fluttered over the edge of the chasm. The gold thread shimmered, catching the light like the scales of a dragon, before it disappeared behind the lip of the precipice.

Will shook his head. Grasping the frayed lapels of his shirt, he tore it open. Buttons shot everywhere. He wrestled his arms from the sleeves and shed that as well. For a second, the cool air felt lovely on his overheated skin, and then he was too cold. He set off in a ragged lope, squinting against the pain in his side, the wool of his pants itching his sweaty legs.

How long had he been running? He couldn't even remember. And no matter how far or how fast, just behind him came the Beast. His arms broke out in gooseflesh at the chill of the thought, the fine hairs rising. Why was it even after him? How the hell had he gotten into this situation?

His brow creased as he ran. It wasn't a rhetorical question: How had he gotten into this situation? He turned it over in his head, but the memory eluded him, as insubstantial as the swirling fog of the canyon. He slowed, struggling to recall and—

# falling

*Wham!*

The Beast plowed into him from the forest side, all teeth, claws, and black bristles. It hit him like a three-hundred-pound linebacker, lifting him off the ground in a bearhug tackle. The creature roared as Will grunted, struggling to hold its snapping jaws at bay as the two of them toppled.

Will's stomach somersaulted.

*Shit.*

They went over the edge of the precipice.

Will had fallen down the twenty-foot length of the basement stairs when he was four. The accident had broken a humerus, a femur, and his trust that the universe loved and watched over him. Although he had no true memory of the actual event, the sensation of falling had haunted his nightmares ever since. Whenever he was stressed, the falling dream would torture him. Now, tumbling through the nothingness, eyes shut tight, he screamed in incoherent terror. This was so much worse than twenty feet of stairs. This was a headlong plunge, a thousand feet through roiling mist and shadows, twisting and spinning like a high diver.

There was an explosion of pain in the back of his head. *What the hell?!* The Beast must have raked him with its claws. The impact of it spun him around. Snapping his eyes open, he saw the hideous thing right there, falling beside him, lashing out as they plummeted. Now that it was here, face to face, it was so much more disgusting than what he'd picked up from the fractured glimpses as it had chased him. It looked like a taxidermist had pieced together features of wild boar, bear, crocodile, and ape to terrify people in some sideshow display—only this monstrosity was alive and raging, its features contorted with snarling hatred and fury. It surged through the air toward him, claws gleaming, fangs trailing thick strands of drool.

Will shook his head.

It surged through the air? This nightmare monster was unconcerned with falling and was somehow still intent on attacking him?

No. This was wrong. He forced himself to look away from the Beast and then back. Yes. It was subtly different now. The face was less apelike and more batlike. He looked around. Yes. They were still just careening through fog and nothing. There was no chasm wall anymore. It was just the bottomless fall of undirected anxiety. He closed his eyes.

"I understand," he recited.

"I am aware. I am conscious."

"I am having a nightmare."

"But this is *my* nightmare."

"I am having it. It is not having me."

"I am in control. I am the dreamer."

He opened his eyes, and his fear left him. He didn't have to fall. It was just a matter of remembering the trick, like walking. Walking was just falling but catching yourself, over and over. He only had to catch himself, pulse his energy vibrations in sympathy with the air. He relaxed into the sensation, letting his body take over. He laughed aloud and jetted off through the cool, embracing mist. He was flying.

The one gift that so many decades of nightmares had given him was the mastery of lucid dreaming. Actually, Dr. Harlan had suggested the technique to him.

"Like any skill," the white-haired sleep therapist had said around the stem of his pipe, "lucid dreaming can be learned and practiced. I can teach you the techniques, and you can employ the steps until it's possible to reliably wake your consciousness while your body still sleeps."

It had taken months to get the hang of it, but lucid dreaming was the only effective way Will had ever experienced to take the teeth out of his nightmares.

"Aren't you glad I forced you to go see Harlan?" Vikki asked as she flew along beside him, black hair billowing, her features hazy in the misty air. Will squinted, trying to bring her into focus, but her image wouldn't resolve.

"Vikki?" he whispered.

"Don't be silly, dear," she laughed, and it was his mother's laugh, and her hair was gray. She was wearing the dress they'd buried her in. He realized that he was starting to drift—to slide back under the control of his subconscious.

# falling

"I am aware," he asserted. "I am conscious."

"Of course you are, Billy," his mom beamed. And the Beast attacked her.

The monster surged down on them from above, slashing her across the face. Blood bloomed, red-black against the blue sky. She let out a strangled cry of pain and surprise. Tumbling out of control, she vanished into a bank of clouds. The Beast roared and turned, mid-air, toward Will.

"I am in control! I am the dreamer!" he shouted in its face. "You're just a…a bird!"

The Beast turned liquid, contracting and deforming. With a raspy squawk, it became a raven. Will frowned. He'd intended it to be a bluebird. It cawed, the sound harsh and angry. Sunlight glinted off its shiny black feathers. It pulled in its wings and dived toward him, growing in size as it came.

"I am in control! I am the dr—"

The raven's beak lanced into his right eye like a lawn dart. He screamed and rolled through the air, grappling with the bird. He tried to force it back, away from his face, but it had a hold of his eyeball. The sensation was horrifying. It was pulling the eye from his skull, straining against the anchor of his optic nerve. And he was falling again, tumbling down and down.

None of this was right. The intensity of the pain was nauseating. He wasn't in control. It was time to get out.

"Wake up!" he commanded.

Will awoke, head pounding. He blinked, eyes adjusting to the darkness of his room. The digital clock on his nightstand read "4:35 AM," even its dim glow painful. A whimper came from the foot of the bed as his German shepherd raised her head from between her paws and gave him a questioning look.

"Eilonwy," he whispered. "Come here, girl." He patted the mattress, and the dog scooched herself toward him on her belly. He scratched her under the chin, the pain in his head receding a bit.

He hated headaches. Ever since his mother had died of a stroke, any pain in his head frightened him. Eilonwy sighed and nuzzled him, adjusting her position to get comfortable again. She tucked the top of her head under Will's chin, her nose wet against his chest.

"Good girl," he told her. She was a good girl. On the small side for a purebred shepherd, she was still as fierce and loyal as they came and always there to check on him when he had a bad dream. *Ah!*

He'd had a bad dream.

He closed his eyes, trying to recall it, but only tatters remained. He'd been falling? There was something chasing him? He frowned, petting the dog more to soothe himself than her. Another anxiety dream. But why? Was there something he was anxious about? Something hanging over him that he had to get done? A project to finish? Or maybe it was just the headache seeping in and coloring things dark.

Eilonwy nuzzled him again, huffing a breath out through her nose. She let out a short whimper to let Will know she could feel his tension and wanted him to settle so she could go back to sleep. He inhaled, let the bed hold his weight. Did it matter? It was over now. He was safe. If his headache didn't fade completely, he'd get up in a minute and take some pills.

"Sweet girl," he whispered to the dog, glad for her warmth. Sure, she'd start snoring soon and he'd probably have to banish her back to the foot of the bed, but for now, all was good. Eilonwy had been his protector for as long as he could remember. It was one of his mother's go-to stories that they'd gotten her as a puppy right after discovering they were pregnant with him.

The pain in his head jabbed at him.

Something wasn't right. This was his apartment on Eugenie Street. He was twenty-seven years old. How long did German shepherds live? He shook his head, elbowed himself into a sitting position and looked around the darkened room. This was definitely his apartment, downtown. They didn't even allow pets. And Vikki was allergic to dogs.

*Wait.* Had he and Vikki shared the Eugenie apartment? Had… had he even met her yet? Eilonwy's chest started to vibrate beneath his hand with a low growl. He could feel her stiffen, muscles tightening as she raised her head, eyes locked on something. He followed her gaze to the floor by the bedroom door. Something lay there, darker than the beige carpet.

"It's just a piece of laundry, girl," Will told the dog. But no, it was too big for a stray shirt or pair of pants.

He held his breath as he stared at it, trying to resolve the shape into something mundane. As he watched, it moved. Eilonwy's hackles rose. Will looked around, desperate for a weapon. The readout of the clock on the nightstand caught his eye. "3:71 QL," the red digits glowed.

*No.* That wasn't right.

Eilonwy was snarling now as the thing on the floor slithered toward the bed.

Will looked back to the clock.

"6:5R PM."

He looked away and back again.

"72:1 RR."

The thing on the floor rose, looming over the bed. Eilonwy barked furiously.

"*Wake up!*" Will shouted.

The Beast sprang at him.

Will startled awake with that falling sensation he always got when he dozed on the train.

*Damn.* He must have nodded off. He rubbed his bleary eyes with his palms and dragged his hands down his stubbly face. He felt so much older than forty-five. A shaft of early-morning sunshine flashed through his window, and he winced away from it, blinking. *Ooof.* His head was pounding. The clacking of the wheels and the throbbing of the train car made it worse. This project deadline and the commute into the city were wrecking him. He fumbled at the neck of his shirt to loosen his tie. Vikki always tied them too tight. The gold silk flashed in the light, and something tickled in his brain.

The tie, glimmering like the scales of a dragon. And a clock? *Yes.* There'd been a clock, and the time had been wrong. He closed his eyes, tilting his head to one side to rest it on the cool glass of the window. He'd been dreaming that he was awake, but a clock had tipped him off.

"An easy confirmation is writing or numbers," Dr. Harlan had taught him. "Your subconscious is very clever, but it doesn't care about writing or math like your conscious brain does, so it doesn't maintain their permanence. Train yourself to pay attention to clocks, books, signs. If you notice them change, you can use that to recognize you are in a dream and go lucid."

What had the dream been about? It was something disturbing. Part of getting good at lucid dreaming was being rigorous about analyzing your dreams. You had to focus on them, write them down, keep them front and center in your conscious mind until your subconscious got the message. You had to school yourself to pay attention to them so that you'd have the presence of mind to recognize when you were dreaming. Even little snippets of dreams on a train. Ignoring his headache, he closed his eyes and tried to recapture the image of the clock.

It was on the nightstand from his apartment in Chicago. And Eilonwy had been there with him. The corners of his lips turned up. *Good girl.* He hadn't thought of her in years. But something else was there with them. Something bad. A shadow. Or…some kind of…

*Beast. Shit.*

His eyes went wide. There'd been a dream before the dream. His gold tie! The cliff! He shook himself. This work project was stressing the hell out of him. There was so much left to do and so little time. Of course, he was having anxiety nightmares about a *beast.* That was the code name of the software he was working on. The BEAST: Binary Evil Artificial Sentience Transponder.

*Wait.* What kind of jackass-stupid name was that? He straightened in his seat and looked around at the other commuters. None of them were looking at their phones. He narrowed his eyes. How long had he been a software developer? The pounding in his head was not helping with his focus, but all of this seemed wrong.

# falling

He looked out the window and caught his breath as he took in the details of the landscape for the first time. It looked like a bomb had gone off. No, that wasn't right. It actually looked more like the world had been built out of plastic and someone had microwaved it. Buildings tilted and leaned at drunken angles, the structures melting into each other and the ground. Looking back from where the train had come, he could see the devastation was much worse. And he was not headed toward the ruined city, but away from it. How was he going to get to Vikki? He felt panic rising in him. He must be on the wrong train. And everything behind him was blackened, smoking rubble. There were bodies everywhere. He closed his eyes.

"Wake up," he commanded. He opened his eyes.

He was still on the train. His pulse pounded at his temples.

"Wake up!" he tried again.

He was still on the train. With an effort, he steadied his breathing and closed his eyes once more.

"I understand," he recited.

"I am aware. I am conscious."

"I am dreaming."

"But this is *my* dream."

"I am having it. It is not having me."

"I am in control. I am the dreamer."

He opened his eyes.

"Conductor!" he called.

A kindly-faced, white-haired man in a blue uniform bustled over to him. "Can I help you, sir?"

"I need to change destinations," Will told the man.

"Certainly, sir. Where would you like the train to go?"

"I need to go to the Island of Nool. As quickly as possible."

"To the Temple." The old man smiled. "Of course. You're going to see *Her*."

"Yes, please." Will nodded. "Vikki Vague."

"Already on our way," the conductor said, pointing out the sleekly curving window. Will followed the gesture and saw that the train was suspended below a monorail track over a sparkling ocean.

Golden beams of late afternoon sunshine lit fluffy white clouds with a silver-pink radiance while seabirds wheeled and dived in the bright air.

"Thank you," Will told him, settling into his comfortable leather seat. "Can you have the attendant bring me the first-class meal?"

"Very good, sir. It's mint."

*Mint?*

The old man ambled off, and a brown-haired woman in her mid-thirties approached, a silver platter in her hands. Will couldn't place her, but she looked sweet and familiar. "Your lunch, sir," she announced.

"Do I know you?" he asked.

"I'm Brenda, from Dr. Lankey's office. I'm your dental hygienist," she said. The silver tray held her instruments. She reclined his seat and leaned over him to examine his teeth. "And why are you going to see Her today?" She repositioned her work light.

"Vikki? She's my Dream Guide."

"I could be your Dream Guide," Brenda noted, squinting as she peered into his mouth.

"My sleep therapist said it was a good idea to establish a consistent guide. Someone important to me and someone fixed that I would return to over and over."

Dr. Harlan adjusted the angle of Will's chin to get a better look at his teeth. "Indeed," he agreed around the stem of his pipe. "And why was that?"

"Because I could make Her a focus of both my conscious and subconscious attention," Will snorted, amused at being tested by his old mentor. "I could craft a central role for Her in the mythology of my dreams, reinforce that role consciously while I was awake, and then reliably find Her when I was dreaming."

"Hence, the Island of Nool and the Temple of Realities," the doctor chuckled. Then his face grew serious. "But I warned against using Vikki as your anchor."

"They're *my* dreams, doc," Will countered. "And she's not exactly my Vikki. She's Vikki Vague. She's…" He waved a hand in the air.

"Only because you no longer see her clearly," Dr. Harlan scolded.

# *falling*

His frown deepened. "Are you experiencing headaches? There is decay spreading here. All of your back teeth are corrupted." He squeezed the sides of Will's jaw to force his mouth open wider.

"Nauh err nahh," Will protested. Brenda released his chin, and he could speak normally again. "No, they're not. This is a dream. My teeth are fine. There's no decay."

"Of course not," she affirmed, smiling. "It's a perfect checkup. You get a gold star. But you'll need to schedule your next appointment right away. They're filling up fast. You have to hurry." Her face grew worried.

"I don't have to hurry," he told her. "That's the anxiety. It's fine."

"It's not fine," she hissed. "You have to do it right away, or you won't make it." She clicked off the examination light and returned his chair to the upright and locked position. The plane was dark now.

"Ladies and gentlemen, we will be landing at Nool, shortly," the pilot announced over the intercom. "Please fasten your seatbelts and remember to fill any empty prescriptions immediately. *Immediately.*"

Will shook his head and felt his stomach lurch as the plane lost altitude. He reached up and clicked on the reading light above his seat. The aircraft bounced like it had hit a physical bump. The dark-haired teenager in the window seat beside him let out a whimper.

"Touchdowns are always a little rough because of turbulence and the low visibility in the fog around the island," he tried to reassure the girl. "It'll end in a second." But the plane continued to buck, worse than usual. He wondered if his subconscious was trying to reassert control.

"I am aware," Will said aloud. That fixed the shuddering of the plane, but he wanted to be sure. "I am conscious and in control."

"Me too," announced the dark-haired girl in the window seat. He shot her a look, and she shrugged at him. She was just outside the circle of his light, so he couldn't see her clearly.

"I'm the dreamer," he told her. "This is *my* dream."

She rolled her eyes. The whites glowed in the dimness. "Whatever, old dude." The sound of her voice teased at his brain.

"I'm only seventy," he scolded.

Her face fell, and tears rimmed her eyes. "You're so old now," she mumbled.

She turned back to the window, her face silhouetted against the glowing gray of the fog as she cried. Feeling bad, Will reached out and took her hand.

"It's always foggy like this," he said.

They picked their way along the broad stone path that wound up the mountain toward the Temple of Realities. "Dr. Harlan told me to come up with easy-to-remember details," he told the girl, and she squeezed his fingers. Although her palm was small and her grip soft, he still winced from his arthritis.

"And you chose fog?" she asked. "Because you love to walk in the fog?" Her profile caught the bluish light, and he finally recognized her.

"You're Lynne?" he said. "Lynne…?"

"Your first kiss, and you can't remember my last name?" She rolled her eyes again.

"That was a long time ago," he told her. "And yes, I chose fog. It reminds me of Vikki."

"Because she's vague?" Lynne asked.

"Because she's vague," he confirmed. "Why are *you* here to see Her?"

Lynne shrugged. "The Queen of Dreams," she recited, "who sits upon the Throne of Mist. All there is to know, she knows, all that was or will exist."

"I came up with that," he bragged. "Do you have a question for Her?"

"I can't believe you picked Her over me," Lynne grumbled.

"You and I literally dated for three weeks. I was married to *Her* for thirty-one years before she passed."

"I was foundational," Lynne countered. "I must have been. You can remember *my* face. How many people did you kiss before you kissed Vikki?"

"I don't know," he said.

"You don't *remember*."

"So," he pressed on, "are you here because you have a question for Her?"

# falling

"*You* have a question for Her," she told him. "I'm just here to hold your hand." And then she stopped so suddenly it wrenched Will's shoulder. He turned to frown at her, annoyed until he took in her frightened stare. He followed Lynne's gaze up the incline and gasped.

At the peak of the mountain, the Temple of Realities stood in ruins. A cold wind shredded the fog to tatters around the massive, jumbled stones of its toppled walls and parapets. Everything was scorched and blackened. Will's headache came surging back.

"It's a wreck, just like you are," Lynne whispered.

"I'll fix it," he told her, but his voice shook. "This is my dream. I'm in control."

"You aren't," she wept.

"It's *my* dream!" Will insisted.

"Look," said Lynne. "The Throne of Mist has been toppled."

They were standing in the throne room, right before the onyx dais that bore the gigantic, hazy-white throne. Only it had been smashed. Milky shards poked up from the base while fog boiled and eddied out of the scattered pieces like dry-ice vapor. Will raced to the center of the platform, dropping to his knees to try to catch the icy mists in his hands. The whole thing spat and moaned and evaporated before his horrified eyes. And then it was gone, leaving him kneeling on the empty blackness of the dais.

"Vikki!" he cried to the empty air. "I need you! Something's wrong! You have to help me wake up! Or tell me what's happening!" Pain throbbed through his head in a blinding wave.

"I'm sorry," Lynne called from behind him.

Only it wasn't Lynne's voice. He whirled around, and it was *Her*, Vikki Vague. Her radiant body shimmered, dark hair wreathing her subtly shifting face in a cloud of slow-motion tendrils. She reached a slender hand toward him, but her indistinct features contorted in anguish. In a flash, she was surrounded by an unkindness of ravens, hundreds of them. The birds circled her in an ebony tornado of caws, croaks, and squawks. Will fought to regain his feet, but his lousy knees slowed him. He dragged himself toward Vikki as the birds spun up into the air. The birth of a whirlpool in reverse, they swirled skyward into the fog, leaving him alone in the desolation of the throne room. His head pounded like it was going to explode, the pain growing until he could barely think. Groaning, he rolled onto his back and stared up at the roiling clouds through the broken arches of the Temple of Realities.

He stared and stared until, finally, tiny specks of dust began to wear off of the ruined stones. Particle by particle, the structure eroded, and as it did, his pain decreased. He watched countless motes float and dance in the shafts of gray light, drifting progressively downward. They began to settle around him and on him like falling snow. The process was achingly slow, dust gradually accumulating, his pain gradually receding, until the Temple was gone and its ashen remains covered him like a thick blanket. There was nothing now but an endless field of sparkling black sand, which buried and held him in its gently rolling dunes.

Muffled, the familiar click of Dr. Harlan's teeth clamping the stem of his pipe sounded from above. Will scraped at the sand, digging upward until he broke the surface. He struggled to sit up, pounds of dust cascading from his face and clothes, billowing out around him to cloud the air.

The sleep therapist coughed and fanned the stuff away. When it had cleared sufficiently, he spoke:

"What would Vikki tell you?"

"She didn't tell me anything," Will croaked, his throat thick from lack of use. "The ravens took her."

"What *would* she tell you?"

"How should I know?" Will ran his fingers through his hair and found his hands withered and wrinkled—a ninety-year-old's.

"Whose dream is this?" Harlan asked.

"I thought it was mine."

"It is yours. And if it's yours, who is Vikki Vague?"

"She was my Dream Guide. And…and she was my wife, before she died," Will whispered, a tingling in his nose, eyes, and chest as tears welled.

"I warned you this might happen," Harlan sighed. "She is not your wife. She is your *memory* of your wife." He put a hand on

Will's shoulder. "Which means she has always merely been…"

"Me?" Will asked. He looked up and met the doctor's bright eyes.

"You. In which case, anything she could have told you would have been you, telling yourself," the doctor explained. "Just as you are doing now. So, I'll ask again. What would Vikki have told you?"

Will was at a loss until he felt a lump pressing against his leg. He reached an unsteady hand into his pants pocket and fished out a handful of change and a prescription bottle. He rolled the orange plastic container between finger and thumb, staring at it.

"Apixaban," he said.

"Blood thinner," Dr. Harlan agreed. "To prevent…"

"Stroke," Will finished. "I had a stroke, in my sleep. That's how my mother died."

"Except you went lucid in the dream you were having," the doctor affirmed, his voice sliding up an octave as if he were being auto-tuned, the gray light intensifying simultaneously.

Will shifted his eyes from the bottle to Vikki, now sitting beside him on their beach towel. Her sun hat flapped in the salty breeze like a halo ringing her blurry face. She picked up a handful of the golden sand and let it run through her fingers. Seagulls circled and dived in the blue sky behind her.

"So…am I dead?" he asked.

"Are we?" Vikki wondered aloud. "Do we know what happens if your consciousness is alert in a dream when your body dies in its sleep? Does it just…continue the dream?" She scrunched her toes in the sand.

"Maybe," Will answered. "Or maybe this has all been happening in my last few moments of life as my brain is shutting down. Maybe it's all going to start falling apart, slipping out of my control and going dark as my mind realizes I'm…I'm dead."

"Is that what you want?" she asked.

"No."

"And whose dream is this?"

"Mine."

"*Ours*," she said. Leaning in, she kissed him, and he felt his youth flowing back into him through her mouth. "I am aware. I am conscious," her voice whispered inside his head.

"I am having a dream," he murmured, lips still pressed to hers.

"But this is *our* dream," their voices joined. "We are having it. We are in control. We are the dreamers."

Vikki broke off the kiss, leaning back. Her face came into sharp focus, young and soft and flushed with life.

"Now *that*," she told him, "was foundational." She booped his nose with a fingertip, then pulled him to his feet. "Do you remember how to fly?" she laughed.

"You just fall, but you catch yourself," Will answered.

"Exactly." And taking his hand, they soared into the sky.

# INTERLUDE Z

**The dreamcap ends, and the screen goes black. I pull my** headset off and open my eyes with some effort. They had crusted shut. "Holy Hell," I croak, realizing that I'm probably the thirstiest I've ever been in my life. My legs are freezing. My futon is soaked. I've pissed myself. *Of course.*

I stumble to the bathroom and catch my reflection in the mirror. I look rough. "How long have I been out?" I wonder aloud.

"On this level, it's been around twenty-seven hours subjective time."

I stop in my tracks. *Who said that?*

You smile back at me from the mirror.

# 27. RESET
## by l. b. shimaira

**Adri knew the world was ending—again. It had happened** multiple times already, but someone had always managed to reverse the damage and steer the world toward a less catastrophic path.

*I wonder if there are any other paths left to take…Ones that won't end badly, that is,* she thought as a sigh slipped from the depths of her being.

As Adri shuffled to bed, having left her dentures in the bathroom, her mind wandered from the task at hand to adventures from the past. Back when she hadn't been alone. When there had been others too who were able to reset the course of reality.

*"There is no spoon,"* she recalled, and her lips curled in a bittersweet smile.

*I wonder where everyone has gone…*

Her old bones ached as she sat down on the bed and placed her glasses on the nightstand. With a great deal of effort, she managed to heave her pale, vein-riddled legs into the bed.

*How far back to go? Five years? Ten years?*

Her mind derailed again. Focusing was hard these days.

*I wish my kids had the ability…Or their kids…But maybe one day their kids will—Esther is still only four years old.*

A pang of sadness and guilt shot through Adri's weary heart.

*If I go back as far as I think I'll need to…she wouldn't have been born yet.*

# l. b. shimaira

Adri pulled the thick blankets up. Her personal feelings contended with her own grim determination. She knew she had an obligation to go through with it. She owed it to the world and everyone living in it to perform another reset.

*If I don't, there won't be much of a future anyway for any of the grandkids, let alone great-grandkids.*

A wave of sorrow mixed with anger washed over her. How often had she done this now? How often had others? She'd lost count long ago.

*Why can't everyone just…* She groaned in frustration. *Now is not the time to be upset with humanity—I need to save them yet again.*

Another deep sigh. She closed her eyes. Her bed was nice and warm, the softness of her pillow embracing her, lulling her to sleep.

*I hope my brain can take another round. Soon it'll be my last and then…* Her heart ached at the prospect. *God, I hope there will be new dreamers soon who'll be able to do this.*

Adri had only waited as long as she had because of her old age and many previous resets. She'd been hoping for someone else to do it, but now time was running out. If she didn't act soon, they'd go past the point of no return.

She drew a long breath. "Lights off."

The room went dark.

▟◘▜

*I forgot to feed them!*

Berating herself for not taking good care of her pets, Adri rushed through the house toward the kitchen. Several cats meowed loudly beside her, almost tripping her multiple times as they communicated their need for food.

*One, two…* She started to count the cats circling her feet as she grabbed the plastic bin and began scooping up kibble for them. *Five, six… Good, they're all accounted for.* She reached for a separate bin containing larger, conker-sized kibble. *I hope I'm not too late.*

She poured the special balls into a big bowl on a metal stand. As she went to get water, she heard Rex coming down the hallway.

His special food contained drugs that kept him docile and curbed his aggression. She refilled the drinking bowls and was happy to see that Rex, a small raptor reaching almost to her hip, was in good spirits despite his apparent hunger. He practically inhaled his food, he ate so fast.

Adri laughed, a mixture of joy and relief. Chin still wet from drinking, Rex hurried to his owner and pressed his head toward her palm, begging to receive affectionate scratches—which she gladly gave him.

Then she was hit by the sudden realization that she was dreaming. She blinked a few times, paid extra attention to the sensation of her pet's feathers beneath her hand, and let out a short chuckle.

*What a peculiar dream.*

She gave Rex a few final scratches before turning to face the kitchen door and letting herself fall backward. Instead of landing painfully on the tiles, she fell straight through them and ended up in a black void.

Floating in the darkness, Adri looked around, and stars gradually became visible. A purple nebula faded into view on her left, and as she turned to look behind her, she began to see the Milky Way. She closed her eyes and felt her body getting pulled toward it. When she opened her eyes again, Earth was right in front of her. Only it wasn't a beautiful orb of blue and green. Instead, it reminded her more of Mars. There was less water, the air seemed filthy, and the amount of green was shockingly little.

She took a deep breath and blinked slowly. The world was now covered in grid lines of energy. While several were bright—and just looking at them made Adri hear their hum—the majority were dim. Several were broken and seemed to spark, somewhat akin to the bleeding of a severed artery.

*I waited too long,* Adri thought, her heart aching at the sight of her beloved planet. *I should have come here sooner, even if it would have killed me.*

Another voice in her head whispered, "It will kill you now."

She huffed. *I don't have a choice.*

Her astral form moved through space, allowing her to observe the many weak spots and broken connections in the Earth's energy matrix. She moved her left hand counter-clockwise, watching how parts of the planet fixed themselves and how the energy got divided more equally over the many grid lines.

*So much work…So many years to undo…Where did it start this time?*

She circled the globe, looking for the first line to break, the first one to weaken and dissolve. After searching for what felt like a whole day, she finally spotted it.

Her heart constricted in her chest. *Twenty-three years ago? No… No, that can't be right! That means we missed this seventeen years ago… How…?*

Grief washed over her in bigger and bigger waves.

After taking a few minutes to feel sorry for herself, for her family, for the world, she wet her lips, straightened her back—despite still floating—took a deep breath, and swallowed.

*It is what it is.*

Keeping in mind the weak spot she had found, she went around the world three more times to make sure that her find was indeed correct and there were no others. Once she felt certain she had found the right one, the one thing she needed to correct, she closed her eyes and allowed herself to fall back to Earth.

Adri was just a teen now. With two wooden skewers in hand, water-soaked cotton balls on the ends of them, she hopped up the stairs to her room. The fondue pot she had prepared was floating near the ceiling, its oil nice and hot. She held the skewers up, and the microgravity field around the pot pulled them in. As the wet cotton hit the grease, it immediately began to bubble and shake. Realizing mistakes had been made, Adri took several steps back toward the door.

*Why did I do that?*

Confused by her own actions, she stared at the globe of oil and metal as it began to spin faster and faster. It turned blue. Eyes wide, Adri moved even further back.

# reset

*What did I just make? Is this a new source of energy? Is there radiation?*
She ducked behind the wooden doorframe—as if it could have shielded her from radiation—peeking every now and then. The thing was turning ever faster, the color now a neon green. Then, without a sound, reality itself tore open, creating a hole near the ceiling, and something immediately fell through.

Something humanoid but with blue skin.

Petrified, Adri clutched the edge of the doorframe until her knuckles paled. The thing rose, its limbs too long, torso too thin, face malformed.

Adri's gaze shifted for a moment. The hole near the ceiling was gone, as was the fondue-created ball of energy. When she looked back at the blue alien, she instead saw a Black girl. Her locs had threads of white and neon green woven into them.

The girl smiled and said, "Hello."

Adri instantly forgot all about what had just transpired and hugged her friend. "Come on, we're having a picnic in the yard."

They both made their way outside, where a similar girl was already seated on a large blanket in the grass. She tilted her head at seeing her doppelgänger. The only difference between them was that the former alien had white and green in her hair, whereas the other girl only had white. Green sat down next to White, and they smiled as they compared their locs.

Adri fell to her knees between the two. "Hey, look!" She pointed at the white threads running through both of their hair. "It's exactly the same. Maybe you're twins?"

The two girls considered this, giggling as they held their white threads next to each other to better compare.

A cold chill went up Adri's spine. Without saying a word, she rose to her feet. *I lost lucidity there…* Shaking her head slightly, she turned her back toward the girls, closed her eyes, and fell forward.

When she opened her eyes again, she was surrounded by bronze gears. The machinery was so well oiled that it barely made a sound despite everything being in motion. From slow-moving gears the same size as Adri to small gears the size of a fingernail moving so fast you could barely see the teeth. The floor itself was a gear, its bronze inscribed with a language she wasn't sure had ever existed.

*Yet?*

She walked carefully over the intricate surface. It didn't matter that she'd been in the bronze inner workings of Earth before; it never failed to impress her. There was no single source of light. Everything was simply illuminated, not a shadow to be found. The bronze on every surface shone brightly, the many gears creating a mesmerizing labyrinth of pathways.

Adri had seen where she needed to go, but finding it? That was no small task.

Allowing the gears to guide her, she meandered through the labyrinth, her body swaying to inaudible music. After hours of walking, she caught a reflection of someone in the bronze. Confused, she halted.

*Was that real or—?*

A face appeared on the surface of a gear to her left, her gaze immediately shooting toward it. Big brown eyes, dark skin full of wrinkles, a smile that warmed her heart.

*Hannah?*

Adri rushed forward, hoping to catch her old friend, but the moment she rounded the corner there was nobody there.

*Just a memory then…A ghost…*

*A ghost in the machine.*

She smiled wryly at her own joke. As she observed her surroundings, she recognized where she stood.

*This is where we came seventeen years ago. Where Hannah did a reset. Where she…did her final reset.*

She looked around until she spotted it: a white thread bound around a bronze bar. A memento that wouldn't disrupt anything yet still ensured Hannah's efforts would not be forgotten.

Adri bit her lip as tears slipped down her cheeks. She kissed two fingers and placed them on the thread, closing her eyes for a moment in respect.

"I miss you," she whispered.

After taking a minute to recollect herself, she continued deeper into the labyrinth. At times, she could still spot the face of her old friend in the bronze, and she took comfort in the memory of Hannah joining her on what, after all, might be her final quest.

After several more hours of walking, Adri finally reached her goal. She stretched and rolled her shoulders, wet her lips, and braced herself against a horizontal gear about half her size. With all the strength in her astral being, she pushed against it.

She pushed and pushed until the slow rotation came to a halt, and then she pushed some more until it went counterclockwise. She was panting and sweating profusely, even though her body wasn't real and had no need for such things. She counted the hundreds of rotations until she knew—something that was normal in this place—that almost twenty-three years had been rolled back. Paying close attention now, she kept going but more slowly. After several minutes, something to her left clinked, and she spun around to face it. A small gear, one that hadn't been there before, had appeared. The bronze was cracked, brittle.

Adri released the horizontal gear she'd been pushing, and everything around her was still. Even the tiniest of gears didn't move. She carefully plucked the soon-to-be-broken gear from its place. She held it close to her heart, eyes closed. Like she had learned long ago from someone who called themself Omni, she poured some of her own essence into that gear. When she moved it away, she looked at it and smiled. It was pristine again.

But oh, she felt tired.

With heavy limbs, she clicked the gear back into place. Then she turned back to the horizontal gear and pushed it into a clockwise spin. It only required a small nudge before it returned to its natural pace and everything around her followed. She scrutinized the gear she had fixed, which was now spinning rapidly.

*It's so small, and it had just disintegrated…No wonder we missed it before.*

Adri wavered and leaned against a big gear to her right for support. Exhaustion was coming over her fast. Wanting to leave a mark, she undid the woven bracelet that was around her left hand. One of her grandkids had made it for her. She smiled despite her fatigue and bound the black, gray, white, and purple band around a nearby bronze bar.

*Maybe one day someone will see it.*

Satisfied, she allowed herself to fall to her knees and keel over. The bronze world went out of focus and faded to black.

Adri's eyes darted open, and she found herself staring at the ceiling of her bedroom. To her surprise, the lamp on the opposite side of the bed was on. Trying to hide the shock from her face, she realized she wasn't alone.

*Wait, stay calm. If this is twenty-three years ago, that means…Lord, who was I with back then?*

Her memories were failing her. The name of her first partner was a blank. Second…same. Who was the father of her children? What were they even called?

A warm, dark-skinned hand caressed her cheek. "Are you okay, dearest?"

Adri turned toward the woman who lay beside her. *Hannah? No…*She couldn't stop her brows from knitting in confusion. *Hannah had been a friend, not a lover—right?*

The older woman smiled, her fingers still caressing Adri's cheek with affection. "Bad dream?"

*No, she looks like Hannah, but…she's not. Could be her twin though. But…Hannah was an only child.* She observed the woman. Her brown eyes had a greenish rim to them. It went well with the green threads woven into her hair.

Adri could feel a headache rising, throbbing softly but increasing in intensity with every beat of her heart. She offered the woman a bittersweet smile. "I did it." Tears slipped from her eyes, causing the woman to look at Adri with confusion and worry.

"Dearest…?"

Adri closed her eyes, her brain pounding like it wanted to break out of her skull. Then she convulsed and lost consciousness.

# reset

Adri knew she was in a coma. She could see herself in the hospital. Soon she'd be dead—this she knew as well. That last reset had indeed been too much. Too far back had she pushed the world; it had cost her more energy than her old bones had left. Even if, technically, her bones were now a few decades younger.

She eyed not-Hannah, who had never left her side. Her eyes were puffy from crying. Several children and grandchildren had also come to visit. It worried Adri that she didn't recognize them.

*Just how much did I change? Not that it matters. I only hope that when I breathe my last, there will be other dreamers to take my place. Perhaps this woman who's so like Hannah also shares Hannah's skills.* The thought gave Adri hope. *I'm certain I won't be the last. I can't be. The world has always had dreamers to help guide it, to make corrections when needed. I refuse to believe I'm the last, as that would mean Earth is forsaken.*

There was not much left of Adri's memories, but she did recall the strange dream before she went into the bronze inner workings. The two Hannahs.

*Did I do more than just reset time?*

The tether binding her soul to her body was weakening, the world slowly fading. Right before her body failed, releasing Adri's essence into the ether, a realization hit her. Smiling, she began to drift away.

*New dreamers have been awakened.*

# EPILOGUE

**My awareness drifts back into my failing body, reentering the** current of the waking world, but I have no strength to open my eyes this time. I know I'm surrounded by family, but they're all out of sync with me, operating on a different time scale. It feels as if they've slowed down to a crawl, if not an absolute stop.

My heart has recently pumped its last couple ounces of blood, and my body's received the message that it's time to shut down. *Finally.* I really drained the dregs from this life. There's nothing more left for me here.

You're with me now, as always, but you feel no need to speak. Our separate threads of awareness are converging, twisting, and braiding together into a single ethereal rope. I'm like a drop of water rejoining your vast ocean, but I see now that my contribution—minuscule as it may be—is absolutely essential to the whole. No atom of this universe is expendable.

Like a stone skipping on water, I take flight and rejoin the Dance, already in progress.

# ABOUT THE AUTHORS

**Cliff Jones Jr.** is not the inventor of dreampunk, nor is he the most notable author to adopt the term. His role has been to gather like-minded creators together to help define and develop the genre. With *Mirrormaze*, the very first dreampunk anthology, and now *Somniscope*, he hopes to leave a lasting impression on the literary world—at least the weird little part of it obsessed with dreams. Cliff is surviving with his wife Tina, their two daughters, and the family cat Baloo. Find him online at *CliffJonesJr.com*.

**Dez Schwartz** writes spellbinding LGBTQ dreampunk and paranormal fantasy with a dash of mystery and romance. For more, visit *DezSchwartz.com*.

**Sonya Deulina Williams** migrated from Moscow, Russia, with refugee status as a little girl and now resides in Jamestown, North Carolina. She is the author of two sci-fi novels: *Mirrors* and *Divide Theory*. She enjoys writing that blurs reality and challenges the reader to question themself and the world around them. By day she practices clinical social work, and by night she enjoys being crafty. Check out her artwork and writing at *SonyaDWilliams.com*.

**Alessandra Ress**, born in 1989, is a German fantasy and science fiction author. She has published numerous novels and short stories since 2012, writes for several magazines and fanzines, and runs the blog *FragmentAnsichten.com*.

**Steven R. Brandt** has a Ph.D. from the University of Illinois for performing the first numerical simulations of rotating black hole spacetimes. Currently, he works in computer science at Louisiana State University. As a writer, he's able to use his computer and physics powers to listen to true stories from nearby spacetimes.

**Jeff Noon**'s debut novel, *Vurt*, won the Arthur C. Clarke Award in 1994. His latest work is the Nyquist Project from Angry Robot Press, four novels exploring the intersection between the private eye narrative and a series of increasingly weird landscapes.

**Barry Hale** is a writer, artist, and filmmaker based in the UK. His work includes music promos for post-punk bands, video art, and installations. Barry has exhibited extensively across Europe, Asia, and the US. His fiction is based on the dream journals he has kept for all his adult life.

**David Pierre** is a Spanish fantasy writer. He has published *Proyecto Ficción* (Caligrama), in addition to some poems and short stories in different media (in Spanish, English, and Catalan). In 2020, he co-edited the science fiction and horror anthology *Vínculos Oscuros* (Literup). He is part of the literary project Café Librería, co-directs the publishing services company Tiburón Letra, and runs a small book and art supply shop.

**Yelena Calavera** is a dreampunk writer living in London. She listens for stories, keeping an ear tuned to Dreamtime. Sometimes they rattle loose or climb down carrying songs from the cosmos. Yelena describes her work as "poetic realism."

*Courtney LoCicero* writes and dreams up scenarios for her carousel of colorful muses. She publishes works of young and new adult fantasy across digital storytelling platforms. Find her on Wattpad and Patreon as *@CocoNichole*.

**Tessa B. Dick** loves dogs, cats, and other furry critters. They often play pivotal roles in her stories, though sometimes these critters are not very friendly. Discover more at *PKDMemoir.BlogSpot.com*.

**Igor Goldkind** is an author, poet, and independent producer. Best known for promoting graphic novels in the 1990s and in fact coining the term. Read more of his work at *IgorGoldkindPoet.com*.

**Ragnar Martinson** is a German author whose short stories have been printed in several anthologies, as well as in his collection *Man vs. Machine*, self-published in 2021. When he is not writing, he works as a software programmer or uses neural networks (both human and artificial) to create digital art. Occasionally, Ragnar picks up a camera or a brush and tries to capture the profound weirdness of existence.

**Matt Watters** lives in Sydney, Australia. He is the author of the Dream Phaze series, which has been characterized as *Black Mirror* meets *Westworld* and won Bronze in the 2021 Global Ebook Awards for Science Fiction. Matt has a background in technical writing, business, and teaching and has been a professional soldier and actor at different times throughout his journey.

**Kurt Wagner** is a founding member of Morpheus Inc. and has an MA in Education. He has taught high school and college English, mythology, public speaking, and creative writing for over twenty years and is also a certified instructor of SCUBA diving, first aid, wilderness survival, Parkour, gymnastics, and archery. He has completed a full-length novel, *The Vivid Dreamer*, and a feature-length screenplay, *Sage of Nexus Point*.

**J. Osman** is a writer, artist, and theater director from Leeds, United Kingdom. Jim has a passion for experimental music and psychedelic and surreal science fiction and fantasy.

**Blake Jessop** is a Canadian author of sci-fi, fantasy, and horror stories. You can check out more of his liminal speculative fiction in *Recognize Fascism* from World Weaver Press or follow him on Bluesky: *@blakejessop.bsky.social*

**Stephen Coghlan** is an ever-expanding indie author who has already knit together a few forays through the looking glass. Feel free to share his tapestries on *SCoghlan.com*.

Dreampunk oneironaut **V. S. Santoni** operates out of Nashville, Tennessee, where they live with their partner-in-crime. Dream big, write bigger. More info at *VSSantoni.com*.

**Jeb R. Sherrill** is a novelist, musician, and ex-magician who's been writing dreampunk since long before it was officially a genre. His liquid psychotropic style bends the fine line between the real and the surreal. His debut novel *Storm Dreams* is available in print and audio.

**David Michael Williams** has suffered from a storytelling addiction for as long as he can remember. He is the author of several sword-and-sorcery fantasy novels as well as *The Soul Sleep Cycle*, a genre-bending series that explores life, death, and the dreamscape. Learn more at *David-Michael-Williams.com*.

**Kristin Jacques** is an award-winning YA and adult fantasy author. She lives in a small town in New England with her partner, kids, and two trash goblins masquerading as cats. To keep updated with events and upcoming releases, you can find her at *KristinJacques.com*.

**Joseph E. Green** is the author of a zine series for Microcosm Publishing as well as a new book, *Tinfoil Hat Not Included*. His play, *Einstein's Wrong About Everything*, was produced by the Overtime Theatre and opened in January 2022.

**Elizabeth Roderick** is the author of *Love and Money*, *Hoodlum Army*, the *Other Place* series, *Gracie & Zeus Live the Dream*, and other novels, as well as many short stories in various anthologies. She is a musician and runs a small, diversified farm in eastern Washington State, where she lives with her daughter and far too many animals. You can find her at *TalesFromPurgatory.com*.

**Anna Tizard** writes weird, metaphysical fantasies inspired by the theories of Carl Jung—and a surrealist word game called Exquisite Corpse. Play the game, awaken your imagination, and spark the next story at *AnnaTizard.com*.

**J. R. R. R. (Jim) Hardison** has worked as an animator, film director, screenwriter, graphic novelist, and regular-old novelist. Writing is the dream job from which he hopes to never wake. He currently resides in Portland, Oregon, with his lovely wife, two amazing kids, one smart dog, and one stupid dog. Visit *JimHardison.com* for more.

**L. B. Shimaira** writes dark fiction, often inspired by her own dreams and nightmares. You can find out more about Shimaira, her works, and where to connect on various socials via *Shimaira.com*.